The Chess Queen

By

Valerie A. Edwards

Copyright © Valerie A. Edwards
All Rights Reserved
ISBN-13: 978-1514253281
ISBN-10: 1514253283

DEDICATION

To the memory of my husband, Donald Ward Bennett Edwards, and my great appreciation to him and my daughter, Leslie Edwards for the endeavors to make my writing live.

Foreword

In 1986, Elizabeth Ward Hoskins died leaving the contents of her home on Cape Cod to my husband, Donald Ward Bennett Edwards. He grew up in California unaware of his Ward family history in Boston. He had the opportunity while still a young boy to meet his great aunt, Elizabeth Bruen Perkins (Bessie), who speaks for the family in this biographical book which begins with her grandfather, Samuel Gray Ward, a prominent member of Boston's society and patron to many writers and artists. In Ralph Waldo Emerson's book, Letter to a Friend, the friend referred to is Samuel Gray Ward with whom he had a lifelong friendship.

Elizabeth Hoskins, like many New England families of that era, never threw away items such as letters, news articles, scrapbooks and post cards. While working to dispose many of the items in the house unaware of the many famous people acquainted with the family, I discovered a manuscript dated 1928 written by Howard Ridgely Ward, the brother of Elizabeth Perkins. In it he described his life with the Thomas Wren Wards of New York and his Bostonian grandparents. It became obvious that there was a fascinating story to be written and so I began. It took two years to transcribe all the material at which time I began to relate closely with the course of the life of Elizabeth Perkins. Events, except for very few, in The Chess Queen actually took place, only the dialogue with its emotional content is my own. I know Bessie spoke through me to tell her story.

Prologue

NEW YORK TIMES, May 13, 1936

Paris, (AP) - Colonel George Cabot Ward, age 60, prominent lawyer and clubman, died today of pneumonia at his villa in Cannes. Colonel Ward was a prominent member of the American colony in France, where he had lived since the World War. He was Acting Governor of Puerto Rico in 1909 and was decorated by three governments. His war services, including a detail as chief of the intelligence section of the line of communications of the A.E.F., brought him many decorations.

He became attached to the General Staff in France and did liaison work with the British and French high commands in Paris and at their respective grand headquarters. He was decorated by both the French and British governments and in addition to the Distinguished Service Medal received the cross of an officer of the Legion of Honor and the Distinguished Service Order.

Colonel Ward was born in New York, son of Thomas Wren and Sophia Howard Ward. He studied at Harvard and was graduated from Harvard Law School in 1901, when he began to practice in New York.

****

NEW YORK TIMES, January 20, 1946

HOWARD RIDGELY WARD of Auburn, California, was reported missing and presumed dead on November 11th when he did not return from a trek in the Sierras in the area of Eureka in northern California. Mr. Ward was born November 10, 1881 in New York City to Thomas Wren and Sophia Howard Ward. For three generations his father's family from New England had represented the great English banking house of Baring Brothers.

After graduating Harvard, he went to California to begin the practice of mining engineer. As he himself wrote to us, "I have been in and out of that profession several times. Beginning in California in the old gold camps my wanderlust moved me progressively to Arizona, Alaska, Europe and New Caledonia." This great diversity of interests made him an agreeable companion who could adapt himself to many conditions and climates. In that sense he may be considered as a typical American, a jack of many trades and a master of several.

For the past several years Mr. Ward had lived in Auburn where he had an assay office. He left his wife, Mary E. MacInnis and three children from his previous marriage to Beatrice Kidder. Mrs. Kidder's mother was at the time of their marriage, president of the Grass Valley Narrow Gauge Railroad. They had two daughters, Elizabeth Kidder Hoskins and Beatrice Bennett; one son, Thomas Wren Ward; and a grandson, Donald Ward Bennett.

****

BESSIE

Early one November morning, gray-laced with snow threatening clouds, in our home at 15 East 9th Street in New York, I heard the first birth screams of my brother Howard. I was just eight years old and my brother George was six. It was a startling experience for us and we thought the new baby to be very red, very fat, and very ugly. Never would I have thought in my overactive imagination this baby born with dreams of wanderlust would impact and interfere with my life. Later in the afternoon the storm broke, turning to thunderous, skin biting sleet, ending what was for me my first real traumatic day. A day to be firmly forever embedded in my memory.

Mother was born in Baltimore, raised in aristocratic gentility as a strict Roman Catholic. She is a delicate, nervous woman and has at times taken to her bed with nervous prostration. Dr. Polk is always called in, holds her hand, shakes his head, and orders the usual sedatives for her. He is the delightful, dependable rock on which the family can lean in times of stress but offers me only a sympathetic pat on my shoulder. Over Mumsie's bed is the embroidered motto, "As thy days, so shall thy strength be." My eyes come to rest on that motto when Mumsie takes to her bed. At those times the awesome weight of family responsibility falls heavily on my young shoulders and many days I have to summon strength that, at times, is elusive and remains so. I am the mistress of this family.

Papa is off every weekday to Wall Street where he works for the investment firm his grandfather started; walking with that strange air of resignation, books crammed into his portfolio and the ever present newspaper under his arm. Then there are times when the aura of the dreamer envelopes him while he revels, I imagine, in the thoughts of what might have been if his family had not been so insistent upon him to establish a New York office. The academia of Boston was his cherished milieu.

My brother, George, has developed a rather stoic personality, hiding feelings in moods I don't understand. He spends a great deal of time in his room from where I can hear plaintive notes from his violin sneaking from behind the closed door. He attends Cutler's Academy uptown and is always at the top of his class. He reminds me of one of Howard's toy soldiers. Everything in place. Always checking to make sure Rose, our housekeeper, ironed the creases to knife-edge sharpness in his pants, and put just the right amount of starch in his shirts. Checking in the mirror, adjusting his tie, and making sure the brown curls of his hair are carefully pomaded down before he leaves the house. I know his routine by heart.

Thanks to Bonpapa's and Papa's urgings, Mumsie relented and I've been allowed to attend Brearly School in midtown Manhattan. The school has just been opened and there is furious talk that it defies the usual education expected of a young lady. The powers that have wielded the hand of education dictated that girls were to be learned in the proper social graces expected of New York's social register - music, art,

French, literature, English and, of course, etiquette. Much to my astonishment one evening, I overheard Mumsie's and Papa's friends say that intellectual activity took the bloom from young ladies. Can you imagine? If anything were to make me bloom, it was the anger that such an absurd irrational attitude aroused in me. My cheeks turned a burning red and the glow was still evident when I entered the room to stiffly give them my cordial, `good evenings'. Eagerly I left the room, having done my family duty, with angry injustice still burning in my head.

Brearly's curriculum was designed to provide young girls such as myself with an education comparable to that available to my brothers and allow me to intellectually advance along with them. The headmaster even encourages us to take the college admissions examinations and continue our education. God in heaven! Really a revolutionary attitude!

Inspiration for me was the famous journalist Margaret Fuller. Bonpapa has talked about her incessantly ever since I was a little girl. He more than admired her. He idealized her as the consummate thought provoking philosopher-scholar of his time. I can just imagine him as the young Harvard student sitting in her Cambridge salon listening with that steady gaze of his, intent on every word. I remember his laughter when he told me that she once said to her enthralled gathering of students: "I know all the people worth knowing in America, and I find no intellect comparable to my own." Bonpapa said he was taken aback by such audacity, especially in a woman, but had to admire her forthrightness in expressing her own convictions. And as he said, after some thought, she, for all he knew, might have been correct. Bonpapa apparently encourages me to carry on her struggle to rise above the deprecating attitudes toward the world of women. To resist the mentality that a woman belongs to her husband instead of creating a whole with him. After studying Margaret Fuller's writings, Bonpapa's challenge became apparent to me: to follow my own mind, create a sense of my own self, and to command my own destiny. So I have thrown myself vehemently into my studies and deal with my responsibilities at home in the best way I can. Secretly, hidden in my deepest thoughts, my desire is to live and study in Europe after graduation from Brearly, as all the men in my family have done. No faded bloom will I be!

Evenings we spend in the library with Mumsie usually writing letters to our many family members scattered from Boston to Washington and to her sisters who are now living in Europe. She is always chatting about something that amuses her. Papa, when not helping us with our lessons, is, for the most part, lost in reverie in one of his many books. When he was small he suffered a severe hearing loss due to a bout of scarlet fever. Bonnemaman told me he surprisingly adapted quickly to his silent world as if it had always been there waiting for him. Over the years he has used some hearing aid devices but like this evening he retreats into that silent world he has created for himself: distant, quiet solitude. Many times I envy him that world. His shutting out irritating noises from the streets, the prattling of voices, an excuse to be unaware of others. But there are evenings when he decides to entertain the family as a storyteller, enchanting us in rapt attention for hours with his adventurous tales of his Amazon expedition with Professor Agassiz when he was a student at Harvard. Something always sounds troubling in his voice when he tells us about how he and his friend, William James, witnessed smoke above Richmond when they sailed past in 1865 on their way to Brazil. Not until a year later when he returned did he find out that they had witnessed the burning of Richmond by the Union troops. All the horror of the Civil War had not touched him. It was as if he had been living in another distant world while the people of his country were massacring each other. But the old excitement always returns to his voice when he speaks of the rare zoological specimens he saw while drifting down the Amazon with native guides. His father, Bonpapa, being quite the adventurer himself, was inordinately proud when Professor Agassiz wrote him telling him that he thought his son was, because of his intelligence and energy, the best man of the expedition. I think Papa regrets that those adventures have long faded into the past.

  The quixotic moods of Papa take on a special aura on the weekends when he has planned one of our many jaunts to the country, either to the beaches of Long Island, or to New Jersey, the Hackensack Meadows, Fort Lee, or Nyack and Westchester County, New York. Several times Papa would rambunctiously put Howard on his back and run for miles with the rest of us trailing behind him, unable to keep up with his dog trot. He seemed so carefree! Sometimes we take lunch with us and sometimes we buy it at some little hotel or inn. I shall never forget when we took along the first grapefruit, never seen before in the markets. Oh! How sour it seemed, and how we wondered how anyone could eat it with any pleasure.

  Monday mornings I watch Papa walk slowly down the street again, off to Wall Street with the proverbial book in one hand and his portfolio in the other.

  By the time Rose Doyle had come to live with us and help with household chores I had become quite taken with my youngest brother and adored amusing him with silly games. He is easily placated and exhibits a charming mischievous streak.

Mother, as she had done with George, sent Howard off to drawing lessons that he hates. He takes dancing lessons that he hates still more. Above all else, he confided to me, he hates the little girls that he has to be polite to and dance with. The idea of having to dress up infuriates him and a real terror seems to beset him when having to attend a children's social event. His deportment seems self-conscious; and the idea of socializing, which comes naturally to his peers, becomes a gigantic task for Howard.

Behaving restlessly one night as I was reading him one of my many attempts at poetry, while turning a toy soldier over and over again in his hand, he confessed, "You know something awful Bessie? Everybody at school picks on me. I hate them! Do you think it's because I'm so little? I'm not as big as my friends, you know! I like to be left alone to do what I like. I don't want to worry about what other kids think."

He started pounding his pillow with his fists and I was astonished how quickly he worked himself into a fit of rage. He picked up his favorite toy soldier and began smashing its head against the iron railings of his headboard. I grabbed his arm and took the toy soldier and laid it on his night table. His body was heaving from sobs. I stroked his forehead and waited for the calm. Finally he looked up at me with that sad, poignant look that only a child can evoke and said, "You know I've learned where all the fire stations in the neighborhood are and all the fire boxes too? I can even tell the special sounds of all the bells and whistles when they go to a fire. I like playing with my fire engines and not think about all the horrible dancing and art classes or those silly parties Mumsie makes me go. I would like to hit all those bullies at school who tease me. Just sock them once, good."

I believe that mournful confession created in me an even more maternal protective feeling toward my youngest brother. I have become more convinced I must jolt him out of his melancholy before it does real damage to his self esteem. I've begun spending more time singing songs, playing anagrams and bringing little toys to him when I can afford a little extra from my allowance. Still I am resolved to going to Europe regardless of Howard's childish dependence on me. Wherever I go, he will always be rooted in my mind.

****

GEORGE

January 6, 1890

Dearest Bonnemaman,

Half of your glorious present I am going to turn into the thing I have wished for more than all the others - a dress suit case, or valise to carry when I go visiting. I am going to save the other half. Mama gave me a box of visiting cards which will be most useful now that I am beginning to have a proper social life.

I had one of my friends, Bayard Cutting, dine with me on the eve of the tenth, and we went to a very funny comic opera afterwards, and laughed till we couldn't laugh any more.

School has become irritatingly strenuous now. I am taking Solid Geometry, Trigonometry, Advanced Algebra and Analytic Geometry, also French, German, Latin, Ancient History and Physics. I'm still heavily committed to my music lessons and my violin playing is steadily improving. At least the notes do not sound so excruciatingly painful. My college entrance exams will be upon me before too long and I expect that you, Bonpapa, as well as my parents are expecting me to attend Harvard. I have been giving it some thought but have not decided definitely on a major.

All our attention has been turned to football games lately and, of course, the elections. In lecture hall this morning it was very interesting to hear Mr. Cutler refer, in his usual short tedious morning speech, to "Teddy" Roosevelt as one of the first graduates from his instruction. I do though laugh to myself when I envision the weighty Mr. Roosevelt bulging in his safari jacket, posing over the carcass of an elephant looking like the cartoonish political buffoon.

We are all hoping that you are daily regaining your strength, and that Washington D.C.'s milder winter will benefit your recovery.

With lots of love to you and dear Bonpapa,
Your loving grandson,
George

Howard is recovering again from one of his many illnesses. I cannot remember myself being ill as many times as he seems to be. Bessie and Mother pamper him too much; rushing to his every whining call. Manipulation is the name of his game. My fingers feel stiff and numb, difficult to bend. Damn! Maybe the bandage is too tight. I don't know whether to be angry at Bessie and Howard or myself for such a stupid accident. If Bessie had not prodded me into playing "Throw the Broom" to amuse Howard this would never have happened. Worst of all was trying to explain to Papa the broken glass in the bathroom door. Howard darted into the bathroom so quickly and slammed the door in my face that in my stupid haste to grab him I thrust my hand through the glass panel. Maybe I play too rough with him. He complains continually about his size and that I pick on him because I'm bigger. He is small for his age. I admit he annoys me with his demanding demeanor especially those times when he tries my temper and patience by bursting in on me and my friends with one of his silly tales of fire engines.

The snow has been piling up all day against the front of the house. Poor Papa, I can't help him shovel. Looks like it might be another horrific storm like the one in '88. I sure had my fill of shoveling then. I probably won't be able to practice my violin until my hand heals. Damn! The frustration of hearing phrases in my head and there lies my violin. It's so remarkably beautiful - its long neck cradled in my hand, the glow of the wood, my cheek caressed in its curve, my hand pulling the bow across its tight strings......mellow, flowing sounds erasing my confused feelings, confused thoughts, not to have to think today, tomorrow, or the day after tomorrow. Just let my mind roam through the music. Blissful release! Shhhhh! Shhh! I can hear Bessie reciting that strange, insidious little poem again to Howard.

> There was a little devil once.
> Some people thought he was a dunce.
> He ate some cake on Tuesday
> Which made him sick with small delay.
> He ate so much of jelly cake,
> It made his little belly ache.
> He used to go with his Papa,
> And see the children burn in tar.
> And when they yelled and shrieked in pain,
> He clapped his hands and said, "Again!"

****

HOWARD

November 13, 1890

Dear Bonnemama,

Thanks ever so much for the electric battery that you gave me. It is the nicest present I ever had. I was so glad to get your letter. I am quite well again. On my birthday Mama invited Hugh Minturn to lunch and took us to the horse show in the afternoon.
With love to Bonpapa,
Your loving little grandson,
Howard

The snow is clearing. I wished it had snowed like it did two years ago. Boy, did George get himself in hot water that day. It took Papa a month of Sundays to cool down. The schools were closed and though he never told me where he was going, I had bet it was uptown to Justine's. He didn't think I saw him, but I did! He tried tiptoeing down the stairs, sneaking past the library where Papa and Mumsie were reading, and closing the front door ever so quietly. I ran to my bedroom window and saw him running down the street. I found out later he had taken the Sixth Avenue line and it got stalled just north of 14th Street. Some men got some ladders for people to climb down to the ground but they charged everyone a dollar. George only had thirty five cents with him. I can imagine he panicked thinking he was going to have to sleep all night on the train and what would Papa do to him. He finally saw one of Papa's colleagues who paid for him to get down but as luck would have it... lucky for my own self-interests that is... Papa's friend told Papa a few days later not knowing that Papa was totally unaware that George was even out of the house. Bet George thought he was home free. Papa confined him to the house for two weeks and he had to clean our front steps and walks including our neighbors. Even more to my delight, Papa told him he could not accept any money for his services. I thought it was funny because it took a long, long, long time for all that snow to melt.

Papa will insist I can make it to Miss Miller's school tomorrow. If the sidewalks are clear maybe Elie and I can roller skate to school. I hate taking the elevated. What if it got stuck again! Even though the school is on 42nd Street, lower Fifth Avenue is asphalted and the rest is Belgian blocks. We skate mostly on the flagstone sidewalks - we sure cover ground! We like hollering, `Comin' through!' to all the people walking to work. I think when I grow up I will skate to work.

I made a new chum at school, Junius Brown. He beat me playing "Catch one, catch all" in Bryant Park. But he made me laugh when he started teasing about Miss Miller's assistant, Miss Small. He said she looked like a tall, splintered toothpick with a pimple for a head. Then he started to imitate her mincing walk, holding his knickers out the way she does with her schoolmarm's gray skirt and his head bobbing up and down like a chicken just like she does. She would have switched his hindquarters raw if she ever saw him. My sides ached from laughing. Anyway, I like him!

Elie's mother and mine have made us take singing lessons. I can't even hum a melody in tune but I think I can whistle Yankee Doodle to everyone's satisfaction. Elie and I had to sing an awful duet, "On Monday morn I love my love the deepest". What stuff to make us sing! We sounded like two croaking frogs caught with their legs stuck in the mud. Wish they would leave the musical performances to George and Bessie.

****

BESSIE

June 6, 1891

Dear Bonpapa,

Amy met me at the station in her family's high-swung buggy. It is an extraordinary experience to ride with Amy as she manages their old horse with that unique stern authority of hers, and she is quite capable of remarkable speed whenever she wishes to pass another vehicle. She takes no one's dust and gives liberally of her own to any close following cart or carriage. I held my breath all the way home and thanked God that I was given the chance to see the magnificent apple blossoms and lilac bushes that are now in full bloom.

After regaining my shaken composure from the wild buggy ride I took my place in life at the Lowell's house, Sevenels, whose atmosphere is like a daily Shakespearean drama.

Unaccustomed terror fell upon me the other morning, spoiled only daughter that I am, when I left a portfolio on a forbidden table, and I arrived breathless and apologetic five minutes late for breakfast. My faux-pas caused a pall to fall upon the hospitable spirit of the house and they greeted me at the breakfast table with chilly `Good mornings!' The reproach was taken and I ate in silence eager to finish and be off with Amy. But I like the human climate of this old house and discount the weather even when the high winds and thunderstorms of temperament drive us to the shelter of the gardens.

But not to mind, I do enjoy the company of Amy's older brothers and sisters. The men are all very well versed in the affairs of government and the intricacy of science and the women are very keen for civic *betterment and public interests. What every thoughtful person looks for in human intercourse is found in this house, a perpetual flavor of continual interest behind every important incident of the day. When we gather for meals one dispenses with listening that becomes superfluous. Any two members of this family can talk and listen simultaneously, effecting a great economy in time and patience, for conflicting opinions might be stated, registered, and answered at the same moment. How the essence of that opinion is argued matters little whether from the mouth of a sibling, parent or guest, such as myself, although at times I am reticent to the challenge. The usual New England reserve does not prevail at their table. No hot-blooded Latin could discuss more fervently, or with more expressive gesture, the local happenings or the larger questions of the day.*

Funnily enough, I can't help but giggle to myself sometimes when I find myself in the midst of their discussions reciting that silly little rhyme,

> *And this is good ole Boston,*
> *The home of the bean and the cod,*
> *Where the Cabots only talk to the Lowells*
> *And the Lowells talk only to God.*

But it is all quite invigorating and enlightening for me. Being involved in such intense discussions hopefully will serve me well in my studies in Europe. Mr. Lowell and Amy plan to accompany me to Boston to make certain that I am well situated on the boat for the crossing.

I hope to visit George at Harvard before I leave for

Paris on the 20th. I must get a letter in today's mail to Mumsie and Papa. I will surely miss little Howard. Give my love to Bonnemama.

Lovingly, Bessie

    Please Mary Mother in Heaven; free me of this persistent worry that frets my every waking moment. Why do I constantly have to reassure myself that there will be no family crisis while I am in Europe? Howard will have to start growing up, for the first time in his life, act responsible and manage without me as his confidante. Mumsie's strength will just have to hold up and George will have to help her deal with the household. George! He does not offer even the remotest possibility of help. He keeps to himself so much these days acting more than ever the eccentric recluse. Something always seems to be bothering him. I wonder if the pressure of entering Harvard is making him so moody and irritable. Whether the family is aware of it or not, their not so subtle pressure on George and myself to always maintain the family's reputation is suffocating at times. I must find the opportunity to capture Papa alone some evening and hope I have the courage to tell him what worries me.

    There's Amy over in the pasture beyond the lilac arbor on her horse. It's so exhilarating to watch her outdoors with her horses and dogs. Always with her hair pulled up in that funny little topknot, hating to be bothered with fussing over long hair. Look at her! She sits so tall in her saddle, riding like her brothers, putting her physical courage to the test, especially jumping. What courage it must take to be a Lowell! I dislike riding. I have too much sympathy for the horse to have to carry the weight of a human besides having to take orders on which way to go by the pull of a bit in his mouth. I am sure any horse that I would ride would revolt.

Some friendships have a bizarre uniqueness about them. Such is mine with Amy. What is the irresistible need for each other when we are apart and why are we still friends? We're so different from each other. She deals with life so easily with such directness and that enormous vitality of hers. Whether she's moving about the dance floor at social functions, or talking with the other girls' young men, she's so generous in her empathy and so comfortable with herself. Her persona questions my own insecurities. I want a freedom, a freedom I don't understand. My own soul, separate and untangled from my family. I struggle to keep my anxieties suppressed and under control. Control! Control! Amy is always expounding on self-control. To her mind, the highest moral virtue. Doesn't too much control strangle spirit? Choke free expression? Rob one of what might be those breathless moments of real freedom and joyousness in their life? Deceit is what Amy hates the most, but doesn't excessive self-control sometimes harbor deceit? I wonder if we were to let go of our self-control, especially in this familial structured, well-disciplined household, what emotions and mysteries it might unleash?

I adore the times we spend moon-gazing from the roof of Sevenels. After the house has gone to bed, like two conspirators we creep out the bedroom window onto the flat tarpapered roof, carrying a quilt to spread beneath ourselves. We become bathers in the moonlight letting the silken night air caress our bodies. Our whispered conversations, like a cat that steals upon his prey, suddenly reveals our most intimate inner selves. The profusion of thoughts wash over me like continuous waves sometimes so overwhelming I struggle for breath as in a rough surf when Amy whispered,

    `For the world, which seems to lie before us like a land of dreams.

    So various, so beautiful, so new,
    Hath really neither joy, nor love, nor light,
    Nor certitude, nor peace, nor help for pain.'

But our intimacy was harshly torn when after a few moments of contemplation drinking in the poetic impact, in my passion I said one's pain could be eased and peace found in oneself by confession and absolution in Christ's name. Amy's outburst caught me by surprise. She sat straight up, snapped the book shut and said, "Bessie, how naive! You are talking the jargon of a sect!" My mind reeled in confusion, then outrage, but I did not answer. I felt no need to defend myself. I can only surmise that it's Amy's New England Puritan inheritance that made her react so angrily and lash out at me. Maybe I'm naive but sorrowfully, when I think about it, I question the parochialism of the most gifted of my friends. I feel a sadness now, never before felt, that there exists a rift, an impassable chasm that our two lives will never again enmesh as one in our quest to explore life's mysteries... all because I offer my pain to Christ?

              ****

GEORGE

February 20, 1892

Dear Bonpapa,

I received your allowance and bought some new sheets of Bach's violin concertos with part of it. I have been invited to spend the weekend at the Cutting's country place at Oakdale, Long Island. I discovered that Bayard's sister, Justine, also loves music as much as I do. She has some interesting ideas on interpretations of Bach - so I am looking forward to her ideas on my new sheet music.

Bayard and I hope to do some quail hunting if the nice weather holds out. I have my deer head that I bagged last fall hung in the library, and it is so superb. I do wish you were able to see it.

The family sends love to dear Bonnemama and hope that you are getting better and stronger each day.

Your loving grandson,
George

Now that Bessie's in Europe I should teach Howard how to shoot and maybe a little fly-rod casting. Bessie acts like such an old biddy mother hen with him. Where did she get the absurd notion that she had to become Howard's mother, nurse, confessional priest, even to the absurdity of tucking him in at night. Whose needs is she really fulfilling? She has catered to his every whim that if left to his own devices I believe only trouble would follow. All the time she has spent reading and singing to him, encouraging him in academics, achievement is an enigma to him. Although to his credit, he's becoming a fairly accomplished figure skater according to the newspaper articles, which he so carefully cuts out and pastes in that scrapbook of his. Luckily for him, it's a sport where size doesn't take precedent.

Usually when Howard and I find ourselves alone together the atmosphere is strained and stultifying for me. But there was that one instance when we both became enthralled in a conversation about how it must have been to be a frontiersman, exploring the unknown, facing an unknown world, confronting the terror of an unknown savage people, the Indians. The conversation arose because of his passion for Henty's books on the West. We thrust our imaginations far into the night on the sands of Navesink beach gingerly traversing the imagined wilds. Odd to think that we both might have the same aspirations. No! No!

My envy of Bessie's trip to Europe is eating at my liver. I can't imagine what it must be like to be amidst such life - to engage in talk about the renaissance of art, music, architecture. To converse long into the night over a bottle of Chianti exploring the depths of man's thought. A poor American's undernourished intellect must be stretched and strained to compete in such an atmosphere. I'd love to test my French. I think I'd do quite well although my accent leaves a great deal to be desired. "Gargle the `r'! Grrrrrr! Encore! Mon Dieu! Votre accent," my French prof continually laments. Admittedly, Justine's French is far superior to mine. Will I ever get to France? Life can be so precarious. It can change in an instant. Like that incident last summer at Navesink Beach when we were having such fine weather. All of a sudden out of a seemingly calm day, an easterly squall broke near evening. There had been this medium size power boat just offshore when it disappeared into the squall. Ten minutes later, after the squall had passed, the sea was blank. We heard that the seven or more fishermen and crew aboard when the ship turned turtle had all drowned. For several days we stopped swimming while patrols combed the beach for bodies. What must it be like to stumble upon a body on the beach? I was stunned when I thought how easily one's life could end so abruptly. In just ten minutes one is there and then one not! Ten minutes! Death made me shiver. My mind spun furiously with Keat's words imploring, "What am I that should so be saved from death?"

****

HOWARD

April 11, 1892

Dear Bessie,

    When are you coming home? Bonpapa has given me thirty five dollars to get a safty bycicle with, but I have not got the safty bicycle yet, but I am going to get it very soon. I belong to a Club. We meet in the Park. I am Secretary. I am going to school every day and I go to carving every Saturday. I hope to be soon in a higher class. I love you and whish you were at home. With love to Aunt Bessie and Uncle Ernst.

Yours lovingly,
Howard

P.S.

Dearest Bessie,
    Howard's letter to you has set his ambition on fire. Writing is not his best and the spelling has to be improved but such as it is, I send it, that you may see how he grows. The composition is entirely his own. We have the plumbers out of the house at last and the Board of Health assures us that everything is now in perfect order. I sincerely trust that they know.
    With love from all,

Ever devotedly,
Mother

    They've flooded a vacant block on 8th Avenue and 57th Street to start a skating school. Papa thinks it would be a good idea if I took lessons after school. Mumsie says I have a good sense of balance. Maybe they're right. I would like to excel at something athletic. I don't have much success at the other sports at school. Junius and Elie seem to do so much better than me. Oh, how I'd like to beat them at something. Just once to show them. I hate going to Durlands for horseback riding lessons. I feel stupid sitting in that English saddle just like I felt when I was a real little kid and George took me out on the river when it was so rough. I just hung on to the side with both hands while it bobbed up and down and my stomach went with it. George just laughed and said I'd get used to it. Well, riding that silly horse bobbing up and down, up and down is that same nauseating feeling. I haven't gotten used to it and my stomach still flip flops. My complaining to Mumsie about 'why' do I need riding lessons irritates George. He rides so well. He does everything so well! I hate trying to do as well! I think Papa is always comparing what I do with what George does. He hardly spoke but I heard it in his tone of his voice when I asked him if I could quit all Mumsie's silly lessons. "Mother knows what a young gentleman should know and you will be a gentleman!" was all he said. I know he's disappointed in me.

    I wish Bessie was home. I miss her stories and poems, especially the ones she made up. I liked it when she sat at the foot of my bed at bedtime with her beautiful silver decorated hairbrush and watch her brush her long brown hair one hundred times. I made her stop after every twenty-five brushes and tell me a poem, when she reaches a hundred she has to tell me a story, then she tucks the covers in real tight for me. She always has that understanding look and is the only person in this family that really listens to me and never, never, never snaps at me like George does. I can't wait until this summer when we all go to Seabright again. I'll have so much to tell Bessie and I hope I can have her alone a lot, just for myself.

****

BESSIE

May 10, 1892

Villa Celimontana
Roma

Dear Bonpapa,

I'm here! My dream, a reality! Here, amidst all the stories you told me about Italia. Roma, the Eternal City - a vast museum of the old world's history. Sitting here in Aunt Lily's beautiful garden, I can look across the lawns and gaze upon the magnificent noble Arch of Constantine and let my imagination take flight through all the historical, powerful figures that must have passed triumphantly under its portals.

I am beginning to take exception to your words about Italy being a good place for Americans to visit and study, but not good for them to live in. You said we must live in the future and the present and not in the past. Furthermore, that an American living in Europe has no "raison d'être"; he loses much distancing himself far from home and all that's new in a young country's growth. He gains no place for himself in the old impenetrable order of European society. Remember saying that our consciousness is based in growth and life in the future and that we are part of that American consciousness while in Europe we have no part of the past?

You may either laugh or reprimand me for I've thrown your words to the Roman skies while I gorge myself in the past, revel in the present and am thrilled by the future. Since arriving in Rome and being so graciously greeted by Aunt Lily and Uncle Ernst's hospitality I have felt such a marvelous sense of freedom. *Walking in the footsteps of the past in the narrow back streets of Rome I can plunge myself into a new found sense of curiosity - pushing the door of a tucked away church in hopes of discovering a little masterpiece. One evening I stumbled upon a most unique, little piazza just off the Via del Corso where I found a jewel - the church of San Ignacio - faux pearl that it may be! I pushed the door and stepped into a fantasy of frescoed ceilings filled with trompe d'oeil marvels, fooling one's eye and mind at each step down the nave -angels and saints toppling from the sky - accompanying you like giggling, naughty children as you walk toward the altar with its domed ceiling. Then laughter fills one's throat as you look up to find that the domed cupola is all an illusion. The ceiling is flat! Flat! Then spasms of laughter strike because you have been so exquisitely fooled. The windows of the cupola are painted right at the edge of what appears to be a dome. Walking back down the nave the sun started to set and its rays of fading light streamed through the upper windows bouncing off the mosaics of multicolored marbles in the floor and columns -filling the nave with dazzling displays of color. This little church's eclecticism and illusions defy the mundane order of things. Maybe that's why I fell so quickly in love with it.*

Woven into the fabric of their everyday lives the Europeans have created a tapestry of music, poetry, and have forever immortalized the art of the past. The arts are their bloodstream, naturally functioning as every breath they take. I quite vividly remember you saying that if we stay too long we will decline into lotus eating. Well, the energetic remnants of Renaissance life have consumed me with feelings that can only enhance my pen and my paintbrushes on the waiting empty paper and canvas. I don't feel that I can ever stay too long here.

Dictates say that I do have to return home soon and I expect that I will be needed again to help Mumsie. I dearly love my family and miss all of you; but secretly, I express to you that I fear the greatest adventure of my life will soon be over. Somewhere deep inside, a part of me will grieve that it was all too brief a romantic sojourn. Perhaps the only one in this short life that God will grant me!

This epistle has, to my surprise, been a literal flooding of thoughts I was not aware of - I must close. I have so many stories to tell you when we are together again at Seabright this summer. Please give my love to Bonnemama.

*Your loving granddaughter,
Bessie*

I remember Bonpapa telling me how struck he was by St. Peter's sheer massiveness. How it still maintained a beauty and comfort, exclusive of all discord. A climate that was so seductive to a believer in Christ. It's no small wonder that even those who have not rendered themselves to the Church would find comfort in St. Peter's. There's a very spiritual side to Bonpapa but he holds so tenaciously to his esoteric intellectual approaches to life. Thanks to his friend, Mr. Emerson! Being that he was raised a Unitarian, at times I sense a ghostly chasm between us when it comes to Catholic dogma. Amy's accusation that I speak the jargon of a sect keeps haunting me. He never mentions Bonnemaman's conversion to 'the one true faith' after they were married. There must have been some tense, quiet moments in their home because I cannot believe that it did not bridle Bonpapa. I know her strength of conviction won because Papa was raised a Catholic, though I'm not convinced that Papa takes the Church to heart. Why is it that I would even question that those outside the true Church would not feel the power of Christ in St. Peter's?

The dichotomy of life in Rome is a beautiful paradox! While glorifying itself in the death of Christ and the saints, the musical cacophony of Italian life plays and echoes through the streets. The human condition permeates every brick, cobblestone, the very air one breathes. When tiredness overtakes me, I close my eyes and images, colors, forms, flash behind my lids. It makes me anxious - so ready to express those flashes of life on canvas.

> Why linger you so, the wild labyrinth strolling?
> Why breathless, unable your bliss to declare?
> Ah! You list to the nightingale's tender condoling,
> Responsive to sylphs, in the moon beamy air.

Keats must have written those words to lift my dragging spirit when my feet feel cast in cement. I have fallen in love with the labyrinth of Rome. Here in these stones is what I want. Here is what satisfies my search. Here is the way to unsilence my voice.

****

HOWARD

May 20, 1892

Dearest Bonpapa,
 Thank you so much for the photograph and the book on skating. I have already placed the photograph in my frame, opposite Bonnemama's. I have found so many figures in the book that I never knew of before, and the descriptions of how one should hold one's self are so good. Last week I skated in a figure skating competition and got the third prize which was a bronze medal. I am also playing on the hockey team of our school and so far we have been always victorious.
 I am looking forward to sharing the good times we have at Seabright with you and Bonnemama again in June. I wish I had been there during the big blow when the bathhouse went to pieces. Mama has been having headaches but is better at present.
 Mama tells me that tomorrow is your birthday and I wish that I was with you in Washington having a good time. Many congratulations and kisses are sent to you by Papa and Mama and I wish I was with you to kiss you eighty times.
  Your grandson,
  Howard

 Latin! Ugh! Why Latin? I'm always struggling to learn these 'dead' languages and I can't understand why the need? Amo, amas, amat, I love, he loves, they love. Well, they can love it, I don't! History causes my head to throb. Maybe it's because I have to bang it against the wall to remember all those silly dates. Ten sixty-six, somebody invaded England and it wasn't Julius Caesar! Had to be some French guy! Those guys hate the English; or is it that the English hate the French?

George is commissioned at times to help me with my homework by Papa but he keeps berating my slowness and lack of interest. He's planning to enter Harvard Law School so he can use the Latin. The last time he became frustrated with me he said in that uppity manner of his, something like, "One cannot have mastered the Latin grammar at any early age without a speaking acquaintance, at least with Virgil, Horace and Cicero." Then he went on to say something like, "a single one of whom makes all educated men kin and establishes a free-masonry like no other." I don't even know what he means when he said 'establishes a free-masonry' much less am I planning on trudging through all those writers. I bet Papa pressured George into the idea of law school because it doesn't make sense otherwise. George does nothing but talk about his music and that stupid Justine. Rather him than me! Oh, summer come. I beg God at Mass every Sunday to make June arrive quickly so I can run over the dunes and the highlands at Seabright again. I can learn to love the ancient histories of the sea, the rivers, and the stone that makes up the earth. I can sit for hours and listen to the old-timers tell stories about shipwrecks, devastating storms and other bizarre disasters. I suppose some of the family find the wildness of the shore rather lonely and unsociable but to me it's paradise. My private Garden of Eden!

****

GEORGE

October 25, 1892

Dear Bonpapa,

I have just returned from a house party over the weekend and found your cheque awaiting me. The house party was with the Vaughan's at Hallowell, Maine and we had a glorious time coasting, tobogganing, snow-shoeing, etc. Mr. and Mrs. Vaughn talked continually of you and Papa and old Boston days.

We are having Indian summer weather here at Cambridge. Sunday I went skating and today it is hot enough to put on summer clothes. This afternoon the Circle Francais is giving a lecture by Mr. Gaston Deschamp, and I am to usher. My French is improving and I have developed an insatiable appetite to learn French history. I hope to find time between my law courses to take some courses in French history. Those times you reminisced to me about your love affair with France when you toured Europe with Bonnemaman and Aunt Bessie, and my sister, Bessie's, never-ending stories enchanted me and set my mind to the hope of following all your footsteps some day.

I must close and dress for this afternoon's event. With much love to Bonnemaman.

Your loving grandson,
George

I can visualize Howard struggling in the water last August at Seabright. It remains vividly etched in my memory, flashing its terrible scenes behind my closed eyelids as night descends. A shadowy unreality persists about that day. Howard's thrashing and my reactions all slowed in time. I wrongly thought by the time it happened Howard had become adept at swimming. No one was home so I decided to laze in bed a little longer. I can still hear the new sailboat that Papa and I had bought making that harsh grating sound as it rubbed up against the dock. The new paint was probably being scraped and marred as it hit the dock. I could hear Howard outside playing, batting a ball around with an old stick. I yelled down to him to push the boat away from the dock and I pulled the sheet up again over my head. To this day I don't know what compelled me toward the window to see if everything was all right. The next moment I found myself in my pajamas grabbing Howard's outstretched arms. The look of terror in his eyes still haunts me. I had never felt such strong feelings toward Howard as I did at that moment. I tried to explain to him with utmost calm how he should have tackled the job of mooring the boat more sensibly. My feelings were totally bereft of anger. Coming so close to being a witness to his death has fostered some eruptive confused feelings that I didn't know were there - hidden somewhere in my deep psyche. I had an intense compulsion to put my arms around him, hold him close to me, feel his physical presence, assuring me his heart still beat. I can't fathom that compulsion.

During the hubbub of the near drowning incident a strange coincidence occurred. Mumsie happened to be glancing out the window of the commuter train returning from New York that morning and saw me on the dock in my pajamas talking to Howard. She seemed to be more upset about the impropriety of my dress rather than the near tragedy. What in life should take precedence, propriety or action? Always act the gentleman, make no open display of embarrassing emotion, and keep the family pride intact, on and on and on! I will! I will! Grit my teeth, I will. But the memory of Howard's terrorized face beneath the water's surface will linger forever.

****

BESSIE

October 31, 1892

Dearest Bonpapa,

I arrived at Sevenels late yesterday afternoon to be greeted by several of Amy's young nieces and nephews imploring me to admire their costumes for this evening's Halloween festivities. The excitement, as ever, is catching - so much youthful life to celebrate the passing of the dead! This house when filled with all of Amy's brothers' and sisters' families virtually thrives on life. Remember telling me to be a keen witness of life in all its forms? More importantly, to learn and act upon it as I see fit. There is an abundance of life forms in this house, a tremendous on-going learning process at the dinner table, and a necessity to keep my self-control in rein, not to act too impulsively. As I have experienced before on my visits, when the family departs and the house is left to us and Amy's parents, a reserve descends like a fog carried by the local east wind. Amy's mother's invalidism and her father's stern conventions as to time and order pervade the atmosphere as if the sun has disappeared. It is obvious to me that my generation is trying to experience life with a little less formality and rigidity to convention. Our behavior is certainly threatening to the conventions of the older generation.

I still try to keep pace with Amy. It fascinates me how her penetrating eye is not satisfied with just seeing. Her most emotional arguments are about the society into which she was born. A society being too well satisfied, complacent about society's ills, and above all a deathly smugness that kills the possibilities for creative solutions. Among her acquaintances, still in their middle years, there exists a certain smug pride. In spite of excessive time and money that offers them complete freedom of activity, many of them have never been outside the Commonwealth of Massachusetts. If they only knew what treasures are to be found in the rest of the world; I can only sorrow over how provincial their lives must be.

Their self-complacent atmosphere is not one in which a thirst for the unattainable is fostered. Such hunger and thirst suffers with one's feet on ancestral ground, and is considered by many Bostonians equivalent to an unhealthy appetite for the moon. My appetite surely suffers since I so love the moon and nothing pleases me more than my discussions of Keats' poetry with Amy by the light of the moon streaming into the library in the evenings. I am a true granddaughter of yours, since it was you who introduced me to the marvelous words of the poets. These are your ancestral grounds and yet your footsteps failed to follow in theirs and I am hoping mine will set a different course too.

I am expecting Charles' carriage tomorrow to take me to his parents home for dinner. His constant attention lately leads me to believe that he has serious marriage intentions. Needless to say such a commitment causes concern and anxiety in me. How would I know what I would be losing if I said `no' OR if I said `yes'? I still hear Margaret Fuller's words that you read to me: `I wish women to live, first, for God's sake. Then she will not take what is not fit for her from a sense of weakness and poverty. Then if she finds what she needs in Man embodied, she will know how to love, and be worthy of being loved.' How will I know when I have lived enough? I could use your counseling so I look forward to seeing you at Christmas in New York.

Give my deepest love to Bonnemaman and tell her I promise to write soon. I expect some of my outspoken ideas in this letter might be upsetting to her.
Your loving granddaughter,
Bessie

The argument with Amy this evening is reminiscent of the storm brewing outside the library windows. As long as I have known Amy she has had an all consuming love affair with words. She is always embattled in that constant search for words with diamond cut precision which will speak with that impressive sheer power given to the page, printed with impact to remain embedded in your consciousness. Flipping through the dog-eared pages of the books piled on her nightstand, reading her furiously penciled marked passages, her endless scribbling in the margins, her mind must consume the ink that prints those velum pages. The chasm that separates our thinking could be attributed to the fact that Amy bases her arguments from her own strange cerebral analysis of the written words. It's an obvious inherited habit. Amy's family involve themselves in continual competitive intellectual exercise. They hammer away at all facets of life, examining it with a critical analysis void of human emotional and physical reflexive response. Amy claims that man is always a rational being. I cannot accept that! The proof of Amy's own irrationality lies in our prolonged discussion of Keats' love letters. We almost know the poems by heart. It started with the question of whether Keats treated Fanny Brawne according to our code of relationships which we have discussed since we were young girls. Amy's reaction was intense and I thought totally out of character for her when I said I thought Keats was not an over-zealous lover as Byron might have been. No surprise if Amy is living in vicarious tryst with Keats' poetic love poem to Fanny. She would probably respond that man is rational but women are prone to irrationality. That is our wont!

The wind! I like the soft movements of shadows the wind creates across the shelves of dusty books - books with written words in their tight well-ordered jackets. The shadow of that long gnarled oak branch that stretches across the library window is bowing with the wind like a maestro waving his baton across the heads of the symphony. Would it not be ecstasy to give words to the movement of the shadows? My words behave like prisoners on paper.

That wind! Listen! It's howling! Sounds like the rebirth of an evening last summer at Navesink Beach when the remnants of one of the West Indian hurricanes wreaked destruction on our little vacation home. That storm also played havoc with me. The tide was unusually high, with a light east breeze that evening, and at bedtime I could hear the little lapping waves in the river which rose almost to our back door. When I awoke in the early morning, there was a furious gale from the east, a heavy sea, and as the tide rose, I saw our protective sand levee crumbling with each wave. As the levee disappeared I could see the gigantic waves piling on the beach, the house was shaking and trembling in the gale, and the tide kept rising until the ocean was pouring into the river between all the houses. The river was rough enough, too rough for boats and we were marooned. I felt an exquisite exhilaration. No one could touch me! As long as the water surrounded me, I answered to no one. No need to say the right thing. No need to think about the future. I could dream dreams of wild fantasy, of other lives, of other times, of other futures. Let the storm rage, winds so strong I could hardly stand against them. I loved the feel of the wind pushing strongly as it wrapped itself around my body. The surge I felt as I pressed against it with no fear of hushed reprimands. Keat's plaintive words sighed on the wind,

> Ah, love, let us be true
> to one another! For the world, which seems
> to lie before us like a land of dreams.
> So various, so beautiful, so new,
> Hath really neither joy, nor love, nor light,
> nor certitude, nor peace, nor help for pain.

Charles loomed only as a ghostly figure of my past, an actor in my life. He did not have to be! I needed a zealous Keats to love more, deliciously more! My singular night of passionate fantasies was lost with the dawn as the tide had receded and we, three women and children, were all carried by the men to the Forrester's home on the other side of the river where it was slightly more protected and then later to Seabright to my grandparents' home where life reclaimed its normal tight paced march once again. I could not even whisper to Amy the moments of ecstasy I had had but will hold tight in my body to summon when I need to relive them. Irrational or not!

****

HOWARD

November 15, 1892

Dear Bonpapa,

Your cheque arrived safely in time to buy lots of Xmas presents. When I come to Washington I will bring all the photos of the Adirondacks with me, some of them are pretty good. I wish I could have taken some pictures of East River Falls that are way up in the source of the Hudson. They take a drop of about sixty feet and are wonderfully picturesque.

Even though I have a few years at Cutlers Academy left I am dying to go into the Navy through the Naval Academy and become a line officer. Every day the Navy idea grows more on me, and I so wish that I could get an appointment; though I don't know who I could get it through.

With much love to dearest Bonnemama.
Your loving grandson,
Howard

P.S. Dearest Bonpapa, I know it's rather early to ask, but with all the people you know in Washington do you think you could use your connections to help me to get an appointment to the Naval Academy. Better to start early, don't you think?

Bessie has stopped coming into my room at bedtime. She doesn't read her poetry to me anymore.
I often times see her writing in the library. She's begun her art classes at the Metropolitan uptown in the mornings. The other day I caught her staring at one of Bonpapa's watercolors and asked her what she was

thinking. She sounded annoyed that I had treaded on her reverie and pointedly said that she was just studying his technique. The look on her face seemed to say there was something more. Barriers seem to be building between us like boulders sliding down the mountainside. It is so upsetting. I just don't understand girls.

Last summer when Charles Perkins came to visit (I nicknamed him Carley) he was so obvious in his all too affectionate interest in Bessie. I was surprised that she seemed to like it! What an 'enfant terrible' I must have been! With my usual curiosity, I was interested, and I suppose I butted in when I shouldn't have and repeated things I shouldn't have heard. But I thought Bessie was happy!

What an exciting summer! What with the hurricane but most of all in August Papa told me that we were going to New Hampshire for two weeks and George was going to take me on a hunting trip in the Adirondacks! I couldn't believe my ears! Since my accident with the sailboat, for some reason George has taken an interest in what I do. I was an intruder if I went into his room whether it was just to play or talk with him. Preparing for our camping trip he taught me the basics of shooting a rifle and shotgun and fly-rod casting, and after the joys of assembling our equipment we were off to the Tohamas Club near Mt. Marcey. One night when we were comfortably camped near the lake, we talked late into the night huddled over the campfire. I am still muddling over our talk. Is it that George does not want to take up the law? Justine, I think, has become an obsession. It was always, 'Justine plays the violin so well!' 'Justine speaks French as if she were Parisienne!' 'Justine is so intelligent!' How does one love another person who is not family? Especially a girl! George tackles everything so matter-of-factly but he sounded confused about pursuing a law career and his future with Justine. I made a pact with myself never, never to allow someone of the opposite sex to confuse my life.

The next day George was his usual disciplined self as I watched him catch some gamely fighting trout in Lake Golden and Lake Sanford. I shot my first deer; a beautiful, tawny colored buck. He stood there so regally framed by the surrounding glade as if he were invincible. Such an easy shot that I am still somewhat ashamed of it.

We tramped trails and gorged on hotcakes. I believe I could go back today and still find my way through those trails whose windings are still like photographs in my mind. Hungry or tired, rain or shine, with a bag or empty-handed, I will forever tramp the woods and streams and lakes and mountains I love so much.

****

Christmas, 1892

"Why don't you children take Bonpapa and Bonnemaman into the library? He has brought his special applejack from Lenox. I'll help Rose clear the table and join you later," Mumsie said as she rose picking up her plate.

Pushing back her chair Bessie took Bonnemaman's arm and helped her into the library. She settled her before the fire and pushed a cushion for herself beside her chair. Bonpapa settled himself in the big wing chair with his usual snifter, turning it in his hand while admiring his applejack. Looking at Howard reclining on the settee he inquired, "Tell me, my dear Howard, what were your surprises this morning under the tree?"

"Oh, George gave me a tray to hold pens. I think he hopes the pens will prompt me to do better at school. Bessie gave me a box of preserved fruits and Mumsie gave me a nail cleaner, a box of prunes, and a spool of silk to clean my teeth. She's always so practical! But Papa did hide a little musical instrument in my stocking, probably thinking I would join them in the evenings around the piano. Pray to God, Bonpapa, that you'll never hear the horrible sounds I can wring from musical instruments. My singing should have been torture enough for everyone."

Bonpapa's eruptive roar of laughter startled everyone. "Howard was just complaining about his tortuous singing. I can certainly attest that he will never be an applicant for the Vienna Boys Choir."

Sitting up on the edge of the settee, Howard said, "Wait a minute, I'll sing like a nightingale if it would get me a trip to Vienna. I'll practice the octave above middle C and stop drinking milk to retard my growth for the next year if I could go!"

Papa having put down his book during the ruckus,

said jokingly, "It's times like these that I can appreciate my poor hearing. If you could show me that you have the discipline to practice ANYTHING for a year Howard, much less singing, I will gladly think about sending you to Europe." He picked up his book again and thumbed through the pages.

Perplexed, Bonpapa not knowing if Papa was truly amused or irritated, returned his attention to Howard. "Do you still have your mind set on attending the Naval Academy?"

"Well, I still work on my scrapbook of naval vessels. I know the guns mounted on each one, her armor, speed and all else there is to know. I've been talking about going to the Naval Academy at the dinner table but Mumsie keeps talking about engineering, especially about George Morrison and the bridges he's built, and Papa says nothing. It's not clear in my mind now what my thoughts are."

Picking up his cane, Bonpapa tapped Papa several times on the knee to get his attention. "Is that true, Thomas? You've not given Howard any encouragement about entering the Academy? You know the boy's insatiable interest in boats and the navy. I would think you would foster it. After all, it's never too early to encourage your son on a career choice."

Bonpapa's perfunctory tone of voice interrupted Papa's absorption in his book. Clasping his hands on top of his book he said in a resigned voice, "I have left it to Howard to know his own mind and choose how he wishes to spend his future. Life doesn't allow room for second choices. So his first choice has to be the best."

Papa, slowly running his hand up and down on the leather binding of his book with downcast eyes continued, "I think his decision should best be his own without my undue influence. I only advise him to consider his options carefully. Too many times guidance is a purely subjective opinion of the one giving it, and often is of one's own unfulfilled dreams. Adhering to the influence of others and basing your decisions for your future on such guidance can lead to another unfulfilled life," he said in a tone of voice glinting with an edge of unusual anger. "Now, let's lay the subject to rest."

Ignoring the angry tone in his son's voice, Bonpapa said, "I still believe Howard needs your guidance." Turning to look out the window Bonpapa continued in a quieter tone, "I remember my first choice was to spend my days in my beloved Berkshire hills, plowing my fields, writing in the late of the day but one day I thought I saw an apparition of my father in the garden and at that moment I thought I foresaw my destiny. I was going to be asked to take over my father's position in his company." Bonpapa appeared to reflect for a moment. A shrug of his shoulders seemed to stiffen his back as he turned and looking directly at his son, speaking with an emphatic, prideful voice, "As a matter of duty I yielded and to this day I am proud of my success. I more than tripled the company's business during my tenure when I turned it over to you, son. That company has provided both my family and yours with a very comfortable life. I knew myself well enough to know my literary and artistic yearnings were only that - yearnings. I realized I never had the talent to wield a pen like a Hawthorne, a Longfellow or a paintbrush like John Singer Sargent or a Renaissance painter. I'm content with what I've achieved even though it was my second choice!"

Bonpapa reached inside his jacket pocket and pulled out one of his favorite cigars and began to stoke it. Seeming to continue in his reflective mood he continued. "There was a poem I wrote years ago the last two verses of which are brought to mind."

> Forged were those arms for men of other mould;
> Our hands they fetter, cramp our spirits free;
> I throw them on the ground, and suddenly
> Comes back my strength, returns my spirit bold.
> I stand alone, unarmed, yet not alone;
> Who heeds no law but what within he finds;
> Trusts his own vision, not to other minds;
> He fights with thee. Father, aid thou thy son.

Thinking that he had previously put the conversation to rest, his right hand clenching the arm of the chair, Papa in a deliberate tone of voice said, "As I recall it was your friend, Henry James, who advocated the need for freedom, spontaneity and innocence. Didn't he declare that he desired his child to become an upright man in whom goodness shall be induced not by mercenary motives? And that his character could not be forcibly imposed upon him but one freely assumed and he believed he could achieve this by surrounding his children with an atmosphere of freedom. I took his advice to heart and I believe my children's choices will be their own. I hope they have the courage to make them. Courage - that's the obstacle in their way - the most difficult and the most profound of all human qualities. The courage of direct, personal choice is the essence of the individual. Courage is what I wish for my children. God wishing I had had more!"

Bonpapa, startled at Papa's response to his poem, leaned back in his chair without taking his eyes off Papa. "I did take exception with old Henry Senior on the lack of course he allowed his children and I think it is well evidenced by William's behavior. Being his close friend you know all too well how William vacillated from one thing to another never making a decision. What was it, painting? Chemistry?

Anatomy? Then withdrawing from medical school to go with you on Agassiz' expedition. As if that wasn't enough for him he goes sailing off to Germany to study God knows what. I remember how William's letters terribly concerned you in which he wrote how depressed he was and suffering from nervous prostration. I can't help but believe his problems stem from Henry's lack of setting a discipline, a direction, and exacting decisions from his children." Bonpapa looked down and shook his head. "Poor William."

Papa reached for his snifter and took a long sip and savored the taste of the applejack. "No, not poor William. William, with all his problems has been able to exercise his creative genius. I believe his writings on the human animal, his failings and successes will be on the library shelves long after we are gone. And what have we left?" Gazing into the snifter he said, "That's a strong batch of applejack this year, Bonpapa." Then he picked up his book from his lap, adjusted his reading glasses and began reading again.

After a few moments of tense silence, George sat down at the piano and began to play a Mozart sonata glancing up once at Papa as if he wanted to say something but only his music could speak for him. The door opened and Bonnemaman stepped into the silence. Sensing something was amiss; she shuddered as if there was a chill in the room, and threw her shawl over her shoulders. She picked up her embroidery from her basket on the end table and sat down next to Howard on the settee. Finally, Bonnemaman's low, calm voice broke the unspeaking stillness.

"Did you children attend midnight mass at St. Patrick's last night?"

Howard, feeling a twinge of guilt for possibly causing his father's outburst, knowing Bonnemaman was attempting to calm the tension in the room, answered, "Yes, we all went. It was a sung Mass and the church was bursting to the very spires with people."

"Christmas Eve does seem to make the Church irresistible to those who are errant the rest of the year. If I could but take back a day of my life to relive again it would be as a young girl in New York when we lived on Beekman Street. The Christmas Eves with my family, riding in the carriage to St. Patrick's for midnight Mass is still vivid in my memory. All the windows with the lighted candles and later the smell of the church with all the evergreen boughs tied everywhere. When we moved to New Orleans and I was sent to the Sisters of the Sacred Heart at St. Michael's, Christmas was never quite the same without the snow, the lights, the excitement on New York's streets. As fast as the years slip by, I think those Christmas Eves will be just as strong in my memory, until the day comes when I close my eyes for the last time."

"Bonnemaman, you're not thinking of leaving us?" asked Bessie half-amusingly, wanting to lighten the tension in the room. "Don't tease us. It makes me shiver."

"I expect I shall stay a little longer... if, for nothing else, to keep Bonpapa out of mischief," she responded with a reprimanding tone and a sideways glance at Bonpapa.

Christmas reminds me of a very full life. No regrets and death can no longer frighten me. Life for me is like the brook in Lenox which flows more rapidly as it streams over the rocks through the woods falling faster on its way. The more falls I suffered in life the faster life fell on me, changing years into moments. But those lessons I learned are pocketed safely away in my bosom. After a life as long as mine I can allow myself to contemplate the past and say, `Such was life, times of ecstatic happiness which is so fleeting and times of abysmal despair that lingers too long. But the contradictions fade like shadows in the distance while the high moments, the blissful times shine like lights, as bright as ever.'

Sitting up a little straighter on her cushion beside the fire, Bessie thought, how kind and gentle age has been to my grandmother's face though time has wrung the vitality from her body. Bonpapa told me a writer friend of his described to him the first time he ever saw Bonnemaman when she was a young girl. It was one Sunday morning as he was going to church with his mother and as his friend passed the gate she said, 'There is young Mr. Ward going up the steps, to see the beautiful Miss Anna Barker.' He told my grandfather the little incident impressed itself on his memory because the beautiful Miss Barker had been at his house and had made him, a boy of ten or twelve, captive by her charms. She obviously has a stronger power than mere beauty to have captured my grandfather's heart and the hearts of his friends.

She gently squeezed Bonnemaman's hand. Bessie had always presumed Bonnemaman, much like her mother, did not pursue intellectual activity, spending most of her time taking care of her family. Suddenly it occurred to her that maybe Bonnemaman had also suffered the conflicting feelings that Bessie was experiencing now: what choices had she for her future? Did she really have a choice?

Two generations separated Bessie and her grandmother. She was well aware that her generation's vocabulary had much changed from her grandmother's. The difficulty arising in the chasm between the differing ages of the two, making words so slippery that she thought of the potential of a language not existing between us with the same meanings. The thought struck Bessie that they each had had a common experience -- Europe. Surprised, she thought why had she not spoken to Bonnemaman about it since she had returned last October. What little I know of this woman!

"Bonnemaman, you met Bonpapa while you were visiting Europe. I've talked to him often about his travels but I don't believe I've ever asked you about your memories. Forgive me for never asking but now I'm eager to hear."

Bonnemaman smiled, resting her chin on her closed hand, said, "Oh, yes, I well remember my impression of the old countries. So full of glamour, especially to us visitors from such a young country. The sheer magnitude of the history that surrounds one is at first, incomprehensible, but then one realizes actual life in Europe is weighed down by the memories of a tremendous past. Bonpapa and I have been disturbed by the papers lately and discussing the ominous political storms rising again in Europe between France and Prussia. One presumes to believe that Europeans live only with the memories of their past. Bonpapa's belief is that we have made our American history alive in which we all share an awakening future. At any age or point in time, he says, we must guard against inhibitions to act while maintaining an innocent eye. Otherwise, we drift back to seeing by custom only. What we expect to see, not what is there. Your grandfather and I have no use for dead issues and me none for stagnant souls."

Bessie, amazed by these unexpected articulate revelations of Bonnemaman's pondered, How sad! Somewhere, some time ago, I must have succumbed to the male myth that only knowledgeable, well educated men could have insights on the human condition? Am I one of those stagnating souls?

Reaching for Bessie's hand and kissing her fingertips, Bonnemaman said, "I need not worry about your soul, my dear. You have a marvelous reserve to hold tightly to what you value and an expectancy that I have seen you hold in excited anticipation." With a barely audible sigh, she said, "My eyes are feeling heavy. I think I shall go upstairs and crawl under that warm comforter Sophie has laid on my bed." With a louder tone of voice, "I believe your grandfather should also be thinking of turning in!"

Bonpapa put down his snifter and opened the library door for Bonnemaman then turned and gave us a knowing wink as he closed the door behind him. Bessie thought for the first time that Bonnemaman might have a great deal of influence on Bonpapa. She had always assumed that the relationship was much like the one her parents had - one of just quiet resolve.

George thumbed through the pages of a music book and again started to play a more lilting piece. Bemusement crossed Bessie's face with the sudden discovery of an inner person in Bonnemaman she had never known. What loss that I did not know! What wasted time have I spent talking on trivial, inane matters. Have I been blinded by habit? I've been seeing my grandmother and my mother as properly behaved puppets that blithely go about their lives without thought? How many view me in the same circumstances? Do I have a choice? Oh, someone tell me!

The snow had stopped falling outside and the gas lamp from the street flickered across Papa's face. It was obvious that he had been intent on listening to Bonnemaman even though his eyes had been lowered to his book on his lap. He slowly rose and put down his reading glasses on the side table. George stopped playing and looked across the room and caught Papa's eye. Papa moving toward the library door stopped and placed his hand on George's shoulder. "Play on son. You play so well." Papa's difficulty in hearing prevented him from the fullness of the music but he swayed back and forth anyway. George finished the piece with a flourished run up the keyboard and a final dramatic chord. Papa smiled. "Music can express immense grief, George, but it also has the marvelous power to heal the deepest pain."

George began to play a Mozart waltz. "I hope this makes everyone dance, Papa."

Bessie stood to give her father a goodnight kiss. He held her a little longer than usual then spun her around in a little dance step. Pulling her back he whispered in her ear, "No bird flies too high if she flies with her own wings."

"I'll remember Papa."

He extended his hand to Mumsie but she said, "You go along dear, I would like to sit by the fire a little longer."

"Goodnight, children," Papa said, looking down at Howard who was preoccupied with his new Henty book. With a slight nudge from Mumsie's insistent foot, under her breath, she remarked, "Howard!"

"Oh, goodnight, Papa!" he muttered without looking up from his book.

George noticed the snow falling heavily now. He hoped it would not fall too deep to stop the carriage from getting through tomorrow. Justine lived uptown on East Seventy-second Street. He was anxious to see her. He had been unable to since coming home for the holidays from Harvard. They both had family commitments but she had promised him she would spend the entire day tomorrow with him.

Annoyed by Howard's indifferent goodnight to Papa, George thought how it exemplified his insolent attitude.

The family is still too indulgent with him. Sitting around the campfire during Howard's and my camping trip last summer it was extremely difficult to talk to him about any subject that required some depth of thinking. He could not seem to comprehend or verbalize on any important topic, certainly not his future. It was easier to let him run on about shooting a stag.

Mumsie put down her embroidery and rubbed her eyes. She sighed. "Well loves, it has been a wonderful Christmas. I savor each one now because it won't be long before you have all gone your separate ways and I suppose it will be a rare thing to have us all together to celebrate a Christmas Day."

Howard sat up sharply. The thought had never crossed his mind that things in this house one day would be different. He knew he dreamed about the day that he would be gone, but the others! Wild thoughts darted through his mind. Bessie and George gone! Where? Who will I talk to? What will it be like in this big house alone with just Papa and Mumsie? I never thought about them going. Sure, George has been infatuated with Justine and Bessie has been involved with Carley. But marriage! Children! Nieces and nephews?

Mumsie tapped Howard's knee saying, "Howard, did you hear me?"

"No, I'm sorry, what did you say?"

"I said dear, I think you should turn in also. You have to be at the rink early tomorrow for practice. Didn't you say you were thinking about joining the ice hockey team?"

"Yes, I've been giving it some thought. I like it better than doing figures. It's more exciting and I can skate with my friends. The men in the figure skating club are all so much older than me. They insist on referring to me as a youngster. Even that article in the newspaper about the competition said, 'Ward, a clever youngster'. When will they let me grow up?"

George turned his head away to conceal a smile thinking, not until you decide to grow up. I know I'm waiting.

Bessie, without paying any attention to Howard's whining, said, "Yes, Mumsie, I've been thinking the same thing. I wonder where we'll all be? I just had a bizarre thought - imagine Howard at attention in a naval uniform." She started to laugh but catching a glimpse of a tear in Mumsie's eye she quickly added, "We won't ever be far from you." Mumsie bent down to kiss the top of Bessie's forehead and blowing George a goodnight kiss she ushered an irritated Howard out of the room.

Bessie's gaze was intent on the fire but she seemed not to notice the ebbing flames. George stopped playing and rose to stoke the fire. Bessie did not move. He felt strangely compelled to talk to her. Leaning against the mantel watching the fire he said with a faint trace of a laugh, "Bess are you here or are you drifting into your love affairs with dead artists?"

Bessie's head jerked up. She could feel the heat of a blush rising up across her face. A sudden sense of fear that someone might have penetrated her thoughts - confused, embarrassing, and intimate thoughts. Looking intently at George she realized he was not really asking a question of her but was making fun of her.

"You're seeing Justine tomorrow, aren't you?"

"Yes. What did you think about Papa's little outburst?'

"Surprised, I guess! Papa so seldom says what's on his mind. It's kind of refreshing. Do you think he tells Mumsie his secrets? I can just see him putting his pipe down and saying, "Sophie, I'm thinking of canoeing down the Amazon again. You don't mind, dear, if I'm gone for a year or two?

George laughed and pushed at the fire with the poker. "No, I can't imagine. But I can just see Mumsie's reaction. 'Yes, dear. Do take your raincoat. You remember what a heavy rainy season they have? Do you think I can have the painters in while you're gone? The bedroom ceilings are in such terrible condition.' She's so, so practical. Thank God, she gave Howard the prunes for Christmas! I think she believes it will get him out of the bathroom faster in the morning. What if Carley said he was going down the Amazon?"

"It would not likely be Carley but me that would be canoeing down the Amazon. Like Mumsie, Carley would be picking out paint colors. Will you listen to me! You're making me say wicked things."

"But is it wicked to wish? I can see myself lounging happily on a rock in the south of France, lazily watching the Mediterranean lapping at the feet of pretty French girls."

"I'm not so foolish to think George that you would look at anyone else but Justine! Instead you would be playing your violin beneath her balcony in Verona."

"You're not the only one mocking me. Bayard was teasing me the other day and he had the sheer gall to say in that false haughty tone that he uses to mock, 'You're such a persistent chap, old fellow, that you'll win in the end, I am sure.' I'm just afraid she will not come out on the balcony."

"I think I understand Justine. Have you ever thought about what she would have to give up if she marries you?"

"What does that mean? It sounds like you might be having second thoughts about marrying Carley, Bess?"

"Well, I may too, have a difficult time opening the balcony door!"

****

BESSIE

November 15, 1896

*Oakwood
Perkins Street
Jamaica Plain, Boston, Mass.*

Dearest Bonnemaman,

Life takes its usual enigmatic twists as I pen this to you as Mrs. Charles Bruen Perkins, a new title, a new life but still your loving granddaughter. I remember Papa saying, "No second thoughts allowed, the first thoughts have to be the best." I am bathing in happiness in my decision to share a life with Carley. His strength of character is a good balance for my own unbridled one. His direct simplicity draws a power of attention. It is a subtle quality which I have found in my favorite artists, in children and most of all, in the wise. As a wise old grandmother said to me the day before my wedding, "Most women betray their indecisions as to the style of the hour through dressing by piece-meal. Such a manner of dress sadly lacks style and unity. Remember where in life one needs to put the accent." Every morning before rising I will remind myself of that wise woman.

 Wasn't the wedding beautiful? Mumsie decorated the house so beautifully. Everyone remarked how they loved the choristers from the Paulists Church. Howard was the only one who seemed annoyed describing them as bellowing with their endless verses of "Filie et Filice". Howard is never one to mince his words.

 Our trip on the Ile de Normandie was smooth without being troubled by bad weather. Retracing one's steps through Europe is reliving a wonderful *dream one has already had but the political reality is unsettling. The unthinkable idea of another war would certainly be greater in scope and turn its pristine landscape into a nightmare. The ocean which separates us also insulates us. The nightmare, if it comes, will only be theirs.*

Life is going to be very hectic for me while I try to settle us into Oakwood. I hope to convert one of the rooms into a studio. I have an aching desire to get my hands on a canvas. The last months have left me filled with expectancy to see if I have a new expression in the midst of paint.

Do give my love to Bonpapa. I will write again soon.

*Your loving granddaughter,
Mrs. Charles Bruen Perkins*

I adored being the center of attention. Mumsie fussing over me while I was putting on my wedding dress. With all the excitement I didn't worry about anyone. Such lovely, delicious narcissism! Just me! The house was decorated for me! I didn't feel guilty. And I didn't feel like the blushing bride. Mumsie seemed to be a blushing mother. While she was fluttering about I would catch her glancing at me apprehensively. I knew she was searching for words. Honestly, I was glad she could not find the words. I cannot believe that we have the same feelings. Sex is not a word in Mumsie's vocabulary, or anyone else's for that matter.

I thought I would feel differently? I didn't have any idea what to expect. Was I to experience instantaneously overnight some kind of transformation? From virgin to Mrs., a feeling of purity to impurity, white to black, the absurdity of never wearing a white wedding dress ever again. Who made me feel like this? Am I just imagining that people look at me differently?

Mrs. Charles Bruen Perkins, Mrs. Elizabeth Ward Perkins, Mrs., Mrs., what? Elizabeth! Elizabeth! Bessie! Have you ever felt when saying your name over and over and over again in your mind, you can't relate to it. As if the name belongs to someone else. If someone calls your name you know you will answer. But how do I associate those written letters, those spoken syllables not to a physical body but to another reality which is really me?

Papa kept patting my hand as he accompanied me down the staircase into the front parlor to be married. Even in the carriage on our way to board the Ile de Normandie he held my hand but said nothing. Did he feel a bond was about to be broken? What do men feel when their daughters are given into a physical relationship with another man and they are no longer able to protect them? Anger? Jealousy? Impotency? Papa's face had a look of sadness when he waved goodbye to me from the dock and yet still he said nothing. What were the words I wanted to hear?

We had a nice cabin on the boat but it wasn't the romantic trysting honeymoon hideaway I had always dreamed about. Maybe such a place doesn't exist! I was nervous but Carley is not a passionate man. He had only kissed me lightly on the mouth a few times. Carley makes me feel safe and our first night together he was very tentative, to say the least. I didn't know what to think! Is it only in my books of poems that I have felt that rush of passion. That wave of tension, heat and ache that begins in my loins and travels up my body like a spasm. Is this the man who could make me feel that passion?

****

HOWARD

November 20, 1896

The "Ava"
9 East 10th Street

Dear Bonnemama,

Fifteen years old. Fifteen dollars in presents, fifteen everything. It was such fun when I opened your birthday note to find five whole dollars. It made me feel very rich. I am so sorry that you have been suffering so much and I hope that you feel ever so much better now.

Moving into our new house is taking its toll on Mama. She is working herself to death. Every day she says she will rest on the next, but she never does. And to think that Bessie, or rather, Mrs. Charles B. Perkins is coming home so soon. She writes that she is bringing me a mysterious present, but she will not tell me what it is. George gave me a book by "Henty". With love for Bonpapa and lots of kisses for yourself,

Your loving grandson,
Howard Ridgeley Ward

Can't wait for Sunday. Junius promised me he would go out to the island again in New York harbor. It's like being involved in an unsolved mystery ever since they started unloading the crates from the docked French ship several months ago. Some of them were opened and I could make out some strange kind of sculpted iron pieces. They were all marked with numbers. Since then they have started to construct them and one of the construction men let me inside to see the interior. Some Frenchman named Bartholdi was supposed to have designed it as a gift to the United States but it is hard to imagine just what it will look like. One worker said it will be a woman holding a raised torch. Why a woman?

    Bessie coming home so soon after her wedding! I wouldn't be surprised if it's Mama's doing. She worked herself into one of her usual fits of frenzy, flitting up and down the stairs, telling the movers "Put that dresser here. No, put it there." Then complaining that she didn't know what to do with it. Thank God for Rose! Her Irish eyes just smiled at Mumsie and winked at me while she kept on about her business of unpacking. I tried my best to make myself scarce while Papa gritted his pipe between his teeth and with one hand over his good ear, endured Mumsie's complaints. We were here only two days when she took to her bed complaining again about not feeling well. I wonder if it could be just a ploy to make Bessie come home. It was curious when at the dinner table the other night Papa mentioned he hoped Bessie was happy in getting adjusted to her new home. Mama looked up at him and a grimace crossed her face. I've never thought about it before but could it be that Mama didn't want Bessie to leave home.

****

GEORGE

November 25, 1896

Dear Bonpapa,
A law book sits open in front of me but I found myself reading the pages as if they were blank. My thoughts turned to you and your revered Harvard. I'm well into my junior year at the 'Yard' with no clear purpose yet as to what I wish to do with my life. I suppose that when I finish my undergraduate studies I shall study law, but to what purpose? I can't see myself arguing obscure points of jurisprudence in the courtroom, and still less researching case histories for someone else. Father always says that it isn't important so much what studies I pursue, and even less the practicality of what I am learning at the moment. He tells me that this is the only time in my life that I can try to become EDUCATED. Educated to do what?

There has been an early snow here in Cambridge, and unusually cold for this time of the year. I wakened early this morning (5:00) and could not go back to sleep. I finally dressed and went for a walk, down by the Charles. The water has a thin sheet of ice on it. I can imagine it fully frozen and ice skaters everywhere, a sort of Bostonian Holland. Too early for that, although it reminded me of Howard and his skates. I watched him while he was practicing on the ice the last time I was home. I don't think he knew I was there. I stopped in on impulse and didn't want to distract him. He's good, isn't he? I'm so used to thinking of him as the baby that it takes some getting used to think of him as talented or graceful...or human.

My envy of Bessie has increased twofold since she was able to return to Europe this time with Carley in tow. I wonder if she views the European society differently now as a married woman? I shall be having dinner with them on Thursday evening before she goes to New York. I understand Mumsie is ill again so Bessie is going to manage the household again. How difficult for her with her own new home to settle!

While walking back to my room along the river, I began to muse. I always look forward to the summer, the beach and water, the laziness...but the winter is more like me. Overcast, sharp winds, serious. You see, Bonpapa, my mood at the moment, perhaps because of exams next week?

I will be able to see Justine in several weeks. She is visiting friends during the early holidays. I wish we were closer.

Your affectionate grandson,
George

Winter, it crawls inside your bones! Cold, dormant, shrill winds. I love Cambridge in the winter. The cutting contrast of the pristine white snow on the green branches of the tall evergreens. Evergreens that remain untouched by the seasons. Each winter they continue to prove their enduring nature, hanging on to their green spark of life, that small part of nature which remains constant, seemingly unaffected by the winter dying of the sun's light, while all else sleeps. I become obsessed with the need to daily inspect the stark, denuded trees for any hint of green to see if they will be awakened by the equinoctial sun or will the angel of winter death have strangled the sap that gives them renewed life. Energy to renew themselves. That seems to be the nature of man too. What is it I need to awaken me? I can't seem to control these obsessions of mine. I walk the same path every morning, my eyes inspect the same limbs of the same trees, I return back to my dorm room and play the same violin piece, it must be played twice, then I arrange my pencils and pens, all sharpened and according to size on the right side of my desk. I feel trapped by something. I lay in bed at night unable to sleep out of fear. I don't know what fear! The cold night brings with it my own struggle with the angel of winter death in a battle to keep my lifeblood alive. I put myself in a meditative state in a struggle to make my mind and body numb so I can sleep.

In contrast to my state of numbness, Bessie's enthusiasm kept her ranting for hours about the excitement of her experiences in Europe. She is the usual epitome of decorum and propriety but I think she had one too many glasses of wine. Much to my amazement she started talking excitedly about the intimate details of Michelangelo's male nudes, their expressive power that made her feel an ecstasy beyond religion. Carley looked startled and recanted the wine. Possibly I am the only one who knows her secret side.

She caught my eyes following Carley as he replaced the decanter on the sideboard and admonished me. "You're not listening George. Where are your thoughts fleeing? Do you not have something to say?"

"I'm not slighting you." I was rather enjoying her tipsy state. "I was just envying your footsteps on the cobblestone streets of Paris and Rome, stopping at all those little cafes, savoring the subtleties of regional wines while drinking in the sights. I was envisioning myself enjoying the crimson richness of a glass of vin rouge at a Left Bank cafe as you obviously did. Do you think I have a chance soon to do the same?"

Bessie tried to assume a sense of seriousness in an effort to overcome her tipsy state. "Have you talked to Uncle George? I know you're concerned about your future and who else but your namesake might be able to help."

"Because I carry his name gives me no cause to

think he would have any concern for my future."

Bessie tilted her wineglass to sip the last red droplets left in the bottom. She slowly turned it around and around by its stem while her eyes fixated on its prism glints. "Maybe you're right. Maybe no one can help you with your future. It seems to find its own course no matter how hard you try to guide it."

I instantly regretted my somber response about my future that provoked her mood to change so quickly from playing the evening's delightful blithe spirit of lightheartedness. I felt I had wounded a nightingale.

****

BESSIE

December 6, 1896

Dear Bonnemaman,

I have a very special early Christmas gift to give you. I will be bestowing the title of Great-Grandmother on you come next July. I am expecting in July!

It's such a bizarre feeling - pregnancy - it's as if I have been separated into two beings in the same body. I am creating! Or is it re-creating?

I have been here in New York now for a couple of weeks. Mumsie seems to be getting her strength back. The new house's library is a fabulous place to retreat to and lose oneself in a long forgotten, once beloved book.

I'm hoping to find an appropriate time to talk with Mumsie and Papa. I don't know why I feel so apprehensive about telling them. Deep inside I feel the news will upset them - as if I'm breaking some unspoken sacred bond - losing me forever. They can no longer call me home to manage Howard and Papa when Mumsie has one of her spells. How did you feel when your daughters, Aunt Lily and Aunt Bessie were married? Am I wrong in wanting to put my own new little family first in my thoughts, needs and priorities? Should I not now look to thoughts, needs and priorities? Should I not now look to Carley and my children to come to fulfill my life?

I must tell them I can only stay another week then I must get back to Boston to prepare the house for the holidays. I have not yet told them that I promised Carley that we would spend the holidays with his family in Boston. My first Christmas away from home. Remember the time we talked on that Christmas night in the old house about the time when we would be going our separate ways. The time has come and it is difficult.

Please write me soon. Your wise words will be a comfort.

Affectionately,
Bessie

A baby, so quick, so soon! Carley is so pleased with himself. Thirty-four, and he was anxious to become a father. He had told me that because his own father was past forty when he was born he thought he missed a real father-son relationship. But so quick! Can I really be pregnant? I wish someone had told me about this. Nobody talks about it. It's as if the men hold all the secrets. How could I have been so naive to think that you had to have relations with your husband over some period and it, whatever it is, would build up and then it would happen? Absurd! I should have known better!

I'm afraid! Lord, I'm so afraid! I remember the screams from Mumsie when Howard was born. The blood, all the blood on the sheets that I saw when Rose hurried them down the stairs to throw them into the washing tub. She caught me looking from behind my bedroom door and couldn't help but notice my fearful eyes but she didn't say a word. I remember George perched atop my bed during the birth and his face turning ashen like he was going to be ill. When Papa came to tell us we could go in to see the new baby I was terribly apprehensive and then overwhelmed by how exhausted Mumsie looked. George took only a glance at the baby then turned abruptly and left without saying a word. Later in his room he told me that the smell, I think it was ether, sickened him. He didn't understand what happened but he was afraid that Mumsie might have died. He said he never wanted to hear those sounds, smell that stench, or see that wretched, tired look on Mumsie's face ever again. He asked me, "Why is someone born with such pain?" I could not answer him.

****

HOWARD

Thursday, April 28, 1898

Dearest Bonpapa,

It is so exciting here, to hear everyone talking about the war and extras coming out every hour. I have written the names of the warships on slips of paper and we are following their movements with great interest. Recruiting tents have been pitched in Union and Madison Squares.

This morning the "Evening Telegram" had an extra out at seven o'clock in the morning.

I think that my plans for the summer are to stick to George as much as possible after my examinations in the spring. I am going to try Latin, French (both elementary); Elementary Algebra, Plain Geometry; English, Ancient History which includes both Roman and Grecian.

I have read the article on bicycling in the Fortnightly Review, and found it most interesting. Powell does not seem to like the chainless wheel, but I cannot believe that it is not going to supersede the chain wheel. Several people I know ride the chainless, and they all agree that it runs easier and smoother than the other model, and now that they have come down to seventy-five dollars, they should be more popular. A bicycle show has been held here all last week, and about fifteen manufacturers exhibited chainless wheels.

I have been skating this morning and practicing for the figure skating competition which takes place in the middle of next month. I had the good luck to make the Cutler Hockey team this winter. It is great fun to practice early in the morning twice a week.

We have so little news from you or Bonnemama, but

we hope that it means that you are growing stronger. I did not write to you before this, dear Bonpapa, because I thought that you were too ill to want letters. Mama and Papa are dining out tonight and I am alone in the house, which seems so very large without Bessie and George. With much love to Bonnemama,

Your affectionate grandson,
Howard

P.S. I wonder if Miss Angier would be startled to know that my cyclometer has registered 1500 miles since she gave it to me.

    September! Harvard! Me! At Harvard! In step with all the others, Bonpapa, Papa, George. I feel like a damn cutout cardboard copy. It's like a magnet, you get so far out and bang! You get zinged back. All the muscle in Bonpapa's lengthy financial reach did not get me into the Naval Academy. It could have been my grades but he still is a powerful man. I bet he could have twisted somebody's arm a little bit harder.

    Well, I'll tell them one thing, I'm not going to be a lawyer stuck in one of those musty old offices with some crooked Tammany Hall politician with his stogie clenched between his gummy teeth wanting me to represent him on some charge with a few added perks thrown in. Of course, under the table. Or maybe I'd represent one of Papa's classy friends down at the Union Club on a property deal. I'd probably favor the Tammany Hall guy. He's got the girls!

    Thinking of girls, I really enjoyed the musical Junius and I saw last night. I was especially enamored of a chorus girl on the left end and I was also attracted to one in the center but my distant admiration is about the extent of my research in their direction. Later in the evening when we got back to our rooms my nerve was severely put to the test. I had picked up a book and was reading when a senior happened by with two very chorusy, chorus girls. I was on tenterhooks and frightened to death until they went, such was my fear of the proctor. I'm never very courageous in such matters.

Look at the line over at the recruiting tent. Some of those guys look younger than me. I could make Mumsie take to her bed without a wave of her handkerchief if I joined up. What if I did? I'd make a damn good officer. Good-looking one too! I think ole' Teddy was right when he said, "McKinley had no more backbone than a chocolate eclair." They blow up the Maine and McKinley is still scratching his head. I'd gladly trade my schoolbooks in for an army duffel bag if I could go with them to Cuba.

Well, Harvard, you've got me. But the devil better believe me, I'll find a way out. I need money. No need to tell me it's a tired cliche that money is the root of all evil but it gets the job done. It gets you where you want to go and in my mind, that's out. Out in the world! Around it! On top of it! And hopefully below it where the gold lies!

****

GEORGE

RECEIVED at the WESTERN UNION BUILDING, 195 Broadway, N.Y.
April 15, 1901
Mrs. Charles Bruen Perkins
Oakwood, Brookline, Mass.

Am taking the 1:00 PM train to Boston Friday. Have important news. Wait dinner.

George

If only I could see the dust of George's carriage rising from the drive. Waiting like this is excruciating, especially when someone tantalizes you with the phrase 'important news'. Last evening's rain has finally filled Neptune's fountain basin. The showers of April so refresh our winter weary lives. How many, many times have I stood loving the way the raindrops course their way down the curves of Neptune's body making it glisten as he remains unbending. Why is it man needs to constantly create images of himself so erect, taut muscles, unbending, no trace of human weakness and always the weapon in his hand, slingshot, sword or Neptune's trident? Who is he fending off? Who is the enemy or is it to shield him from the emotional trespass of all others, enemy or not? Why is it that man is so terrified of emotion? It's more than water the body needs.

Bessie was startled to hear little Francis rushing down the stairs screaming, "He's here! He's here!" She had forgotten how excited he was about his coming. Francis had barely allowed the driver to stop the carriage before he reached up to open the carriage door. George dropped down to the gravel and grabbed

Francis and swung him around in the air much to his glee. Two-year-old Mary stood quietly on the porch holding Rose's hand, shyly hiding her face behind Rose's apron wondering what all the fuss was about.

Bessie waited at the top of the stairs. A moment ago she had thought of flying away. Now she was basking in the joy of watching her oldest son lovingly greet her brother. What a contradiction life is!

George climbed the stairs with Francis still in his arms and gave Bessie a kiss on the cheek. She thought he looks so relaxed and unusually happy. "How mischievous of you to telegraph `important news', and then make me wait. Come in and get settled quickly. I can't wait much longer to hear."

"It's still fun to tease my sister. But you are the first to hear my news, so feel yourself honored. Go twiddle your thumbs in the library and I'll join you in a minute as soon as I take my bags upstairs and give the children their presents."

Bessie went instead to the dining room and poured two glasses of sherry from the decanter. George finally descended the stairs and Bessie was waiting impatiently.

"Does your news deserve a toast?" handing him his glass.

"Certainly! Allow me!" George raised his glass to touch Bessie's and said, "Here's to July in Paris where Justine and I will take the long anticipated walk to the altar."

"Paris! Why Paris? How marvelous! How delicious! Paris!" Bessie's arms swung around George's neck spilling sherry on his jacket. In her excitement he grabbed her waist and twirled her around the room. They fell laughing on the settee, feeling like children again.

Bessie caught her breath. "After all these years, she

finally accepted your proposal. You've been in love with her since we were teenagers. What changed her mind?"

"Persistence, I guess. I didn't want to wait any longer and I wanted to get on with my life. I felt I couldn't do that without Justine. Out of desperation, I told her if she did not accept my proposal she would never, and I meant NEVER see me again."

"She didn't for a minute believe you? Not Justine, with your long history!" Bessie laughed. "You have always been the quintessential puppy dog when it comes to Justine. You men, all of you are like books without covers. So easy to read. You, George, not see Justine?" She laughed heartily.

"Okay, okay! You've made your point. Probably not! Believe me I'm aware all my practiced, controlled notion of discipline blows away with the westerly winds when it comes to Justine."

"Well, tell me. What did she finally say after such a strong ultimatum?"

"She seemed taken aback. I guess I had never been so outspoken in all the years we've known each other. She finally asked me to give her a few days and promised me she would give me an answer then. Needless to say, I waited with grrr-eat anxiety. As you now know, she accepted but with a strange request."

"Strange! How strange?"

"She wanted to be married in Paris in the Episcopal Church with only a few members of our family present. She was adamant that it not be turned into a big celebratory occasion."

"George, this is difficult for me to ask but I have to know for not only your sake but my sake since I hold you dearly as a brother. Does she love you?"

"I love her. Perhaps irrationally, but I love her."

"You didn't answer my question."

George looked at her, his thin lips tightened, he turned abruptly and walked over and sat down in the wingchair. He picked up his glass, sipped the rest of the sherry in his glass then began turning it around and around in his hand. Obvious irritation crossed his face.

Bessie decided to check on dinner in the kitchen, giving herself a chance to recover from the unexpected news. How over the years George's stature became like Neptune. Always erect, like poured steel unbending in virtue, immediately defensive when he feels challenged. Does he hide in this obsessive love? I don't know! He washes his love over Justine letting it wrap her into his cocoon. He has built that cocoon all his life. Nearly impenetrable. Never allowing anyone in. Not even me. I've unwittingly watched him do that and have said nothing. I've always been here for him but I don't really know my own brother. There's something wrong. An inequity in this relationship and I don't know who's at fault, Justine or George. Maybe Justine senses this marriage might be wrong and that is why she waited before she accepted. Love! People need it and most of all I want my brother's life to bask in it. I don't want him paralyzed like Neptune hovering over a dry fountain waiting for it to fill again with water.

Bessie picked up a spoon and dipped it in the soup, taking a taste. "Ouch! My God that is hot."

"Well, what did you expect, my dear? When soup is on the stove it's usually hot. What is the matter with you?" Rose handed her a glass of water.

"I'm sorry. This was not the joy I had expected when I received George's news. If you had been listening at the library door you would have heard that George is marrying Justine in Paris."

"No, I didn't do my usual tiptoeing if that is what you are asking? You know the children tiptoe too!"

"Sorry again, Rose. Don't mean to be accusatory. I don't know if I understand what love is better than the next person. I've always liked and admired Justine but there is something ominous about this impending wedding. It's like a sudden revelation to me. What have I missed in their relationship over the years? Please Lord, help me understand! You better hold off dinner for awhile. I'll make some tea. Maybe it will calm us both before Howard arrives."

As Bessie put the tea tray down on the table, George had his head bowed with his eyes focused on his hands outstretched on his knees. "What can I say to you?"

"Nothing!" Noticing the excitement and enthusiasm gone from Bessie, he said, "Just wish me happiness."

The doorknocker banged loudly. Bessie reached for her glass of sherry and quickly finished it off. She stood up and smoothed the front of her dress, straightened her hair and while obviously trying to regain her composure said, "Well, now you will have to explain your professed love and marriage to Howard. I invited him to dinner but I only told him you were coming. I did not warn him about your important news. I don't know what his reaction will be. Not that you don't know he always seemed to bear a certain resentment toward your attachment to Justine. I don't believe he's ever shown an interest in a young lady. At least he has never spoken of anyone to me. Has he you?"

"No."

The doorknocker banged insistently again. Not anxious to answer the door, George placed his book of Keats back on the table. "I'll go. I'm sorry my news has upset you."

Reluctantly he walked toward the front door muttering, "I'm coming! I'm coming!" The knocker banged once again. Bessie sat back down on the settee still smoothing her skirt. She stared at Keats' name but no words or images soothed her mind. Just a sense of nothingness. I don't want to think anymore. I feel completely helpless. It's his life!

"George, how are you ole' man?" Howard came into the library grinning and gave Bessie a kiss on the cheek.

"George looks great, doesn't he Bess? Like a man with a future."

"Yes, he certainly does! While you two catch up on news I'll check with Rose to see how dinner is coming. The children are probably upstairs playing with the gifts George brought. Go up and say hello before dinner. I want Rose to give them their supper early so we can have a quiet evening."

As she closed the door she heard George say, "Forgive me Howard but I guess I'm a little behind in the news about what you've been doing."

Howard reached into his suit pocket and pulled out a silver cigarette case and attempted with an air of sophistication, tapped a cigarette on the case, put it into his mouth then looking at George said, "Do you have a light, ole' man?"

While George reached for the box of matches on Bessie's tea table, with a somewhat sardonic smile he said, "Okay, I'll ask. When did you start smoking?"

"Surprisingly enough, ole' man..."

"Wait, before you go on, what is this 'ole' man' remark although you do make me feel doddering at times?"

"Sorry! As I was saying, the last visit home Mumsie asked me why I didn't smoke. She said I was certainly old enough now, and men seem to get such relaxation, enjoyment and sociability from it. I couldn't agree with her more. Don't mention this to anyone but I started to experiment with cornsilk and some other imitations until I felt myself an expert. It does add a certain flair to one's character, don't you think?"

"Character involves a lot more than one's ability to flick a few cigarette ashes, Howard." George's amusement turned to irritation as he thought about the superciliousness of Howard's behavior. He walked over to the window where his eyes, like Bessie's, fell on the Neptune fountain. "How many years has that silly mythological god been standing in the garden? Stoic! That's what he is. Rain, sleet, snow, August sun, nothing changes him. Maybe burnishing his bronze a little more." George noticeably straightened his shoulders.

Howard, in a slight state of confusion being faced looking at George's back, tried to encourage a more lighthearted conversation. "Junius told me to send you his regards. He and I have quite a nice little suite now in Ware Hall, not far from the Yard."

George appeared not to have heard so Howard moved toward the window clearing his throat, he raised his voice and said, "I made the rowing team as cox and we have had a number of wins. I thought you would be rather proud of me since it was you that always encouraged me to stay with sports. So I want to thank you personally."

Howard reached out for a handshake and George shook it accepting Howard's gratefulness. "Of course I'm proud you have stuck with it and not given up. It's too easy to give up."

"The irony of it is that all these years I've been trying to grow taller, put on some weight and fill out. Now in order to remain cox I have to watch my weight and hope I don't grow until I graduate. Life sure doesn't give a damn, but seems to enjoy playing satanic tricks on one's self! Well, damn, I am going to eat like hell after graduation."

George noticed the dropping of curse words and thought, One more affectation. Is it for shock effect?

"This isn't a business trip, George, is it? Bessie looked a little strange, slightly upset when I arrived. Was it something you said?"

"I told her Justine and I were going to be married in July."

"Oh, my God, you did it!"

"God had nothing to do with it. Why don't you congratulate me now?" George said with a noticeable edge of irritation in his voice.

"Certainly you have my congratulations. I didn't mean to offend you. You just caught me by surprise."

George turned back to the window. A sense of discomfort hovered over the two of them. Howard dropped into the wingchair and felt a nerve wracking sense of guilt for the tension in the room but was not sure why.

Bessie found them still in silence when she opened the door and said that dinner was ready to be served.

****

June 1901
New York

Howard's uproarious laughter could be heard coming from the library as George put his umbrella in the stand. Brushing off the little drops of moisture still lingering on his shoulders, he shuddered and headed for the library. His irritation with Howard had been nagging at him ever since Howard had arrived home from Harvard. George had neither seen nor heard any signs that Howard was taking any steps toward deciding on a reputable profession or obtaining a summer job. All he had heard was Howard spouting at the dinner table incredulous schemes and ideas of mining and finding gold.

"Gold! Gold! Gold! What does he think? That Papa has the Midas touch for all his extraordinary fantasies?" George muttered as he opened the library door.

Howard looked over the top of the paper and seeing it was George said, "George, have you seen the paper? Obviously you haven't! Forgive me, ole' man, but it is rather a kick. Did you know you are stealing Mr. William Bayard Cutting's greatest treasure? His daughter Justine?"

Will he ever stop calling me 'ole' man'? Still hasn't dropped those awful affectations. George sat in the wingchair across from Howard. He braced himself for Howard's inevitable repartee.

"Listen to this," Howard chuckled, folding back the page of the Christian Science Monitor. Sitting more erect and with a pompous tone he started reading the headline. *'Young Bayard Cutting, Jr., falls in love with the witty, pretty, piquant Irish beauty, Lady Sybyl Cuffe, in London. While George Cabot Ward, his friend from boyhood, falls in love with Justine Cutting,* his *chum's musical sister in New York.'* Can you believe that?

Headlines! Your little love affair has made the headlines. Pictures and all!"

George reached out to grab the paper but Howard snatched it back laughing. "Wait, there's more. Da-da-da-da-de-dah!" he mused, glancing down through the article. "There's all this stuff first on your boyhood chum, good ole' Bayard. Ah, wait, here it is. *But the little God of Love hasn't spent his time with Mr. Cutting. No, indeed. Instead he has purposely ignored him and devoted himself exclusively to Mr. Cutting's greatest treasure - his daughter Justine.'* Ah, that I can attest. Your exclusive devotion to Justine. I have lived with that devotion it seems like all my life."

George could no longer contain his rage for Howard's mocking attitude. He jumped out of his chair and angrily snatched the paper.

"Get out! Get out! What would you know of love! You just hang around the bawdy houses or the dance halls hoping to see God knows what!"

Howard's face turned ashen. He started to sputter, "That's unfair! My going to the theater to see the new musicals has nothing to do with your love affair."

"You call that theater! You'd only see Macbeth if Lady Macbeth did a high kick in a tutu."

Howard jumped out of the chair and turned toward the door at which moment it opened and he came face to face with Mumsie. The air was still ringing from the invectives and Mumsie seeing the paper crumpled in George's clenched fist and his pencil tight mouth knew she was intruding upon a scene again between her two sons.

"Howard, did you not tell me you had some letters to write? I'm expecting you to make better use of your time while you're home, young man." Glancing at George's rigid stance before the front window she continued, "And I have a suspicion that you, young man, are somewhat responsible for the atmosphere in this room at the moment. And clean up that mess you've made with your pipe."

Feeling somewhat little boyish, Howard swiped at the ashes on the endtable. Picking up his pipe and pouch he tried to assert a victorious manner and said, "I'm finished with the paper George. You may have it now."

Mumsie placed her hand on George's stiffened arm and reached down to take the paper from his hand. Seating herself next to the fireplace she smoothed out the rumpled pages. Reaching into the pocket of her dress for her reading glasses she looked quietly up at George's back. Silently she started to read to herself. A smile crossed her face and she said, "Have you read this, dear?"

"No, Mother." Anger still smoldering in George's voice.

"You should dear. It sounds rather delightful."

"Well, it certainly delighted Howard!"

"I know at times his childishness can be rather annoying but in time he will grow up, dear."

"Grow up! Good God, he is twenty years old. When will you and Papa decide he is grown?"

Realizing that something more than just Howard's behavior was bothering George she tried to soothe the tension and picking up the paper again. "Listen, dear. This is charming. *As the result of Cupid's visits came the formal announcement the other day of the engagement of Miss Justine B. Cutting, daughter of Mr. and Mrs. William Bayard Cutting, to George Cabot Ward, son of Mr. and Mrs. Thomas Wren Ward and grandson of Samuel G. Ward, who for many years was prominently identified with Lenox and New York.'* Oh, that comment will please Bonpapa."

George was still standing at the window with his

hands clenched behind his back as she continued reading aloud, `And those who know say it is just what they expected. For young Ward has loved Justine Cutting, and her alone, ever since the days when he and her brother Bayard were first school chums together and Miss Justine herself was little Justine and wore short skirts and her hair down her back. The announcement of Miss Cutting's engagement was expected by those who had watched the shy little girl grow into a tall, lithe, reserved young woman.'

"She's more than that George. She is remarkably beautiful and talented as well. I could not be more happy for you. I'm sure she will make you a marvelous wife and mother of your children."

George still did not move. The streetlights flashed on throwing their glow across the library floor. Mumsie slipped her glasses back into her pocket knowing that dinner would be soon and she should tidy her hair before Papa's steps could be heard coming in the door. Whatever was bothering George she hoped Papa could handle. She had tried but hesitated at the idea of having to deal with what was evidently a perturbing problem.

Let Papa handle it, she thought as she climbed the stairs to her bedroom.

George picked up the paper that Mumsie had left on the chair and stared at the pictures of Justine and him. Graphic drawings of dogwood surrounded their photographs but curiously a nymph playing a lute among the dogwoods lies next to Justine's picture under which was printed Little Miss Justine Cutting.

George shuddered. Damn! It makes me sound like a conniving monster, tearing their sweet, innocent daughter from the safety of that goddamn fortress they live in.

He started to read where Mumsie left off glancing

quickly through the writing about Bayard's engagement when his eyes fell upon the paragraph starting *'Very different was the romance of his old schoolboy friend and college chum, George Cabot Ward. One was a courtship of six years. The other of six weeks.'* Good ole' Bayard! Never was one to take his time. "Take what you want when you see it", he was always telling me. I wonder if he would have done any better with Justine? Is she really committed to this marriage? In marriage, at least, I can keep close to her with her passion for music. There is so little need for us even to talk.

With a knot of tension still lingering in his chest he continued reading. *When Bayard Cutting, Jr., and George Ward wore short trousers and reveled in playing hooky they were fast friends. And, though separated, they are loyal friends now. They were chums at Dr. Peabody's famous Groton School, and still chums during their college days at Harvard. And if there is one member of the Cutting family who is not surprised at Miss Justine's engagement it is her brother Bayard. Time and again he has said to his friend Ward: "You're such a persistent chap, old fellow, that you'll win in the end, I am sure.*

"Well, I won, Bayard," Howard muttered dropping onto the settee. He sat staring at the photograph of Justine. "But won what?"

Disconsolately, he continued reading. *Perhaps, because he knew his secret was one of the reasons why every summer for many years back Bayard Cutting, Jr., insisted upon George Ward spending at least a month with him at "West Brook," the Cutting country place at Oakdale, Long Island. Here Miss Justine led the life that she cared for most. She is not a society girl. Though her debut about three years ago was one of the most exclusive and smartest functions ever given in*

New York. *Yet the debutante herself was glad when it was over. At that time her father gave her three strings of wonderful matched pearls, each string representing a fortune, and her mother, gowns fit for a princess, and they both hoped that their young daughter would be a society belle.*

But for formal, fashionable society Miss Cutting cared nothing. To be a musician was her sole ambition. Nothing could thrill her like music, and even during her first year as a debutante she would spend a good half of every day practicing in her music room and setting her thoughts to music.

It is well known that Miss Cutting is one of the best of the younger amateur musicians in New York. She is passionately fond of organ music and is an organist of exceptional talent. Mr. Ward is also a musician. And in his wooing Miss Cutting he has let his violin whisper more than mere words. This she understood and liked. During the past few years it has been their mutual love of music that has drawn them together.

But they had other mutual interests as well. They were both fond of outdoor life. It was George Ward who first taught Miss Cutting how to manage a horse. Now she drives tandem like a professional.

But Miss Cutting never thought of such a thing as falling in love with George Ward, so she told her intimate friend, "Dolly" Kernochan, as long back as two years ago.

Distraught, he read on. *And so she told the same "Dolly" Kernochan not more than two months ago. But since then, for some good reason, known only to herself, she has changed her mind. It is whispered that the last time that Mr. Ward proposed to Miss Cutting he strongly intimated that he wanted her love or nothing. And furthermore, if she didn't marry him she wouldn't see him. To this proposal it is said that Miss Cutting incidentally remarked before saying that she had grown so accustomed to him that to be with him had become one of those unfortunate habits she really couldn't break.*

And now the wedding is planned for the Fall.

Slamming the paper down on the endtable, George's body shook with rage. Damn it! So I'm just a habit!

****

HOWARD

June 8, 1901

Dear Bonpapa,

We feel quite settled at last, in a nice, comfortable little hotel called "The Garland" at the head of Suffolk Street quite in the center of everything.

This afternoon Mumsie and I went for a little exploration stroll down the Strand a few blocks - and saw lots of interesting shops and people and buildings. On the way back we found ourselves near the parade ground where soldiers were drilling and about who we made all sorts of speculations - and finally found out that the men were waiting for Lord Roberts to present them medals for bravery. So we waited about five minutes and "Bobs" looking as splendidly as he should, came by, and took off his hat to us.

George is at present helping the Cuttings so we are alone till dinner time and we plan to go to bed early and get a real rest.

From the window in our sitting room which is on the ground floor we can see the Strand crowded with busses almost hidden with advertisements, hansoms, four wheelers and fine carriages, all mixed in apparently hopeless confusion. It is wonderful how the police manage the traffic - just by lifting a finger. I can hardly realize that I am really so far from you and home.

Much love to Father, who I will write to next, dear Aunt Lily and Miss Angier.

Your loving grandson
Howard

Smell that air! Even laden with smoke and dankness it smells jolly good to me. Imagine me, Howard Ridgeley Ward, unattached, loose from the burden of family with their endless prattling of formalities, feet on English sidewalks, free to wander London like a spectator just passing through. Remarkable! Let's see, I have to get off at Queen Station according to the concierge's directions to the Metropolitan Fire Brigade's headquarters. Riding in the Underground, or as the English say, 'the tube', certainly a more descriptive word; makes me feel like a register receipt being shot through a Macy's pneumatic tube. This is it, Queen Station. Now, to find the Southwark Bridge. The fog is moving in. Sure puts a chill in the air. Well, will you look at this my good man, a total iron bridge. Extraordinary engineering. Standing here in the middle I can look up and down the Thames. The murky water carries old coal barges downriver at a snail's pace. Makes me shudder. The sooty brick covered factory buildings along the banks, the blackness of this heavy iron bridge, the moist droplets of the fog eerily disperses the light from the gas lamps, even though it's early in the day. Dicken's ghost is surely haunting nearby. Makes me believe that someone must be lurking around a dusky corner ready to kidnap me and ship me off to a slave factory soling old shoes. Ha! Wonder if the family would rescue me? Better stop daydreaming. It's getting late.

Finally, here's the station. Wow! Look at that beautiful steamer engine. I have got to get my hands on it. Will you feel the high polish they've rubbed on this beauty. The redness shines like the brightest of fires. They have the fire-box warm. It must be from this gas tube feeding it.

Suddenly brutal sounds reverberated off the walls of fire station. Oh, my God, it's an alarm!

"My ears!" Howard yelled at a running fireman as he clapped his hands over his ears.

Firemen were sliding down the pole from the upstairs barracks, throwing on their tunics, pulling on great knee boots and slinging their burnished helmets atop their heads. Howard shouted at a tall firemen as he raced across the firehouse floor toward the horses' stalls, "Where's the fire?"

"Whitechapel!" he shouted over his shoulder as he worked the lanyard and swivel holding the horses' harness.

Howard raced out to the street to flag down a hansom cab. As one turned the corner, he shouted to the driver to follow the fire engines to the blaze. As he fumbled in his pocket to find a shilling to pay the driver, he could see smoke pouring from a second floor window of what appeared to be a factory of some sorts. Looking up he spied some people trying to force open a third floor window. He could feel his heart start to race and a rising panic.

Oh, God, I wish these men would get that steamer in position faster. It looks like the blaze is only on the ground floor. I bet it's an overheated furnace.

"Do you see those people on the top floor?" Howard yelled at one of the firemen who was yanking a hose toward the front of the building.

"Don't worry, my lad, keep back! Our men are getting the ladders. We'll have them down in bonnie sweet time."

Howard bristling from being called `lad' and a feeling of helplessness consuming him thought, that fireman can hardly be but a few years older than I. If I were fire chief I'd have his uniform and he'd be out the door in his `bonnie sweet time.' I can see a man leaning out the window trying to get a hold of the top of that ladder. His hand looks bloody. Must have cut it on window glass. There's a woman behind him. My God, there's two of them. The other looks no more than fifteen. I wish to heaven they would work a little faster. The smoke is appalling. They must be choking and gagging, even holding cloth over their mouths. This is not the excitement I thought it would be. It's deathly! I never thought about dying in a fire, wrapped in that black smoke -- all light and air shut out while you are still seeing and gasping for breath. Thank God, they're bringing the last woman down. Pray to Jesus there is no one left in that bloody hell hole.

Howard pulled the heavy door of the pub open and stepped inside. He saw a vacant stool at the end of the bar and wearily settled himself down. I must get my wits together. Calm down! Calm down! Boy, do I need to sit here - a pint of strong ale, stout should do me just fine.

"What'll you have, lad?"

"A pint of stout, please. And don't call me lad!" Whew! The atmosphere of this pub smells good. Masculine smells. That strong smell of a man's history. Breathe deep. Howard took several long hard breaths. Just let me put my hands around a beer mug, feel something strong slither down my throat, listen to voices talking about the day, anything, anything but the horror of that fire.

The bartender placed the pint down in front of Howard and went back to talking to two laborers seated at the bar. Howard sipped his stout and listened.

"Well, this Dr. George Fordyce for twenty years sat in an old tavern near here, the Essex Head, and drank a jug of strong ale, a quarter of a pint of brandy and a bottle of port daily with his dinner and STILL lectured to his students afterwards! Now there's a man who can hold his drink," the bartender guffawed, slapping his towel against the bar. The two laborers shook their heads in agreement.

Howard feeling a little better thought he'd have one more before going back to The Garland. I'll have a great story to tell. I was only a step away from being a hero. I could have easily carried that young girl down the ladder, and kept her skirt just as tightly wrapped around her ankles as that old upstart Irish fireman!

Howard spied Mumsie and George seated at opposite ends of a sofa in the lounge engaged in what appeared to be somewhat of a tense conversation when he arrived back at the Garland Hotel. The concierge was tiptoeing around them turning on the lamps. Pulling his shoulders back and taking a deep breath he strode into the lounge trying to maintain his composure hoping to hide the unsteady feeling he had from the too many pints of ale he had consumed over the past couple of hours. Howard feeling a little dizzy thought, funny how you don't seem to feel the effects of drinking while you're having fun but as soon as you see someone who you know will disapprove the room seems to reel. He sat down in a large chintz covered wingchair opposite them. Mumsie and George's hushed conversation stopped and their startled eyes stared straight at Howard. Happily, he noticed one of the hotel waiters and catching his eye, Howard beckoned to him. Howard kept his eye on the waiter as he made his way across the room in order to avoid the stares of Mumsie and George.

"May I help you sir? Can I get you a drink?"

"That's a very lovely, interesting tray you have there. Is it a George II piece or Victorian?" Howard asked the surprised waiter.

"I'm sure I don't know sir, but I will be glad to ask if you wish?"

"No, no! That won't be necessary. I was only curious," Howard said with his eyes still on the tray.

The waiter bending over a little further toward Howard said again, "Would you like a drink, sir?"

"Oh, yes!"

Taking his eyes off the waiter and struggling to sound in complete control of himself he said, "What are you drinking, Mumsie?"

"I'm sure I don't know dear! George and I have not ordered anything yet," she said, eyeing Howard quizzically.

The waiter shifted uncomfortably wishing he was back in his tiny, quiet bedsitter instead of being an unwilling participant in this little Ibsen drama. Bending from the waist again, a trifle more emphatic, he said, "Sir!"

With a backhand wave of his right hand, Howard said, "Brandy!" With a slight pause, he added, "Changed my mind. Napoleon."

"In a snifter?" By this time the waiter had decided to drop his politeness.

"Of course! What else would you pour it into? A mug?

"Some people have strange requests, SIR!" The waiter straightened up, clicked his heels and marched off.

"Howard, whatever is possessing you to be so rude? Have you been drinking? Your eyes look a little red, dear!"

"What makes you think that? Today, I saved someone from eminent death!"

"Har..umph! With a sense of impending ennui, George said, "Is this one of your attempts at a joke, Howard?"

"It's quite true, George. It was one of those strange circumstances of being in the right place at the right time. If I had not been there, a pretty young girl's life might have been snuffed out by the flames."

"Aha! I knew a young pretty girl had to be involved! So where was this pretty young thing?"

The waiter returned and without looking at Howard put down his brandy on the low table in front of him and quickly started to turn away. Howard, reaching for his drink, said to the waiter's retreating back, "Wait, my good man," while reaching into his trouser pocket.

The waiter turned back and looked warily at Howard, wondering what strange request might come next.

At that, Howard looking at several coins in his hand picked out the largest and tossed it onto the waiter's tray, saying, "That should take care of you, my good man."

The waiter stared at the pence, then at Howard, then carefully at Mumsie and George. With a slight nod and a look of puzzlement he walked away muttering, "These rich Americans! Do they think I can enjoy the high life tonight on a pence?"

George leaned back his head, closing his eyes, laughed to himself thinking, good Lord, what will come next? "Well, Howard, tell us about this amazing rescue feat of yours."

"You needn't be so superior George. That girl will sleep safely in her bed tonight, thanks to happenstance that I was there."

"Alright boys! I would like to hear about this experience of yours Howard," Mumsie said, watching him critically as he downed what looked like a large gulp of brandy.

"Well, I just happened to be taking a pleasant stroll over the Southwark Bridge when I saw a rise of very black smoke curling up through the fog what looked to be in an area near the end of the bridge. I decided to investigate and just about two blocks off the south side of the bridge I turned into a mews and saw a dilapidated building with flames shooting from the windows. My God, it was exciting!"

"Dear, were there any people killed?" Mumsie asked now intent on Howard's story.

"No, Mumsie, thanks to my quick thinking."

"Oh, what did your quick thinking do?" George said sarcastically, thinking this might be one of his best whoppers yet.

"I did see three people screaming from a third floor window. There was an older man whose hands were streaming blood and staining the black bricks of the wall. Then there were two women gripping his arms, one gray-haired older woman and a young girl. When she saw me she started to scream for me to help them. I tried the front door but something was blocking it and then I ran to the side of the building to see if I could find a way to climb up to them. There was none."

"You must have panicked, dear, when you couldn't help."

Howard took another long sip of his brandy and with a great pensive look said, "No, Mumsie, I told myself to remain calm. At that moment I heard the fire engines so I raced to the corner and hailed them down, then directed them to the fire. The fire chief was quite impressed with my cool demeanor. When the firemen started to unwind their hoses I told the chief I would help with the ladder. He seemed pleased with the extra hands. We held the ladder steady while one of the firemen went up. The women wanted him to take the man first since he was losing a lot of blood and he started to become limp. When they brought him down I helped lay him on a stretcher. By that time another firemen had rescued the old woman and she would not let go of his neck. I guess the situation had made her hysterical."

"I can hardly blame her, dear. I'm sure I would have

fainted. It was surely lucky for them that you kept your wits about you."

"I tried my best, Mumsie. But more importantly, I noticed that because the fireman could not set himself free from the old woman, no one was rescuing the young girl. As I looked up she pleaded with me to help. I climbed the ladder as fast as I could and when I reached her she sobbed, "Thank God for you!" I leaned over the top of the sill and picked her up. She felt very light in my arms. I wrapped her skirt tightly around her ankles as I balanced her on the top of the sill so that she would not be embarrassed. You know how those firemen behave?"

"Really, Howard? How do they behave? Different than you?"

"George! No need for sarcasm. Your attitude right now is in question. Behave! Do you think Howard is lying?" He gave his mother a condescending look recalling the conversation he was having with her before Howard arrived. He shrugged his shoulders wondering how his mother had created that insular world of hers, so invincible but so gullible.

"Go on, Howard. Finish this remarkable story."

"Well, I hadn't noticed but a big red-haired Irish fireman who had been handling the hoses had climbed the ladder behind me so I was able to hand her down to him then he in turn handed her to another fireman until they reached the ground. When I got down the Irishman shook my hand and said he didn't know what they would have done without me.

"I bet the girl was grateful, too?" George said staring again at Howard.

"Well, she did give me a timid hug."

The waiter disgustedly picked up the empty glasses without a word or thank you, turning his back on Howard and left.

****

GEORGE

July 1, 1901

*Grand Hotel
rue Scribe
Paris, France*

Dearest Bessie,

 Three more days before I am caught in the human web of what some call "wedded bliss." The Fourth of July, Independence Day, fateful irony it may be - my independence usurped by a new responsibility - Justine's happiness. Have I always made life so complicated? Would that you had knocked on my door more often and pressured me out of my monastic self. But here in my `cell' at the Grand it feels easier with pen to put words on paper that can speak for me. Words that hurt too much when spoken.
 These are the words that have long been my painful secret. I have always envied your relationship with Papa. I suspect you never knew that. Maybe my feelings of inadequacy arose from trying to eavesdrop and interlope into Papa's world and unsuccessfully could not understand him. Some evenings in the library I would catch his eyes fall upon you over the top of his ever constant book while you were indulged in your Keats' poetry. I envied those loving goodnight kisses gently placed on your cheek. I wanted him to be proud of me, hug and hold me. I felt if I disciplined myself to achieve things that I thought Papa's world would respect -- hunting, riding, academics, law degree and now marriage to a daughter from one of New York's finest families I would capture his pride. But inside that is NOT me! The discipline that I tried so hard to

attain shields and protects me (but it also wounds me).

Understand me -- dreams and reality blur and twist in my desire to control the jolting turns of life. Somewhere, sometime gone past, maybe it was only a moment, I missed an important turn, either a significant word, action or gesture, I was either unwilling to see, hear or believe and traveled on sublimely in the creation of my own dream. I am a tired traveler. The love I was so sure of and professed for Justine seems like an eternity ago and has fallen into confusion these months since our engagement announcement. My desire was so insatiable to keep the one relationship that I thought I understood because of our mutual love of music, that it's possible that I may have suffocated her own sense of free will to choose. Now it's late in the day. I've set the stage. The Cuttings have made all the arrangements at the American Episcopal Church. Their family and friends along with Mumsie and Howard have arrived in Paris and there is no turning back. I know your presence will be with me on Sunday, if in spirit only, and God knows, I need your presence. Send me your prayers to give me strength and send me happiness - that elusive state!

Always your loving brother,
George

Finally, my feet on French soil, in Bonpapa and Bessie's footsteps. My wildest dreams would not have dreamt that my marriage would be the circumstances why I'm here. Breathe! Take a deep breath! Hear those voices surrounding me. Muted vowel sounds can be anger or joy if one does not understand. Whatever a Frenchman's emotion, their inflections tease the ears like music. They speak like the woodwinds of a symphony orchestra. Oh, listen to me!

Justine is late! I haven't posted Bessie's letter yet. She must have looked up at these magnificent spires of Notre Dame. The arches and spires seem to glide with an ethereal speed against the sky's sea of blue. One can imagine Abelard in his brown coarse muslin habit, crossing the plaza toward the tall wooden doors, pulling on the iron latch to enter that religious inner sanctum, his thong sandals quietly moving down the aisle, thoughts of Heloise heavy on his mind. Was his obsessive love of her the same as mine? Did she not also obey the desires of her father and enter the convent to keep her a virgin, away from the reputation of Abelard? Here I am in Paris because it was Justine's father who insisted we marry in the Episcopal cathedral. We Catholics are still held in disdain underneath the superficial politeness of those stiff grande dames. When I objected, Justine said, "We must." I feel a sense of paralysis seizing my determination to direct my own life. Slowly it's being chipped away.

Oh, Christ! Here come those dirty gypsies. Ugh! They're like a virulent disease contaminating this Eden. Look at them hanging on to the arm of that elderly gentleman with one hand stuck under his face, begging. That's not begging! It's extortion! The stink of their bodies, their clothes, and unwashed hair forces one to give them money just to get rid of their repulsive stench. But they survive! They survive in their filthy way of life.

Whew! It's hot. Where's Justine? I hate being kept waiting. I should not be kept waiting!

****

HOWARD

July 3, 1901

Dear Bonpapa and Bonnemaman,

Everything in London went well. Mumsie had a chance to have a long visit with her sister, Aunt Nina, which has kept her in high spirits. They had been too long away from each other and they for a morning, giggled and laughed like two little children.

Paris is still arrayed in glorious splendor with the leavings of the Exposition. Most of the other nations' pavilions are torn down or are in the process. The Eiffel Tower stands as an engineering miracle in the midst of the rubble. It's truly wonderful! With all the fracas, and critics screaming about it as an iron mess against the skyline; I love it! The French have a way of arguing from a stance based on the classical notion of the arts, the ideal form composed of perfection and beauty - they are ever the innovators of the future!

In contrast to the French, a colleague of Justine's father who is assigned to the United States Embassy here, told us the other night that the U.S. pavilion built for the Exposition was only equipped with tables, chairs, newspapers, and letterboxes - this is what we had to show to the world! Americans visiting the Exposition had the assurance that they would not be out of contact with their monetary investments since the pavilion was equipped to follow the prices on the Stock Exchange both in New York and Chicago. Nor did they have to suffer the inconvenience of European life, since the Congress had allocated enough money to insure that ice water would always be at everyone's disposal.

George is behaving nervously and seems very irritable, but I guess that is normal for a groom.

Justine, I imagine, is in hiding until the wedding. You know how every other word out of George's mouth is usually Justine. Justine does this, Justine does that! Well, he has been strangely quiet, off in another world. His usual regimented, well-ordered self remained on all accounts.

Anyway, I have had about enough of Mumsie trekking me along on endless shopping, churches, art galleries and museums. I do enjoy some individual paintings, some sculpture and some history. BUT ENOUGH! I cannot bear them in large doses. I'm looking forward to my August trip to Maine with Dick Hammond. The great outdoors is beckoning me!

Keep well and I will see if I can sneak some good French cognac through Customs for you.

Au revoir,
Howard

Paris today is typical of a hot New York July day. The sky is clear, the sidewalks still not cooled down by the night air, holding their heat from yesterday's humid weather. As Mumsie and I entered under the portals of the church coldness seeped up through the soles of my shoes, a sniff of cold air brushing past my face made me stiffen. Mumsie's fingers dug into my arm as if she also was bracing herself against something unknown whispering from the cold granite walls of the cathedral. Walking Mumsie down the aisle to her seat in the front pew seemed an indeterminable distance. Its length growing longer and longer, footfall after footfall. What has happened from yesterday afternoon's rehearsal to today? Did I not notice in all the commotion? Is it my imagination?

George looks rigid. He didn't speak a word to me back in the rectory; just, "I think it's time to go." I had thought in my bed last night some words I might say to him before the ceremony. After all, it's a big change in his life, husband and possible future father, although I have never heard him mention the possibility of children. We don't have the greatest relationship as brothers but what little we have I want to hold on to. I didn't think of any words though. Well, all to the better, I don't think he would have heard me anyway. He has not even glanced at Mumsie. She keeps trying to catch his eye, I guess to reassure him. One really needs reassurance in THIS situation!

****

GEORGE

The sounds of Mendelssohn's wedding march disturbed the solemnity of the cathedral. Justine and her father emerged through the sanctuary doors. George's shoulders straightened as he looked up the aisle. At last, we can get on with this, he thought, sighing with a sense of relief. Oh, my god, how beautiful Justine looks. She moves like a dream I've never dreamt. What is it about her? George's attention riveted on the vision of a young woman moving with elegant grace down the long aisle. The translucency and shimmering of her veil softly cascading over her head revealing only the soft glow and tracings of her face. Every step she took made the folds of silk and lace falling from her waist rustle like spring warmth fading away the gloomy coldness of sooted grey stone. Do I really know this woman? The loveliness of her. This elusive mystery beneath that whiteness. For me to have her, my wife. What enormous pride I feel.

****

HOWARD

August 20, 1901

Dear George,

I still have enough light left from the setting sun to scratch some words to you. Dick and I have set up camp in that favorite spot of yours along the Penobscot River here. We loaded up the canoe with the usual things that you and I used for our escape from home, Harvard and life's little harassments. We had a fantastic day....Dick poled up and paddled down the "quick water" while I played the fish. We caught a couple of trout and fried them over the campfire. The smell of pine needles, frying fish and the last rays of the sun glinting off the river makes the memories come roaring back and that knot that arises in your chest wanting desperately to hold on to the moment forever. Time can stop now!

I had become concerned with Dick's health at the end of the school term last year. Dick, as you recall, has always been very intense in whatever endeavor he undertook. He was a pitcher on last year's team. He would pitch hour after hour and day after day during varsity practice when the other pitchers were laid up. You know how wiry he is and he worked too much on his nerve when tired. I certainly am not the perfectionist that Dick is but as we settled in tonight I was surprised to find out how tired I was....not from the trip but from all of the events of this summer. Anyway, Maine's bracing air seems to be doing us both some good. At this moment I feel so far away from all pressures that it has given me the courage to write hopefully to clarify some of my muddled thoughts.

You and I have never had a close relationship. Maybe it was age, or personalities or possibly just the differing pressures on us. My life these last years seems to be in constant flux so much so that I have had little time to reflect on who I am, where I'm going and worse, what am I going to do? Must I keep up with you? Be as creative as Bessie? Do what Papa expects? Hell, that's a lot to deal with!

I keep reliving that moment standing next to you at your wedding. It seemed time hung balanced between our boyhood and our manhood. What had happened to us? While you were repeating your vows I suddenly realized the awesome commitment you were making to ONE person for the rest of your life. Shock slithered through my body and my feet felt cemented to the floor of that cathedral. Why? Love can't be that strong!

I can understand the need for a woman to want her own home, have her own children, be the mistress in her own secure nest without the worries of the outside world...letting her husband worry about making money, paying bills, finding a respected place in the working world. What happens to freedom? Are you free? Have you ever been free? I am not being presumptuous. I want to know. Sure, I like women...certainly some more than others. I love their teasing ways, their delicate smells, the fall of their hair and its softness streaming down the small of their backs ....BUT vows?

So much for my meandering mind on the subject of women! September will be on me before I'm ready. I realized that I will have to stay another year at Harvard for a mining degree. After all I want to supervise the digging, NOT do it. Jack and Budd are heading out west and I hope will make some connections and lay some groundwork for me when I get a chance to join them.

The sun has set and my light is fading although the

questions I am asking linger. I hope the future will bring the two of us back here and you will provide me the answers I want about you.

Although it might sound hypocritical, my misunderstanding, confusion, puzzlement, whatever having to do about women - please give my love to Justine.

Your loving brother,
Howard

I don't know how it happened! Dick and I woke early and over our coffee decided to go hunting deer. The leaves had started turning into their arrays of colors. The air had that freshness that keeps you taking deep breaths as if you want to store it up for the winter months to come. So we packed a lunch into our knapsacks, checked our guns and ammunition and took off into the woods. We started to climb a ridge that we obviously misjudged. It was higher, steeper and the underbrush heavier than we had thought. By the time we reached the top we were on our hands and knees, exhausted. We slid our knapsacks off and rolled over onto our backs on the ground and just gazed at the clouds rolling overhead hoping we would recover before the sun reached its zenith. As we started to survey the ridge we found that it curved around us on both sides and we were looking down into a lightly wooded glade with open pastures beyond toward the west. We saw a number of jackrabbits and I thought I had caught a glimmer of a deer in the glade. We decided that Dick would follow the ridge around to the north and I would go around slightly to the south keeping each other in sight, find a place to settle down and wait. We thought we had all options covered for any animal going through the glade. I found a perfect perch for myself from where I could see Dick's black and red jacket across the hollow. I leaned back against a boulder, adjusted my rifle, and settled myself in for a wait with my eyes fixed on the glade.

What happened next I can only speculate. My mind started to drift back to my letter to George. The more my attention fixated on that glade the more its shapes transformed themselves into images floating through the morning mist of the glade. As my imagination became more vivid, streams of the sun's rays broke through an opening between some tall trees in the glade reflecting the same aura of the sunlight streaming through the rose window of the cathedral in Paris. Desperation started to grip me for no apparent reason. Justine is going to change George's life forever, taking him into her own world; a world dominated by her father. The Cuttings. America's self-appointed aristocrats with all their trappings. How could he give himself up to all that? A shudder convulsed me as I saw the image of George walking up the aisle with Justine on his arm, husband and wife. He was walking away. Leaving me behind. I felt the water enveloping me again, falling below its dark surface, then George reaching for me, pulling me up, his arms holding me tight while he shook. For a brief instant, leaning against that cold rock, I felt George's strength and fear but I was safe. Death had not come! We should have been hunting together. Then and now! Again as times before! Why would George allow this to happen to him. Give his life, his freedom, his mind to a woman? Who is she? What is she? Justine! Justine! At that moment I hated her.

Anger mixed with a hidden obscure fear, a fear I didn't understand had me gritting my teeth and constricting my throat when I saw a stag emerge from the glade and stop in back of a fallen log. I jerked my rifle up and I guess aimed too quickly and shot. I must have hit the stag in the rear right leg because he dragged it over the log and I shot again and he kept moving forward toward another part of the sheltered glade, so I shot, and I shot and I kept on shooting all the time moving down the ridge toward the glade. At some moment I stopped caring about the stag and kept on shooting. It felt good for those moments. The stag was down and bleeding profusely, only his forelegs quivering and his body heaving as his last breaths were leaving him. I stood over him and just watched him die without feeling anything. Nothing!

****

Christmas Eve 1902

Oakwood
Jamaica Plain

"Is that the clock striking seven Bessie? Weren't you expecting Amy at six? My stomach is beginning to grumble," Howard said offhandedly to Bessie while dropping a small wrapped gift under the Christmas tree.

"Have you ever known Amy to be on time? All the years you've known her, has she ever been on time? No! So to keep your mind off eating, try storytelling to keep the children amused while I see if Mumsie's headache has gotten any better." Exasperated, Bessie sighed with an overwhelming sense of deja-vu of past Christmases with Mumsie and her seemingly lifelong headache, Howard with his self-centered childish needs of attention, overexcited children and the endless preparations the holidays demand. Oh, to be a little girl again just to enjoy the simple pleasure of waiting for Christmas morn. Age certainly clouds the joy of youthful memories. Your ears hear so much more, demands come from all directions and that beautiful glistening Christmas tree only becomes one more mess that has to be cleaned up. Tiredness overcame her as she started to climb the stairs. "Temper, temper, temper my impatience," she muttered to herself. Looking up she saw six year-old Francis throw his leg over the banister and start to slide down.

"Francis!"

Startled by his mother's voice Francis jumped back onto the stair landing. "Straighten your jacket, young man, and go downstairs and keep your Uncle Howard company. I expect you to act the gentleman tonight, not only for me and your father, but to show your grandparents what a good boy you can be. And don't tease your sisters!"

With his back as straight as a ramrod, Francis walked down the stairs, lips pursed, assuming a military attitude. He sharply rapped once on the parlor door and without waiting for a reply entered and saluted his uncle.

Howard laughed and said, "Oh, I see you must have had one of your mother's sound reproaches. Act like a gentleman! Am I correct? Well, let me say, two can play at that game. Are you with me?"

Francis broke into a big smile and shook his uncle's hand. "Right sir! I'm game!"

"Okay, just follow my lead and we'll make this Christmas Eve a memorable one for all the blossoming gentlemen of the world."

At that moment the doorknocker sounded loudly. Howard pulled out his pocketwatch and muttered, "Quarter past eight and dinner has been ready since seven!"

"What did you say, Uncle?"

"Just talking to myself, Francis. Now remember what I said, do everything I do." Pushing Francis ahead of him they started for the front door. Howard assumed a military stance, winked at Francis and opened the door.

They were confronted by a very ample, substantial Amy Lowell dressed in her usual tailored dark suit with the lacy white collar encircling her rather heavy neck. Howard swept his arm up and then down and across his chest bowing as he greeted Amy. "Good evening, Miss Lowell. How very nice and well you look. Please come in out of the cold." Howard gave Francis a little kick and a nod at which Francis' arm swung wildly out and down as he bowed to his waist.

"Good evening, Miss Lowell."

"What is this 'Miss Lowell' and bowing nonsense?" Amy said as she swept past the door. "Francis, how nice you look all dressed up in your suit. Come give me a kiss." Francis looked uncomfortably at Howard who gave a quick nod. Francis marched forward and Amy bent down for a kiss. Francis had a change of mind and quickly stuck out his hand to shake Amy's. She straightened up and roared with laughter. "I understand. Up to your old tomfoolery, are you Howard? Playing games? Well, three can play as well as two. Shall we?" Amy started toward the parlor, chuckling to herself.

Bessie was coming down the stairs when she saw Amy in the hallway. "Amy! Oh, Amy, I'm so glad you could come."

Amy looked up and as Bessie stepped on the last riser Amy holding her skirt out with both hands curtsied low, bowing her head and with great formality said, "I am honored to be a humble guest in your gracious home." Francis giggled and Howard quickly passed by them and into the parlor.

Bessie remembering the fun they had as young girls playacting said, "Amy, here you are again after all these years still trying to imitate the great Bernhardt. Well, I can tell you as your favored critic, your performance leaves much to be desired but your attempt at British royalty was just what I needed. Throwing her arms around Amy she said, "I can't tell you what a relief it is to have you here."

"This is marvelous to spend a Christmas Eve with all the Perkins and Wards. I am looking forward to a vigorous conversation with your father and grandfather. Is everyone here and well?"

Bessie answered in a voice that was almost a whisper, "Yes and no. Mumsie is suffering from one of her headaches. You know the kind? But it's nice to have Papa here and Bonpapa is in top form and certainly ready for that vigorous conversation you mentioned. I'm sure he will regale you with all his usual favorite quotes from his beloved writers. But I hope we can find a few moments to ourselves. Just you and me."

"I know, like old times. I'm ready but tell me about Howard. What new escapades has he been up to lately?"

"I'm sure he will lambaste you with all his latest schemes. He talks about the world as if he is its new Cortez, out to find undiscovered gold. Of course, festooned with all the trappings of luxury while others do the digging."

"So, he's looking for a stake! Fair warning. I'll keep my hands on my purse strings. Well, come on. Let's start the festivities." Amy took Bessie's arm and led her into the parlor.

Bonpapa's eyes lit with a sparkle when he saw Amy. Little Mary was seated on his lap while Bonpapa was turning the pages and reading from one of the many children's books. He always enjoyed Amy's intellectual aggressiveness, her eccentric style with which she had battled the Boston Brahmin aristocracy into which she was born. Although he had a great admiration for the Lowells and their accomplishments, Amy had that special quality of incisive insight into the literary giants that his beloved Margaret Fuller had. He looked forward to the challenge of rhetoric, sometimes adversarial but most of all, those times when two minds work in creative harmony. He put little Mary down on the chair and stood to welcome Amy.

Papa who was perusing the books on the bookshelves turned and smiled when he saw Amy. He had found the William James book he was looking for. Turning toward Amy he took her hand. "Merry

Christmas, Amy. I'm hoping this evening you will give me the opportunity to edge my penny's worth of thoughts between you and Bonpapa. As you can see, I'm already trying to prepare myself," as he showed her the book. Lowering his voice, he winked and said, "You know how hard it is to get a word in with Bonpapa when he is allowed to embark on one of his literary diatribes!" Amy was startled but genuinely amused by his very uncustomary wink. She had always known him to hold a posture of withdrawn sedateness. Maybe age does soften and humor one, she thought to herself. Anyway, she was delighted.

Bonpapa warmly welcomed Amy. "And what was that about, pray tell. Are you two in cahoots? Maybe I should borrow Tom's hearing aid so I don't miss any mischief. You do look in good spirits, dear. It must be hard for you now rattling alone around in that big house your father has left you. We do miss the company of your parents. They were such good friends and we all enjoyed being kept on our intellectual toes when in the company of your family."

"Need you not worry about me, my dear Mr. Ward." Having arranged herself on the sofa and with a generous smile lighting her face she said, "Tomorrow Sevenels will be filled with my brothers and sisters and all their numerous children. The rooftops will be raised by noise of older children teasing younger children and the usual clashes of adults challenging each other on their child raising philosophies. You may be certain I will be in the middle of it all, romping, ravaging and relishing in all the events that Christmas envisions. The smell of pine needles, crumbs from Christmas cookies and footprints of all sizes impressed in the carpets; scraps of wrapping paper scattered behind sofas, heat registers and other hidden nooks for weeks to come. I'm an old fool when it comes to Christmas but, be assured, my sanity returns when I can rattle around my own home at my leisure. By now I'm sure Bessie has told you my delicious sin of staying in bed till noon. But that old Protestant work ethic forces this old body to work so I do spend my afternoon in the library poring over my tomes. Evenings I can settle into my favorite chair with Keats in hand and scribble my ideas on paper with which I litter the floor late into the night. Only my housekeeper has to put up with me. Can you imagine anyone else doing so?"

"You're lucky you found such a disciplined housekeeper. She must have been sent from the heavens with instructions on the caring of such a messy angel. On another topic Amy, I do want to tell you and Bessie of a young painter Carley has become acquainted with. A Mister Charles Woodbury. I met him the other day in Carley's office. We had quite a long talk on New England painters and especially Mr. Woodbury's interest in the dynamics of the ocean. He was visiting from Maine where he now spends most of his time painting. Carley said that you had met him briefly at a dinner party. I thought you'd be very interested in what he had to say."

"I do recall meeting him but we had no opportunity to talk. I believe he said he came down from Ogunquit. Have you seen any of his work? Is he another in your collection of dilettante American artists?"

"Don't tease an old man on his meanderings through the local galleries. You may be surprised one day, my dear young lady, when one of these artists rises in accomplishment to the top of the art world. This Mr. Woodbury just might be the one and I would only be too delighted if I had a hand in his future. He brought along a few sketches in his brief. Certainly not enough to judge his true talent but I was impressed. I thought he mentioned that he would soon have a gallery opening over on Newbury Street. Isn't that true, Carley?"

Carley looked up from a book he was thumbing through. "Yes, January 15th if I remember correctly."

"Aha! You see sweet Bess, Newbury Street is always the first prominent step. I'd be honored to have a granddaughter escort this frail, old man with fading eyesight who still delights in the marvels of paintings to view this young man's work."

"I'd be charmed. We can spend the day in delightful colloquy on whether American artists will ever achieve the genius of the European artists or will he forever remain an imitator."

Howard, who had gone upstairs to check on the children came in holding Nancy in his arms. At the sight of Amy she squirmed and put her arms out to her. Amy lifted her from Howard onto her lap. "Oh, Nancy! A dress fit for an angel," she said as she straightened Nancy's white lace dress. I imagine you can sing like one too. Howard are you going to accompany us tonight in some Christmas carols?

"Are you sure? You don't remember my screeching?"

"Yes, my ears are still recovering but we need the volume so God, if he truly does exist can hear us."

"He'll hear, and I'm sure he'll release his thunder to drown us out."

The family had settled into enjoying their Christmas Eve dinner with undue relish. After helping himself to a second helping of turkey breast, Howard was caught by Amy looking amused at him. "I've heard, young man, you plan to take Horace Greeley at his word and head West."

Howard seemingly caught unaware, cleared his throat while placing his elbows on the table and clasping his hands, he said, "You might say that. Dick and Budd and I have been making plans. Budd also got his degree in mine engineering so we thought our futures lie where the ores lay."

Carley spoke up. "Well, this comes as a surprise to me, Howard. How well have you planned and financed this expedition. Have you made contact with the right people? Have you got interviews set up? Do you know what to present in a job interview? Just curious."

"I'm sorry I didn't mention it to you, dear." Bessie said noting the irritation in Carley's voice.

"I didn't mean this to come as a surprise to you, Carley," Turning his knife over and over on the tablecloth Howard continued. "To help put your mind at ease we have put a great deal of time in planning. First we're going through Chicago then Kansas City where we will take the T&P for Bisbee. We've been invited to visit the Copper Queen Mine and then to Douglas where Phelps Dodge is beginning to build a smelter. We hope to manage to get to California if our money holds out. It may be wishful dreaming, but maybe we will hit it rich. Look at all those guys who took off in '49. They're sure sitting midst the yellow and green now."

"And who's financing this glorious expedition?"

Everybody shifted uneasily in their chairs. It was so uncharacteristic of Carley to speak so pointedly. Bessie took an audible breath. "Well, dear, Howard has been saving his money this past year and Papa and I decided we could foot some of the bill. After all, this might be a great opportunity for Howard to possibly find the place for his life's work."

"I hope he finds it in my lifetime," Carley said under his breath.

Bonpapa seated at the head of the table knowing to change the subject, said, "Amy, my dear, would you please pass me the gravy and in the passing I would delight in hearing how your manuscript is coming on Keats."

"My manuscript? It's certainly a challenge to my constitution. If anything were to try my soul, it's Keats. The manuscript has become my nemesis. I don't know where my head was when I began but it's become a formidable struggle and Keats wrestles with me in a ferocious battle for every page. My pen has been at it for six long years. Imagine! Six long years in the writing and what's worse, lately I've begun to surmise that I may be inadequate to the task. It must be my audacious persistence that has kept me going."

"Persistence is part of your inherent nature as long as I've known you, and that begins at birth, you have never, never exhibited inadequacy in my presence whether it's a hearty debate or handling that horse of yours. Why, in heaven's name, are you feeling inadequate?"

"I most appreciate your undying support but I think my anxiety rises from the fact that no matter how minutely I have read, dissected, analyzed each line of Keats' verses I'm afraid the depths into which he reached to write those immortal lines has eluded me. Floating out there in infinity just outside my grasp." Amy wiped her hands vigorously on her napkin. "Frustration! Sheer frustration! I fear my subjectivity has entangled my own beliefs, my inner feelings, thoughts, what have you, into my interpretation of his poetry. How could someone really know another's intimate thoughts and understand their life's course which they've woven so intricately into their poetry? And I've taken it upon myself to unweave that web! Isn't that pure arrogance on my part?"

"I trust that's a rhetorical question. I, of all people do not have to remind you that another's essence is inaccessible to direct knowledge. I do think in our exuberance to share a love of ours, such as your love of Keats, we tend to over praise that which we feel to be undervalued. You understand that original thought comes from and refers to the heart of a people. Those thoughts can only address itself to that segment of a society capable of receiving it. If great works do not find such a class in their own time, they wait till time and their own influence create it." Bonpapa paused rubbing his forehead for a moment. "Ah, for example what immediately comes to mind is Lincoln's address at Gettysburg. No more powerful piece of writing of our time was ever written that spoke directly to the heart of the nation but it took a generation before we truly understood the lasting power of that speech."

"I understand your point. The Gettysburg address is a curious example. Lincoln's words echoed across a terrifyingly, bloody battlefield in which his words could not possibly contain any subtlety to the horrors which war wrought. Although he had the advantage of being ensconced in the seat of highest political power in this country. From that elevated seat he was able to unloose a political force from which emerged a new social order by the sheer power of his carefully chosen words, written or spoken. Thinking back it is as if I had been alive in the aftermath of his presidency, knowing full well how Lincoln surprised the nation. A nation caught unaware! I know my parents were unduly surprised to find that beneath that tall, gawky, ungainly figure of a man lay a power of words. At first they flashed like a silent streak of lightening across a midnight sky but their ensuing thunder rolled across those flamed and impassioned minds, both North and South, that to this day I, myself, hear the resonance of that man."

Amy moved her dessert spoon back and forth across the tablecloth trying to find adequate words on the issue of writing. "I think poets and writers suffer the same anguish as Lincoln about the sacredness of life and the sorrow of death. How does one create that forum or, shall we say, hallowed platform from which the words of the poet will have a lasting, eternal impact?"

"Very well said, Amy. Asking me you cannot find the answer and is it possible the great writers not know themselves?"

Amy stopped swinging her spoon back and forth and Bessie placed her napkin on the table. The conversation had been left unresolved. Bessie thought how she wished she had the eloquence of dialogue that her dearest friend Amy had.

Papa, who had been listening intently, poured himself some more wine. "Amy, you have the enviable luxury of time to struggle with the problems of interpreting the poets. A questionable problem, to say the least. You have so many avenues to choose from. Does the poet choose his words with the reader in mind, his loved ones, a specific lover or only what he is driven to form from his own inner self? Is it important to know?"

Amy, still concentrating on her spoon said, "Your question is a provocative one. Are you suggesting my first decision is to solve the mystery to whom Keats is speaking? To whom was he speaking when he wrote of the 'unravished bride' in Ode on a Grecian Urn? To the world of women or men? My critical world could be overwhelmed by your questions. By my questions. I would like some answers. Remember Keats' words, *'Bold Lover, never, never canst thou kiss, Though winning near the goal - yet, do not grieve: She cannot fade, though thou hast not thy bliss, For ever wilt thou love, and she be fair!'*" Amy paused, looking around the dinner table. "Let me ask you members of the male world, why is the poet more attracted to the characteristics of the virgin? Even male dominated

Christianity dotes on the Virgin Mary? Where does Keats sense of knowing come from to write about female celibacy? Where is the well that he plumbs to reveal a woman's repressed feelings then turns them into a glorified blissful eternal state? Where?"

"Oh, my dear, who could possibly contemplate all those questions, much less answer them? But it might be of interest to you what my friend, Mr. James claims. He says that no thoughts leave the mind of one and cross into the mind of the other. James went on to say that in order to understand another's thoughts, you must reconstruct his thought within yourself which then becomes your own and therefore original within yourself. Now obviously the difficulty lies in your differing genders and how differently the female mind works as Mr. Freud has suggested. It would certainly be of interest to male readers to have your feminine interpretation of Mr. Keats. Anyway, you can console yourself Amy that anything you write about dear Mr. Keats will stand as original thought emanating from the very essence of you."

"Oh, then my writing will be subject to interpretation, and I can conceive of a barrage of criticism from men, and on and on it goes, ad infinitum. Sounds tiresome."

"Don't count me out Amy, as one of your expectant readers," Howard interjected. "I'm very interested in your pursuit of man's interest in the concept of the virgin."

"Concept, grandson, is the wrong word to use when speaking of a virgin. One conception, no more virgin!" Bonpapa roared back in his chair in laughter.

"Bonpapa!" Bessie said with a low voice. "The children! Remember!"

Everyone seemed caught by surprise and amusement. Howard said with a slight shrug, "Well it's just a purity that men seemed to have always envied because in our masculine world she's an enigma. You know, unattainable, untouchable. Much like Keat's unravished bride in Ode to a Grecian Urn."

Young Francis who had been listening intently to the conversation, not being able to restrain himself any longer piped up, "Who owed this Grecian guy and how much did he earn?" Startled eyes fell on Francis who looked puzzled when all the family fell into laughter.

Bonpapa after wiping tears from his eyes, tapped the side of his wine glass with his dessert spoon and called for quiet. Raising his glass he said, "Francis has reminded us all again how difficult the English language can be and how easily we can misunderstand each other. But now I want to toast all my family and guest. First to my great grandchildren. May Francis find that acting the gentleman opens doors unknown to many." Francis picked up his napkin and gingerly wiped off his pursed lips then with an imperious manner lifted his glass to Bonpapa. "And may Mary's nose come out of the books long enough to smell the garden." Mary pushed her nose up with her finger and gazed at the ceiling. "May Nancy's mischievousness find her a pleasant nook for herself in life." Nancy peeked at her mother and giggled. "And to my grandchildren; may Howard chase his rainbows, find his gold and keep us all in riches. May Carley find the ultimate design for Boston to rival the Eiffel Tower and may Bessie find a peaceful, quiet corner in her life to fulfill at least one of her dreams. And to our honored guest, may every library have a copy of Amy's renowned dissertation on Keats. And finally to my son, may he rapture in the beauty that his family has wrought and to his wife, my dear absent daughter-in-law, may she be released from the pain she is suffering to join us tomorrow to celebrate

Christmas."

"Here! Here!" said Carley drinking down the last of his wine.

Amy still holding her full glass said, "While I have been blessed with sharing the joys of this family I most wanted to share a special gift I have to my steadfast friend." Unfolding a piece of paper she had taken from her skirt pocket, and raising her glass to Bessie she read,

Dear Bessie, would my tired rhyme
Had force to rise from apathy,
And shaking off its lethargy
Ring word-tones like a Christmas chime.

But in my soul's high belfry, chill
The bitter wind of doubt has blown,
The summer swallows all have flown,
The bells are frost-bound, mute and still.

Upon the crumbling boards the snow
Has drifted deep, the clappers hang
Prismed with icicles, their clang
Unheard since ages long ago.

The rope I pull is stiff and cold,
My straining ears detect no sound
Except a sigh, as round and round
The wind rocks through the timbers old.

Below, I know the church is bright.
With haloed tapers, warm with prayer;
But here I only feel the air
Of icy centuries of night.

Beneath my feet the snow is lit

And gemmed with colours, red and blue.
Topaz, and green, where light falls through
The saints that in the windows sit.

Here darkness seems a spectred thing,
Voiceless and haunting, while the stars
Mock with a light of long dead years
The ache of present suffering.

Silent and winter killed I stand.
No carol hymns my debt to you;
But take this frozen thought in lieu,
And through its music in your head.

Amy raised her glass to Bessie as the rest of the family raised theirs. Drinking the last of her wine, Bessie thought, "What happened to the ache of our wild dreams in the comfort of that soft quilt on the rooftop?"

Bonpapa, rising from his chair said, "Besides a superb meal, my dear Bessie, I must say to Amy that we cherish your thoughtful Christmas gift to our beloved Bessie. Now how about trying my new batch of applejack in the library."

"That's an idea that I would not pass up," said Howard putting down his glass.

"I think your heads are nodding and they are going to hit the table if I don't muster you off to bed. Santa Claus comes early," Bessie said, removing their dessert plates.

There were sleepy goodnights, kisses, and Carley, telling Bessie he would help her put them to bed. The rest of the family headed for the library while Rose started to clear the table.

Papa lit a match and attempted to light the kindling in the fireplace while Bonpapa poured his applejack into snifters. As he handed one to Amy who had settled herself on the settee she reached into her handbag and pulled out one of her well-known cigars.

Bessie and Carley returned from putting the children to bed. Bonpapa had poured them some applejack and handed a snifter to each of them. Carley picked up a set of blueprints that were left on the couch. He carried them over to the library desk, smoothed them out with his hand, then picked up the pen from the inkwell and began making notes, sipping his applejack.

Bessie found a comfortable chair by the window where she could see snow starting to fall while Carley pored over his blueprints. "I know what is going on in that mind of his and I am nowhere to be found." Carley pulled his silver pill case out of his vest pocket and popped one of the pills into his mouth. Bessie's heart skipped a beat as she watched his unexpected action. "Oh, my Lord, he could go so quickly with his bad heart. How guilty would I feel? He's kind. Certainly a good father. He's done nothing to deserve my feelings of neglect."

Papa and Bonpapa were engrossed in a chess game. Howard had pulled up a chair to offer advice, wanted or unwanted, on strategy. Bessie relaxed for the first time in the day as she also became engrossed in the game observing Bonpapa carefully contemplate each chess move. She remembered his friend, Ralph Waldo Emerson, saying that when he first saw Sam Ward, he was only about twenty-one, and he thought him to be a prematurely old man, but he grew young, and has been growing younger ever since. And that he has with more spunk than ever. He's such a charming man filled with very unique paradoxes. She smiled remembering that he was supposed to have said one day, `I have harvested a hundred bushels of excellent potatoes and am thinking of translating Goethe's autobiography this winter.' And he did!

"Your move, Bonpapa. Watch it! Papa nearly has you checkmated. I'd watch your bishop if I were you," said Howard.

"But you are not him, Howard! Smoke your pipe! I would like to once beat Bonpapa at his own game," Papa said with a touch of irritation. He picked up his own pipe and looked at Bonpapa. "Your move."

Laughing to the point of choking Amy grabbed her snifter and quickly took a long swallow. While Amy was patting her chest with her hand trying to regain her composure, Bessie had quickly come to her side and threw her arm around her friend's shoulder. "Are you all right Amy?"

Amy still gasping nodded her head. Taking a deep breath and noticing the looks of consternation on the faces of the stilled family members said, "Please, please go back to your games. Forgive my interruption. I'm alright."

Puzzled, Papa and Bonpapa turned back to their game and Howard with furrowed brow commenced studying the chess board. Amy, her face still lit with the evidence of amusement, said in a low confidential voice, "This evening has been like a night at the theater. You know watching all the marvelous posturing for position. Listening to all those subtle and not so subtle innuendoes cast loosely across the table. Those whizzing barbed arrows of remarks that seemingly slide off the intended's back. Family squabbles are so filled with delicious insidious material for my pen."

"Family idiosyncrasies sure toughen one's skin for life. And you, my dear, and I have certainly had a lot of toughening. We're like two old stewing hens. Can you believe I was born with alabaster skin and now look at all the cracks, marks and wrinkles in it. They all have their own history to tell."

"Your move, son," Bonpapa said with a wink as if

he had just made the ultimate move of the game. As Papa contemplated his next move Bonpapa putting his hand on Howard's shoulder said, "You know, my boy, chess is a strange game. Did you ever consider who and what the chess pieces might represent?"

"No. Can't say that I ever did, Bonpapa. I've just thought of it as an advanced game of checkers which just makes you think a little harder. Why? Have I missed something?"

"Maybe an important lesson. A very important lesson. Look at the board. Do you notice anything?"

Howard stared intently at the board. Papa, while still deciding on his move, also stared at the pieces wondering what in the world has he got up his sleeve. Howard shook his head. "I guess I just don't see it, Bonpapa. So knock me off my seat with your insight. What is it?"

Bonpapa took his pipe from his mouth. "Didn't you ever notice that there is only one female on the board and she can move like any other piece on the board except the knight?"

Howard frowned and peered at the board. "Huh, you're right. Why? What does that mean?"

"Well, I can only speculate but I think that men, which certainly includes me, have always been aware of the remarkable strength and power of women. Possibly out of a fear of her power he devised societies of laws and roles for women meant to keep in check that awesome power. Look at the chessboard and I bet you will see a resemblance to those societies, whether it be the eastern or western world. In both those worlds there were soldiers, knights, castles, a religious figure, and of course, a king. All men. And then there stands the queen."

Papa, who had his fingers on the queen, pushed her forward confronting Bonpapa's knight. "Okay, let's see just how powerful she is. Your move."

"Now there is a confrontation to consider. That knight is the only piece on the board that the queen cannot move in a similar fashion. She can move like all the other male pieces but not the knight. Did they create him to try keeping her in check? Dance rings around her? Two over, one back. Two over, one forward! Just like all of us men. Don't know what to do when confronted by a powerful woman."

"Okay, you've got my curiosity. What are you going to do with your queen?" Papa said, twiddling his king between his fingers.

"At least she has options. Not that king you've got there. What can he do? The highest position on the board and everyone is out to get him and yet he is the one who is shackled. He can only make moves on four squares around him, unless he needs to escape to the walls of his castle and then he uses his rook to hide him. The joke is on men."

"I bet you learned that lesson from your astute Margaret Fuller. Knowing her she probably engaged you and all your friends in a game of chess. Isn't that true?"

"She certainly managed to chastise our masculine world."

Papa moved his bishop challenging Bonpapa's knight. "I think what he is trying to tell you Howard that to always give the women in your life a lot of room or you will pay the consequences."

"True, son. But I'm also implying that you can kill the heart and soul of a woman if you try to keep her in her place. Then he leaned forward and moved his queen across the board in front of Papa's king. "Check and mate," Bonpapa said emphatically. Papa looked at the board in surprise and found that he had ignored the position of Bonpapa's other knight and castle and shook his head in disbelief.

"That's what a good woman can do. Check and mate." Bonpapa puffed on his pipe for a few minutes. "You know when I fell in love with your grandmother her father was not truly fond of me. I was persistent in my pursuit of her and when he thought I might be close to winning her hand he called me into his library. He still did not look too happy about the possibility of me being his son-in-law but then in that serious protective fatherly tone of his he said I was never, never to encage her intuitive instincts of life in marriage because it would have killed that sacred spirit which was her. And I never did."

Having become interested in the conversation, she noticed Bonpapa's face. There is no sign of pain that must linger inside him from Bonnemaman's death. What an affair of love they must have had. She carried that amazing presence of hers walking into death. It was hard to know if that aura of beauty radiated from her pure physical stature or was it all inner beauty. The eyes can be so deceiving! I envy Bonpapa. What must it be like to have loved like that?

Bonpapa picked up his queen and turned it over and over in his hand. It was an exquisitely carved piece of ivory. "She's beautiful, isn't she? Helps me win every time," Bonpapa said triumphantly. "I guess some cleverness still remains in this ole' boy. It's been a pleasure 'whuppin' you son." With that he pushed back his chair and while rising said, "And it's about time for this ole' man to turn in. So let me say my goodnights."

"Amy, please address yourself at our door more often. I would like to talk more about your poets while these old eyes can still read. Goodnight Bess. And son, keep the chessboard out and I'll let you try again. Maybe tomorrow! By then you may have learned how to protect your king," he chuckled. Papa grimaced and reached for the chessbox. Howard handed Bonpapa his cane who leaned lightly upon it and with a slightly weary shuffle left the room.

Papa started putting the chess pieces back into their walnut box. "Wait! Aren't you ready to challenge me to a game? I'm ready to duel."

Papa looked up at Howard at first rather amused then with a tired sigh said, "Not tonight, son. One challenge is enough for a day and I didn't do too well at that. Bed sounds pretty good to me too." He closed the top of the chessbox and placed it on the sidetable.

Howard glanced at Bessie and Amy seated on the settee, instantly drowning him in that old knowledge that he was not welcome when these two got together. He went over to the sidetable and picked up the chessbox and sat down in the wingchair in the corner. Opening the box he picked up the black king. It was carved ebony. Ebony and ivory, two precious elements from the world's darkest continent. It was one of Bonpapa's treasures that he had brought back from Africa in the 1850's. He picked up the ivory queen with his other hand. The black king in his right and the ivory queen in his left. The queen is exquisitely beautiful. Pure and not from any world I know. He moved his thumb up and down the form of the queen. He sat quietly for awhile. "I guess I'll go up and read my book," he said resignedly.

"Sounds like a good idea," Bessie said.

"Do keep me posted on your western misadventures, Howard. You know us Lowells. Our feet don't stray far from the hallowed ground of Boston. Our pioneering days ended in the last century and thank God for that!" Amy said stretching her feet out in front of her. "These fine leather shoes I bought for the holidays were only made to keep my feet covered and not to tread down any wayward path."

"Well if I run into any Indians I'll bring you back a scalp to make another pair of shoes. Goodnight." He went out the door and the sound of his footsteps taking the stairs two at a time could be heard drifting back into the room.

"Same old Howard," Bessie sighed.

"Did you really think he'd change, Bessie? After all, you are the one responsible for mothering him all these years."

"I know. You needn't remind me. What should I expect?"

"What really intrigues me is what's happening with George and Justine? It was apparent at the dinner table that something is going on because I didn't hear their names mentioned once. Where are they?" Amy said, her eyes lighting up with expectation.

"Amy! You don't fool me! I know that facade of yours. Beneath that delver into the literary classics of the centuries really lies the heart of a giggling, nosy, little incurable gossip."

"That shouldn't surprise you. So let it out. You know me. It will go no further than this room."

"You want me to believe that, you old gossip? All I know is that after their honeymoon in the south of France they went back to Paris for a week. George is at a law firm in New York now and has an apartment on the West Side. Justine remained behind in France supposedly to pursue her interest in early religious music. That's all that George had to say. You know how tightlipped he is."

"Isn't that rather odd, to say the least?"

"Of course I do. But Amy I'm too tired to even want to contemplate the possibilities of what this all means. George has always been an enigma to me. That stolid posture, uncompromising from his every waking moment. I thought Justine might have slipped inside his skin and was privy to his private reality."

"Maybe she found that reality after she marched out of that cathedral into the marriage bed."

"Amy!"

"Oh, Bessie, don't act so shocked. You're not naive. Nor innocent about marriage beds. That's why I love my bed so much. It's all mine. Mine alone. No snorts, grunting, sweating body thrashing back and forth. Only mine. My cats are the only ones that can complain and thank God they can't speak back. Just meow and scoot out the window or curl up under the bed. My bedroom is my venerated sanctuary. I recall Justine being a very private girl who liked being alone. Maybe her sanctuary being violated was too much."

"Amy, your imagination is running away with you."

"That's all I have to write with Bess. If my imagination does not run rampant my pen lays on the pad."

"I cannot let my imagination run rampant, as you say, with George and Justine's problem, if there is one."

"You look gray around the edges, sweet Bess. You're too young for that. Isn't it about time you start looking after yourself?"

"Huh!" Bessie sighed, "Tell me, how I do that? Don't answer! I just don't have the courage to stop taking care of everyone. Don't you think I've told myself over and over I have to have a life of my own? But who's going to give it to me?"

"Who am I to say anything Bess? Here am I, selfishly guarding my own pleasures; locked away with my books, dreaming of the life of a mystic. Ha! As if I could ever be one. Can't stand still long enough to hear the muses."

"You've come closer to it than I. When I lie down I hope to be carried adrift on fantasies but when my eyes close exhaustion becomes my bedmate. What happened Amy? What happened to our nights on the rooftop?" "That was an eternity ago, another life, my sweet Bess."

****

HOWARD

June 10, 1903

St. Francis Hotel
San Francisco, California

Dear Papa and Mother,

At long last I've found some decent writing paper with some breathing space to write. When I picked up my pen my head began to spin not knowing where to begin. It seems like I've lived a lifetime the last three weeks. To start, we got off the train in Chicago and expected to spend a couple of days exploring. But we were back in the train station the next day. Jack and Budd were holding their noses, breathing deeply trying to rid themselves from the smell of the stockyards while sitting in the depot. The city literally reeks with a pall of stench. It's overwhelming. Depending on the way the wind blows I'm sure homes hundreds of miles away keep their windows closed. Certainly all of Chicago does. Why they rebuilt it after the fire is beyond my comprehension. I would have canonized Mrs. Murphy's cow. We were delighted when the "All aboard!" sounded and the train started to chug out of Chicago. Relief certainly ran across our faces and I noticed the color coming back into Dick and Budd's faces after a couple hundred miles.

We changed trains in Kansas City for Bisbee - that's where the excitement for me started to pick up. We looked over the Copper Queen Mine and even considered staying awhile and taking a mining job. But Budd was anxious to push on. We tramped through the beginnings of the town of Douglas where Phelps Dodge are beginning to build a smelter. *Good investment!* The last night Jack came tearing into our room all excited, looking like a frantic mammy whose lost her chilluns. It seems a man was shot right in front of him over some silly quarrel in one of the gambling halls Jack was roaming around in. I guess the West is still a bit wild. Jack started throwing his clothes into his carpetbag all the time muttering, "We've got to get out of here. No telling who they'll shoot. I can just bet they sure don't like Bostonians." So on we went without a look back.

In El Paso we walked over into Mexico. Dusty, dirty and hot. Once is enough. As we stepped off the train in Los Angeles we headed right for the beach. Before we knew it our bodies turned redder than hot coals. I guess there's some truth in what they say that the sun is hotter in the south. We drenched ourselves in witch hazel and headed for San Francisco from where I now sit in enchantment. The crashing sound of Pacific waves, the divine vista of a city rolling over gentle hills, the vibrant colors of flowers glimmering through the salty misty air. The people here welcome visitors with open arms filled with generosity. They will not let you spend a penny. Heaven!

On to the Hammond Lumber Company in Eureka tomorrow where Dick is suppose to start work. Will write again later.

Thanks again ever so much for the extra $50. I still have it tucked into my fob pocket. We will have to talk when I return about investing in the future of some of these mines I've seen. The possibilities are endless. Good insurance for the long run of life!

                Your loving son,
                Howard

Hold on legs, hold on! This old lumber steamer can surely roll. God, San Francisco was great. Didn't have to spend a red cent. What a little charm will get you! Poor Dick and Budd back there in the stern. Still have their heads hanging over the side. Keep my eyes on the horizon and pray to spy Cape Mendocino soon and keep my money dry. Two hundred dollars! A lousy two hundred left. Goddammit! Money. It's so damn elusive. Like trying to hold snowflakes lighting so gently on your open hand and then slipping away. Nothing. An empty hand. Only a memory of how beautiful they were. Then you waste your time trying to remember where it went. Still scratching my head over that bunko game in Mexico. Lost five bucks. Never again. First and last time. Dirty Mexican's hand was too damn quick. Thank God, I'd be a hell of a lot worse off if Bonpapa hadn't slipped me that extra hundred. All I can hope for is a bonanza on those twenty bucks we invested in that Copper Glance mine in Arizona. I expect the return on that should lay a good cement foundation to my financial future. I'll make those stuffy Union Club members sit up and take notice. They'll be clamoring for my advice.

Aha! Eureka! There's the Cape. Eureka - here we come! Ha! Ha!

****

PAPA

July 1, 1903

Dear Howard,

Every day since you left your mother has waited to hear the sound of the mail dropping through the mailslot, so when I heard her gasp of joy I knew you had finally decided to write. Whether writing is just a duty to you or not, you cannot believe the joy it brings to your mother.

Your written words force upon me the past and the future and I feel caught, wavering between the two - memories of myself shivering with excitement and trepidation setting off with Professor Agassiz for South America; my eyes willing to drink in everything, my tongue willing to taste anything, indulging every moment, unwilling to sleep for fear of missing something, knowing the inevitable - I would never regain those miraculous moments. Times were different in my generation. The nation was being torn apart with issues of cotton and slavery. When I embarked from Boston Harbor I pushed away the knowledge that the country was on the brink of Civil War. I convinced myself it was only a political problem. Slavery was an abomination and beneath the character of all educated, thoughtful men. I absolved myself from the struggle between men, believing neither I nor my family would be affected by this domestic policy dispute. How easily we can delude ourselves. I sailed away secure in family and finances - Bonpapa had done well in the marketplace.

Upon my return home, feeling like I had conquered the world, I spent days purging myself to all who would listen of my adventures. In the back of my mind was the possibility of continuing the life of an adventurer, writing great treatises on new undiscovered rare zoological and botanical specimens. In search of flora and fauna sounded like the life of a poet tinged with apprehensions of danger as one enters unopened doors on dark continents. One evening your grandfather called me into the library and poured me a strong dose of harsh reality.

It seems that at the onset of the conflict between the North and the South, Baring had withdrawn a large share of their American interests to a mere holding of railroad bonds. They warned that those who had been rich may find themselves poor from the great depreciation of property. There had been an ominous truth in those words.

Your grandfather hung on using courageous diplomacy between the growing animosity with the Brits and the American government during the war years. But the truth, he suspected, was served by the economic devastation wreaked by the Civil War. The rich aristocrats were scrambling for new sources of wealth. Bonpapa had faith in the growth of the railroads and the opening of the West. In the early 80's he finally convinced Baring to invest in the Atchison, Topeka and Santa Fe Railroad which at that time was earning 12% on its stock and then later to invest in the St. Louis and Iron Mountain Railway. A few years later a serious cash shortage was discovered in the Atchison's books. The directors had falsified their records about a floating debt....payment for cars and locomotives. Gross mismanagement and charges of nepotism rocked the St. Louis line. The railroads were in chaos. Your grandfather - my father - was a man of the highest integrity. It was unconscionable to him that men of high standing would lie in their greed for money. Bonpapa, in concert with Kidder Peabody, tried to oust the directors and force a massive reorganization. Battles ensued, charges lashed back and forth until it ended up in the courts. Bonpapa finally convinced Jay Gould to intervene, who, through his strong, manipulative financial power was able to impose his will. Bonpapa had said that the man's power was uncomfortably great, whether for good or evil, but they had to take him as they found him and thanked heaven he was on the side of law and order.

But the pressure through all the wrangling had taken its toll on Bonpapa. To maintain his ability to transact business he retreated to his beloved Lenox more and more. In 1884 during all the turmoil, Kidder Peabody took over Baring's New York office and Bonpapa told me he wanted me to work in the New York office so that he could keep his hand in its management. Words and politics flared between London and New York with Bonpapa insisting I be given a partnership; but I was denied and was given a comfortable salary though little power. I stayed for Bonpapa's sake, never wanting to see his years of hard work and sacrifice go for naught. I did the best I could but Wall Street started on a continual downward spiral in the 90's. By 97' conditions had worsened to such an extreme that Baring said they could no longer afford Bonpapa's pension, claiming that they felt he was financially comfortable and possible richer than any of them at the present. Nothing could have been farther from the truth. Bonpapa had always been too generous with his money and the cost of living today drains one's bank accounts quickly.

That brings us to the reason for this long dissertation. Maybe I did not do as well in the financial world as I could have. I never inherited the business genius of your great-grandfather or even the practical financial approaches of your grandfather but even though I was lacking in expertise I struggled to never allow any of my children to suffer any disadvantage in life - whether it be education, travel or learning experience. I wanted all of you to be well prepared to challenge life. You have had all the advantages without the pain, without the burden of financial worry but now is the time for you to take the reins of your own life. Find your place. I will be your support for whatever it is you choose to do in life. Now is your time.

Your loving father,
Papa

****

HOWARD

Dearest Howard,

What joy for us to read your letter. You know how I worry especially when I know you are encountering so many savage, uncultured peoples. I sometimes fear for your life from what all I hear about the Wild West. Your letter astonished me - is it really true people will shoot just because their skin was rubbed the wrong way? It all sounds so hostile. I was so glad to hear that you are safe and well. I know the Hammonds will see to your well-being.

Bessie has been devouring the little free time granted her lately with painting. She and Bonpapa always have their easels close at hand, ready to set up in distant meadows, gardens in bloom, paths along Jamaica Pond, any day the New England sun decides to bless them with its light upon the landscape. Bessie continues to regale us with the wonders of Charles Woodbury's work. We were enticed and finally did succumb to purchasing one of his oceanscapes which is now properly gracing our mantle. It will be comforting during our cold, unremittingly bleak winter New York days begging us to remember the pleasant days of summer beaches to come.

We are expecting George for dinner tonight. Justine, unfortunately, is visiting her parent's estate on Long Island so we will miss the pleasure of her company.

Please, please dear, write more often.

Your loving, devoted Mother

Sounds wild in here. I wonder if I can even get an elbow up to the bar. Dick and Budd must be in here somewhere. Boy! Everybody seems to know Dick. Must be nice to be welcomed home with all this shouting, noise and joy. Hell of a lot different than my homecomings - stiff handshakes and formal pecks on the cheek. Hey that must be Dick's arm waving over there. Let's see if I can climb over all these bodies.

"Hey, Howard! Howard, over here. Barkeep! Pour my friend a beer. What about this place Howard? California! Gets in your blood, doesn't it?"

"It certainly tells me a lot more about you, Dick, than I knew before. You covered yourself well with a Boston 'high hat' all those years at Harvard. You've even dropped your well-tempered Back Bay accent."

"When in Rome do as the Romans do. You know the old saying. C'mon drink up there's more beers to pour."

"What's happened to Budd? I thought he came in with you?"

"He's over in the corner there. I introduced him to two old lumberjacks who've worked for my father for years. He got hooked on their stories. He should be waterlogged with logging stories by now. Wait here, I'll go rescue him." Dick picked up his beer and shouldered himself through the crowd.

Howard turned back to the bar to pick up his beer when a tanned, muscled arm with an extended hand slammed down on the bar top. "Hey, barman, pour me another beer and one for this green Yankee here. Pour a good head on them too, if you want your money."

"Well, thank you, but I still have some beer left to drink," Howard said rather startled by the gruffness of this man's voice and noticing that the man was missing a couple of fingers.

"Well, boy, you have to keep that elbow bent on the

bar around here. So swill it down and hoist yourself another." With that he picked up his glass mug and proffered the other to Howard. Howard hesitated a moment, irritated by this imposing man calling him 'boy', but realizing he might be in the middle of a situation he wouldn't know how to handle, picked up the new drawn beer. This rough-hewn man's face lit with a large grin revealing the loss of his two front teeth and clanked his mug against Howard's.

"Cheers! Belly up!" he laughed, and then downed half his mug in large gulps. He thumped his chest and belched. "Ahhhh! Now tell me, boy, you plan to stick around here? Try your hand at a little logging? Pay's good but life can be short if you're not quick on your feet. Believe me when one of those big fellows goes, one of those eight to fifteen feet in diameter redwoods, if you don't get out from under fast enough, they don't have to worry about burying you. That sucker pushes you so far into the ground they just stick a cross over you and if you're lucky they'll scratch your name into it." The man looked down into his beer mug on the bar and was silent for a moment. Then he muttered, "Like poor ole Billy."

Howard feeling a little unnerved, sipped from his beer. "I better see if I can find my friends. Nice meeting you." The man didn't look up, just nodded his head over his beer. Howard elbowed his way through the hubbub toward Budd and Dick's table. He was taken aback by the amount of empty beer mugs on the table.

Budd, seemingly well past his limit, upon seeing Howard yelled, "Another round for my buddies!"

Dick winked at Howard. "I'll have a smoke instead." Dick reached over for Budd's cigarette case, snapped it open and took out two; one he extended to Howard. Howard lit his, took a long drag, pushed his chair back until it leaned against the wall and let his eyes wander over the room.

Well, excitement surely reigns here. No doubt. A different life. Wild, unabashed, unfettered, a little rough but I think it will suit me just fine. As the guy said, the pay's good. At least I've got an in with Mr. Hammond. Keep on his good side and maybe I can get a management job out of this. Ha! Imagine me. A lumber baron. I'll wear the crown well.

"Howard! Howard! Hey, quit dreaming. Get off your damn duff. Give me a hand with Budd." Dick was struggling to pull Budd up from his chair who was still gripping a beer and mumbling incoherently. Something about home. I managed to wrestle the mug from Budd's grasp and hoisted him up. Then Dick and I dragged him toward the door and once outside the night air splashed across our faces and we stood frozen for a moment and just inhaled.

"Hey, once we're back at the logging camp let's pull our sleeping bags outside. That bunkhouse smells like the inside of a ripe, late night bathhouse down on the lower East Side. This night air is too good to leave and maybe we'll get a good night's sleep and God only knows, we need it," Dick said, trying to get a better grip on a slumping Budd. "I don't think Budd here will even notice but the air can't but help a hangover and he's gonna have a rip-snorting one."

Budd's snoring could contest any logging saw. It was a helluva struggle Dick and I had trying to get him into his sleeping bag. Dick had Budd slung over his shoulder and as he tried to hoist him higher; Budd just slid down Dick's back and when he hit the ground he curled up and began snoring. Dick collapsed laughing, picked up Budd's sleeping bag and threw it on top of him and said, "He'll never know the difference."

"I guess he won't but he's got to be confused in the

morning with the taste of dirt and stale beer in his mouth."

After Dick climbed into his bag we rambled on about watching the gigantic logs arriving on cars and rolling into the bog with immense splashes, then drawn up an incline to the insatiable humming, singing mill where they sawed them into all sizes of boards, timbers and shingles. I started to tell Dick about the man in the bar with the missing fingers and his tale about being crushed to death. I tried to hide my apprehension and really wanted to know how dangerous it was going to be working at the mill but I noticed Dick's head drop and he was out to the world. I decided to drag my bag into this circle of giant redwoods. It's like laying on the floor of a cathedral. Looking up at these tall limbless trunks, their heavy tops only letting an occasional trickle of moonlight gleam on the bare ground coated with cool silent needles. It seems criminal to cut these wonderful monarchs of centuries growth, and miles of cut ground is left in the rear; useless fields, no trees, no undergrowth; just stumps, left like a dead, overwhelmed, defeated army.

Howard, with his coffee mug in hand, had settled himself down on an old tree trunk. He suddenly noticed the sunlight flashing across the dank ground. Tree limbs shook violently, the air became cyclonic, the forest roared. Then silence. Quietness settled once again through the woods.

A shout came from the forest. "Why the hell didn't you get out of here? What the hell were you thinking?" A logger with his axe slung over his shoulder moved toward Howard. "Damn! What the hell do you think you're doing, buddy? If you didn't hear them holler you sure as hell should have heard the rumble or at least felt the ground shake. Where's your senses man?"

Howard could see a man's big, angry mouth moving

but the words floated past him. He closed his eyes and felt his numb body start to shiver. It felt like eternity passing slowly. There was no reality to what he had felt or witnessed. The downed tree lay across the old tree trunk upon which he had just been sitting.

Finally he recognized the weathered face of the missing-fingered man from the bar coming through the woods. The other logger who had been yelling at him slung his axe into a stump.

"Mac, you wouldn't believe this guy. He just stood there. Stood there like a goddamn planted oak. I tell you, twenty years out here and I've never seen somebody freeze like that. He had all the time in the world but he froze. Get him out of here. I don't want to plant anymore crosses. Get him out!"

"That true, boy? You froze? Didn't I warn you about these suckers?"

Howard realized the words of this weary-worn man, devoid of anger, was asking him a question. His voice was strangled in his throat and words were stricken in his mind, that is, if there existed any words to express what had just happened.

"Boy, what's wrong with you? You dumb or something? You're not hurt or are you?"

Howard shook his head back and forth, no, no, no. His eyes were affixed on the enormous trunk of the downed tree. Suddenly his knees buckled and he slid down to the ground next to the giant redwood. His hand tentatively reached out to grope the ground under the trunk. Then he frantically started to scoop out the dirt as if he were searching for something.

"C'mon boy. It's over. C'mon," Mac said in a quiet tone. Mac picked up Howard's axe that lay in front of his feet and said, "Come on now. Let's go back to the bunkhouse."

Howard looked up at Mac's face. Confused, he

looked at the hole he had dug then at the dirt in his palms. Then he reached once more in the hole under the trunk and his hand closed over something. He pulled it out and kept it in his clenched hand.

"You find something, boy?" Howard did not answer but leaned his head back and stared for a moment up into the blue sky space created by the felled tree then he let his head drop. Slowly he rose to his feet, his body still shaken.

"Well, whatever it is, better it was buried under the tree rather than you. Let's get a move on." Even the resentment he had felt at this man for referring to him once again as 'boy' was gone. With tired, slumping shoulders, he followed Mac's footsteps meekly down the slope.

The bunkhouse felt like an eternal resting place. Howard lowered himself gently onto his bunk. He held the cloth wrapped item close to his chest. "Thank God I haven't lost it," he murmured. He relaxed for a moment, and then the shudder racked his body. His chest heaved and another shudder hit. Howard just let the spasms take him. The lifeblood of his body seem to drain upon the bed and when it finally quieted, the sobs came. They washed down his face, his neck, soaking into the pillow until they finally cleansed him. The terror was gone, the experience lingered.

Dick came into the bunkhouse, having heard the news of Howard's imminent leave taking. Budd lay sprawled across his bunk watching Howard trying to shove his things into his duffel bag. "Gee, Howdy," Budd's pet name for Howard, "I'm sorry to see you go. Seems like your breaking up that ole' gang of mine," Budd said as he kicked off one of his logging boots.

"Yeah, Howard, that's true. Remember when we all sat around in Charley Wirth's pub in Harvard Square mapping out this western voyage and after one too many beers we dubbed ourselves The Happy Family and pledged to stick together. Remember?" Dick pulled himself up onto his bunk.

"Yeah, I remember," Howard replied with an air of dejection. Howard had not said anything to either one of them about the event in the woods only to say that he was leaving. He was afraid if he said anything more they would pressure him to stay by making him feel guilty for leaving them behind. But the room was quiet. The troubled air could be cut with a knife.

Dick watched Howard try to pull the drawstrings tight on a now over-stuffed bag. Finally, he jumped down from his bunk and took a hold of one of the drawstrings. "Here, if the two of us pull maybe we can get it a little tighter." They both yanked then Dick tied a knot and leaned the bag against the wall.

"Howdy, Budd and I don't blame you for wanting to leave. We heard about what happened. Believe me, I know, it can be sheer terror out there. Don't forget I grew up in the midst of this. I've seen the bodies."

Howard just nodded. He felt empty, wasted, as if his heart was still trying to find its normal beat.

"What time does your train leave?" Budd asked.

"Six."

"My parents are sad to see you go but they understand. Dad told me he got a hold of a Mr. Haynes for you. He's a friend of your father's, isn't he?" Dick asked.

Howard nodded. "Uh, yes. He wired that he could put me on at the Empire Mine over in Grass Valley."

"Safer job, I suppose?" Budd said. Dick fired him an angry glance. "I don't mean anything by that, Howdy. God, I had my kick in the butt out in that damn forest today, too. I had stepped out of the way of a falling tree but a branch caught me and slapped me a good one across the back of my head. Took me five minutes before I could think clearly again." Budd gingerly felt the back of his head. "Sure makes you think about loving life or the loss of loving women, whatever." Budd let out a little laugh. A slight smile crossed Howard's face and everyone felt a little relieved.

Dick picked up Howard's duffel and said, "Come on, pal. Let's get you on that train."

A look of concern crossed Howard's face for a moment and he checked something in his inside coat pocket. Whatever it was the concern vanished and Howard said, "Okay, I'm ready. Ready to move on."

****

Beatrice had been dawdling about her bedroom all day romanticizing about the young Howard Ward. She fussed with her sandy blonde hair and changed her dress several times. She posed in front of the mirror creating imaginary conversations all afternoon. She had the maid brush her hair a hundred times and pile it on top of her head. She had pulled out a couple of long curls, winding them around her finger then pulling them out to trickle seductively down the back of her neck. She kept turning her head to see in the mirror, pursing her lips in various poses.

I wonder what New Yorkers talk about. I'm sure he is used to all those society girls from those snooty Eastern finishing schools. They probably only speak French at the dinner table. "Comment allez-vous, monsieur?" That's all I know how to say. If he answers, "Tres bien," I'm fine. If he dares to carry on a conversation any further in French I'm lost. Hmmmmmm! I wonder how New York men kiss.

She had just decided which side of her profile was

better shifting back and forth several times on her boudoir mirror stool when she was startled by the front door knocker. She waited to see if someone was going to answer. After a few moments she heard the knocker again so she went down the stairs and opened the door. "Howard, how nice of you to drop by. Do come in." Taking a deep breath and trying to lower her voice hoping it would have a more sultry, genteel quality. "Please why don't you make yourself comfortable. Would you like a sherry?"

"I'd be delighted," Howard replied thinking I do believe she's playing the coquette. He watched her swish her skirt across the room and pour two glasses of sherry. She turned her head to glance at him and she caught him watching her. Howard felt a little embarrassed and uneasy as he reached up to take the glass from Beatrice. He had never been alone with her before on his visits to the Kidder home. He took a sip and said, "How is your mother. I had hoped to see her." Beatrice feeling a little perturbed thinking he had not come to see her but her mother.

"I'll go see if she's available." In the hallway, she stopped and fixed her dangling curls in the mirror and pinched her cheeks to bring the pink to the skin surface. Oh, think of something intelligent to say, Bea. How many chances am I going to get to catch a young eligible New Yorker. Think! Think! Think!

Howard finished his sherry and thought, that was stupid. Why didn't I think of something intelligent to say? At least engage her in a witty conversation. Now I have to think of something to say to Mrs. Kidder. I sure didn't think this out when I decided to drop by. Stupid! Stupid! Stupid! Okay, think now while I have a moment. Wow, this is a marvelous old mansion. Look at the detail in the woodwork. All that redwood in the ceilings. Luxury! Life must be sheer luxury here.

Oh, my God, I hear them coming. Think, Howard. Think!

"Good afternoon, Mrs. Kidder. I hope I have found you well?" Howard said as he attempted to rise to his feet.

"Yes, dear boy. Please don't get up. I see Bea has poured you a sherry," Mrs. Kidder said. "And it looks like you are ready for another."

Howard looked at his empty glass a little embarrassed. "No, thank you. I think I've had enough."

"Nonsense, dear boy. You're in the West now and we're into a little bit of the hard stuff, especially this time of the day. It's four o'clock, isn't it?"

Howard nodded yes, a little taken back by her masculine manner of speaking.

"Bea, don't just stand there. Fetch our good scotch. I could use a good shot after a morning of haggling in the office with my foreman and spending the afternoon in a hot kitchen. Although the smells of good food cooking is God's aphrodisiac for a hungry soul. Don't you think so, Mr. Ward?"

"Yes ma'am." Howard fidgeted in his chair wondering, why am I here? Please, please, please think of something to ask. Bea had come back with a tray of shot glasses and a bottle of scotch. She put it on a low table in front of Mrs. Kidder. She picked up the bottle and poured the scotches. She handed one to Howard then picking up one for herself she swigged it down and poured herself another one.

"Don't let me shock you dear boy, but I need a good belt to keep my heart ticking some days."

Howard eyes had widened as he watched her. He quickly took a big gulp from his own glass, gasped, took a deep breath, and then took a smaller sip. "It's alright, ma'am. I sometimes need one myself."

"Mr. Kidder used to say after God made Adam and

Eve and then he created the grape so that Adam would taste the mystery of its juice to help him survive life's pain. It was probably Eve who was fooling around in her kitchen one day and pulled out of the cupboard some six month old juice she had salted away, served it to Adam that night and when Adam started to giggle and wink at her every turn, she realized she had something good on her hands. That apple story was just for the puritans." Mrs. Kidder laughed and took another drink.

"I've heard some stories about Mr. Kidder around town. He sounds like he was a very unique man," Howard said. "I'd more than enjoy hearing more about him."

Mrs. Kidder grinned widely, thumped her glass on the table and said, "Oh, there's some great stories but let me tell you this one."

Thank God, Howard thought to himself, relaxing now since he found something to talk about. Beatrice flashed him a coy smile and seeing that he looked comfortable felt relieved knowing he was going to stay. She reached around to the back of her neck and pulled the dangling curls over her shoulder.

"Back a good number of years ago when John, that's Mr. Kidder, was engineering the road bed for the railroad through Grass Valley he had convinced the stagecoach line to give him a free pass to travel the road back and forth from Nevada. I don't recall what he promised them but you can bet your last gold nugget it was something worthwhile. Mr. Kidder never went back on his word. Well, it seems that Mark Twain got wind of this privilege and being an impish character decided he would yell to the driver that he was Mr. Kidder. I gather he had been doing this for some time when one afternoon he jumped up on the driver's seat and said casually, "I'm Mr. Kidder". My husband's reaction was quick, like the crack of a horse whip. He reached up and yanked Mr. Twain back to the ground and bellowed, "You're who?" Mr. Twain, with that Mississippi twang of his, convinced Mr. Kidder he meant no harm. Mr. Twain's charm has a right to be known as legendary because if he could charm my husband he could charm a rattler out of its hole. They even became fast friends after that stage ride. Of course, Mr. Twain paid." Mrs. Kidder rocked back and forth in her chair for a moment lolling in the memory of the story.

"He sounds like he was a man of principle but also understanding of a man's foibles," Howard said.

"He certainly was that. He was born with that damn Yankee backbone but he was not an uncompromising man and always gave a man the benefit of a doubt. He always said if one is so set in their principles no telling how many great opportunities they might miss in learning from or about another man. I was born with that western grit in my teeth, not trusting everybody coming down the pike, so to my own misgivings, I don't give a man that much elbow room. He better prove himself well before I'll move over. I can tell by how they look me in the eye whether I can trust him or not." Mrs. Kidder looking straight at Howard continued, "Tell me, Mr. Ward how are you finding our western way of life. You've had a couple months of experience now. I know you've been supervising that tennis court over at the Starrs. What about mining? That's your profession isn't it?"

Howard fidgeting in his seat again began to feel a little uncomfortable wondering if this formidable woman could read his thoughts. His mind reeled. Boy, I need her to trust me if I want a position in this community. Should I mention a few famous intimate names? I have got to impress this woman. But be subtle. Subtlety is the name of the game. He tried to focus directly across the room at Mrs. Kidder assuming a posture of supposed sophistication and a projection of proper upbringing.

"Yes, I have a mining degree from Harvard. My male forebears have always matriculated from Harvard and to this day are major financial supporters of the institution. It's always been known for its prestigious faculty whose virtues my father was always extolling."

"Harvard, hmmmm! Mr. Kidder was a graduate of Rensselaer, a prestigious, your word Mr. Ward, engineering institute also, don't you think?"

"Oh, I don't wish to demean Rensselaer. I'm sure it's a great school." Howard hurriedly said. "I guess I mean to say that my father and grandfather had the opportunity to study the classical arts at Harvard. I guess if it had not been such a family tradition for the men to attend Harvard, I might have considered Rensselaer because of its engineering reputation," Howard said trying to retrieve the situation from the slight tinge of irritation he heard in Mrs. Kidder's voice. "My grandfather had his circle of friends at Harvard and was encouraged by Mr. Emerson to engage in philosophical writing and discussion. Mr. Emerson thought my grandfather had much to offer the intellectual world. I know I was influenced by my father and grandfather's circle of friends and I suppose I thought I could challenge some of Mr. Emerson's premises at Harvard."

"Oh, really! Mr. Emerson. Emerson. Is that Mr. Ralph Emerson?"

"Yes, ma'am. Ralph Waldo Emerson."

"Now there was a man with a Yankee mindset. Mr. Kidder had read a number of his essays which he enjoyed very much in regards to Mr. Emerson exploring the nature of man's existence. He liked his imploring mind to think beyond his own self. But as I recall, although I know he lectured at places far from Boston, he didn't believe there were any other culturally civilized areas outside of Boston. I gather he deemed it the American cradle of civilized thought. I think he would find life here rather rough. With your intimate knowledge of Mr. Emerson, wouldn't you agree?"

Howard laughed nervously. "Rough, yes. But I think he would call it savage. I remember my grandfather inviting Mr. Emerson to his home in the Saddleback Mountains in western Massachusetts where my grandfather had several fields under tillage. Upon his return to Boston he wrote my grandfather a memorable letter claiming that the isolation of life in the wilderness was self-immolation, maceration lending oneself to those rocks. He was thankful that he could hurry back to Concord before the charm of his visit wore off, hoping never to see the mountains again."

Howard saw Mrs. Kidder smile and thought, it's rough matching wits with this woman. She's like a bear trap. One false step and I'll never make another. He glanced over at Beatrice who also looked a little relieved.

"I know, Mama, unlike Mr. Emerson, Mr. Ward is quite taken with our hills."

"Oh, yes. I've been trying to weave myself into its history of the 49' gold rush. What excitement that must have been! I've sought out and searched the ruins of the deserted mines, You Bet, Malakof, Deadman's Flat. The names themselves entice one to roam their tunnels hoping for your eye to catch that glint. That's why I feel lucky to be in the employ of the Empire mine where those rich pockets of gold, which Mr. Starr calls "jewelry shop" or "bonanza" ore, are still being found. I always have my eyes open.

"I've never been inside the mine. Mama has never

let me near the miners calling them rough, crude men."

"No place for a young, pretty girl," Mrs. Kidder replied.

Howard saw a chance to prove his worthiness in this household. "Maybe your mother would entrust your safety to my care? I would be delighted to show you how a gold mine works. Would you do me the honor, Mrs. Kidder?"

Mrs. Kidder was taken aback by the extreme polite propriety of his request and found herself momentarily lacking an excuse not to allow Beatrice to go. "I guess Beatrice is old enough now to be escorted on the arm of a gentleman. I know I'm overprotective but a woman has to be careful in this neck of the country. There's a lot of uncouth, uncultured, uncivilized men out there just waiting to take advantage of an innocent. But you, Mr. Ward, appear to be more than trustworthy."

Beatrice beamed. Howard stood up and said, "Would tomorrow at four when I am free for the day be okay?"

Trying not to look overanxious, Beatrice said, "Certainly, I will be ready."

"Wear some good, strong shoes. The dirt and mud can sometimes ride up your ankles."

"I'll search my closet. I'm sure I can find something. Thank you, Howard."

"Beatrice will show you to the door, Mr. Ward. And do be careful with my daughter. She is like crystal, she breaks easily."

"Mama! I'm sure I can handle myself. I have strong bones and I've not yet broken one."

"Thank you for your kind hospitality Mrs. Kidder. I promise you she will return in one piece. I will see you tomorrow."

****

"Watch that step there. All this is makeshift stuff. Never meant for a woman's tiny feet. You better take my hand and hold your skirt up with the other because I can assure you that pretty dress will get muddied."

"Yahoo Yankee. Who's that pretty thing you got wrapped around your arm down there?" a lanky miner, lunch pail in hand, hollered down from a slope on the hill over the mine entrance.

Howard looked up the slope and frowned. At least the men here had nicknamed him Yankee and didn't refer to him as 'boy'. He hollered angrily at the amused man, "None of your business, Red." Howard pulled out his pocket watch and glanced at it, then looking back up at Red yelled, "You've got another twenty minutes to round up your crew and start that blasting area I laid out for you this morning."

"Aye, aye, sir!" Red saluted, laughed and turned pulling himself further up a path on the slope.

"And mind your language when you speak to a lady," Howard continued to yell after Red's retreating back. "These are rough hewn men around here not used to pretty cultured young women. If I were you I'd keep a good distance unless I'm near. Trust me, I'll keep them in line."

Bea turned her head away. 'Where does he think I've been all my life? Locked away in my gabled lacy bedroom, waited on by liveried servants and fed sweet things slathered with gentility? Well, I'll let him think that! Papa is probably roaring his head off wherever he is. He always let me trip after him over the railbeds, lifting me up into the engine cab sometimes to ride down the rail line.'

"Watch out!" Howard yelled.

A startled Bea lost her footing and fell back against the mine wall. Howard lunged forward grabbing her forearm and with his other hand grabbed her around her waist and pulling her back to her feet. She had regained her balance but Howard did not let her go. The moment extended into awkwardness. Howard kept looking down at her confused face which she felt like burying in his shoulder. She felt a twinge of pain in her ankle. "This is dumb! Stupid!"

Strangely Howard still had a tight hold of her. She put her hands on his chest and started to exert a little pressure to push herself away. She looked up and confronted Howard's eyes.

Oh, my god, what the hell do I do now? Howard felt slight panic overcome him. Do something, do something now. If he loosened his grip in any way he would lose his chance. Chance to do what? Kiss her? Yes. Yes. Do it now. NOW!

"Howard, I'm okay," Bea said slipping her hand down to his wrists and pushing them away.

"Well! Well! Well! I guess there is more to be found in a mine than gold." Howard swung around and saw Red standing in the mine entrance with a smirking grin on his face. "Looking for a reward for your attentive, personal guided tour, Boss?"

Embarrassment conflicted with anger rising in his throat. Through clenched teeth he started to speak but heard the stammering of his first words. He stopped, his eyes glaringly fixated on this red-bearded, muscled man. "You'll be picking up your last paycheck if you don't start swinging that pickaxe. That's what you were hired to do, not to stand around insulting a lady."

Red grinned. "C'mon guys," he yelled to the men outside. "The boss says to get off our butts and start swingin' or there will be no money for pints tonight." He sidled past a blushing Bea.

Bemused, knowing eyes glanced sideways at Bea as the miners edged past. Howard, hoping his voice was carrying to the miners and that their shenanigans had interrupted his explanation of mining to Bea, continued with an air of authority and knowledge. "Now much of the gold mined is found in these nearly invisible fine particles, but we often find rich pockets with massive gold holding the quartz crystals together. Those finds are called the 'jewelry shop' or 'bonanza' ore. Howard raised his voice even more, "I think those finds are where the miners confiscate their illicit share of gold to pad their paycheck."

Bea's head started to swim with the notions of nuggets of gold possibly lying a few feet below her feet. Just to hold a few of them in my hands. Experience their glow. Their richness. What a world they would buy me. Freedom. Go anywhere I want. Do what I choose. People beckoning to my every whim. My father always called me his little princess. The gold in these walls would make me a real princess. She looked at Howard, who was trying to recover a pickax from a hole the miners had made, with a different perception of his future possibilities. Yes, maybe he's the one who has been sent by fate to rescue me from this deathly boring valley. He's clever enough. With a little encouragement from me maybe he could become president of this mine, or better yet, owner. Mama's got the connections if I pull the strings.

The innocence that had powdered Bea's face was now rouged with that of a cunning young woman. Feeling more than the usual discomfort in the company of a woman, Howard coughed a couple of times and said, "I'm afraid the dust is too much for me in here and it is certainly not good for you." He took her arm and started to lead her to the mine entrance.

The ride back to the Kidder household was quiet. Both silent as Howard escorted Bea to the front door. Before his departure he took her hand and told her he hoped to see her again soon. Bea was sorry to have the day end but anxious to get to her room and mull over the events of the day and think strategy. I must be clever, not too pushy or obvious, but I must think what could I dangle in front of his very blue eyes to keep his head turned my way? Bea pulled out the hairpins, loosening her curls and started to brush her hair with an energized determination.

****

July 20, 1903

Mrs. Dibbles Rooming House
Grass Valley, California

Dearest Bessie,

Grass Valley is the most naturally beautiful mining town I have ever seen. I'm about two thousand feet high among millions of pines, overlooking the Sacramento Valley and dim in the distance I can see the Coast Range. Where the pines have been cleared away, the manzanita bushes spring up and scattered here and there are pear orchards. The soil is deep and very, very red. I'm told the winter months can be miserably rainy but right now it is dry, clear and not too hot. Paradise!

I think this is going to be my kind of job, just to my liking. Out in the open, surveying, mapping and using my real skills, engineering. I know I can smell gold just like a dowser after water. Mr. Bourne, the owner of the Empire mine, invited me over to dinner the other night. He has the kind of house I will own some day - a beautiful stone house, very English, with ivy climbing over it and gloriously beautiful grounds and gardens surrounding it. He offered me my first job endeavor - to lie out and superintend the building of a concrete tennis court. I was ecstatic. I imagined myself smashing swift serves across the net. You recall I am not a bad netman and I must say I do look handsome in tennis whites.

I can see you smiling as you read this - every morning I can be seen trudging a mile and a half to the mine with my tin luncheon bucket in my hand like all the other miners who are funnily enough called cousin jacks, as I understand the Cornishmen are usually called. The buckets are made of trays, in the bottom is tea, next sandwiches as a Cornish 'pasty', and on top is pie, cake or fruit. Half an hour before lunchtime, we put a small candle or 'snuff' under the bucket and when it 'tapered off' our tea was hot and so was everything else.

  Mr. Starr is superintendent of the mine and my boss. He and his wife have taken it upon themselves to look after my well-being. Mrs. Starr is more than motherly taking any young man under her wing. I personally believe she is an inveterate matchmaker always citing the qualities and beauties of all the young girls she knows. I do think she cannot abide the idea of unmarried young men. It becomes her personal duty to see that they find a wife. I bet she charges!

  Lastly but not least, I have met a fascinating family, the Kidders. Mrs. Kidder is the present President of the Narrow Gauge Railroad which was built by her husband. He died a number of years ago much to my chagrin because I would have loved to have met this legend of a man. All I can assume now about the man are the tales Mrs. Kidder tells me of his exploits which keeps me enthralled for hours. All these stories my friends and I hear while she cooks up Bacchanalian feasts. She's a marvel at throwing anything together, put in on the fire, murmur a few incantations, and then come forth the most epicurean feeds imaginable. All this is enhanced by the presence of her daughter, Beatrice, adopted from Mrs. Kidder's brother. Mrs. Starr's ranting about her beauty had a ring of truth. Beatrice is full of life, a good dancer and a fine horsewoman. Yes, she does pique my interest.

I am sure you are reading this to the entire family. So give them my love and now they know that I am well.

Your loving brother,
Howard

The late April morning sky was painted with grey but had that unique tinge that augured a change in the day to come. Howard was sitting tall on his horse, a new leather jacket's collar pulled up to keep the chill away. This little spontaneous weekend trek had been the idea of George Starr and his wife. The girls were to pack the food and the men were to haul all the paraphernalia for a trip to Bowman's Dam about a two and a half hour journey. He was amused at everyone's obvious discomfort with the cold. He thought how enduring and braving Boston's treacherous winters with winds off the bay that would make one's bones ache had toughened his skin and thickened his blood. Bea shivered and clutched her fur muffler tighter. Her fingertips were starting to tingle but she had no way to let go of the reins to warm her hands. What a stupid idea this is. Mother should have been more adamant about not letting me go but no, I had to play the frontier woman faking that I could ride a horse to Bowman's with no trouble. As if I did it every day. God, it's cold. Howard isn't even shivering. He hasn't even waited up on me to see if I'm cold.

Howard turned in his saddle and looked back at Bea. She managed a little smile but then shuddered as a blast of cold air blew across the path. Howard glanced up at the sky and saw the first flurries of snow. Well, it should warm up a bit. But this was surely not what Mr. Starr expected for a picnic. We've only been on the trail an hour and that sky does not look too promising.

Two hours later they crested the western side of the mountain and now could look northward up the valley. Howard was startled by a heavy force of blowing snow roaring down the valley, blinding him for a moment. He pulled his horse up short, rubbed the wetness from his eyes and looked up the mountain range again. He could see that it obviously had been snowing quite some time on this side of the range as high drifts had already been piling up covering the trail. He gave his horse a little kick to force him forward on the trail to catch up with Mr. Starr.

"I'm afraid, Howard, this doesn't look good", Walter Starr said as Howard pulled up alongside of him on the path. "Let's wait up on the others. We'll have to decide what our options are. I'm afraid we can't turn back. This storm is moving too fast and it would soon catch up with us. I don't want to frighten the girls but we must get out of this storm as fast as possible. The sooner the better."

"Isn't this rather odd? A snowstorm in April? How bad can it get?" Howard asked pulling his neck scarf up over his mouth.

"No, it's not that unusual up in these Sierras. Sure not picnic weather. I guess I was just too anxious and longing for spring and Mother Nature decided to smack me back to reality. That's what these ole' mountains will do to you."

Oliver and George Jones pulled their horses up. The girls were just a hundred yards back on the trail. Oliver shouted over another roar of wind-bearing snow, "I know there's a small clearing about two hundred yards up ahead. Why don't you keep going and see if there is anything with which we can build a shelter and I will push the girls along." George Starr started to object leaving the girls behind but Oliver waved his hand at him and turned his horse back down the trail.

Oliver saw the frightened looks on the girls face. Frances, his sister said, as he pulled up, "We're frozen through, Oliver. We've got to get out of this wind."

Bea, on the verge of tears, said, "Where's Howard and the others?"

"I told them to go on ahead to a clearing I know and see if they can find something to make a shelter for us. C'mon, push those horses." Oliver turned back up the trail trying to conceal his concern.

Mrs. Starr felt her heart starting to race, suddenly feeling responsible for putting the young people in this dangerous situation. The trip had been her idea believing it would give the young people a chance to be away from the usual formalities of social life and let their hair down. Get to know each other better with looser ties. I wish George had argued me out of it but he just nodded his head okay. With motherly concern she yelled to the girls, "Don't worry, we'll make it. Just keep your heads down and spirits up." The snow was now drifting very fast making it slow going for the horses.

Howard and the others had found the clearing and had spotted a little makeshift lean-to up a slope among some trees. Mr. Starr was barking orders. "Cut those branches fast! I've got a scout knife and a hatchet. If you've got something better, use it! Get as many as you can. Let's go! Let's go!" All the men scrambled up the slope and started hacking at low branches.

They had dragged a good number of branches into the lean-to by the time Oliver and the women arrived. Mrs. Starr slid down from her horse and yelled to the girls to hurry and take the horse blankets from under their saddles. Bea, looking confused, began pulling at the saddle's strap, fumbling with the hitch. Frances and Mrs. Starr had deftly removed theirs and came to help.

Bea, not being able to hold back the frightened tears, began to cry.

"It's alright, dear, Mrs. Starr said as she pulled Bea's saddle off her horse. "Calm yourself down and take your saddle and blanket up the slope. Hurry and make yourself helpful. There will be no time for tears."

"I'll make some tracks in the snow. Just keep right close behind me, Bea," Frances said calmly. "We'll be okay. I trust my brother and Mr. Starr to keep us safe."

Funny, Bea thought, she didn't mention Howard would keep us safe.

"Pull those horses over into that stand of trees, Anne, and tie them together!" Mr. Starr yelled at his wife. Bea, hearing Mr. Starr yell, looked back and stood frozen in a mesmerized state staring at the awesomeness of the whiteness of deep drifted snow, not feeling it anymore as it fell upon her face.

"Hurry, Bea." Bea did not move. "Bea!" Frances yelled louder. "You'll freeze standing there like Lot's wife." Frances stepped back down the trail and tugged at Bea's arm.

Bea turning, all expression vanishing from her face, picked up a broken branch and dragged it toward the shelter where the men had already piled up a slew of cut branches. Howard trudged up the path dragging several large branches. He stepped inside the lean-to and pushed the snow away from the center of the hut with his boot.

"Bea, fetch me that small shovel from my horse and Frances, you start breaking up small twigs for tinder. We've got to get a fire started." Frances, exasperated by Bea's helplessness, irritatedly said, "Here, Bea you break up this branch, I'll go down and get the shovel." She gave an irritated look at Howard as if to say 'You take care of her.' and set off down the slope. Howard, feeling sympathetic, took the branch from Bea, broke it apart and started a pile of tinder. Bea grabbed a branch and started to break it up. Howard said nothing. He picked up a large branch and started to prop it up against the outside wall of the lean-to. He stripped some saplings and leaned them against the open end of the lean-to, slanting them toward the ground as far as he could in order to provide more room inside.

"Good work, son," Mr. Starr nodded approvingly. He and Oliver started laying their branches against the framework of saplings. Bea had come back with Mrs. Starr and began helping Frances shove her small branch pieces in openings between the lean-to's timbers. Howard started digging a fire pit. They moved as fast as they could, working hurriedly before the darkness invaded them. Mr. Starr and Oliver dropped several logs they had found on top of the tinder then covered the logs with more tinder.

"Well, let's all pray I can get this to start. They're awfully wet logs." Mr. Starr said as he lit the driest branch he could find to use as a torch. He lit the tinder in several places but after a few minutes and a lot of choking smoke the tinder died out. He tried again, and again, and again. Bea stood staring at the continually dying sparks. Her feet were numb and she was shivering uncontrollably. Suddenly, she turned her back to the group, pulled up her skirt and yanked off her petticoat. Without saying a word, she handed it to Mr. Starr. In amazement and with a quiet 'thank you' he started to tear the petticoat into strips.

"What a good idea, my dear. I should have thought of that," said Mrs. Starr while turning around and pulling off her petticoat. Frances followed. The men looked at each other and Oliver said, "C'mon men. If they can do that, we can contribute." With that, the men followed him outside. Shortly, they returned and dropped their undershorts on the pile. Mr. Starr lit another torch and touched the clothing. It caught fire immediately and he managed to push it down among the logs. Moments spanning time like years passed, all eyes focused on the embers, not a breath passing clinched lips until finally a spark exploded, one of the logs caught and flames darted up. Bea started to laugh, then cry, then laugh. The infection spread and they all put their arms around each other and laughed.

The morning light seeped through the cracks in the lean-to and Bea opened her eyes to find Howard's arm around her and his horse blanket thrown over her. Obviously, in her exhausted sleep, her body still wracked by the cold, she had crept up to his warmth during the night and he accommodated her. She smiled, and then the sound of movement made her adjust her eyes to the misty early light of the lean-to. Mr. Starr was trying to quietly put another log on the fire. The new log flared up and crackled loudly. Startled, the others started to stir and sit up.

Mr. Starr grimaced and quietly said, "Well, good morning all. Sorry about the noise but I didn't want to let this good fire die out. I think we're out of underclothes to start a new one." He laughed. "I see we all survived the storm alright." He looked over with a knowing glance at Howard and Bea. Embarrassed, Howard sat up and brushed off the dirt and leaves from his new jacket,

"While I was outside getting another log I thanked the Lord because the sun is shining. I think it will be slow going but if we get a good start now I think we can make Graniteville by ten."

Howard helped Bea up on her horse and handed her the reins. He mounted his horse and they rode gently down the snow covered trail. Nothing ever looked as marvelous to all as the sight of Graniteville nestled down in the pass. They pulled their horses up in front of the inn where they had expected to stay the night before. As they entered the lobby, Bea spotted the roaring fire in the fireplace and hurried toward it pulling Frances along. They rubbed their arms and turned their backs to the fire's warmth. The other guests at the inn looked perplexed at the two girls 'oohing' and 'aahing' in the ecstasy of a roaring fire.

The innkeeper, rushing down the stairs, grabbed Mr. Starr's hand, and excitedly exclaiming, "Blessed be, I'm sure glad to see you and Anne. Couldn't sleep last night waiting to hear word of you. What a storm! Shades of the Donner party! I had nightmares but you must have lived one." He threw his arms around Mrs. Starr. "Hey, let's get some hot food down your throats. Mary!" he shouted toward the back of the inn. "Mary, get some grub out here."

Mary came hustling out from the back and hugged Mrs. Starr. "Oh, my dear, we were up all night watching the trail. I kept the soup on the stove all night. Come on dears. Sit down quick."

Howard slipped into the chair next to Bea at the table. He took a few sips from his bowl of hot soup, looked up and down the table, finally turning to Bea who was looking at him. "Feeling a little warmer now?"

"Yes, thank you."

There was an awkward moment of silence as they looked at each other. Howard took another sip of soup while slipping his other hand over hers under the table. With his eyes downcast toward his soup in a whisper said, "At least your hands have come back to life."

Bea looked around the table and saw the rest of the group absorbed in eating and conversation. She smiled at Howard and squeezed his hand. "I guess you kept me warm last night. The cold so numbed me I felt I lost all feeling in my body. Now I know how easy it is to go to sleep and die quietly in the snow."

"I couldn't let you leave this earth just yet. I think there might be too many adventures ahead for you."

"Now what kind of possible adventure would that be?" Bea said amusedly.

"I don't exactly know. Surely, not another winter picnic in the mountains. Maybe next time not such a perilous one but a more romantic one. You know, the type with a full moon."

Unexpectedly, Bea laughed loudly which made all heads turn and look curiously. Howard's face reddened more than usual.

The group spent the rest of the day in front of the fire telling tales and teasing one another about their harrowing experience. Tiredness fell on them and they said pleasant goodnights, laughing that a warm bed would never ever again be taken for granted. Bea had been in bed only a few minutes and was just drowsing off when she thought she heard a knock at the door. She sat up and listened but the inn was silent. Suddenly she heard a floorboard creak and another quick knock on her door. She slipped out of bed and whispered, "Who's there?"

"It's me, Howard."

Bea opened the door. Howard stood there in the hallway, head bent, not sure what to say. "Howard, is something wrong?"

"No." He shifted uncomfortably. "I guess I just wanted to be sure that you're okay."

"Yes, I am."

She looked up at Howard who was not making a move in any direction. "Howard, would you like to come in?"

"Yes."

Surprised at his quick response Bea moved back from the door. It was only a tiny room. Besides the bed there was a small dressing table and a fragile looking boudoir chair. Howard tried to sit in it but looking terribly uncomfortable, Bea giggled. "Why don't you sit on the bed next to me? At least your knees won't look like they're tucked under your chin."

Howard moved over next to Bea. Though it was a bold move of his to come to her bedroom, his obvious discomfort made Bea realize that she was in control of the situation. She turned her head to look out the window. "Oh, look it's snowing again. It's so beautiful but I will never ever forget the aura of cold death it carries with each fallen flake. How did we make it through the night? Although I felt a strange warmth this morning when I awoke and it was wonderful to find that it was your arms wrapped around me."

Howard seemed even more uncomfortable but reticent to make a move neither toward Bea or the door. Bea picked up Howard's hand and running her hand over them said, "They're strong hands. Not rough like the railroad men. They say something more. Maybe the ability to make all things possible."

"What things would they make possible?" Howard said, finally finding his voice.

"Well, the future. A good life. An exciting life." Bea stopped. She kept running her hand over Howard's. She whispered, "And they could be loving."

He removed his hand and ran it gently up her back to the nape of her neck. She could feel his hand tremble on her back and knew she had to move closer to him or he probably would not make any further move. She leaned closer to him and laid her hand on his cheek, then let her finger run along his lips. Howard could stand it no longer. He felt his body rise into a hot fever. He quickly pushed her down on the bed and forced his mouth upon hers. Bea felt herself caught suddenly in a violent struggle. Howard was pushing her nightgown up to her waist. His mouth was still upon hers as he rolled back and forth on top of her.

"Stop, Howard. Stop!"

Howard was struggling with his pants. "It's okay. It's okay." He started kissing her up and down her neck then to her breasts, his hands holding her waist. He started to move more violently and Bea became more alarmed. She felt a stab of pain. She closed her eyes. Howard finally groaned and collapsed on top of her. He kissed her again, then her ear and let his hand run through her hair. Bea turned her head to look out the window. Large snowflakes were adhering themselves to the windowpane then melting, one by one. One by one.

****

HOWARD

June 15, 1905

Dearest, dearest Howard,

The letters have just arrived and I am quite faint from excitement and joy - and shock a little because you have kept your plans so secret we have not been prepared by a single word.

Beatrice must be as perfect for a sister-in-law as Justine. I can hardly say more and all I want is an opportunity to know her but I can love her (and do) without that.

How very clever of you to see that what we most needed in the family was a blue-eyed fair-haired fascinating person.

It is maddening to have you so far away! I see Mumsie on the 24th and that will be a great comfort - though Carley is a comfort now. He is so very fond of you and is in himself such an exposition of permanent true love. This is a confidence to you as to love and marriage to the right person not that you and Beatrice need to be told anything - but only as a point of view of the same thing from the other endless end. It will be ten years next autumn since we were engaged and there is not one day that has not brought out some new and wonderful development of that great fact. As to your feelings about the Church I am more concerned about Mumsie (through her letter I have that she takes it like a trooper and just as you would wish) than about you - though realizing how much you must have gone through to come to such a decision. I rely absolutely on your straight forwardness and singleness of purpose - and honesty and sincerity can never go far wrong. Therefore I am as sure as I can be of anything that it *will only be a matter of time, experience and deeper thought. I cannot help wishing we had talked more of those things - only that it might have saved you some wear and tear - for I must confess to a short period of the kind when I was eighteen and that it took thought and reading with the grace of God to bring the conviction that unless Christianity is discarded altogether and how can one deny what it has done for the world and that it is the highest ideal we know. The Catholic Church is the only logical church and therefore <u>the</u> Church.*

This is a very hurried letter as we move to Swampscott today but I had to express my joy in your joy. I will write to Beatrice soon and hope to see Dick Hammond any minute.

Your devoted sister,
Bessie

P.S. *There is not a day that we do not miss you.*

Howard, having read Bessie's letter for the second time, reached into his desk drawer where he had placed his cherished scrapbook along with a few other personal beloved things that he had packed when he left Boston. Sticking his finger in the pot of new white paste he had bought that afternoon at the stationers in town he lightly dabbed the corners of the letter and centered it on a new page. Then he rifled through his desk drawer till he found the scissors Mrs. Dibbles had loaned him. He looked at the pile of newspapers with the countless accounts of his and Bea's engagement announcement. He picked up the top paper, found the item and started to cut. When he had pasted the last article into the scrapbook he sat staring at the San Francisco paper with Bea's picture with a drawing of a coy, little flirtatious angel balancing on Bea's shoulder. Despairingly shaking his head, he started to read the headline.

NEW YORKER TO WED MISS KIDDER

Grass Valley girl is famous for beauty. Howard Ridgely Ward of New York City is to marry Miss Beatrice Kidder, daughter of Mrs. Kidder of Grass Valley. The engagement has been formally announced.

Miss Kidder's mother is president of the Nevada County Narrow Gauge Railroad. Her mother is an extremely wealthy woman in her own right, prominent as a leader of society and lauded in social circles for her charming manners. Miss Kidder is a girl of unusual beauty and attainments. She has many friends in San Francisco who will wish her happiness as a matron. For several years Miss Beatrice was a boarding pupil at Miss West's School.

Miss Kidder is a blonde, a perfect type of that fair order of beauty. Above her faultless face there glows a wealth of golden hair, abundant, charming, the perfectly appropriate setting for the features below. The Ward family is connected with prominent and highly connected Eastern families. The date for the wedding has not yet been set, but it is stated that the ceremony will be performed sometime this coming fall.

Howard sat staring at the picture. George and Justine flashed in his head... remembered feelings of that cold cathedral shuddered through his body. How did this happen? Happen so fast? How did I lose control of this situation? Graniteville! God have mercy! That night in Graniteville.

He slowly began to flip through the pages of his scrapbook again reading the letters from his grandparents when he was little. Then he turned the pages to all the clippings about his skating honors. His eyes fell on the caption, WARD A CLEVER YOUNGSTER. He shook his head. Where is that cleverness now? Continuing to turn the pages he glanced at the pictures of himself on the hockey team, articles as a cox on the rowing team, letters written to him at Harvard, playbills from favorite shows, a program citing him as a member of the Cutler Comedy Club. Suddenly his eyes fell upon a letter Bonpapa had written to him before he set off on his western journey. The words felt illuminated as he read,

Lights seem only bright when shadows are near, and mountains high only when valleys can be seen. Peace may only be realized when oppressed to turbulence, an interesting adventure only enjoyed when compared to bored inactivity, all being mental perspective and relative, if one cannot glimpse occasionally a bit of ugliness, how can one possibly appreciate beauty or joy?

Howard slumped and dropped his head into his hands. Slowly, he began to apply pressure to his temples to assuage his fear. He reached over to the open desk drawer and picked up a small object. Carefully unwrapping it and then turning it over and over, he contemplated its intricate shape, its beautiful features, as the wind of distant memories carried him beyond the walls of his small rooming house bedroom. He felt the tear slowly course its way down his face as he set the object on his nightstand and closed the book.

****

BESSIE

June 21, 1905

Perkins Cove
Ogunquit, Maine

Dearest Bonpapa,
* The children are spending the afternoon with their nurse playing on the rocks in the cove and basking their sun-starved white bodies in the summer sun. Watching them from the window I can vicariously enjoy their delight when the waves crash themselves against the rocks and sprays them with their delicious taste of salt sprinkled water. What joy to see them scurry back from the ocean's edge with that childish mischievous pretense of not wanting to get wet.*
* I am sure that you and Bonnemaman have heard the news from the West. It took me by surprise as I am sure it did you. From my heart, although I wish him the very most of life and happiness, I am concerned as you must surely be. Howard is so young a man to make such an onerous decision with all the responsibility that marriage entails. What stresses me is how can he manage financially since he has not worked long enough to have amassed a sufficient amount to maintain a proper household? I am deathly afraid that I hold myself responsible for this spontaneous proposal of marriage that Howard has made. When he was a student at Harvard he always had an open invitation to our home. He accepted that invitation often and much to my dismay he always came with an empty wallet and I knew he played on my sympathy for an advance on Papa's allowance. Carley always disapproved and chided me for not making him more financially responsible. I do maintain my family's budget to allow*

Carley the time to spend on his architectural firm and clients which is so necessary for our own economic survival. In my books, I can find no space for Howard and his ensuing family when he finds himself in difficulty again and I know it will come. It is so hard for me to be mean-spirited and in my fears I might succumb to his entreaties if only to insure that he is safe. Oh, doesn't that sound motherly. When will I stop?

My other concern is something about which you and I would differ but I need your solace. The Church! Beatrice is not Catholic and I am aware of your feelings that spirituality above all is the most important virtue. But I anguish over the fear that Howard might stray from the Church. Please, Bonpapa, I implore you to try to make him understand how important it is to his family that he keep his immortal soul from sin and solemnize his marriage in the Church.

To brighten your day from my commiserating epistle I, by chance, have met Mr. Woodbury the other day while strolling the beach. He had his easel perched on a marvelous vista of the dunes. I was enchanted, as I was before when you and I visited his showing, how extraordinarily well he captures the colors of the sea and with one brushstroke can make a simple wave turn into a vibrant, alive one. How I envy his eye and his brush. I invited him and his wife to 4:00 tea today and am longing for a conversation on the art of painting. Do you think I can restrain my enthusiasm and not make a fool of myself in the presence of a true artist?

Your very loving granddaughter
Bessie

"Rose, have you got the tea service prepared?"
"Yes, ma'am. I prepared cucumber sandwiches and

hid a few cookies from the children from yesterday's baking. Little hands are so fast when the smell of cookies baking hits their little noses."

"Oh, I see the Woodburys coming up the walk. Would you please get the door Rose."

"Certainly, ma'am."

Bessie looked quickly in the mirror, excitedly patted a stray hair back into place, then stepped into the parlor. "My dear Mr. and Mrs. Woodbury, I'm delighted you could come."

"Please call us Claudia and Charles," Claudia Woodbury said shaking Bessie's hand.

"Agreed. And you must call me Bessie," she said gesturing them toward the settee. What an exquisite woman, Bessie thought to herself. Claudia was a slight woman with softly carved delicate features. She had an ethereal aura about her that bewildered Bessie. She looks like a china doll, breakable if touched too hard. A Madonna serenity.

Charles was a distinguished looking man who carried the demeanor of a professor. His face was enhanced by his neatly trimmed mustache and goatee. His intense blue eyes gazed at one through rimless glasses, as if he were taking detailed notes. But when he spoke his hands moved with a rhythm to emphasize what he was saying. "What a fabulous view you have of the cove. Look quickly, how the sun rays are breaking through the clouds and bouncing off the waves on that reef just offshore to your right. Do you see?" he pointed excitedly. "That fusion of sun and water color is exquisite. Yes, it's the perfect painting. You can see a new canvas every day as the sun paints the sky. I never tire looking at it. Add those children scrambling over the rocks and it breathes even more lively energy."

Claudia laughed. "Children certainly have a palette of their own. They can mix white to brown faster than any formidable painter. Charles complains continually about trying to keep them still while he tries futilely to capture them, but they run like quicksilver. So you will see them on Charles' canvases as just swashes of color.

"Do you have children?" Bessie asked.

"Yes, we have a beautiful son. He just turned three. That age where curiosity follows him from morning to bedtime. Charles and I love his interest in everything but we relish the quiet that comes when he is asleep. Isn't it funny how much more angelic children can look when they're finally asleep?"

"Yes," Bessie replied. Claudia looks as angelic as any child Bessie thought. "I can't begin to explain my delight when my grandfather and I saw the gallery showing in Boston. I was especially intrigued by Charles' ability to capture the thunderous power of the ocean. And Claudia, your European work made me shiver with memories."

"Work! I wouldn't have called that period 'work'." She walked toward the settee speaking with increased animation. "You can't imagine how memorable that time was spent painting. A pure crystal dropped into the sands of our lives. My imagination still reels with the charms of cultures from country to country, colors, languages, faces, landscapes made one anxious to paint and paint and paint until your body was covered with its smells and your fingers ached from holding the brush." Claudia paused. "But I longed for the smells of home and it grieved me to leave those enchanting foreign shores. I'd set sail in a minute to return."

"I can understand why you left your heart there."

"I believe she did," Charles said. "And paint she does and well. She laments about her talent but she does have that unique ability to capture that charming, intimate side of an individual's singular, soulful expression in her portraits. She is quite talented,"

Charles spoke admiringly, reaching up to take his wife's hand.

"Well, I did learn from a master."

"Oh, who might that be?" Bessie asked.

"Charles, of course!" She looked at Charles with an amused look as if they shared a secret joke.

"Oh, of course, of course." Bessie blushed. "Forgive my unthinking remark."

"No need to excuse anything," Charles laughed. "Only a wife would consider her husband a master." He pulled Claudia's hand to his lips and gently kissed it, then winked at her.

Bessie felt a moment of uneasiness. There appeared to be some unspoken intimate knowledge the two of them shared. "I understand you are an acquaintance with John Singer Sargent. A supreme master! My grandfather is also an acquaintance of his."

"And who might your grandfather be?" Charles asked.

"Samuel Gray Ward."

"Oh, my dear. I didn't realize that the grandfather you spoke of was Samuel Ward. The artists' community could not be more grateful for the generosity of your grandfather as a benefactor. Many of us, working under that old cliche 'poor struggling artists' would never, never have had the chance to paint, write, create, whatever, if it were not for your grandfather's patronage. I understand he dabbles in painting, writing, even finding to his fancy the tortuous, headache producing work of translating German writers. Quite an illustrious man! Unfortunately, I have been told by colleagues that he denigrates his talents while praising other artists and writers. Some of which, presumptuous as it may be to add my own judgment, should have been locked and left in the loft."

While Charles had been talking, Claudia had been

perusing the room's artwork. "You have quite a nice collection of art on your walls. Like this one. Lovely." Charles and Bessie rose and wandered over to look at the painting that interested Claudia.

"That's my grandfather's work."

"Well, now I can see that he surely does have the talent with a paintbrush that I was told. Watercolor is an exceptionally difficult medium to work with. Interesting color contrast in his skies and landscapes. That's very difficult to achieve." Charles said still studying the watercolors. "Do you paint, Bessie?"

Bessie didn't answer.

Charles moved over to another painting. "This canvas of the ocean. It's not your grandfather's?"

"No."

"I can see it's not. The focus is lacking although the effort is there. The problem is in the definition between the sky, water and landscape. But good possibilities are there in the brush strokes. Whose is it?" Charles asked turning to look at Bessie.

Bessie was biting her lip while redness was flushing her cheeks.

"Uh, oh! I think I have treaded on someone's toes."

"No. No. Please I appreciate your comments. It's just a childish effort."

Charles turned back to the painting and tilting his head as if to see it from a different angle. "How much do you enjoy painting, Bessie?"

"Very much."

"Don't the paints help create that private retreat we all long for from the callings of children, house," Claudia lowering her voice to a near whisper, "and husband."

"I heard that. I can't be that demanding, am I? But listen, Bessie, if you are truly interested in pursuing painting I have an opening in my studio here for another student."

Bessie looked startled. "I never thought you would accept such an amateur as I am."

"Everyone has potential. At least those who possess that driven need to paint. As a teacher, that's the challenge - find that soul and help it express itself. Sometimes I win and sometimes I lose but I love the battle."

"The battle with me will probably be one that you have never fought."

"That sounds like you're throwing down the gauntlet."

"Consider it thrown."

From the foyer a clatter of noise could be heard and young Francis burst into the room, dripping wet, excitedly screaming, "Mother! Mother! You should have seen this wave. It was as big as a house." Francis extended his arm as high as he could. "You wouldn't believe it. You should've seen it. I've never seen one that big. I looked up and couldn't see the sky."

"Where were you Francis when this wave toppled over you?" Bessie said, staring at Francis with a look only a mother can contrive.

Francis' mouth tightened immediately. The girls had come into the foyer with the nanny and had been peeking around the door knowing trouble was brewing. They waited for Francis' answer.

"Well, my sweet son, do you have an answer?"

Francis looked up at Bessie and with stiff directness said, "I went just a little ways. Not far. I think there was probably an earthquake under the ocean and it made that big wave come up further than I was supposed to go."

"Are you sure?"

Francis nodded his head up and down keeping his eyes on Bessie's face.

"I think you had better take yourself upstairs, young man, change into some dry clothes and stay in your bedroom until I call you. I want you to think about the truth of your story."

Francis looked over to the sideboard where a plate of cookies had been put next to the tea service. With a slight pleading look at his mother, he said, "Could I have a cookie first?"

"I don't think you should push things too far. Go on now but first say 'good afternoon' to Mr. and Mrs. Woodbury."

Francis turned to Charles and Claudia, both with looks of suppressed laughter on their faces. Francis bowed his head slightly. "Good afternoon. I hope you enjoy the tea and cookies. I know the cookies are really good." Francis turned and marched stiffly past the girls, who had their hands over their mouths to keep from laughing.

After Francis was well up the stairs, Charles roared with laughter. "Now there's a bright, creative young man. An earthquake! That's quick thinking. My Lord, I wish I could have thought that fast when I got in trouble."

"Bessie, maybe you could borrow Charles' tether which he uses on David."

"Children's stories stun me sometimes and it's hard to know what to do without their father here. Tying him up would probably put my mind at ease but I'm sure he would find some unique way to unleash himself. Come on in girls, and introduce yourselves. You may also have some cookies if you remember your manners."

Later the house had quieted down. The Woodburys had left with an understanding that Bessie would attend one of Charles' classes the following Monday. Bessie sipped a last cup of tea and thought with mixed emotions about the day. She picked up a letter from the Tods in Connecticut who had written her mother about Howard's forthcoming marriage. Mumsie had forwarded it to Bessie with a short note how distraught she and Papa were over this marriage to someone whose family they had no knowledge of. Besides the fact that she was Protestant and Howard made no mention of her conversion or acceptance of Catholicism. At least, Justine had been High Episcopalian and had now converted but this young woman was apparently Methodist. She read the letter apprehensively since the Tods had been such close family friends for years and treated she and her brothers like family. Mr. Tod had even tried to teach Howard golf on his nine hole golf course. That must have been a heavy task for him.

****

Innis Arden House
Sound Beach, Connecticut

My dear Mrs. Ward,

It was only a coincidence, but the other morning I told Rea we must preserve Howard's photo from the fingers and thumbs of visitors and, like his father's, set it in a frame for permanent display. So, I went to Stamford with it and left it with the most skillful carver and gilder there. On my return Rea handed me your most interesting letter! I noted that Howard himself had said he would write me but, so far, I have not heard from him; and he is not the brave little gentleman I have ever known him to be if he is going to bother now about writing anyone but <u>Her</u>! So I wait word from him with complete sympathy and understanding, and, meanwhile, turn to offer you the like - and yet how all mixed up! Even Tom, philosopher and psychologist as he is, could hardly disentangle my feelings, much less place them in orderly array on paper. But over and above all - I mean the steady pressure of Tom and you and Rea and me et al: into the background by youth's bold declaration of independence - there mounts an eager desire to know more, to see and to judge for myself, this prairie flower Howard has fastened on his heart. Such is my restful belief in him that I take all in faith and have already conjured up in my mind a Beatrice who makes Dante's look waxen pale.

To your question as to old days seeming far off in the light of such events, I cannot answer "yes", exactly. We can say, with Walter Landor, and in the past tense, that we have - "warmed both hands before the fire of life" without adding, as he does - "It sinks, and I am ready to depart." For it is just such news as Howard sends you that stirs the flames anew and gathers us all around the genial blaze to hear again the old, old story.

Of course, they will pass their honeymoon at Innis Arden. Rea and I will visit Tom and you at the time to comfort and sustain you, and also to let love's young dream unfold itself undisturbed save by the chanting swans.

Ever faithfully,
J. Kennedy Tod

Bessie put down the letter in her lap and began idly pushing chess pieces around on the game table next to her chair. So Beatrice makes Dante's Beatrice waxen pale! Beauty! Why has it eluded me? Bonnemaman was so beautiful when she was young. Even now in her old age she retains the traces of those exquisite feminine features that Hiram Powers sculpted so wondrously. And Mumsie. She and all her sisters. All of Baltimore admired and talked of their beauty. Justine, the golden girl. And I was so fascinated by Claudia today. Her gentle, soft glowing look. I need not look in the mirror to know. Responsibility is my reflection. She looked at the chess board and noticed she had nudged all the pawns forward as if to do battle. She picked up the newly replaced queen and placed it behind the row of pawns.

****

Bessie pulled one of her shoes off and pushed her foot into the warm sand. Granules of sand seeped through her toes as she wiggled them. She shivered, her arms clutched around her, closing her eyes, she felt the ocean breeze blow through her hair and sweep her cluttered mind.

"Bessie! Bessie!" Charles had come up from the water's edge. "I think you had better get started. Do you want me to help put up your easel?"

"No thank you. I think I can manage it." Bessie said, reaching for her equipment. Feeling a little unnerved by Charles finding her still unprepared to start the class, she fumbled with her paintbox. Charles retrieved it and pulled out her canvas stool. He took the easel and forced its legs down into the sand until it was stable.

"Okay, now. You may find me abrasive, overly critical, uncomfortable, whatever, because I'm a hard taskmaster. I want you to get some paint onto that canvas and I don't care how you do it in the beginning but it's a start. Push that paint, pull it, move it. Put that feeling you were just indulging yourself in on that canvas."

Charles turned and walked over to another student who had already begun to work somewhat expansively, making sweeping motions with her paintbrush. Embarrassed at being caught, Bessie's heart beat so hard she put her hand on her chest as if to stop it. Silly, why am I shaking? Just take a deep breath and start. It's not as if he expects me to create a masterwork. Bessie dabbed globs of paint onto her palette. She mixed some white and blue together, added a little more blue, pursed her lips, thought for a moment then added some green. She took a few swipes at the canvas and began to feel better. That's it! Get the notion of the horrors and fear of criticism out of my head! If nothing else, this makes my slumbering creative juices wake up. She began to paint furiously feeling the desire to laugh with each brushstroke.

Charles had set up his own easel a couple hundred yards down the beach. Three young women students had clustered together and dabbling on their canvases while happily chit chatting back and forth. At moments the ocean calmed, the wind stopped and time seemed to stand still while Bessie tried desperately to find the colors to soak her canvas. Then a swell would rise, the wind gust, and time hit her in the face as the scene changed. Exasperated, she stood back from her easel, squinted her eyes, hoping to see something there that would give her confidence. She shook her head despairingly.

"Doesn't look too bad to me. I can tell that it's an oceanscape."

At the sound of the intrusive voice, Bessie turned to see the critic. "George! My God, where did you come from?" Bessie dropped her palette on the sand and threw her arms around him, kissing him on the cheek. George, startled by the quick physical display of affection, put one arm around her, smiled and kissed her quickly on the cheek. After straightening his jacket he bent down and picked up her palette and handed it back to Bessie.

Shaking off the sand, she said, "I certainly didn't expect to see you. Is everything all right? Mumsie? Papa? Justine?"

"Yes! Yes! Yes! Everyone as far as I know is alive and well, including Howard."

"Howard I had put out of my mind for a while. I needed a respite."

"Is that why you are out here slapping paint on that canvas like a whirling dervish?"

"Certainly, one of the reasons."

"And the other reasons?"

"Simple. Charles Woodbury invited me to join his class. My small talent threatened as it might be, how could I rationally refuse the chance to study with a master?"

"I gather that's a rhetorical question."

"Now tell me, why are you here? Not that I don't relish adult company."

"Well, Justine is at the Saranac Inn. Her brother has been ill with some kind of bronchial problem and is recuperating there. I thought I would take a roundabout jump off on my way to join her. I thought my dear sister would enjoy her favorite brother's company to languish awhile in the sun." George looked down the beach at the group of painters. "But I see you've found new company in Mr. Woodbury. Serious, hmmmm!"

"George! Shush! Stop that nonsense. I don't even like joshing even if you're just fooling around. This is such a small, small town. Gossip runs like ivy up a brick wall. It sticks and it's hard to cut down once its tendrils have gripped the wall."

"Please, please go back to your painting. All kidding aside, I think it's great you're attempting to paint again. I just ask that you succeed well enough that I can hang one on my library wall which I can boast about and not have to keep the lights low."

Bessie picked up a clean brush and while adding a few brushstrokes said, "Your story about jumping off here to see your loving sister I'll consider but 'roundabout'? Truly this is off the beaten path. You really came to talk about something. Howard? Isn't that it? Howard? Who else makes us have such troubled sleep?"

"Yes, it's Howard." George stretched himself out on the warm sand and closed his eyes. "Yes, isn't it always Howard?"

Bessie kept painting. She was quiet not wanting to ask any more questions hoping the problem would vanish with the ebbing tide. But the tide always comes back in. Exhausted from the long train ride from New York, George let the sun's warmth shroud him and he nodded off. The sun lowered in the afternoon sky and soon a cloud crossed the sun's rays and George shivered. He awoke, knowing that once again he had dreamt the recurrence of Howard's near-drowning. He shivered again as if to shake it from memory. He looked critically at Bessie's painting effort for a few moments. He had to lift this gnawing onus of Howard off his conscience. "I got a letter from Howard as I expect you did and everyone else he could think of to write, I suppose."

"Yes, I did."

"Have you heard from Mumsie?"

"Yes, of course. More to the point, she forwarded me a letter that the Tods had written her. I'm sure she has taken to her bed. I don't know what she expects me to do about it. I cannot work miracles. Just trying to save my own life is difficult enough." Bessie instantly rued she had said that hoping the pain was not too evident in her voice. She dabbed at some blue and green on her palette and stared at the ocean. She applied a few quick strokes.

"He's asked me to be his best man."

"And are you?"

"That's what I came to talk to you about."

"It's your decision to make."

"Come on, Bessie, you've always given me good counsel. I was depending on you to help me make that decision. You know she's not Catholic."

"Neither was Justine."

"Episcopalians could hardly share the same church with Methodists. What's more the same mass. We don't even know these people. Did Howard tell you anything about her family?"

"Not really. Although he did write in his earlier letters that the Kidders owned the railroad in Grass Valley and that Mr. Kidder had died some years ago and Mrs. Kidder took over the presidency. It does appear they have money and we can only thank God for that."

"Do you think she'll come with a dowry?"

"Times have changed but we can pray the custom of a dowry no longer being a necessity has not caught up yet in California."

"Seriously, do you think Howard is an opportunist? I can't believe that he would willingly commit himself to a marriage openly."

"Who's the opportunist? Why not her?"

"Now, now, I did not mean to tread on your feminine toes."

"Howard is not my territory." She dabbed at the canvas then turned to stare at the sea's horizon. George noticed Charles Woodbury flitting around the other young women's canvases appearing to make critical remarks by his emphatic gestures. George smiled to himself wondering how vicious his pointed finger might be when he peruses Bessie's work. Does he have any idea how the softness of her femininity evaporates like dew on a hot August morning. Her chin juts out; her eyes focus on the subject offering what they believe is creative help, her lips purse. Oh! Oh! My advice to Mr. Woodbury would be to tiptoe gently across the sands of Bessie's painting.

"George, I did write Bonpapa the other day opening the old floodgates again. Poor Bonpapa. I shouldn't do that to him now that he's confined mostly to his bed. He's always been there for me and I know all too well his last years should be respected. They're suppose to be golden, aren't they? But once that ink hit the paper I couldn't stop. He hasn't responded yet so it's given me time to reflect. Remember that Christmas eve in New York some years ago when Bonpapa and Papa got into an argument about Howard's career choice. Bonpapa thought Papa should have been involved more in Howard's decision. Do you recall what Papa said?"

"I remember that prickly situation. I recall Papa talked about courage."

"Yes. More specifically that courage of direct, personal choice is the essence of the individual. And that's what he wished for his children. I believe that! Howard's life is in Howard's hands, not mine! He will have to find the courage to fulfill his life if this marriage is truly his personal choice." Bessie started to again furiously paint as if her anger flowed through her hands. "There is no earthly power that I have to stop Howard," she said vehemently.

"Okay. What do you think I should do? Tell me and I'll say no more."

Bessie concentrated on shaping an old bathhouse onto her canvas. She mixed some red with black and brushed it on with some small strokes. She stood back and looked, then took a glob of black and slashed it across the roofline. Her shoulders slumped as if she had survived a battle, not winning or losing. "I think you should go."

Summer breezes stealthily wafted across the sands lulling both painter and basker.

****

July 1, 1905

Camp Edgewater
Saranac Inn, N.Y.

Dear Old Howard,

Of course I accept with the deepest pleasure the office of best man. You can imagine there is nothing that would give me greater happiness to do. Before I knew I was to stand up with you I arranged to arrive at Grass Valley on the afternoon of the 17th of September. When I got your letter I telegraphed you to say I would come earlier in case you needed me or cared to make use of me. But as I have not heard from you I will assume that the 17th is O.K. I will come west from Omaha leaving St. Paul the night of September 14th in time to catch the "Overland" at Omaha. Also should you find before the 17th, that you want something bought or something done at Frisco you might get a note to me on the train at Reno-Sacramento, and I could go right on to Frisco on the 17th to execute your order and return to Grass Valley on the 18th. I do hope that both Beatrice and Mrs. Kidder are keeping well. This must catch the daily mail boat so goodbye. Love to you both. I am staying here a few days on my way West - having just arrived from N.Y. to cheer up Justine's brother who is ill.
George

George sat back on the deck chair on the porch of the inn and read the letter again. "Deepest pleasure" are hardly the words I would like to write but white lies will have to suffice.

****

The screeching of brakes and the sudden jolt shook George awake as the train pulled into the Grass Valley station. He straightened his jacket, brushed off his sleeves and pulled his valise down from the overhead. He sighed resignedly and thought, "I have finally arrived in this God forsaken country. If Ralph Emerson thought Lenox was savage he would have thought this the epitome of hell. It's hot enough!"

As the porter reached for his valise, George stepped onto the platform. Looking around he noticed people seemed immensely different than people found on any eastern railway platform. Some of them looked as if they had been lolling around there for years. Some were certainly laborers of some kind, whether miners or what he could not discern. Hearing rough language made him cringe.

"George, over here. George!" As he turned he saw Howard stepping down from a buggy, rather an elegant one at that. In fact, the only one of its kind at the station, as far as he could see.

"I'm glad to see you arrived in one piece. Not too out of sorts I hope. I know it's a rugged, long journey and I do appreciate your coming," Howard said, shaking George's hand. He knew not to hug his brother, having known since he was little, George was not the hugging type. The grasp of his handshake would tell you if he was happy or not and his handshake was rather limp today. "Oh well, at least he came and I have some member of the family here to represent me."

George's eyes kept scanning the old wood buildings as they moved down the main street of Grass Valley. He kind of smiled expecting some type of gunfight to break out from a rooftop. Although not his type of reading material, he had picked up some of Howard's books on the west back home and one night became engrossed in a high action drama. Now, here he was expecting gunfire to start at any moment. Times have changed but some of these men look like they could pull a trigger without a second thought.

Howard kept glancing at George, but decided to say nothing. Better leave him to his own thoughts, whatever they might be. Disapproval, I'm sure. They finally pulled into the rooming house where Howard lived and had managed to have a room ready for George. George still uttered not a word as he pulled his valise from the back of the carriage and followed Howard up the steps. After Howard settled George in his room, he invited him into his own room where the landlady had set up tea for them.

Howard, feeling very uncomfortable took a few sips of tea. "George, I have to get the carriage back to the Kidders. Please relax and make yourself at home here in my room. Your room is so small, but it was all they had. I hope you don't mind. I'll be back as soon as possible, and then dinner here is served at seven. I'm sure you will want to turn in early and get a real night's sleep after all that train travel. But I must warn you, the bed will keep on moving and seemingly bump along in the night just like the train. The brain does not adjust easily."

"Fine, fine! You go on. I'm exhausted. Food will do me good and a long, long uninterrupted sleep can only do wonders. Until dinner, I'll enjoy just sitting here looking out at the mountains. The landscape is intriguing, Howard. I hope I can see more before I go." Those were the most words Howard had heard in the last hour. He breathed a sigh of relief and left thinking maybe this will work out all right.

As the door closed, George leaned back in the overstuffed chair and surveyed the room. He spotted a bottle of whiskey on a little side table. Good Lord, I could use a strong jolt. He picked up a shot glass and poured some, taking a sip and a second later downed the rest. Taking a deep breath he poured himself another one. Spying a pile of letters on the table, he recognized Bonpapa's writing. Knowing he should not, he picked up the pile of letters and with his drink in hand, sat down again in the overstuffed chair.

Dear Howard,

Your letter received yesterday took away my breath. This morning I have letters from your father and mother and I assure you will be pleased to see how ready we all are to give a welcome to your fiancée. You have been brought up among so many charming women, your Bonnemaman, your mother, your aunts, your cousins, your sister, and your sister twice has expressed confidence in your choice.

The $5,000 is yours and you will be glad now that you have not encroached on the family fortune. I suppose we must accept the fact that this makes you a Western man. On the whole I am glad of it and to have one member of the family growing up in the West where there's so much room and such a new world.

Excuse the pencil. You know I write on my back and ink will not flow upwards. Don't forget to write.
Ever affectionately,
Bonpapa

P.S. Please give my love to the young lady and respects to her mother.

George picked up the shot glass and downed it. He held his bowed head in his hands and tried to hold on to his anger. Calming himself, he picked up the rest of the letters, and glanced through them. One from Jack in Boston who wrote, 'I couldn't have received more unexpected tidings.' and then a very interesting one from Budd.

July 11, 1905

Hotel Arcadia
Hermosillo, Sonora, Mexico

Dear Howard,

Your letter just forwarded to me from the mines and old fellow how am I going to express myself to make you know how much good luck and happiness I wish you. The first of the old crowd to go. Gee you lucky dog and the lucky girl who has captured you. I do want to meet her. Howdy, I bet you are the happiest engaged "soak". I can just see you. I wish we could drop into Charley Wirth's for a chat and I could hear you soaring up into heaven in your description of her. You bet I shall come to Grass Valley if it is a possible thing and "gee" won't the "Happy Family" be a wreck when they start their Howdy on the road. You must give the "Family" a good reputation for we want to make a great impression and then you know you will have to adopt and care for us poor lonely three until we too meet the girl who can look after us. Ye Gods, after all this is the one of all things to live for. To have loved and lost is sweet enough but to have more must be so much more. What wonderful things you have to look forward to and have much energy it must put into a fellow with that future ahead. Howard I could "digs" a great deal more but I would be no nearer than at the start in trying to express my good wishes. Know old guy that Watson is

whispering to the picture of the "Happy Family" that sits before living; he stretches his imagination a little and he sees them all start and smile at what he says: they jump up and crawling around pat and hug Howdy until he cries enough and then with their heads together sing a close harmony of "Golden Rippling Sunshine".
Budd

"What a strange camaraderie!"

Then one from Dick written from New York on Waldorf Astoria stationery remarking, *"When the news came I fell over with glee. But that you should want me for best man is so good that nothing can keep me away - and little Howdie believes that he is going to leave the fold. It is bad enough to have you share your affection with another. Why we are simply going to annex your better half and we've said it will be done all the faster to spite your attempt to desert. This is the age of combinations and who can stand before such a trust?*

Best man! So I'm a stand-in for a fast updated wedding. I have to stand in for their sacred trust? How fortunate Howard was to have acquired such a bond of friendships with his college buddies. They formed a pact of friendship and trust! How often does that happen? I never had such a bond. With anyone! Bessie has Amy. Papa has William and Eddie. I ache for such a relationship. Just one. Howard is marrying this girl hurriedly. Can she trust him? Has he told his buddies why? I just don't have the trust, confidence and feelings for my brother that others seem to have. But here I have to represent the family, putting on a proper face to keep the family name from being sullied. Thank God it is so far away from Boston that hopefully the gossip vine cannot reach that far. George enraptured himself for awhile in the lush hills of Grass Valley.

Finally he stood up and stretched, looked at himself in the mirror over the bureau, straightened his tie and patted down his hair when he noticed a carved figure on the bureau top. He picked it up, turning it over and over in his hand when he began to realize it was the queen from the family chess set. What the hell is it doing here? His father had always been puzzled as to what happened to it. And here it was: the Chess Queen. It appeared to have been slightly damaged. Why did Howard have it? I'll ask the first chance I have.

It was close to 7:00 so George went down to meet Howard in the dining room. At 8:00 Howard had still not appeared so George being exhausted went to his room and fell quickly into a deep sleep.

Knocking on his door awakened George. Struggling to open his eyes, he called out, "Who is it?" Howard answered. Pulling on his robe he opened the door to a rather distraught Howard. Saying nothing, Howard wearily dropped into a chair. George poured him a brandy from the decanter. George annoyed that his exhausting sleep had been disturbed, said, "Okay, what is it this time?"

"You don't have to speak to me with that tone. Life is just too much to bear some times. One seems to have such limited choices."

"That's a tired cliché, Howard. But people have to make their choices that are limited by their actions. And your action certainly did limit your choices."

"I know! I know! You needn't remind me. I was hoping to tell you about Bea and why I am worried about the responsibility of her as my wife."

"Why? Is it any more of a responsibility than I have with Justine?"

"You might say so. You see, Mrs. Kidder could not

have children of her own so she bought Bea from her brother. Actually bought her. So she treats her, not as I think one would treat their own biological child, but as a possession. She is a doll that has been carefully dressed, primped and shown as if she were a private treasure. I don't want to marry a doll or someone's private treasure. How am I suppose to live with that?"

George winced. "That's a problem I guess you will have to work out yourself, Howard. I don't have any answers." George opened the door to the hall. "Get some sleep, Howard. There is nothing you can do about it now."

****

As the carriage moved along the road, George brushed off his suit and tried to compose himself. Howard looked frazzled but George thought it was no time to talk to him. Looking out the carriage window he could see the mansion atop the hill. It was quite impressive. As they turned through the gate he felt an unpleasant tremor through his body. He could not fathom what the cause was but was uncomfortable as he descended from the carriage. They were greeted at the door by a butler and seated in the library to wait. Howard began to fidget as he had done all his life. He, still like a young child, could not sit still. There was nothing to be said. Suddenly the library door opened and to George's surprise, a formidable woman stepped in, walked across to George, who promptly stood up. She did not extend her hand. "I am very pleased to meet you Mr. Ward. It is a welcome gesture to have someone from your family present. Please sit." Then she nodded to Howard to take a seat.

She looked straight at George and Howard, sipped from a glass of water on the side table, and apparent sternness in her voice, which matched her posture, said, "I have given a lot of thought to the situation regarding this wedding. I want you to understand that until yesterday I was unaware of the circumstances which caused Howard and Bea to move the date of the wedding which was suppose to be tomorrow. I naively thought they were just anxious to be married. Bea informed me last night of her condition. Her guilt overcame her. It did not come into my consciousness that Bea would be in a family way before marriage. My own stupidity did not recognize the signs in my daughter but nevertheless I have come to some decisions."

Uncomfortable, Howard sat on the edge of his seat. He was about to say something when he realized that a discussion was not likely.

Mrs. Kidder waited a moment, knowing that her words had shock value. "Mr. Kidder, my late husband, came from a very prominent Bostonian family that would not countenance such behavior in a courtship, if that is what you want to call your relationship with my daughter. Accordingly, your family also has high standing in Boston society and has had for many years. I was not privileged to be raised in such families and am just a Midwestern Ohio girl with none of the trappings of wealth. I was quite honored when Mr. Kidder asked me to be his bride. California is thousands of miles from New York so my marriage to Mr. Kidder did not raise society eyebrows, as they might if we had been married in the East. Well, that is my opinion so be it."

A somber unease filled the room broken by the ominous tick tock of the huge grandfather clock which stood facing them. Howard began to concentrate on the ticking, apprehensive about Mrs. Kidder's decision.

After taking note of the engagement announcement

laying on the endtable next to her chair, Mrs. Kidder said, "I tried to live up to the standards of the Kidder family which I felt I had accomplished. When Bea came to us from my brother, I tried to raise her in the manner of the Kidder family. I knowingly accept the fact that Mr. Kidder and I spoiled her but I thought she understood what was proprietary behavior. We have over the years attained a high standing in this community, which my husband lovingly endowed with his money and talents." She paused. "I was prepared to have a wedding which I had promised my daughter. But last night, Bea decided to inform me about her condition, I need say no more. Obviously you, Howard, knew but were willing to keep me in the dark." Howard remained speaking not a word.

"This is what I have decided." Howard braced himself. "I will not let shame paint our family. So we will carry on with the wedding and hold our heads high, if you can do that Howard? Lastly, Howard, I would appreciate your looking for another position after the wedding far enough away from gossiping heads and thus I will be able to maintain my position with honor in this valley. Nothing more will be said on the matter."

Without further comment by noticing the look on her face, George knew nothing else would be forthcoming. Mrs. Kidder rose and left the room. She did not bother to close the door. George stood looking at the open door rather astonished. He turned toward Howard, who looked grim. Howard nodding his head said, "You just met the queen!"

"I guess I did!" George took a deep breath, then exhaled, yanked his tie and said, "I thought surely you had informed her of Bea's condition. Well, I guess we better get on with it!" No further words passed between them as they walked down to the waiting carriage.

****

BESSIE

Bessie had taken the morning train down from Boston. Her mother was having a light lunch on a small table by her bedroom window when she arrived. She looked, as usual, quite drawn and seemed to take little delight in seeing Bessie. Bessie kissed her on her cheek and asked after her health. Without looking up, she replied, "Life is quite tiring but I seem to be getting through the days. I am anxious for George to arrive. I want to hear all about the wedding and if Howard is truly happy. It is all I want in life. For him to be happy."

Bessie, feeling herself being drawn back into the depressive mood that cowered in the walls of her mother's bedroom. "So do we all, Mama." Bessie sat down and started to nibble on a small sandwich. Mumsie asked after the children and Bessie amused her for a short while on some of the daily funny antics and remarks that children make. Bessie knew her mother would never tolerate the clamor and rambunctiousness that filled her home every day. Remembering the noise of her children Bessie sat back in the rocking chair and closed her eyes.

Mumsie put down her teacup. "Dear, can you help me with my dress. I do want to sit up for awhile. I hope to have the wherewithal to come down later and join everyone this evening."

She thought she had heard the front door open and voices downstairs. She was anxious to talk with Papa and George before Mumsie joined them. After all, they could talk more honestly about Howard's capricious lifestyle and its impact on their lives, especially the financial implications. With Mumsie, the conversation tiptoed around the reality of Howard. He was still her youngest. Just like a mother cub, Mumsie tended to always shield the baby from the harsh responsibilities of life. As she descended the staircase, Bessie recalled the day he was born, right here in Mumsie's room and his wailing cries. And she was still running to soothe those cries.

George was speaking to his father when Bessie opened the door. "It is harsh country, but the Sierras capture your imagination. I was spellbound by their majesty. But never could I tolerate living in such an uncultured world." George turned as he heard Bessie enter. He smiled as her arms outstretched to hug him. "Well, you have no traces of Western dirt left on you. Regardless of how you feel about the West, I envy you. It must have been spectacular. Anyway, I do want to hear about the wedding and Beatrice and Mrs. Kidder. So get on with it." She settled herself down on the settee next to Papa and patted his hand.

"George, I'm waiting to hear." Then she noticed the look of consternation on George's face.

"George, did something go wrong?"

"Wrong, is putting it lightly."

Bessie looked at Papa to see if he knew. "What happened?"

"It seems that Mrs. Kidder was unaware of Bea's condition until a couple of days before the wedding. As far as she is concerned Howard has brought shame on her family. She informed Howard and me how she felt she had kept the integrity of the Kidder family in Grass Valley and was respected by the community. She, herself, had come from the Clark family in Ohio and had grown up as a Midwestern girl without the wealth of Mr. Kidder. I found out Mrs. Kidder was unable to have children and that Bea was not her natural child but had been bought from her brother. Nevertheless, Bea is pregnant. Who knows what really happened?

Papa said, "What do you mean by that?"

"Papa, I don't mean to sound demeaning but truthfully, I have never trusted Howard."

"Not trusted him! Why?"

"Papa, I don't mean to anger you but Howard has always acted on his own whim, imprudently many times."

"Say no more, George. I will not hear of it if you are implying what I think you are."

Bessie felt as if she had been hit in the chest. "Well, were they married or not?"

Yes, the wedding went on at the Kidder mansion which was decked out like an arboretum. Actually, everything was quite beautiful including the bride. But there was one last thing that Mrs. Kidder demanded and that was for Howard to look for another position somewhere not in the vicinity of Grass Valley. She wanted to maintain her dignity and not have gossip spread their tentacles across her domain."

"Papa pulled his spectacles off his nose and laid them down on the side table. "When is the baby due?"

"Sometime in April."

"How does Howard feel about the baby?"

"I think he's panicked. He didn't say much about the baby except the fact that it's forthcoming. I think he's trying to figure out how to handle Mrs. Kidder. She is a strong headed woman and more than a match for Howard. If he makes it to a second round with her, I'd be surprised. She is calling all the shots."

George stood looking over the chess set which had been abandoned to a corner of the room. He began toying with the pieces, silently moving them. The space for the queen still lay empty. George decided to say nothing about the missing queen but then, without turning around, he said, "Papa, there is a lot of money in that family and you understand how Howard drops to his knees when he smells money. He will reel in any opportunity to put money in his pant pocket. Keeping it there is another issue. You know how I feel about this. You, nor Bonpapa, nor Bessie, nor I should have to spend our lives wondering how long it will take before Howard writes again that somehow, through no fault of his own, he needs money." Now he will use his wife and child as a crutch to beat us over the heads, wielding guilt at every blow." George put down the chess piece and with disgust left the room slamming the door behind him.

Papa fiddled with his spectacles on the side table. Frustration cloyed the walls. Bessie, taken aback by George's anger, felt the chill of nerves in the room. Can it really be that bad a situation for Howard? Am I not willing to look at things straight on? Maybe I am fearful of what it will really bring to me. Maybe I think I can always straighten it out. Amy is always admonishing me about my willingness to jump in when anyone is in trouble. She is always asking, "Did I change anyone?" Howard a father! A father! Bessie heard a sigh of resignation escape from her father.

He slowly placed his spectacles on his nose and said, as if there was no one in the room, "Howard a father!

"Father, did you say something?"

"No."

****

It was just turning noon when Bessie's carriage left the Boston station for home. It had been a tiring train ride back from New York. She sat back and watched the people moving along the sidewalks without much thought. Dazed, bewildered, in a state of flux not knowing how she felt, she watched people sift past her window and mused about their lives. Where were they going? When they opened the front doors of their homes did they feel safe, loved, rocked in a womb of contentedness? If I could run, where would I run to? Knowing the answer to her own question she told the driver to take her to Sevenels. As she walked up the front steps, the door swung open and Amy stepped onto the front porch with her arms open. As they embraced, Bessie felt the comfort of Amy wash through her and she felt as if she had come home. Amy led Bessie into the library and had her sit in her favorite overstuffed armchair ignoring Bessie's protestations. She stepped on the floor bell summoning the maid for tea. Amy picked up her corncob pipe that she had been puffing away at before Bessie's arrival.

With a tinge of forlornness in her voice Bessie said, "What I would not give to go back to those nights when we were young girls and lay on the roof, watching the universe and dreaming."

"You haven't stopped dreaming, have you?"

"In a way I have. Why dream when it only makes you hunger?"

"Well, it's about time you feed your appetite, dear. We must dream! Otherwise, all that latent inspiration, creativity, curiosity within you dies and hope to God you are not willing to die before your soul has left this earth."

"Amy, my soul has been so overtaxed that I think it is willing to leave before I commit myself to death."

"Bessie! Bessie! Where have you been to come to this?"

Bessie lay her head down on the back of the sofa and let her eyes drift across the mounds of books Amy had stacked in every nook and cranny of the room. She crossed her arms across her chest as if to hold herself together, her eyes still drifting over the books. "Remember those times when we thought our dreams would come to life when we were old enough to embark on our own life. We talked about going to Italy, you to write, mostly about Keats and me to paint. Not that I would become a world renowned painter but a painter of quiet landscapes that people love to have on their walls, soothing their tattered nerves from the rigors of the day. I really thought I could do that. Didn't you? Remember how much we talked about Margaret Fuller's struggles and how she achieved a history of her own while in Rome? How horrid the waters of the ocean were to drown her and her husband and worst of all, her precious baby." Bessie shuddered slightly. "But the waves couldn't drown what she had written and it didn't drown the memory she left in the hearts of my grandparents and their friends. Bonpapa talked about her endlessly to me when I was young as if he expected me to continue her legend of what a woman could accomplish. I recall how he told me that Emerson was so crushed and mourned for her until the day he died. I believe Bonpapa mourns her to this day. Don't you remember how much we wanted to have her ambition and tread in her footsteps when we lay on your rooftop?"

Amy dragged on her corncob pipe. "Don't you remember what Fuller said about being a woman?"

"What was that?"

"She said, 'Tis an evil lot to have a man's ambition and a woman's heart.'"

Bessie laughed for the first time. "Oh, yes, you and I know how much a man's world it is! So what are we going to do about it?"

"Did you ever think about cutting your hair short, heaving out all the petticoats and those god awful corsets? That's what I think is the 'evil lot'. Dump the whole lot of it! What a sense of freedom to feel one's own body unleashed. Think of it, Bessie. Naked! Nowhere to hide.

"No, my God, I think not."

Amy stood up and started to unbutton her blouse. She then unloosed her skirt and dropped it to the floor.

"What in God's name are you doing?"

"God has nothing to do with this. Come on, take off that wretched straitjacket you have on." Amy reached over and undid a button on Bessie's blouse. "Come on, let's feel what this freedom is that we've been talking about." Amy took off her petticoat and threw it at Bessie. Bessie laughed and watched Amy reel around the room abandoning her clothes, she started to take off her blouse. Amy, in her nakedness, was now dancing around her desk. She picked up her pipe and stuck it in her mouth and with an air of defiance yelled, "Here I am!"

Bessie, feeling the excitement of it all started removing her clothes at a quick pace and threw them on the tables and chairs as she bounced around the room. Her face lit up with the giddiness, and the dizziness of spontaneity.

"Amy, how great is insanity. I feel insane. Insanity feels wonderful. Insane! Insane! Insanity! What joy it brings!" Bessie started to sing. "Oh, sweet insanity! We're not insane. The rest of the world is insane."

"Not us, Bessie. We know what the damn male world's about. Now they know us in all our glorious naked freedom." Amy fell back into her overstuffed chair and puffed on her pipe, satisfied.

Bessie flounced on the sofa and pulled a wool throw from the arm of the sofa and threw it over herself. She watched Amy puff on her pipe. "What ever happened to that self-control you so continually aspired to?

"Gone! Finally, Bessie, it's gone! Can't write poetry if self-control is holding your hand."

"Amy you look like one of those Aunt Sally effigies I saw at that English fair. You know the woman with the pipe in her mouth that they threw darts and missiles at. I guess it was done for some male aggression to get back at women who pick up male sacred symbols, like your pipe."

Amy held out the pipe for Bessie. "Well, come on, take a puff. Get back at them. Woman aggression, you know. Feels good."

Bessie took a puff then coughed. "My God, Amy. And they like this? Whatever possessed men to decide to inhale smoke? "

"Maybe to contemplate their own mortality. You know that funeral saying, ashes to ashes, dust to dust, then of course, what you have left is smoke. So they ruminate over that."

Bessie took another puff and slowly exhaled the smoke. She handed it back to Amy, who sat back again and inhaled herself.

"Seriously, Amy, where did the feminist movement leave me? I can't seem to get a foothold in it. Look at you, independent, writing what you want, living in your own home, not marrying, and smoking that damn corncob pipe. Happy, aren't you? How did we go down such different paths?"

Amy waited a moment. "Choices."

"What! What did you say?"

"Choices, Bessie. You chose and here you are upset."

Bessie sat up. Angrily she said, "And what choice was that?"

Amy puffed a little longer on her pipe. "I don't hold you at fault, Bessie, but I think you bought into the marriage fantasy. We all grew up on that. Yes, there were changes in women's status as we grew but still we were influenced, or might I say, heavily sold the idea that marriage was the ultimate role to play. And you have found the play is at many times, a tragedy."

"Why did I play and you not?"

"Honestly, I think my family was quite different than yours. You remember how it was around here when we were young. It was a theater of competition, on all levels. It was always a challenge of ideas clashing at the dinner table or on the field of sports. It was every man for himself and I was regarded as one of the members in the battle." Amy put down her pipe. "So you think I have won the battle?"

"Well you are still in the vanguard while I am back cleaning up the mess." Bessie lay back again and stretched her body out the length of the sofa, relaxed and closed her eyes. An essence of reverie floated in the passing moments.

Interrupting Bessie's seemingly tired reverie, Amy asked, "Bessie, do you love Carley?"

"I thought I did. Once. I'm not sure anymore. Maybe I never knew what the feeling was supposed to be. In dark moments I... Bessie's voice trailed off.

"In dark moments what?"

"In dark moments, I wonder if I ever was in love." A tear wound a path down Bessie's cheek.

"Now, my dear, it's your beginning to be you. It's your choice to speak the truth to yourself. Emotion, dear, like love can't be manufactured, fabricated or shaped in a heart. If it's not there, it's not there."

Tears began flowing profusely and Bessie dabbed her eyes with the afghan. "Mary, Mother of God, what do I tell my family?"

"Mary is not going to tell them anything, neither are you."

"Then what?"

"You go home, Bessie. Take care and love the children. That's easy. Take care of Carley. He needs you. But let Howard and your mother go from your care. I never told you but I never liked Howard."

At that Bessie laughed. "And I never liked your mother either."

Hugging each other, they rocked back and forth, laughing. Soon the sound of laughter grew and crept under the doorsill. Footsteps fell on the hallway carpet and the door opened. Ida, the kitchen maid stood in the doorway. "Oh, my God, please forgive me. I didn't mean to intrude." She averted her widened eyes and started to back out of the room.

"Oh, come on in, Ida. Don't be frightened. It's just us girls having fun. Come on, join us." At that, Amy grabbed Ida by the arm and swung her around in a circle. She reeled her faster and faster until Ida began to giggle. "Take off that awful uniform and let's all dance again. Bessie got up and threw the afghan over her shoulder like a Spanish dancer. She grabbed a rose from the side table and put it between her teeth. She pushed one into Ida's mouth and began to tap a flamenco with her bare feet. Amy clapped and Ida stamped a couple of times, then she and Bessie got into the rhythm of the dance. The sun slipped below the window as the three women danced the flamenco.

****

GEORGE

George looked up from his desk to see Justine opening his law office door.

"You looked surprised," Justine said as she slipped off her coat and sank in a chair.

"Yes, I can say that I am. I had told you this morning at breakfast that the office has overwhelmed me with some difficult cases and they do not seem to be offering me any extra help. So I did not expect you unless there is an urgent reason."

"Do you think the firm might be trying to force you out?"

Startled by the unexpected remark, George began to flip through a case file on his desk.
"Why do you say that?"

"You have to be concerned about this undue excessive work which is beyond the capability of the best of lawyers."

"You're suggesting that I can't handle it?"

"You know what I mean. You've not been yourself for the past several months. I don't know what is going on but I do want to know. So that is why I came to take you out to lunch and give you a respite from all this."

"Are you sure that's all it is?"

"Well there are some other things I wanted to talk to you about."

"I thought so! I don't think lunch will be enough time and I, as you can see, do not have the time to give."

Justine grabbed her coat and slipped it back on. "We will find time to talk about this because it does not only concern you but me. By the way, we are having dinner with my parents at Oakdale on Saturday. You will find the time then." Without giving George another glance, she left.

George held his head in his hands for awhile, closed his eyes and took some deep breaths. I don't know if I can deal with the Cuttings just yet. I need some time to think. I don't know what's wrong with this marriage but it's dying before it really has become the marriage I expected. Justine is rarely home herself. Off she goes to Europe as often as possible to study her passion with Gregorian chant. She seems more involved with the Catholic clergy than I ever was and she was not even raised Catholic. Maybe we didn't recognize it was not love but a symbiotic relationship with the notes strewn across a music sheet. My having to run a time consuming legal practice to support the lives we lead has taken my music away. He picked up the case file again. They did not even give me a second chair when I asked for this case. Can it be that Justine may be right? I certainly don't have any strong relationships with any of the other attorneys. He began realigning all the pencils on his desk.

****

Justine and George were greeted at the door by the butler who took their coats and told them Justine's parents were having drinks in the small sitting room off the larger parlor. George glanced into the large dining room as they walked down the hallway toward the sitting room noticing that the table was not set for dinner. A sense of unease shadowed him down the hallway.

Justine's father stood when they entered. He embraced Justine. "How is my favored girl child?" he laughed as he extended his hand to George.

"I'm fine, Daddy."

"And you George."

"Fine, sir."

Justine kissed her father and then sat down next to her mother. Mrs. Cutting, holding Justine's hand, set her glass down before acknowledging George. "How are you George? I hear you seemed to be overworked."

Giving an annoyed glance to Justine, he said, "No, not at all ma'am."

"We must have been misled then."

Mr. Cutting handed a sherry to George. "You and I will have a talk about it later after dinner."

The unease George felt heightened. Justine slyly smiled at him.

Dinner had been set at a smaller table in the parlor. Candles were lit and George was surprised by the intimate setting so unlike the usual large dinner parties they had in the long banquet room. Small talk chattered back and forth between Justine and her parents. George's mind raced with all kinds of possibilities about what Mr. Cutting wanted to talk about after dinner. Are they aware that Justine and I have had rather strained relations lately? Does he know if I am being slowly ousted from the firm? God only knows with the gossip that drifts down the halls and offices of New York and especially Wall Street, anything is possible. I have just never tuned my ear to it. It always reeks of sloppy thoughts and the innuendos are to my mind, ultimately sinful.

"Justine, your brother told me that you were going to Switzerland. What is that about?" Her father said looking at the cake that was put down in front of him.

George dropped his fork on his cake plate. "Excuse me, but do you want to say that again?"

"You didn't know about this, George?" Mrs. Cutting said. She glanced at Justine wondering what was going on in their home.

"Bayard has been talking too much."

"Well, is it true?" asked her father with a stern

intensity to his voice, unusual when it came to talking with his daughter.

"I'm sorry George. I didn't want you to learn about it this way." Justine reached over and patted the top of George's hand. He pulled it away quickly.

Mrs. Cutting sat rigidly. "Justine, as your parents, do you not think it disrespectful to learn of your plans from our son? Your husband appears to have no knowledge of your decision that truly must impact his life. Is this how you conceive of marriage? Doing what you want without the consideration of those close to you."

Justine noticed a spider dropping down on the spindle of its web from the top of the window. Slowly it moved across the windowpane weaving as it went from corner to corner. Justine watching the slow rhythm of the spider wondered, "What do I say now?" A feeling of drowsiness seeped through her body as tiredness traced down her limbs. Everything began to reel in slow motion and the spider continued to weave its web.

Justine's father cleared his throat loudly, obviously waiting for Justine. Justine heard her voice talking but sensed she was somewhere else. She barely whispered, "I have loved music more than anything else in life. It lives in my head. In my dreams. All my waking moments."

George pushing back his chair, went out into the hallway. Returning after a few minutes, he had Justine's coat over his arm. He put it in her lap and turning to the Cuttings said his goodnights. Without looking at Justine, he said, "I'll bring the car around to the front." Justine stood up, pulling on her coat. She glanced sadly at her parents. "I'm sorry! I never wanted to disappoint you."

****

George carefully helped Bonpapa into his favorite chair next to the fireplace. He was now quite frail but that lively, flickering blue of his eyes still captured anyone in his presence. George had not let go of Bonpapa's hand as he kneeled on the carpet next to him. The warmth of this man so comforted him. George felt his grandfather's life flickering. Bonnemaman had passed on several years ago. George still ached for the wisdom that she spread like seeds over the family. His grandparents' marriage, truly a lasting love affair, was interlaced with a unity they created with a mutual philosophy toward life. Both of them though growing frail as age crept up on them, never bowing to it. Bonnemaman came into life, accepted it for what it was, then boldly walked through it and stepped out of it. Along the way, she left remembrances of her spirit which on this cold night was embracing Bonpapa. George saw the glistening of a small tear on Bessie's face as she slipped down on the sofa. George felt his chest tighten. Words that he had so well prepared were laying behind his clenched lips.

"Here we sit," said Bonpapa, "looking like life has deserted us. It's taken off with our joy and hidden it in some secreted box to be found another day." A slow grin crossed his face. "For God's sake, it cannot be all that bad! I had many joyous years with my Anna but we knew that it would come to an end, either me dying first but to my sadness, she went before me." He patted the top of George's hand. "Your Justine will be back."

"No, she won't." George was startled by his quick explicit response. "No, no, no, she's not coming back."

"Why do you say that, George? I can't believe she has left you."

"She's done just that!" Anger bled through George, in his voice, in his eyes and his tensed body. Bessie became nervous expecting an ugly outburst that she so did not want to hear. She was tired enough with familial problems. She already knew that Justine was gone. She had always had a deep sense that something would happen to their marriage. There was never any talk of children or an expectant future. They seemed to live day by day in a silent vacuum. Justine was an exceptionally intelligent woman with many talents, besides being extraordinarily beautiful. A beauty Bessie always envied. She surmised that the same dreams were in Justine's mind that continually haunted her. The images of a world out there which held something for me. Wanted me to become part of it. Wanted me to immerse myself in the true experience of life, far beyond husband, children, home with all its vagaries.

"George, did you hear me. What has happened between you and Justine?" Bonpapa sat up a little straighter in his chair. He gazed sharply at George waiting for an answer.

George started pacing the room. "It's not easy to answer. Marriage, our marriage, was not what I expected."

"And what did you expect?" Bonpapa asked. Bessie pulled her legs up under her on the sofa and reached for an afghan. She felt chilled even though the fire had warmed the room sufficiently.

"I thought our relationship would stay the same. The same from the first time we knew each other, young though we were."

"Did you ever think that marriage was a union blessing the beginning of a family? Did children ever become a part of your thinking when you entered into marriage?"

"No!" George said it so emphatically that it caught Bonpapa by surprise. George noticed Bonpapa's reaction. He sat down on the sofa next to Bessie and looked hopefully at her for a sign of support. Seeing none, he said, "I didn't mean to surprise you but children were never in my future. I witnessed enough by the time I married to know that having children was something I was never conditioned to abide. Look how much trauma Howard has given to all of us with his independent, 'I'll do what I want to do' attitude without ever thinking about the consequences of neither his actions nor the constant incessant worry he has exacted on the family. Now he has a child of his own and this young, childish man is the father. What kind of wisdom and guidance can he give to his children when he cannot guide his own life? I don't mean to be harsh but that is how I feel. Angry? Yes, I'm angry. Angry at Howard. Angry at Justine. Angry at life." With that he slammed his fist on the arm of the sofa.

Bonpapa's face became grim. Bessie stared at George but did not move. Sparks from the crashing of a log from the fireplace spewed upon the hearth. The fireworks slowly died as did the anger spewed by George. In a softer voice, he said, "Besides, Justine never mentioned she wanted children. Her child is her music."

****

HOWARD

Howard leaned over the Western Union desk in Phoenix and rang the bell on the counter. A sleepy clerk emerged from the back room and without a word shoved a message sheet toward Howard and slapped a pencil down in front of him. Howard mused to himself that he would not allow this slovenly example of a lazy man squelch his enthusiasm over his momentous news.

Slowly he began to print:

Mrs. Thomas W. Ward, 6 East Ninth Street, New York. Eight pound girl arrived this morning. Beatrice and baby both doing fine. Have cabled George.
Howard R. Ward

Howard slid the telegram across the counter. The clerk counted the letters and said, "That will be two bucks. Howard pulled out two ones, smiled at the clerk who sullenly nodded, and said, "Congratulations. Kids cost money."

Howard walked across the street where a bar had just opened its doors. He sat down on a barstool and ordered a beer. Even though it was morning he felt the need for something strong as a respite from the last twenty-four hours. He took a sip from the mug when an older, gray haired man crashed through the door, slapped his hand on the bar saying, "Hey, Tom, did you hear about the giant earthquake in San Francisco day before yesterday?"

"Hey, no Mike! Really?"

"Yeah, it's said the whole town is burning."

"My God! Anybody dead?"

"Don't know the count yet but yeah they reported some people were killed."

Howard was stunned. Good God! I just saved our lives insisting we leave San Francisco. Someone's looking over me or us. He slid his hand into his jacket pocket and wrapped his fingers around the small chess queen. He took another long gulp of his beer and sat staring at the two men still talking.

Well, thank God Bonpapa had faith in me to write that five thousand dollar check for our wedding. I think Mrs. Kidder did not want to be outdone, although miserly as she was, wrote that other check for a thousand. My making a lousy hundred dollars a month, the six thousand bucks made me feel quite prosperous, but we still had to live under her roof. She just loved quarreling with everyone. She had to have known that I was looking for another position as she had made the ultimatum. But I think she knew I was getting antsy about that decision and seeing her only daughter leave. As for the future I could not see myself settling down so far away from the city, my family and most of all, my friends. It was definitely over in Grass Valley and I mean over. It did not take much to convince Bea to move on. That didn't take too many words. She was still at odds with her mother. Bea never saw herself wearing an apron. Her mother's overbearing attitude during her pregnancy was grinding away at her nerves.

Wow! One could not explain the look on Mrs. Kidder's face the day I told her I had resigned from the mine. Bea had already packed all our worldly goods not wanting to stay a minute longer after I told her mother. I know I only imagined it but I thought I heard her scream in rage as we drove out the driveway headed for the train. She was now a lonely queen of her empire reigning from her hilltop mansion. Grass Valley was hers!

God almighty, Bea whined the whole month we were in San Francisco. And I had no mine to go to keep away from her harping about how terrible it was to be a woman and having to bear a child. Thought I would never hear the last of it. Child bride. She is that!

The bartender picked up Howard's empty glass and asked if he wanted a refill.

"Yeah, Tom. I could use another one."

"What about that earthquake. Did you hear ole' Mac? Can't believe it. I've never been in an earthquake nor do I ever want to."

"Me neither. Just missed it."

"Really! You don't say. You just missed it?"

"Yes, my wife comes from California and we had been in San Francisco hoping I could find a decent job in the mining industry. Now I know, lucky for me I was just not wanted."

"So how did you end up here?"

"Well, I knew there were certainly mining opportunities in Arizona. But we did stop on the way in Los Angeles and that makes a funny story."

"I'm all ears. Could use a good story now," said Tom while he poured himself a beer.

"I just couldn't make any viable connections for a decent job in San Fran. So we stored everything but our necessary trunks and left for Arizona. I had a letter to a friend of mine's father, John Hammond. who was in Los Angeles. He was a little bit of a man, with shrewd eyes, and I told him my qualifications, experience and what I was looking for. He told me of one possible opening that he had, a position at a little property in Mexico, which he said presented opportunities of advancement. He spent some time describing the place and had me thoroughly interested."

"Sounds like a little piece of paradise."

"Sounded like that to me too until Hammond said, 'But I suppose you could hardly consider it, as it is dangerous country. The last engineer was killed by the Yaqui Indians. Don't think you could take your wife there.' Paradise turned into hell and I was not ready to go. Besides I'm a new papa now. Don't want any

Yaquis around my little girl."

"Well, congratulations! Let's drink to your good fortune. Specifically narrow escapes."

Howard and Tom clinked mugs and drank heartily.

****

June 30, 1906

111 S. Mt. Vernon Street
Prescott, Arizona

Dear Mumsie,

A cheerful letter from you, and one from Papa, enclosing his ever welcome cheque. I have another scheme, to put through if the Senator Mine does not pan out – it may be best anyway. At the suggestion of a Mr. Stevens, whom I met through the parish priest, if I can get the support of the prominent men about, I may go into business on my own book with their expansion, examining mines and reporting on them. It might be slow in starting, but once started, it would be much more of a chance than being at a mine and instead of having a little shack at a mine we could live in town and be comfortable, and in touch with the world. We may start on that line anyway, till we hear of something definite, and then if we don't see a good lookout ahead, we can make our choice.

Elizabeth was baptized last Tuesday, when she was just ten weeks old, and she behaved beautifully, and never made a sound till it was all over. She wore your little medal and Justine's little old Spanish cross reached us just in time. Mr. Stevens was proxy for George and Justine. Betty was so good and funny that we all were nearly laughing – she seemed as interested and amused at everything. Bea thinks that a porridge bowl (pap bowl) would be nicest from George and Justine or else whatever they like best. How nice of the Schoenberg's to make Betty such a nice present. If you send it to us, we will start a savings account in favor of Betty.

    We are making friends fast with our neighbors and all are getting world-wise at last, but it is easy for us, as they are almost all such nice and cultivated people and they seem to accept us without any recommendations. We have heard that we are the "sweetest couple" that ever was. There is a charmingly arranged, little old wooden house next door to rent, unfurnished, and with paint and paper it could be made very attractive if we decide to open shop for ourselves.

Your loving son, Howard

Howard put his pen down and watched Bea swatting at the furniture with a dust cloth. The baby started to whimper in her cradle. Howard peered over at the cradle just in time to see the baby's face contort and a shrill wail penetrated the room. Bea kept swatting at a table then headed toward the kitchen.

"Aren't you going to see what's wrong with the baby?"

"She's all right."

"How do you know?"

"I'm her mother!"

The baby screamed louder. Howard went over and gently picked her up and began patting her on her back. "Moving here was for you, Bea. Remember the doctor said it would be better for your health? He said the cooler air would help you regain your strength and I thought you said yesterday that you were feeling a lot better."

"Yes, I am!" Bea turned on the fire for the teakettle

and got a teacup and saucer down from the kitchen cabinet.

"So don't you think you can take care of the baby now?"

"Seems you're doing just fine."

Howard was struck by Bea's seeming animosity and could not decide whether it was aimed at him or the baby. The baby screamed louder. "I think she's hungry."

"Well, you can give her a bottle," Bea said while she was opening the tea canister and dropping a couple spoonfuls of tea leaves into the porcelain teapot.

"I thought you were nursing her?"

"That's how much you have noticed what has been going on around here. I stopped."

"Why?"

"It hurt."

"Hurt?"

"Yes, it hurt." Bea poured some tea into her cup and sat down by the kitchen window staring out into the backyard.

Howard opened the icebox door and saw some baby bottles of milk. Picking up one he tried to put the nipple into Elizabeth's wailing mouth. She finally tasted the milk trickling into her mouth and thirstily started sucking.

Howard with the now happy, gurgling baby went out and soothed her on the front porch swing. Irritated at Bea he calmed himself by gently rocking the baby in his arms. Within a few minutes, Elizabeth had closed her eyes and had settled down into a deep sleep. Howard gently laid the baby down in the cradle which lay a few feet from their bed. Bea already was in bed with her face turned toward the wall.

Howard picked up his pen and some stationary and went back to the porch where a dazzling night sky blanketed the desert. Staring out at the landscape, he felt enthralled by what he saw. He spread the stationary in front of him and scrawled:

Dear Bessie,

Thought of you just now as I sit here in a scene that screams to be splashed across a canvas with all of God's colors that soak up the atmosphere. I'm railing poetic tonight. Prescott is beautiful country, though it's not as pastoral as Grass Valley. But its air is so fresh I guess because of its 5,000 foot altitude. The air is so clear that ten miles looks like three and seventy miles like twenty. Ah, yes, and look at that sand, that sagebrush and those straggly pines with that endless variety of cactus criss-crossing the valley floor. The immensity of Granite Mountain oversees the whole valley floor and what beauty when the sun drops behind causing night to fall.

Last night we had one of those violent little desert thunderstorms followed by the most extraordinary brilliant sunset. The whole sky was aflame with red, gold then delicate pinks and soft colors, till the wonderful deep purple shades of the mountains gradually deepened into night. This country cannot help but grow on one. It becomes so mysterious and finally soft, friendly and restful but strangely, never intimate. How marvelous it is that it is never too hot and the nights always cool. Numbs my mind and what peaceful sleep until morning.

I hope this country allows me to prosper as I think I can. I trust I am not too much of a burden on the family as I try to succeed. I set myself in the image of Bonpapa……building my domain with all that entails……happy children, society anointing me with their respect, traveling at whim, collecting precious objects to be passed down from generation to generation and leaving an everlasting legacy.

But I go on too much neath this splendid sky. My love to you and will think of you as you lie on the beach letting the sand trickle through your fingers.
My best to Carley and the children,
Lovingly, Howard

Howard slipped the letter into an envelope and dropped it on the dining room table. He tiptoed into the bedroom and smiled as he looked down at a sleeping Elizabeth. "How lucky you are to dream such peaceful dreams", he whispered as he bent and gently kissed her forehead.

He undressed, leaving his clothes across the straightback chair and shivering as he crawled into bed next to Bea. As he touched her back, she shrugged and moved closer to the edge of the bed. Alright, she can't be all that mad. Mad about what? Howard rolled over on to his back and pulled the quilt tightly up to his chin.

"It's cold in here, don't you think?" Not hearing a response, he went on. "Thought I might tell you what happened today if you care to listen. You know Stevens and I have been looking for prospects to develop and capitalize. Well, the last two months while we were gone, we looked at gold, silver, and copper in the Bradshaw Mountains and along the Hassayampa River. Also in the Haluwa and the Harque Hollow to the west and down along the Verde River to the east. Finally we came across the Dunkirk. It's an old prospect with a history of really rich shipments in its early days. Quite a bit of good ore shavings and pretty fair prospects for finding more."

Howard stared at the ceiling for a few moments. "Well, we decided to take over the property on a lease with an option to buy."

"What? What did you say?" Bea rolled over and looked at Howard. "You did what?"

"It's not much, Bea. Just three thousand dollars."

"Three thousand dollars! We don't have three thousand dollars. Are you crazy?"

"I wrote the family telling them what a good investment it would be for them. I'll pay it back just as soon as we get the mine into operation."

"Did you ask my mother?"

"No."

"Good. Just keep my mother out of it. I don't want to hear, 'I told you so.' She has never believed in you and I don't want to give her any ammunition."

"Do you believe in me?"

Bea resolutely snuggled up against Howard. "Sure I do."

Howard remained awake, staring at the ceiling. The baby whimpered.

****

Bea was frantic as she straightened out the silverware on the table. This was her first dinner party since she had been married. She was anxious to show off her new home. It was certainly not like the mansion she had grown up in, but it was hers. She had carefully printed out place cards and now had to think who should sit next to whom. She decided to put the Judge next to her and his wife next to Howard. That should make for interesting conversation. I'll put the Stevens in the middle of the table. I don't want him influencing Howard anymore than he has. Anointing himself President of their mining company and Howard only gets to be General Manager and Engineer. Not right! Not right at all. Bea heard the door knocker and yelled upstairs to Howard. "Howard, will you please answer the door. I'm going to look after dinner."

Bea could hear Howard greeting the guests. "Can I get anyone a drink?"

"That would be very nice, Howard," she heard someone say.

He came into the kitchen. "Where's that bottle of champagne I bought today, Bea?"

"I put it on ice." Bea went back to tossing a salad.

Howard found the champagne and headed back to the front room. She could hear the laughter and the pop of the bottle. She decided to stay in the kitchen.

Soon, she heard Howard say, "I want to propose a toast. Everyone raise their glasses. To the success of the Mt. Tritle Copper Company and all its employees."

Bea heard the click of glasses and muttered to herself, "Amen!"

****

BESSIE

"If you children don't have your valises packed in fifteen minutes, you'll be left behind. And don't forget your bathing suits!" Bessie shouted up the stairs. She could hear the frantic footsteps as her children jostled each other on the staircase. As Francis jumped the last few steps onto the landing, Bessie with a slight grin at her oldest child said, "Francis, I want you to be in charge of your sisters. Papa is not coming with us so you are to be the man in the family. Now that means you are to be on your best behavior and set an example to your sisters. Can you do that?"

Francis straightened his shoulders and put out his chest. "Yes, ma'am. But why is Papa not coming?"

"He has too much business to take care of. He'll come some other time."

"Oh, I was hoping to show him how good I can swim now in the cove."

"You can show me and Uncle Charles." Bessie had told the children several years ago to call Woodbury, Uncle Charles. Charles has become such a part of the family that she wanted the children to be comfortable with him.

"Get the girls now and their valises out on the porch. The driver will be here soon. We don't want to miss the train. Don't forget to say your goodbyes to Bonpapa". I am sure Bonpapa will love the silence of the house for a week. Bessie went into the kitchen to give Rose last minute instructions.

"Mother, the driver is here!" Francis yelled from the drive.

Bessie leaned her head tiredly on the back of the carriage seat while the children settled themselves down with Francis, sitting authoritatively next to the driver. She had not left Bonpapa on his own before and felt uneasy. I have to convince myself that Bonpapa will be fine. I need to be away. I need to hear the wind howl and the waves crash. I need to see the sunrise and the sunset. I need to hear the children's laughter echoing from the cove. And Blessed Mary, I need a peaceful sleep and awake to the gentle winds from the ocean. Most of all, I need myself. Find myself. Recapture myself and be myself again. She closed her eyes gratefully until the carriage arrived at the depot.

****

Woodbury eased himself gently down on the rock next to Bessie. Bessie extended her foot to let a wave wash over it and retreat. She said nothing. Charles reached into his shirt pocket and took out a piece of chalk. He started to sketch on a flat section of the rock that lay to the side of him. Bessie was mesmerized over the water washing over her feet. Nothing was heard besides the sounds of the sea and Charles' chalk scratching the rock's surface. Charles' wife and young son had gone to Europe so she could again paint landscapes and the people of her beloved Holland. Charles needed to remain for his upcoming summer classes and a desperate need to finish some of his canvases. His bank account was quickly speeding again in a downward spiral. If he could ship some finished canvases to the Boston gallery who had promised him a special showing in the fall, he could hopefully replenish the well. Finances and art never held hands. Bessie had been wonderful in her efforts to find him some patrons, although most of them were from her own extended family. She had a passionate way of talking about his art that endeared her to him all the more. But she had not said a word about art or family since she arrived. He stared more intently at the face he was sketching. He began to work the hair with the side of the chalk and rub some sandy grit onto the surface.

"Bess."

Bessie raised her head and looked at the chalk sketch saying nothing. Now Charles was concerned. This was so unlike Bessie.

"Okay, Bess, whatever is bothering you, I want to know. I mean that. I can't have someone so dear to me spread gloom across my rocks and sea."

"Your rocks?"

"Yes, my rocks."

"Oh, didn't know you owned them."

"That's better. Now that you understand you are occupying my world, and as the liege of this land you occupy, my command is to know what is going on."

"I don't know how to unleash myself from all demands of me. Why do women have to clean up the mess of everyone else's lives? Or even through no fault of their own, just age encroaching on loved ones bodies, I have to soothe them as if they were babies again. I nearly find myself singing lullabies to Bonpapa probably just because I love him and want him to have a gentle sleep. Death lies so near him and I don't want it to take him. He has been living with us for a long time and the children are so used to having him around. He never complains about their noise, the clamor they make throughout the house. They so enjoyed him reading Uncle Tom's Cabin to them. You know Harriet Beecher Stowe personally signed a copy for him?"

"Really, that I would cherish. But Bonpapa cannot create all this anxiety I see in your face."

"No." Bessie's shoulders drooped. "It's Mumsie and Papa."

"Are they ill?"

"Well, Papa's firm has been taken over by Kidder Peabody. They have nudged him out. You can imagine how depressed he is. The firm had been in the family for years. Even though banking was not Papa's or Bonpapa's great love. But I am sure Papa feels he has let the family down. There is no income coming in now even though he has some investments. But with Wall Street as precipitous as it is, one has to be very cautious."

"I didn't know. I'm so sorry. What is the future for them?"

Shaking her head, Bessie thought for a moment. "I felt the only way to reduce their expenditures was to invite them to live with us. The New York house will bring them some income that will help."

"My God, Bessie, you have enough on your hands. Can't George help or even Howard. Hasn't his mines brought in some income?"

"Oh, my God, no! In fact, he has written Papa, Bonpapa, and George and probably everyone else he could think of asking them for more money to invest in his wild schemes. I blame myself sometimes when I think how much I spoiled him."

"You can't blame yourself Bessie. After all, you were only a young girl. Discipline was your parent's job, not yours."

"Probably so. But irrational as it is, I still feel responsible. Unfortunately, his behavior might make me harder on my own children for fear they might take the same irresponsible path he has taken."

"The children are fine, Bessie." Charles put his arm around her shoulders as she brushed the tears away. He kissed the top of her head. "So many tears just for Howard?"

"No, no!" Not for Howard but for George. Poor George has been left living alone."

"Left? What do you mean, left?"

"Justine went to Europe. She didn't tell George her plans. It came as a complete surprise to him."

"I thought everything was going well with them. Did something change?"

"I don't think anything ever changed. I had misgivings about the marriage years ago. Actually, from the very beginning."

"Really! You never said anything."

"No, why would I? It was not my marriage. It was their decision."

"So what happened?"

Bessie wavered in answering. She looked toward the cove for a few minutes. In a near indecipherable voice, she said, "There was no passion."

"Do you mean love?"

"No, Justine loves George and him, her. But it was a passionless love." She reached out to run her hand over Charles' sketch. Her finger ran down the side of the chalked face. "It's me, isn't it?"

****

The sun was sliding into the ocean's horizon when Charles and Francis sat down to play a game of chess in front of the big bay window. "Are you up to the challenge, Francis?"

"I've learned a lot since we last played, Uncle Charlie. Watch out."

"Okay, you make the first move."

Francis pushed the pawn that stood in front of his queen forward. Woodbury moved the pawn that was in front of his bishop. Then Francis moved his knight one up and two over. Woodbury contemplated the board and his next move. Francis started to fiddle with his queen as a slight sardonic smile crossed his face. Woodbury made the next move and the game was on. As the game wore on, Charlie would occasionally tap his queen. At mid game it looked as if it might result in a stalemate but Woodbury suddenly began attacking with his rooks taking one of Francis's knights and putting the king in danger. Francis looked at him, smiled as if he expected the moves and moved his other knight over to a nest of pawns.

Woodbury warned, "Better pay attention now. You are in a tough position." He moved his rook towards the king. "Got you now, Francis."

Francis, patting his queen, contemplated the board. It did indeed look as if he was in deep trouble, but suddenly with a cry of glee, he moved his queen to a place where Woodbury had left only a pawn to protect the king. There appeared to be no way out. Woodbury pondered the board for several minutes, then said, "I don't seem to have a move, you little devil. You've got me. Very well played."

The door had opened and Bessie was about to turn up the lamps, when Francis jeered his adversary with an exuberant "Checkmate!" He beamed at his mother as he held his triumphant queen high in the air.

"As Bonpapa always taught us the chess queen has all the freedom and the power. Don't I wish I were she."

Woodbury with a sly wink at Bessie said, "You can be, my dear. You can."

****

GEORGE

Dear Bessie,

I have been negligent in my writing. Please forgive my truancy. Life has been more than hectic since my appointment by the President to be Acting Governor here in Puerto Rico. Thanks to Bonpapa's influence in Washington even after all these years. I knew he had gone back to Washington several months ago but I am unaware why he went. Do you know? I hope it was not just for me. I did not want to burden him with my unhappiness. But I desperately needed to leave New York. Everything and everywhere I went reminded me of my short sojourn in life with Justine. I heard from her in a brief note that she was going to Rome to visit Bayard, who is suffering miserably with tuberculosis. I cannot imagine life when some days breathing takes all your effort. I think of him often and our days at Harvard together when he was always so energetic and ready for anything life would throw at him. But not this! As strong as one's will is, every new day beckons that it might be your last. My unhappiness is trivial in comparison.

Unexpectedly for me, I find Puerto Rico an extraordinarily beautiful island. The white sands of the beaches are like lying on clouds and the ability to swim whenever one desires is an angel's prayer. The warm, soothing waters are an elixir to my despair. As the water cradles you, time floats. Heaven is the word to describe this island of God's.

The exciting event was President Roosevelt's visit. He came to inaugurate the Puerto Rican Reconstruction Administration. The program is geared to development of agriculture, public works and bringing electricity to the island. I will be so thankful to put away the oil lamps. More likely, I will smash them on the rocks with glee. I did get to say a few words with him and he especially wanted to send his regards to Bonpapa.

Lastly, I hope Howard and Bea are safe. I have little, or I might admit, no correspondence with Howard. We did have news of the earthquake in San Francisco, and I did pray that Howard and Bea were not there. I, did in my heart, know that you would have telegraphed me if they had been harmed. So I have slept without worry. It is no secret to you that Howard's constant pleas for monies for his nefarious schemes undermines my sentiments. I do not mean to be so harsh but integrity is an order that I hold in high regard and Howard exhibits none. Secretly, I was always apprehensive that he would approach Mr. Cutting, knowing his enormous wealth. Now that Justine and I are in this marriage limbo, I have little contact with the family. All for the better, maybe.

Give the children, Carley and Bonpapa my love. Tell Francis to have the chess board ready. The next time I visit, I will have my battle plan tucked into my vest pocket, on the ready. And you might tell Woodbury that the first thing I did upon my arrival was to hang his painting of the waves crashing into the cove at Ogunquit. Brings sweet memories when times were blissful.
Your loving brother,
George

George dropped the heavy manila envelope down on his desk. He carefully hung his suit jacket on the wooden hanger, flattening out all the wrinkles with his hand. He then straightened his tie while looking in the small mirror on the wall, and smoothed down his hair. He settled himself into his brown leather chair and opened the envelope. Several letters dropped onto the desktop. Some were obviously bills and bank statements, a letter from Bessie and another from his father. But there on the bottom of the pile lay an Atlantic Monthly magazine. Puzzled, George flipped through the magazine quickly and wondered why it had been sent. Bessie was taking charge of his mail and forwarding it on to him. Why had she included it?

He picked up the letter opener and carefully, with great precision, sliced open his father's letter.

Dear George,

I trust everything is going well with you and your new position should give you great prominence in your new social circle. I understand many American businessmen are extremely interested in establishing offices in Puerto Rico, being a major shipping port from the Caribbean. Wall Street is keeping a close eye on its successes, besides myself. I would like to see our family portfolio make some significant gains to secure our future needs. It has been a troubling ride on the Street the last few years. I have never been pleased with the Kidder Peabody merger. I feel I am being edged out by the young Turks who seem to be willing to take much bigger chances. I never liked gambling, nor will I ever gamble with client's money. I still stand by the conservative approach. Keep that in mind if you have any advice on the present and future situation in Puerto Rico.

I have decided to visit Howard in Prescott to see these mines for myself. He needs investment monies to keep the operation going and I have seen fit to invest. Howard has written again that he needs more investors. This Mr. Stevens, his business partner, as I understand is in New York trying to raise funds. Howard assures me that he can make the operation profitable. Your mother and I are concerned. We want him to succeed to insure that he can maintain his family in a comfortable life. I expect the arrival of more children since he takes delight in writing about his "little family".

Your mother has taken to her bed quite often in the past several months. I have suggested that we take a house for a month on the New Jersey shore but she says she is too exhausted to even think of trying to plan. Her health worries me and I detest asking Bessie for help. My dear, darling daughter has enough burdens with Bonpapa, children and Carley's need to entertain for his business purposes. My guilt has always been that I had to call upon her so often in her growing years when life should have been as gentle as a backyard swing for her.

I need to end and wish you success and happiness. I know it is a struggle without Justine by your side. I pray someday you two will find a way to live a serene conjugal life.

As ever,
Papa

George folded the letter quickly and put it in his top drawer. Angrily, he ripped open Bessie's letter.

Dearest George,

We are all settled in back home in Jamaica Plain and the children have returned to school so the house is quiet. I had a chance to paint my heart out. Woodbury, as usual, was my close confidante and again, as usual, my severest critic. He does not allow me to languish in self pity but tries to strengthen and create a resolve in me to do what he thinks I am capable of. Whatever that is? Self pity is raising its ugly pockmarked head again. He stays by my side everyday on the rocks with his easel as his hand so easily swishes the paints into movements of water and sky. Wish my hand had that inner rhythm to tell it what to do. But I keep up the good struggle, some days good, some days bad. Anyway, we talk about abstract concepts and then reality……life as it passes us by. He always has dreams in his head of what he wants to paint and where he wants to go. And he goes. I wish and I want to go with him. Don't you dare admonish me.

Enough about me. I enclosed the Atlantic Monthly because Justine had written me a note that she had written an article which they had published. I was quite intrigued with her idea of combining prayer and music into one art; the music must pray, the prayer must sing. Otherwise, as she says, the prayer is forgotten in the detached beauty of the music, or the music is forgotten in the detached beauty of the prayer. I paused in her writing when she stated that humans must make their spiritual side evident in an outward form such as words, gestures, actions, that they may be a part of our nature. The truth in that is evident and I must remind myself of acting in a spiritual manner when dealing with everyday stresses.

But I was amused about her paragraph on the Pope attaching importance to this reform Gregorian chant music and why he insists that three hundred million people of his, should listen to a certain type of music and no other. Tell that to my children. Our American culture changes daily it seems and the public is infected with new media on a constant basis whether it is art, music or dance. We ride on a carousel of change and I sometimes do not feel I can keep up with it. I can only influence the children so much then they will ride their own horse.

I do feel sorrow about the distance between you and Justine and hope the article will recover for you some of her brilliance in thought and ideas. I have always admired her in her strong will to achieve what she feels is necessary. I had so hoped that it would not trample on your heart but the footprints I believe have crushed some of your spirit. Let it not be so.
Your loving sister,
Bessie

George folded Bessie's letter and slipped it into his vest pocket. He picked up the Atlantic Monthly and slowly flipped the pages. Finally he found the article and as he started to read, he thought, this is written in Justine's usual pedantic academic style. Tiring! But then his eyes fell upon the sentence, *"Unless the prayer and song thus rise to heaven as a single 'spiritual groaning', unless they become one, merged in a true marriage of the spirit, their association is an offense both artistic and devotional."* There it is! She has it written right there. That's our marriage. It was not a spiritual groaning. Obviously her belief is our marriage has been an offense. To whom? To her and her God, the music. We have certainly not risen to heaven. We have been living in hell. At least that is where I am living in this godforsaken country.

There was a light tap on the door. It slowly opened as a young woman looked in timidly. "Buenas tardes, Señor Ward. I wanted to know if you needed me for something. I put your mail on the corner of your desk. Have you seen it yet?"

"No, Maria. Come in please. I do have some

dictation." George straightened his tie again and tried to regain some sense of calm. He picked up an opened letter from his file box. He scanned it while Maria returned with her pad and pencil. George began to dictate. "This is to Mr. Carlton Walters, Department of Foreign Affairs, Washington, D.C. Dear Mr. Walters," George spent the rest of the day occupying himself with dictation, trying to keep his mind off Justine.

The day dragged on. George put down his pen, put on his jacket and picked up the Atlantic Monthly, pushed it into his briefcase, and nodded goodbye to Maria as he left. Maria looked a little perplexed as George usually left exactly at five o'clock as she had learned was his punctual manner. It was only four o'clock. He strode purposely down the street toward his Gentlemen's Club, reserved mostly for Consulate people and those few wealthy Puerto Ricans who had a command of the English language, a club requirement.

George seated himself in a highback leather chair in a far corner, and Carlos, upon seeing him went over with his tray. Placing a glass of water in front of him, he sensed an unusual gritted tension. "May I get you a drink, sir?"

"A scotch. Make it a double." With that George pulled out the Atlantic Monthly again. Carlos scurried away wondering what caused Mr. Ward to behave in such an abrupt manner. He usually was extremely courteous. George began scanning the article again. Carlos returned quickly with his double scotch. He watched curiously as George picked it up and downed it immediately. George noticed Carlos looking at him. "Damn it man. What are you looking at? Bring me another and then go."

Carlos turned on his heel and this time walked slowly back to the bar. "Nadie puede me hablar de esa manera," he muttered to himself.

The grandfather clock chimed 6:00 as a young man strode across the room and tapped his newspaper on George's knee. "Why the look on your face, George? Been fired? Argument at the office? Not happy living in this paradise which can become hell sometimes? Or are you just contemplating the difficulty of learning Spanish?"

George put down his glass which he had been nursing unaware of the passing time. He stared at Harold as an angry father would stare at a son who had just violated a family rule. An obtrusive interruption! "Harold, I would like some peace, if you don't mind."

"Well, I don't mean to be rude. Sir, if you can excuse me for a moment I actually have been looking for you to discuss President Ole' Rough and Ready's visit."

"That's done with. Over and done with. Didn't you think it went well?"

"Yes, it went well."

"Then what is it?

"Well you seem to have had a good rapport with him as if you had met him before. I don't know. After I graduated Princeton I had hoped to go into politics but here I am in Puerto Rico as a law consultant. It doesn't appear to me I am in the Washington fray."

"No, this is definitely neither Washington nor politics. We are sitting here holding the hands of the natives so they don't revolt."

"Yes sir, that's what I think. I want to get on with a real life, something that I could get my teeth into."

George put down his drink, stood up and took the young man by the arm. "Come on son, let's go talk about our predicaments. I know a nice little bar down the street where there are not as many straining ears. We don't want to find ourselves the subject of local gossip. Damn gossip around here destroys people."

HOWARD

September 1907

Prescott, Arizona

Dear Papa and Mumsie,

I am delighted that you have the trust in me to send me the money for the startup of our company. Stevens has gone east to interest people in the company and dispose of the shares for capital to help us make our payment and develop the property. I am sure there is a fortune to be made here in copper mining.

The good news is that Bea is expecting again and we hope to see a new little one sometime in March. Our "little family" is growing! We have moved into our bungalow and are very happy and deeply in love with each other and our little Betty. The bungalow is not too big and not too small. We are keeping chickens and have now acquired an English sheep dog, a bobtail, whom we call Bob. We have planted rose bushes, and on a neighbor's advice, buried old bones around the roots. That we found out to be a tremendous mistake because a few nights later, very frosty night, I heard strange noises and found Bob busy digging up the bones and the bushes too. I must have been a sight, in my nightclothes, on a cold night, hastily resetting the bushes and filling up the holes. Then to add to our misery, another night we discovered a skunk killing our chickens, so Bea and I crept out like conspirators, she lighting the way with a kerosene lamp and I with a shotgun. We killed the skunk, but it was a week before we could go near the chicken house. We no longer appreciated the sweet smell of the desert and we held our noses most of the week. At night we kept our faces turned down into the pillows.

There are a lot of quail in the foothills and driving around I always take my gun. Often I come home with ten or twenty. Dixon and Amy Jay join us for expeditions in search of wild grapes of which there are great quantities. Then the kitchen hums with jelly making. If the mine does not work out I foresee growing a vineyard and basking in wine. One never knows what the future will bring. Drinking wine out of copper basins?

I trust this letter finds you in good health. I know you are in the best of hands with Bessie nearby. Are you writing now that you have retired from Peabody? I have always wanted to hear more of your wanderings in the Amazon. I know you have so much more to tell and I am the one who most wants to hear. Sadly, we are far away. But I, like you, love the adventure of a new place unknown to many.
My love to Bessie and all,
Your loving son,
Howard

Howard stood on the porch with his letter that he had written a week ago still in hand. He had not had a chance to get into town to post it. Bea had just told him that her mother was coming for a visit. First trying to keep my parents calm about my company and now Mrs. Kidder! Howard was nervous about what she would think of their little bungalow and the aridness of the desert. It was not for everyone especially someone who was used to the lushness of the Sierra Nevada and a life of luxury. She had a huge influence on Bea. He knew that she did not feel him competent enough to create a comfortable, moneyed lifestyle for her precious daughter and granddaughter. He looked out over the barren landscape and hoped he could reconcile the situation. Thoughts flooded through his mind like the flash flood thundering down the gully twisting and turning trying to find a calm outlet to splay across the sands. I seem to spend half my time trying to keep people happy and the other half trying to convince them to trust me. Howard bent down and grabbed a handful of sand and then let it slowly sift through his fingers.

"Damn earth," he muttered, "never seems to give a man a break." He slung the rest of the earth across the yard and started to walk into town.

****

BESSIE

She heard the doorbell and listened as Rose's shoes rushed across the carpet to answer. Bessie was in no mood for visitors as she felt exhausted from the packing, traveling and the general hassle with the children in returning to Oakwood from Ogunquit. She had brought a couple of her oils back with her and sat staring at them as they stood against the bookshelves. I'm a dreadful artist, she thought as her gaze fell on some of Bonpapa's collection of European art which hung on one of the library walls dedicated just to art. What is it that exists between the eye, the mind, the hand, the brush and the color that eludes just me? There is a wide chasm with its jagged ridges between me and the canvas just waiting for me to fall into its crushing teeth. I feel a compulsion to create something, anything just to conquer the chasm. It's a craving, stagnating inside me. I just want to go beyond my being Mrs. Charles Bruen Perkins. Just knowing that I, Bessie, could leave something behind that would be cherished.

"Bessie, there's a chauffeur at the door and he has some valises and wants to know where to put them."

"Valises. What are you talking about? I'm not expecting a houseguest."

"I didn't believe you were but it appears there is someone who plans to stay."

Bessie, in confusion, tried to find her shoes which had been pushed under her chair. She felt ruffled and disheveled trying to straighten out her dress. "Who in the world could it be?"

As she stepped out onto the front porch she saw a chauffeur opening the door of a beautiful LaSalle and assisting what appeared to be a lovely woman stepping down onto the gravel. She was dressed exquisitely in a dark blue traveling suit and a light blue hat with the veil pulled down over her face to protect her from the dust. Smiling, she started to walk toward Bessie who still had a bewildered look across her face.

"Bessie, you look like you don't know me." She pulled her veil up over her hat. "It's me Anna."

"Anna! Anna Schmidt! You, of all people, my God, I never expected to see. Where have you been? I heard you were in Europe. I heard you were studying art and you were not coming back."

"My goodness, Bessie. You surely heard a lot of things. Aren't you glad to see me regardless of where I've been?"

Bessie threw open her arms and wrapped them around her. "I just can't believe it. You have shaken the tiredness from me. You must come in. I'll have Rose show the chauffeur where to put your bags. You remember Rose? She has been my guardian angel and strong anvil for me and still looks after all my family." Searching Anna's face for any clue as to her unannounced arrival. "You are planning to stay awhile?"

"Well I know it is quite presumptuous of me but yes, I hoped to spend a few days with you unless you have reason for me not to?"

"Oh, no, Anna, not presumptuous at all. You can't believe how happy I am to see you. You, of all people who I thought had vanished from my life. Come in quickly and get yourself tidied up. We have so very much to talk about. I want you to tell me everything that has happened even if it takes days, months or years. Again, you cannot believe how happy I am to see you."

"Let me show you your room and you can settle yourself in. I will be in the library anxiously waiting. Do not listen to me. Do take your time to rest up. But I'll be pacing the floor."

Bessie hurried into the library and rang the bell for Rose. As she stepped into the library Bessie was beaming much to the surprise of Rose. "Rose, Anna must be starved. Do you think you can put a tray together until dinnertime? She will be staying but I have no idea how long. What a mystery!"

"I would like to know too. The children have raided the refrigerator so don't act surprised what you might find on the tray."

"Oh, and bring in some sherry. No, bring Mr. Perkins' port. The one he keeps hidden in his cabinet. You know, the one he thinks we don't know about. He will know we know about it now."

Rose hurried out and Bessie straightened the pillows on the sofa. Bessie was anxious to hear why Anna had come. She could not bear any more bad news. Apprehensive and excited she picked up a magazine she had been perusing.

"How much better I feel now, Bessie, with a little warm water on my face and a change of clothes. Nearly a new woman but not quite. Not quite!" Anna said, entering the room now dressed in a light yellow dress. She sat down on the sofa and fluffed a pillow behind her back.

Bessie poured her a glass of port and then one for herself. Handing the glass to Anna she touched her glass to Anna's. "To you for bringing some excitement into my home and lifting my spirit which has been dragging upon the carpets."

Anna raised her glass. "And to you for such a warm welcome to an unexpected friend who suddenly appeared at your doorstep."

"Heaven forbid, you will always be welcome, unexpected or not. Now, tell me where you have been and why you came."

"Remember how you and I always wanted to be

artists, renowned or not? I had great notions of painting exuberant, whimsical paintings wherever and whatever I desired. Nonsense dreams but nevertheless my dream. Then one day in New York I was invited to a gallery opening. My energy was low as I wound my way along the sidewalks thinking of absolutely nothing. I found the gallery and was drawn to a painting with a luminous light. It was of a mother and child. The paint was so rich in its depth of color. I just stood there. The baby was so innocent of life and its newness made me melancholy. Then I heard an obvious feminine voice behind me say, 'Do you like my painting?' I turned and there stood a woman with a steady gaze and vibrancy that I could not resist envying. 'Yes', I told her. I don't quite know the words to explain what happened but there I was in the midst of change."

"I guess I'm having a hard time understanding what you are talking about, Anna."

"I had a difficult time understanding it myself. That incident changed my life with a unique sensation of a life force which I believed came from this woman."

"Well, tell me, who was she!"

"Elizabeth Nourse."

"Elizabeth Nourse! How lucky you were. Good grief, you know she was the second American woman to be accepted as a member of the Societe National des Artistes Francais. Finally, a woman with talent, and great talent at that, gets recognized. My daubing on canvas is a child's scribbles compared to her. So then what happened?"

"That's where my story begins. We went to a café at Washington Square and we spent the next four hours talking. The time felt like a snap of the fingers. Words flew by us like bats from the eaves. For the first time in a very long time I felt connected to a soul that had eluded me for years. She created such excitement in me that before I could fathom the future I was on a boat with her to Paris."

"I can't imagine! That would be a manifestation of a dream come true for me and it happened to you. Luck has befallen you. In all the heavens, I trust you took advantage of the situation. We have to toast your newfound life. I want to drink in all the details and I mean, drink." Bessie took a deep swallow. Anna sipped the port carefully and took a cursory look around the room. Bessie noticed the drifting of Anna's eyes.

"Okay, my dear friend, I think you have a lot more to tell."

"Hmmmmm!" Anna put down her glass. "Yes, you could say there's more. I wonder what really took my life over. I don't know if it was Paris, Elizabeth or Auguste."

"Auguste! Who is Auguste?"

"Auguste Rodin."

"The Rodin?"

"Yes. The Rodin. When Elizabeth took me to Rodin's studio, Bessie, I walked into another life. One that I knew I would be open to. Whatever happened, I would let it happen. I shrugged my old life off my shoulders and drew myself a new persona that only I knew. I was so far away from the structure of my life in Boston, New York or wherever our circles were that insisted we keep silent to ourselves. Rodin's studio smelled of maleness, stone, granite, dust and I heard the power of a chisel hitting something hard just inside the larger room. I was an intruder in someone else's world but I was not shamed. Think! I was not shamed, embarrassed or timid as I walked toward this large imposing man working on a block of alabaster. He ignored my presence but I knew he was aware that I stood there watching. His chisel carefully sculpted the alabaster into an opaqueness that separated the two contemplative faces bonding them together in a shimmer of light that passed through the stone between them. Being in the presence of a creation of human spirits awed my senses. He stood back and stared at the stone, scanning every small mark. I sensed that he thought it was going to speak or move. He just waited. I went back out to the garden where Elizabeth was admiring one of the garden sculptures."

When she thought that Anna had finished all she was going to tell, Bessie sipped her port gingerly. "I know there is more to the story. You appear to be reluctant. I don't want you to say more than you want but, Anna, I will imagine all kinds of things and more than likely, not the truth."

"Yes, there is and was more. Elizabeth apparently wanted me to have my own impressions of Rodin without her interference. She told me the next evening there was going to be a casual dinner with Rodin in his studio. I understood he was a gregarious man and liked the company of women when he was relaxing. I was excited about the dinner but also nervous not quite knowing what to expect."

"Did you go?"

"Of course, I could not, not go. Elizabeth had been so generous to me that it would be an insult not to accept her invitation to go. I did go through my clothes trunk again and again and again. I just did not know what was acceptable. This was Paris. I felt like a churchmouse whose heart was beating too rapidly hoping not to be noticed too much. I chose what I thought was a simple black dress. Though I found the situation intimidating I decided this was Paris and I did not pin my hair up too severely but let it kind of dangle down my neck."

Bessie laughed loudly. "Oh, my dear. Why does it take us so long to do what we want to do? A few dangling tresses and we feel so bold. A couple of glasses of red wine and who knows what would happen."

Anna tapped rapidly on the arm of the chair. Her discomfort was apparent as she picked up her port and this time took several long swallows.

"Why Anna, something did happen. I didn't mean to make light of your dress and hair. I am here at home too much by myself so I imagined so quickly about how I thought I would have acted. I would have been just as excited. My feet would have danced down the Rue. Sorry to have upset you but I meant no harm, dear."

"No. No. I'm not upset. Strange though, it's hard to believe that it was me. I felt like an actress playing a part that I relished. When Elizabeth and I arrived at the dinner, the studio was filled with casually dressed men and women. I felt comfortable in my black dress. I knew no one there. It was like a stage setting with easels, sculpting tools spread on a wooden table. At the other end of the table were dishes filled with beautiful displays of food. Oysters and tiny clams on ice, small strips of rare beef that people were eating with their hands, cheeses and fruit. A sumptuous meal all on a plain wooden table. No silver services, no lace tatted napkins, no crystal goblets, just plain dinnerware. Mostly people just eating with their fingers....and licking them."

"Did that make you uncomfortable?"

Anna picked up a napkin and whisked it across her lips, then patting her cheeks said, "No. I kind of enjoyed it. Actually, the truth is, I slipped into my other skin, the one that had been lurking beneath. I let it come to life. It was me and a me that attracted the man I had come to be enamored with."

"Who?"

"Rodin. Who else would be 'who'?"

"I don't know. But Rodin! Anna, what were you thinking?"

"Obviously I was not thinking, just acting on the moment or moments. Life. Joy. Smells. All were washing over me. All senses became new to me. I let them go."

Intrigued, Bessie asked, "Was this the beginning of an affair?"

"You might suggest it was."

"Suggest! Was it or was it not?"

Anna grabbed her goblet. "Yes, it was!" She swallowed a hefty portion of port. "And I have no regrets. I have nothing to be ashamed of. I was with one of the greatest living artists of our time. He brought energy, ideas, tenderness, bravado and a damning force that would reject anything negative in his life. It was lust, not lust for sexual needs, but lust to unleash the troubled figures of life from the stone. His battle with the world he transferred to the stone which became his ultimate friend and at the same time his nemesis. I just tried to gently drift by and through his work. I wanted to understand his mind. I tried not being a hard, unyielding piece of stone which so many of us are but something that could be carved into beautiful meaning."

"Did he carve you into something?"

"Yes, he did. He broke away the stone in my life. And I know you understand the stone I'm referring to," Anna said adamantly.

"I guess the metaphor is the stone built into our homes dominates our lives. Am I thinking correctly?"

"Did you ever look how carefully the stones are chiseled and fit tightly not allowing any air to flow through? And of course, they're granite. That indomitable, immortal stone. It outlives us all. It slowly steals our breath away." Anna stood up and shook the folds of her skirt. "Are you up to taking a walk, Bessie? I need a breath of fresh air."

"Of course, it would do us both good. After what you've said, I guess the walls of my house are smothering you." Anna glanced at her with a look of consternation and a slight frown.

"Don't look so worried. I'm only teasing. I have to have that breath of fresh air too because I emotionally, maybe more than I want, understand your words. I needed to hear them. I need to hear them again and again and again. Those stones built not only the walls of our homes but the walls in our lives. Come on, let's walk down to Ward Pond. I miss Bonpapa so much that it brings him closer to me just sitting by the pond."

"I remember him as being such an intelligent, empathetic man. I always learned something while being in his presence and from your grandmother as well. I never wrote you my sympathies when I heard of their passings. Strange, the love the two of them had for each other. I could actually feel it when I was visiting them. How lucky you were to have had them. That kind of love is elusive to the rest of us, or maybe just to me."

"No, it is elusive to many of us, including me." Bessie opened the front door, then took Anna's hand and the two faded down the long drive toward the pond, not speaking anymore.

****

The next several days had brought fresh winds of incredible enjoyment and change to the atmosphere of Oakwood. Anna was a charming storyteller to the children and the oldest had lots of questions about Paris. Sitting at an early supper, surprisingly, one of the girls burst out excitedly. "Did you see them do the can-can?" Then she glanced at her mother to see if she disapproved.

"Well, did you?"

Anna laughed. "Of course I did. I went to the Moulin Rouge also with a curious friend and we did see the girls dance."

Francis, with his eyes intent on Anna, said with no compunction or embarrassment, "Did they throw their dresses up?"

"Yes, they threw them up and back, just like they were playing with a fan."

Mary's eyes widened, "I can't imagine. And everybody thought that was okay?"

"Well, yes."

"Did you enjoy it?" little Anna asked curiously.

"You know Anna, I did. And I did because they all looked like they were having a lot of fun and just enjoyed the freedom and fast pace of the dance. The girls danced with abandon. Something we just don't do in Boston."

The children sat in silence momentarily, looking at Anna in awed disbelief. A friend of their mother's was speaking to them honestly and frankly about something they had heard about that had a veil of taboo. Anna spoke to them lifting that veil as if there was nothing to be ashamed about what lay behind it.

"Okay, children, that's enough. I think it's time for all of you to go up to your rooms and ready yourselves for school tomorrow. I will be up shortly to look over your homework and say goodnight." The children pushed back their chairs and politely said their "goodnights" to Anna.

Francis, with his older brother demeanor, said, "That was a very enjoyable conversation, Miss Schmidt. Thank you very much," and with a slight nod of his head, left the dining room.

"My, what a wonderful job you have done with those children and especially Francis. I'm sorry but I could not save myself from laughing at his overtly gentlemanly manner. I envy you so having the pleasure of children. Something barren in my life. Maybe that's why I'm so willing to fall into pleasure, wherever I can find it."

"Why don't you sneak into the library while I look in on the children? One of Amy's new poetry books is on the table. I think it's one of the pleasures you can fall into. I'll join you as soon as I can."

Bessie climbed the stairs with a feeling of lightheadedness. She stopped for a moment and drank in the sounds of the house. The children murmuring gave her a sense of pleasure. Carley was away in Lenox working on a new architectural plan for a large estate. His absence gave her a sense of inner quiet that had fled from her months, maybe years ago. She did not remember the last time she had felt so comfortable in her own home. She continued up the stairs, anxiously looking forward to continuing her conversation with Anna.

****

The day had been a busy one for Bessie. Anna had left for an early morning train back to New York. Anna had told her that she had left her something and she had placed it in the library with the suggestion that she not open it until later that night. Bessie had spent the day dealing with the needs of the children, making doctor appointments for physicals, finding a French tutor with the hopes that they would do better with their language skills. Not that she wanted to push them, only encourage them to the joy of languages and the esteem one feels of being capable to handle the world of Babel.

The children were growing so fast and at times she was astonished at what they said. Her heart seemed to stop for a minute as the realization came that someday soon they would not be here, in their rooms, asleep in their beds but somewhere out in the world absorbing it into their own life. She understood the fast paced changes in life with all the new advances in travel and communication that their lives, their choices would be so different from hers and her generation. She thought how much she envied them.

Then a sensation of tiredness shuddered through her because she had sequestered away in the far reaches of her mind the realization that Papa and Mumsie were coming to live with her. Papa's fortune had taken a downturn, especially with the heavy hits that Howard had made on his father's portfolio. Combined with Mumsie's health problems, they were no longer able to maintain the New York brownstone. There was no other alternative since George and Howard had no possibilities to help so the burden of care was again wrapped and placed in Bessie's arms. She had to start on the arrangements but not today, not today. Bessie still wanted to revel in the last few days in the renewed friendship with Anna.

She picked up the mail from the carpet where it had fallen through the mail slot and saw a letter from Howard. She took a deep breath and decided not to open it until later not wanting to read what she knew would not be good news. Bessie finished her work and glanced out at the garden where the soft light of a dimming sun fell upon the flowers. She was startled that the day was ebbing and heard the grandfather clock's chimes striking the hour as six. She pushed the papers aside and rang the bell for Rose.

"Is the children's supper laid out on the table yet?"

"Yes, dear. Shall I call the children?"

"Please, if you would."

Dinner was eaten with a lot of talk about Anna's reflections on Paris. Francis and Anna decided they were going to go as soon as they could and promised to practice their French.

"Mother, may I be excused? I have schoolwork to finish."

"Certainly, my dear."

Francis kissed his mother on the cheek and with his sly smile said, "Je t'aime Maman."

Bessie put her hand on his cheek. "Je t'aime aussi."

"I can say that too," piped up Anna.

"I'm certain you can, dear. Now I think you and Mary should ready yourselves for bed. I'll come in later to say goodnight."

Bessie, later dressed in a light cotton nightdress, settled herself on a chaise next to the window in her bedroom. With curious anticipation, she slowly unwrapped Anna's present. Once in her hand, she gazed upon a photograph of a marble bust of a beautiful young woman. Gasping, she realized it appeared to be a bust of Anna. Down in the corner of the photograph Rodin had written his name. "My God!" she thought, "Why has Anna given me this treasure which is surely meant for her?"

The moon in all its fullness was meteor bright streaming through her window. She stared straight at its brilliance, focusing on the features of the man hidden within its craters. It had such an ethereal quality, especially this night with the mystery of Anna's gift in her hands. Without another thought, Bessie opened the window wider and like a fawn seeking water climbed carefully out on to the rooftop. She lay back on the shingles of the dormer, wistfully letting herself drift along with the night sky. She imagined herself as Anna, walking along the walks of Rodin's studio. A shiver ran down her body as she felt the touch of this strong man as if she was Anna. Her hand started to run smoothly over the moss on the shingles. She picked a piece of it and pulled it into small pieces and let it drop back onto the shingles. Looking in wonder at the breadth of the moss on the rooftop, she remembered the redness of the wooden shingles when they were new. Now look at them. They have turned that sad gray and the green of moss happens to bring back the color that has been lost. Is that me? God in heaven, I'm losing my color and gray is stealing its way over me. She shivered again and held the picture close to her breast searching for the color that usually flashed behind her eyelids. Search for the red. Is it still swirling? I must find it. She pulled up more moss and held it tightly in her hand.

****

In the early morning Bessie unwillingly opened Howard's letter that she had left on the breakfast table. She took another sip from her coffee and hesitantly began to read.

March 14, 1908

Dear Bessie,

By the time this letter reaches you I have to believe that you will have heard about the birth of our dear second baby, Beatrice Howard Ward. She seems to be very healthy and as good as gold. Now we are happy in our little house, with our two babies, with our growing mine, not much money in the bank, but our mining stock is still rising and shares being sold. The mine has been looking good and we are shipping some ore, though we had to haul it fifteen miles to the railroad and then pay heavy charges to El Paso. That was eating up all our profits so I recommended that a small mill be erected as soon as we could afford it. Stevens wired us to put in the mill, as he has arranged for sufficient money and that his end was going faster. I had begun to think that I could pay back what I had borrowed. Unfortunately, and I know that I can tell you this in confidence, Stevens chose to run the stock up instead of selling it at a reasonable price, and I have found myself forced to put up more money to pay for our mill.

Bessie closed her eyes for a moment and clenched her teeth. It took a moment to continue reading.

So, my dear Bessie, I know with the hardship of Poppa and Mumsie moving to your home that the extra finances will surely be a burden for you. Something I did not want to happen but events have been out of my control and therefore, I cannot help with the costs. I hope George's pockets are not as empty as mine. I keep trying but good fortune does not seem to be my companion. But I do have my little family, now four of us, to comfort me.

I hope I will have better news in the near future.
My love to all the family,
Howard

****

HOWARD

Howard sat slumped in his office chair staring out the window watching the wind blow whirling spirals of sand across the barren landscape. The front page of the local Prescott newspaper lay atop the desk with a headline written in bold type, **'Copper Panic'. "Copper and silver drop to half their value and banks are failing throughout the country."**

Racing through his mind were flashing thoughts and images, not of the copper collapse but reminders of his failures. "How in the hell did I get to this? Why can't I succeed? Everybody else seems to make a comfortable life. Bessie, I need you now. Sing those songs to me again." Howard put his head back and stared at the ceiling. "I was always conscious of being criticized even when I was not in the room. Unless I'm absorbed in something interesting like this whole mining adventure, I'm more comfortable unconscious."

He rolled his head back and forth on the back cushion of the chair closing his eyes. "I'm still at war with inferiority. I thought I had overcome it but it is back and the battle is on again. Would public schools or a different environment have changed this? Was it inherited? Was it environment? When I was young it thoroughly crushed me and it is crushing me again." Howard let his mind drift off again. Soon he was murmuring the words of one of Bessie's songs.

> There was a little devil once.
> Some people thought he was a dunce.
> He ate some cake on Tuesday
> Which made him sick with small delay.
> He ate so much of jelly cake,
> It made his little belly ache.
> He used to go with his Papa,

And see the children burn in tar.
And when they yelled and shrieked in pain,
He clapped his hands and said, "Again."

"I don't know if I'm the little devil or one of the children burning in tar. Possibly both! Who would make such a song for children with nothing but pain? If it is meant to be a warning they sure got their point across. I have been carrying the pain all my life. I need a stiff drink." Howard got up and went to the cabinet where he kept some old scotch and poured a glass full to the brim. Sitting down at his desk he started to rummage through the top drawer. He finally pulled out an object wrapped in several layers of cloth and tied with a string. He undid the knot and unfolded the cloth, gently lifting the chess queen and placed it in front of him. He stared at it for some time. "The king. What can he do? The highest position on the board and everyone is out to get him. Now look at the queen. She has options." Howard picked up the queen and turned her over and over in his hand. He never quite understood why he kept her and what real meaning she had for him. He picked up the scotch and began taking large gulps and when finished he smashed it heavily down on the desktop and said, "We're getting out of here. NOW!"

****

The train pulling into Boston jerked, stopped, jerked and stopped again. Howard looked out the window searching the platform for any familiar face, hopefully from the family. Seeing no one, he stood up and started to get the baggage down onto the compartment's seat. The girls had awakened and were rubbing their eyes. Bea tried to get the baby girls into their coats. She did not say a word to Howard.

Howard managed to find a porter who got the luggage onto the carrier. Bea picked up the baby and took Betty's hand and walked down the platform sensing that there would not be anyone greeting them. That was fine with her since she was in no mood for pleasantries. How many times have I done this? Always on Howard's impulsive whims. He has to beg again to the family. I will not beg! They waited outside while the porter hailed them a taxi. Once settled in and Howard had given the address of Bessie's home, she sat back and watched as Boston floated by. Brick, brick and more brick. Everything is made out of brick. I don't know what to make of this. I feel I've been dropped into a foreign land. It's so different from San Francisco and the West. How nice there seems to be so little dust and sand. I could do without that for the rest of my life. The taxi driver asked Howard if he was to turn at the next corner. Howard told him that he was correct.

Surprised, Bea asked Howard, "What did he say! I didn't understand a word."

"You will have to get use to Boston's accents and there are many of them. It will be like learning an entire new language."

"Really! I thought everyone spoke American English."

"Oh, yes, it's English, but some spoken with thick Irish and Scottish brogues and others spoken with the accents of many countries. Especially difficult are the accents of fishermen coming from Portugal, Newfoundland and other islands. It certainly tests the ear with the carousel of accents."

"It sounded like the driver did not know what an 'r' was."

Howard patted her hand and said, "You'll get used to it."

I hope not, Bea thought.

Bessie was waiting on the front porch. She had seen the taxi turn into the driveway and hurried out anticipating seeing her nieces for the first time. She opened the door of the taxi on Bea's side and greeted her with a kiss. "Oh, please let me take the baby. She looks like a doll and how sweet Betty looks with those marvelous blond curls. I am so excited to have babies again in my home."

"Thank you Bessie. You're most generous but I hope we will not have to intrude too long. Howard promised me we would have a home quickly."

"Well, let's not worry about that now. You must be exhausted and I have the rooms ready for you. I know a bath would feel like heaven for you right now. The filth of trains does not seem to rub off for days."

Howard came around from the back of the taxi with some of the luggage. "I hope you have a welcome for me. A bath certainly would sound wonderful."

"Certainly, Howard. It's good to see you. Carley will be home shortly and is anxious to see and talk with you. And of course, Mumsie and Papa are in the drawing room. They are expecting to have tea with you after you have washed up."

Howard started up the stairs with the luggage. He was not looking forward to any talk with Carley or for that matter, anyone. He could hear the edge of criticism already in their voices. It is the condescending attitude I hate as if I am a wandering pet always wallowing in the mud puddles. He sank down in the armchair in their bedroom. Bea was already in the bathroom running the water. Thank God, Bessie had taken the babies into the nursery and he could hear Rose tsk, tsking and running around as if they had just been born at that moment. Howard took out his wallet and counted a hundred. He looked in another part of his wallet hoping that somehow grace had fallen upon him and another hundred dollars was hidden down deep. Seeing nothing, he dropped it on the table. "Well, that's it! I will have to find some work quickly. Do not want to sleep under this roof too many nights. I will hear them mocking me from the trees."

Bea slipped out of the bathtub and reached for her robe. Thankfully, Howard had found her cosmetics case and placed it on the table next to the sink. She looked carefully at herself in the mirror and felt her shoulders drop as she witnessed the black circles under her eyes and the tired sense of her face. She opened a jar of cream and smeared as much as her skin would absorb and then took her hairbrush and started to brush through her long blonde hair with even strokes. "Count to a hundred and hope that it will look presentable. Meeting Howard's mother for the first time is not the way I expected it to happen. I feel like a dirty ragamuffin coming in from the street with dirty hands." Bea picked up the bar soap and washed her hands again even though they had soaked for a long time in the tub. She wiped her face taking off the excess cream. Then she twisted her hair into a long rope and tied it up in the back with a pearl clasp. She applied a little rouge to her cheeks and light pink lipstick.

"The last thing I want is not to look like a streetwalker with red, red, lipstick and heavy rouge. I don't mind if I look like a schoolgirl and then maybe they will be more reticent in asking the many questions I know will come. I can feel the nerves in my neck twinge already. Calm down! Calm down."

Bea slipped into a light blue dress with lace at the collar and wrists. She smoothed it down and nodding with slight disapproval deemed it fine for the evening. She started to draw a bath for Howard and then went into the bedroom to find him nodding off in the chair.

She shook him awake. "You can take your bath now. I'll wait for you here since I don't want to go down by myself."

"Everything will be okay, Bea."

"That's what you always say, but look where we are. How can this be alright?"

Howard went into the bathroom and slammed the door.

****

Bessie brought in the tea tray and set it down. Then she went to the sideboard and placed the sherry, a bottle of scotch and some brandy out with some snifters.

Mumsie looked askance at Bessie. "Don't you think a little too much? After all, they are tired and you know what alcohol does to Howard."

Bessie poured herself some sherry and without looking at her mother said, "I think we might all need a drink stronger than tea. Have you thought how nervous Bea must feel having to meet you, Carley, myself, and all the clamor that our children make? And besides that, this is Boston, with all its properness and pithiness at times. It all must be so intimidating."

"With that thought spouting from your mouth, do I look presentable?"

"Mumsie, you always look beautiful. It's me that can't keep the wrinkles out of my dress or my face."

"Well, dear, with all the hard work you have to do looking after all of us, it is no wonder you have wrinkles."

"Thank you, Mumsie!" The sarcasm was obvious in Bessie's voice.

Papa put down his book that he had been reading, walked over to the sideboard and poured himself some scotch. Without saying a word, he walked back to his chair, picked up his book, swallowed some scotch and proceeded to read again. Bessie smiled. She knew her father so well, she understood the implication of his action.

There was a tap at the door and Howard opened it. Bea stepped in, with a quick glance she moved toward Mumsie sitting in her chair with a light throw across her lap. Bea reaching out her hand said, "I am pleased to meet you finally. I know you have probably wondered about me. It's a shame it has taken us so long to meet."

She turned and found Papa standing to greet her. He gave her a slight kiss on the cheek. "You look well Bea for having survived such a long trip. Please sit and rest yourself. I know all too well how unpleasant train journeys are."

Mumsie, having surveyed Bea thoroughly as she addressed her said, "Oh, yes dear, please sit and have some sherry. It does the body good sometimes. Seems to calm me down and I'm sure it will settle you too. Dinner will be soon and then you must find your bed early. The coming days will be busy, I'm sure."

Howard stepped over to the sideboard and poured Bea a sherry and then poured himself a glass of whiskey. He took a quick swallow before handing Bea her sherry. She looked at him with a hard look of consternation. He sat down next to her and patted her hand.

Bessie felt the vacuum in the room as no one seemed quite to know what to say. She abruptly broke the silence by asking, "What are your plans Howard?" She quickly thought it was the wrong thing to ask now.

"Yes, Howard, what are your plans now that the mine is gone?" Papa leaned a little forward in expectation.

"Well, I couldn't sell the mine, Papa. So now we, the family own the property."

"Will there be any income from it?"

"No, I don't know where it would come from."

"I had hoped you would have found something useful for it."

Howard took another swig of his whiskey. "No, I didn't."

Bea dropped her head and fussed with her skirt. Mumsie closed her eyes and rested her head on the back rest of the chair.

Resignedly Papa asked, "Where do we go from here, Howard?"

"It's obvious I have to find a job. But first I have to find us a place to live. I know Bea is uncomfortable staying here."

"No, Howard, do not speak for me. I would like you to keep to yourself as many times you forget to do so. Bessie has made our accommodations quite comfortable. Although it's true, Bessie, I would like a home of my own."

Bessie was surprised at Bea's sudden comment and admonishment of Howard. She did not quite know how this marriage was doing considering Howard taking Bea to the deserts of Arizona and then bearing two children in what I would think was an outpost of America. I have to admire her courage. She realized that Bea was waiting for a response from her.

"Of course, dear. You should have your own privacy. But don't be too hasty. Howard tends to make decisions too quickly without taking proper note of the situation."

"Bessie, I don't need a lecture on my life. I'm just trying to do the best I can but fate seems to be against me."

Papa, obviously irritated put down his glass. "I don't think the fates have anything to do with one's decisions in life. It is up to the individual to take responsibility for his decisions not fate. Fate is a tired alibi. Every decision has a following one and it is most important to evaluate it based on the triumphs or failures of the previous ones. I do not think I am overstepping my bounds in stating the obvious but you must show me that you are worthy of my trust again." Papa slapped a book on the table as if to make his point.

Mumsie put her hands on the armchair and reached for her cane. Startling the others, she rose by herself and stated in a direct manner. "I think we should all retire to the dining room where I hope the conversation will be a little more enlightening and enjoyable. We can discuss what shall be done tomorrow. Bea, I would be most delighted if you would sit next to me. I want to welcome a new daughter into our family."

****

GEORGE

George began to walk around his apartment aimlessly. He had just received a short note from Justine that her brother, Bronson, was told that it would be best for him to move to a drier climate. The dry desert air might resolve his respiratory problems which he had been suffering with for years. Justine wrote that she thought it best for her to go with him and help him find a suitable home and make sure he was well settled. She did not know how long it would take but she would keep in touch. He leaned his forehead against the window and stared at the passing people below. He had been devastated when he heard the news that Bayard Cutting had died of pneumonia in Egypt in March. Bayard had been fighting illness for years and finally the battle was over and he had lost. His childhood friend and the closeness of boyhood with all its secrets they had shared were gone. He had never had another relationship like that. After his marriage to Justine, it seemed to have cooled, never to be the same again. Now this! Bronson! So soon after Bayard's death and he is suffering the same illness. He was always aware that Bronson and Justine had a very close sibling relationship. He watched the activity on the street as if he were a foreign observer and not a participant in their life. He felt numb. Alone! "If I was ill, would Justine come to watch over me? I can't feel that she would. I think the love of her brothers and family exceeds the love she has for me, if in fact, she loves me." He sank into a chair and put his head in his hands. "Why did she marry me? She left me so quickly and has never asked for a divorce. This marriage has made my life torturous. I don't think I would feel such loneliness if I had not married. It has shackled me. How can I possibly have another relationship while she's my wife but in reality not my wife?"

The setting sun sent a stream of light through the window and caught his attention. "I can't do this anymore. I'm responsible for what I am and what I do. I'm going back to New York. Puerto Rico is not where I should be nor is it my country. I'm sure I can do something for my country that will do me honor. No more of this life. No more drifting. No more waiting. I don't even know what I was waiting for. Some forgotten fantasy I once had?" He stood in front of the mirror and looked carefully at himself. He smoothed his hair, straightened his tie, ran his hand over his chin and then was satisfied at what he saw. A man with youth still left. He opened his closet door, pulled out his valises and started to pack.

****

The boat pulled into its dock early on a bright, warm spring day. George stood at the railing looking at all the people waving, many of them shouting, "Hola!" anxiously scanning the faces for loved ones. He pushed his way toward the stern of the boat, knowing it would be some time before they let the gangplank down and the luggage off onto the pier. From the stern he looked down the Hudson toward Staten Island. He could see a ferry chugging across to the Lower Manhattan dock where it would spill out all its people, scurrying off to sit in an office chair and handle papers all day. Then back to the ferry to cross once again and begin the same old regime the next day. Thoughts flashed through his head. I wonder if they believe they are doing something good for themselves and their families? And for the world? Or is it just a means of getting by? I wonder if they actually know what the world is like. Who are these other people so different from them?

He turned back to see if the gangplank was down. It was and he saw the glee on faces as many embraced chattering away in a language which would be hard to hear above the cacophony in the heavily populated streets of New York. These were the lucky ones who had the means to obtain visas and not have to come through Ellis Island and prove themselves worthy of being in America. I think I will have to prove myself of being worthy also.

Once having his luggage in hand, he hailed a taxi to take him to the Chelsea Hotel. The desk clerk, slightly taken back by George's colonel uniform and his austere manner handed him the key to a suite on the fifth floor. "I'm sure you will admire the view from your suite. Have a nice stay, Colonel Ward, and enjoy New York."

He took the key with a quick nod of thanks and ascended to the fifth floor in the iron grill elevator. For the first time, he chuckled. Enjoy New York, as if I had never seen it. Maybe I should take his advice and pretend I've never seen it. Look at it through new eyes as if I have no past here.

He stepped briskly out on to the sidewalk and walked uptown. He cocked his head as he became aware that the sounds invading his ears were those of the many Americans passing him on the street, involved in their own conversations as if no one else were there. He had been in Puerto Rico too long that the familiarity of the items in the store windows, the smells of food he knew so well, even the people who one would readily recognize as Americans by the movements, style and habits he found refreshing. He passed a newsstand and bought a Wall Street Journal. Tucking it under his arm he went off in search of a coffee shop. Once settled with a hot American brewed cup of steaming coffee, he opened the paper. Comfort settled in as he scanned the articles with a vague interest when he noticed an advertisement from his old law firm. Not only was it advertising their specialties in the law but at the bottom there was a statement announcing the death of one of their partners and condolences to the family. George was stunned for a moment because he had known him well and considered him one of his mentors. He had told George when he left if he ever changed his mind and wanted to come back he would be welcome. He had given him a Letter of Recommendation which he had tucked away in his files. He quickly drank the last of the coffee, paid his bill and set off for his old law office.

****

BESSIE

The sounds of a motor car could be heard coming up the drive. Bessie had been sitting on the porch rocking calmly back and forth waiting for the taxi while taking in the quiet of the house and the colors of the gardens. It had been a hectic tense two weeks of Howard and his family living in the house while he looked for a place to live and hopefully obtain work. He had found a clerk's job at an insurance company down near Copley Square but it paid very little. He had settled Bea and the children in a small apartment in the village of Brookline so they were actually very close by.

The taxi pulled up in front of the steps and the driver stepped out to open the car door for Bessie. She ducked her head and stepped inside. "Bea, you look so beautiful in that dress." She leaned over and lightly hugged Bea.

"Thank you, Bessie. You look lovely too." Bea looked mildly uncomfortable.

"I know we will have a nice day today. You haven't had a chance to know or really see Boston." Bessie told the driver to take them to the Gardner Museum at Fenway Court. "I wanted to take you to see one of our most marvelous museums built by a friend of mine. It actually was designed to be a house that would house Isabella and her husband's art collection. She opens it to the public only twenty days a year but I did write and ask if we could visit on our own. She wrote a gracious note that said she would be happy for us to have the home to ourselves. She unfortunately cannot greet us because she is off again to Europe in search of more works of art. She has a very eclectic taste as you will see." Bessie kept chattering away. Bea did not know quite what to say and wondered what the word "eclectic" meant. She was content with Bessie filling the void of conversation.

Overwhelmed by the home, Bea thought it looked like something out of a fairy tale. So un-American in its architecture. She felt she should tiptoe like an unwelcome guest. They had come into the cloister area and Bessie began to recite a litany of information about the wall hangings, the sculptures, the paintings. She pretended to listen politely. As they ascended the stairs to the second floor, Bea noticed paintings even hung on the walls of the staircase. There seemed to be an endless array, even what appeared to be paintings from the Orient. They were the only paintings that she felt a familiarity with since they had such a large population of Chinese in San Francisco. She and her mother loved walking through Chinatown fascinated by the ivory carved sculptures and scrolls. Bessie chattered on with great enthusiasm leading Bea into what appeared to be a giant ballroom whose walls reached enormous heights. Again they were covered with paintings, some so dark in color it was hard to distinguish exactly what they were.

Bessie took her hand insistently saying, "You must see this painting of Mrs. Gardner." They stood in front of a painting of a woman dressed in black with porcelain skin and her hands lightly grasping each other in front of her. She stared straight ahead with a slightly bemused smile but Bea noticed what looked like halos surrounding her head.

"What do you think?" Without waiting for an answer, Bessie in a near whisper said, "It caused quite an uproar at the time. Isabella loved it but her husband said, 'It looks like hell, but it looks like you.' Can you imagine? It must have broken her heart because he kept it in his office. But she got the best of him. After he died, she hung it right here in the great hall where everyone could see it. She took back what was her! I have such admiration. She is unpredictable which makes knowing her fascinating. She strides her own path and to hell with what people think."

Bea noticed Bessie's face beaming in awe as she looked upon the portrait and was surprised about how easily 'hell' slipped from her tongue. "What does she mean, wait until I meet her. I wouldn't know what to say to a woman who has created all of this and appears to come from another world. Not mine."

"We must get on. Amy is waiting for us to have tea with her. She never likes to be kept waiting although she would wait forever if it were a famous poet who was coming. And you know, neither one of us are."

As Bea waited at the entrance seated on a small bench she closed her eyes and took a deep breath. Bessie was calling for a taxi. She desperately wanted to go home but she felt compelled to remain with Bessie, not wanting to upset her. I have to make her believe that I am enjoying the day. God help me! This is not my world.

****

Amy was standing on the front stoop as they drove up. "I heard the taxi coming and wondered if it was finally you, Bessie. And I expect this is Bea. My, what a beautiful dress. If it is not too embarrassing to ask, but where did you buy it?"

Bea blushed. "Oh, my mother and I make all our clothes and this was one of my favorites."

"Really!" Amy said with much surprise. "I don't know of anyone who makes their own clothes. How marvelous of you and your mother. Bessie, can you imagine any one of our acquaintances making their own clothes?"

Bessie saw Bea's embarrassment. "I have told you,

Amy, that Howard and Bea have lived faraway from most cities so sewing becomes a necessity and I believe Bea does extraordinarily well. I wouldn't mind if I could do the same."

"Yes, yes! Please forgive my rudeness. I tend to do that many a time when my mouth thinks before my brain. Bessie knows all too well and usually kicks me. Isn't that so, Bessie? Let's go into the library. Tea has been ready and we could all start over again."

Bea was struck by this outspoken, brusque woman. Bessie had told her that her family was one of the richest in New England and her brother was president of Harvard. Howard had spoken of her but he could hardly have described her in the manner of what Bea witnessed. As the library door opened, Bea stepped in and was confronted by walls and walls of floor to ceiling books. Her eyes wandered over the blue and red leathered books with their gold engravings. Many of them tattered and well worn.

Amy asked her how she would like her tea, with sugar or lemon. "Both if you don't mind?"

"Don't mind at all. It is a good thing to sweeten the bitter. Like life!"

Taking a sip of tea she said, "I have never seen a home with such a library. I believe it's bigger than our public library at home in Grass Valley. Wouldn't they be so envious of this! But who could possibly read all these books and why do you keep them all? We have some bookshelves at home but most of them are engineering books of my father's. Now that he is gone they mostly collect dust."

"That's a good question. Why indeed do I keep them? I live alone and even when there were a lot of family members in the house, this room was a retreat. When I'm tired or stressed from daily life, I come in and close the door." Amy drew her fingers across the books. "I just wander back and forth letting my eyes embrace their names, remembering many of them and what they said to me from their pages. I was fortunate to have known many of them. They bared their souls with the written word when they would not speak it. Many were the times their words would say to me what I had been trying to find myself but the words eluded me. Even while in their presence a writer is often too guarded to say what they can write."

Amy pulled a book from a shelf and blew the dust off it. She leafed through it and then closed it. "So they are very much my dear friends whom I can reach out to time and time again when I need them and languish in the feel of the covers, and the turning of the pages. Even when the dust lays heavy upon them. Unlike others whom we have lost to the grave, these authors can reach out from beyond the grave. The beauty of their words float through eternity. My only sadness is that I wish I could write that well."

"Amy! You know you write well. Amy has always had a pen in her hand as long as I have known her. All over her room and dropped around the house are pieces of paper with her scribblings. Don't let her fool you. Ignore her self-deprecating."

Amy took a cigarillo from a box on the table. "You're right, Bessie. I am anything but self-deprecating. I refuse to allow lesser poets to believe they can do better." With that said, she lit the cigarillo much to Bea's horror.

"I hope I don't offend you with the smoke, Bea. I believe women in your end of the country probably pick up a cigar or pipe once in awhile, not to be outdone by the men."

"That might be true, but not in our home. My mother is very strict on what women should do and should not do."

"Really! That's too bad. I don't want to disgrace womanhood but I think we should be able to pleasure in many of the things that men do."

"I don't think we should compete with what men do."

"If you had grown up in this house you could not help but compete with men. It was filled with my brothers and my father's whims. I did not want to be left out. I guess that's why this high faluting society here loves to gossip behind my back, as if I didn't know."

Bea had straightened her skirt several times seemingly in agitation. "I've only lived in the world of women. My father died some years ago and I'm an only child. My mother was very protective of me. Maybe too much so. But I just know that life."

"Look at the clock. Carley will be home soon and I expect that Bea's children and Howard are wondering where she might be. Amy, I'll see you again soon. I'm more than excited to read your manuscript. I promise I will shutter myself away and give it my fullest attention."

"I know I can depend on that. You have my complete respect when it comes to your critique. Let me please drive you home."

"Oh, no. You know it's just a short walk around the pond."

"It was so nice meeting you, Amy. I would love to read your poems and I am sure Howard would be delighted to see them."

"Well, tell that husband of yours, I have not seen him since he has been back. I will feel slighted if he does not show his face around here some time soon."

"I will. Thank you so much again for the tea."

Bessie and Bea walked in silence around the pond. Bea kept her eyes on the boys with their small boats sailing them in the wind, yelling at each other to grab their boat if it capsized. When the house came into view, Bessie said, "Carley will drive you home. I hope it was a nice day?"

"Certainly interesting and to say from my life, different. Very different."

****

The months eased their way into the past. Tinges of color marked the trees. The windows of Oakwood were opened slightly to let in the cool, refreshing breeze that they had lived without during the sweltering summer months. Bessie heard the children playing out in the back garden, yelling, "Give me a push. I think I can go higher." Bessie watched them play from the solarium. Betty and little Bea sat quietly on the ground watching their cousins battle over the two swings that hung from the large oak. She had had the children over to her home often during the summer months. It was easy for her to have them entertained and be out from under Bea's feet in that small apartment. Social activity between the two families had stuttered along and Bessie felt she had done all she could do to make Bea comfortable. But there had been no occasions when Bea seemed to enjoy herself. Instead she continually declined any invitations to teas or luncheons, saying that she did not feel well. It was a common excuse which Bessie finally understood to mean she did not want to be included in Boston's social doings. Bessie felt empathy for Bea. She could not comprehend living in the West but she did know that she would take advantage of the experience. But that was her and not Bea. She heard the front door open and expecting no one this early in the day, she heard someone calling her name. Bessie stepped onto the upstairs landing and was surprised to see Howard. "Oh, there you are."

"Why are you here this early in the day?"

"I took our mail to work this morning because I was late and didn't have time to open them. At lunch time, I was able to find a few minutes and I received something quite interesting."

"Well, what is it?"

"I decided I wanted to have the family present before I tell anyone. So if you would be a dear sister, could you accommodate me and Bea tonight for dinner?"

Puzzled, Bessie said, "Yes. I'll just tell Rosie to expect two more for dinner. I'm sure we can manage. But, is it serious? Should I warn Mumsie and Papa?"

"Absolutely not! I came to pick up the children and take them home with me. Where are they?"

"As usual, they are playing with their cousins. They are such good girls. I am glad they have gotten to know each other."

"I can't thank you enough Bessie. Bea becomes so exasperated with them so quickly. I cringe at times with her sharp tongue when they do something that displeases her and it seems to be a lot of things. Your home is a good respite for them. I have to get on my way and tell Bea to dress for dinner."

She watched Howard go out and gather the girls and help them into the waiting taxi. She shook her head worrying about the coming evening.

****

Howard and Bea arrived promptly at five. Bessie's parents had been told that they were coming for dinner and that Howard had some special announcement. Bessie found a moment alone with her father in the hallway. "I'm quite worried again. Anything to do with Howard and his announcements are usually disturbing."

"If that is the case, it is not for you to handle. After all, I'm still his father no matter how old he is. Remember that Bess."

Taken aback by the tone of her father's voice Bessie knew he obviously was preparing himself for the worst. Howard had always been his prodigal son and now what was he up to? They entered the parlor where they found Mumsie engaging Bea in conversation.

"My dear, the girls are so wonderful to have here. They have so much energy and seem to be in such good health. I hope they never have to suffer the invalidism of poor health. Without my Bessie, I don't know what I would do." She pulled the knitted throw tighter against her shoulders.

"Howard has told me how many times you were kept to your bed when he was growing up. I was quite fortunate in that my mother was always quite strong and healthy."

"I guess one must be in order to survive the area of the West in which you grew up."

Bea turned to pick up her sherry. "Where I grew up is not a primitive or savage place. We do have doctors, a hospital nearby, good homegrown food, even a small library in town. No, we do not have art museums or even galleries but my mother and I do go quite often to San Francisco where society treats us well." With a more indignant tone, Bea said, "In fact, very well."

Bessie suddenly stood up. "Did anyone hear the doorbell?" No one answered as Bessie hurried out of the room. Everyone sat in anticipation when they heard Bessie's voice and the voice of someone else. All looked startled when she came back into the parlor with George in tow.

"My dear," Mumsie cried, "I thought you were still

in Puerto Rico. Has something happened? Come here right now and give me a kiss."

Howard stood and gave him a quick handshake. "Good to see you," then sat down on the settee next to Bea and took a sip of her sherry. Bea glanced at Howard and then back at George. An ominous feeling made her shudder. No one noticed.

"Well, this is a surprise," Papa said, giving George a pat on the back. "You must have had a long trip from Puerto Rico. Why didn't you telegraph us that you were coming?"

George sat down in the high-backed chair next to Papa and straightened the creases in his pants. Papa offered him a sherry that Bessie had poured. George took it in hand and turned it several times before speaking. "Actually I have not been in Puerto Rico for the last couple of months."

"Really!" Bessie burst out. "Then where have you been? Why the big secret?"

"I didn't mean for it to be a secret. Just that I was tired of Puerto Rico. I seemed to be stuck on someone else's career ladder. Isolated on some middle rung, neither going up or down. Anything would have been better than the daily grind of signing innocuous documents of requests for minor things."

"Wasn't Justine going to join you soon?" Mumsie asked. The air deadened as everyone held their breath. Mumsie seemed to believe that George and Justine were still playing the happy couple.

"Justine is in Albuquerque."

"Albuquerque! Why is she not with you?"

Bessie sensed the conversation was floating into dangerous territory.

"Calm yourself Mumsie, George said. Justine's brother is quite ill again and the doctor suggested he go west to a drier climate. You know how close Justine is to her brother and she thinks she is the one most capable of taking care of him."

Unlike her usual temperament, anger flashed in Mumsie's eyes and her lips tightened in indignation. "Never mind, but whatever the case, a wife should be with her husband. First she goes off to Europe on some mission. Something about church music and now this. I care for the well being of my son and that is her marital obligation. I expected her to live up to it. What do you think of her always running off on some imagined mission, George?"

Denying her an answer, George stood up. "I think I will put my valises up in the guest bedroom if that is alright with you, Bessie?"

Before Bessie could respond, Mumsie said, "If you are going upstairs and you have no answer to my question, you can help me to my bed. I don't think dinner would sit well with me tonight. I'm sorry to take my leave so soon and please, Bea, come again and bring the children."

"I'll go check on dinner," Bessie hastily said. "We do have to wait for Carley. I expect him to be home anytime now. We'll have time later to discuss your news, Howard."

After having spoken to Rosie and being assured that dinner would be ready shortly, Bessie met George coming back down the stairs. Lowering his voice he said, "Bessie, thanks for trying to keep my marriage, if you want to call it that, out of the conversation. Let's step into the library for a minute. I have a few questions."

George ushered Bessie into the library and shut the door. "Why, tell me why, and what is Howard up to? I can tell by his manner that something is in the air. Poor Bea, looks like tragedy has already wiped her life clean. She looks exhausted, almost haunted. I don't know her well but the short life she has lived with Howard has obviously already taken a toll. Hauling two small baby girls around the country. What is he thinking? Don't tell me or apologize for him."

"Okay, I don't know either the news he is going to tell us tonight." Bessie sunk down in a chair by the window.

George strode around the room scanning the books until his eyes fell upon the picture of a woman's bust. As he peered closer, he read the name of Auguste Rodin scrawled across it.

"Where in the world did this come from?"

"Just from a friend of mine."

"Which reminds me. Have you been painting? Is Woodbury still teaching you? You should be on the cove in Ogunquit instead of running around like a mother hen. Don't cover for my marriage. What about yours? All the passion I knew you had has evaporated into the air of this house."

"That's enough. Don't take your frustration out on me. Yes, the air is stifling. You took Mumsie upstairs. Did you tuck her in? Listen to all her aches and frailties of life she recites over and over. Did you notice, Papa keeps his ear horn close by only using it when he wants? Fortunate for him, he shuts it all out. What kind of passion can I have or maintain? My passion comes when I'm alone, not surrounded by the needs of others. Even you have come back looking for something. You won't find it here, George."

"Maybe not. I'm not even sure what I am looking for." George wandered over toward the window where a chess set sat on a small table. "Isn't this Bonpapa's set?"

"Yes." Bessie said quietly.

"Why have you kept it? It's still missing the queen."

"It keeps Bonpapa close by for me. He always kept

me in the game. 'Think!' he would say. Remember? He wanted us to think, to strategize. I always knew he meant it to be more than a game. And here we are. We have not figured out how to win the game." Coming over to the table she ran her finger over the space where the queen had once sat. "Maybe she will come back someday." She reached up to smooth away a tear.

George put his arm around her. "I can't imagine not winning. I refuse to lose anymore. I promise you, Bess, when I win I want you to be with me."

"You have the freedom to win, George. I don't know where my gate is to freedom."

George picked up the king and turned it over in his hand. You know the power of the king is protected by the queen. Who really has the power or the freedom?"

Bessie's eyes flashed in anger. "You know you have both to do with what you want with your life. Bonpapa was my mentor but Bonnemaman really knew what the truth was for my life. And now you say I can do what I want? Tell me, do you know what I want? No, because I can't speak to the truth in this house, in this society, in this world of yours. Whatever that queen represents, I hope she sits alone with strength and keeps that power within herself, not to be used again to fight the wars of her men."

Bessie started to walk toward the door when it opened suddenly and Carley stepped in. "There you two are. I was told you were here George. So good to see you after such a long time. I hope you are staying for a long visit. Carley noticed the angered look on Bessie's face and realized he had stepped in unwanted. He put his arm around Bessie and told her that Rosie had announced dinner.

Papa politely waited until everyone was seated while Rosie filled their glasses with red wine. Then Papa raised his glass saying, "I decided on this magnificent bottle of Margaux because tonight is a very special night. We have not sat together for too many long years and my dimmed eyes delight in seeing all my children. My toast is to all of you for a peaceful life. I see the troubled looks on your faces this evening and I want to tell you something that my dear friend, William James wrote. He said that we ought to be independent of our moods, look on them as external for they come to us unbidden, and feel if possible neither elated nor depressed, but keep our eyes upon our work and, if we have done the best we could in that given condition, be satisfied. I want to drink to my dear friend, my children and let us raise our glasses to Mumsie and pray she feels better in the morning."

Carley raised his glass saying, "I certainly can drink to that. No moods, no anger, and let's laugh like the children, though alas we are not children. But with laughter let us joy in George's new job, my dear Bessie and her painting, and whatever the future holds for Howard." With that being said, Carley drank while the others lifted their glasses slowly and sipped their wine.

Papa sipped his wine and with a grin of delight said, "My god, that is a superb wine. Don't waste one drop or I shall keep the other bottle in my cellar for my last days." Bea smiled politely and thanked Papa. Carley and Papa chattered about business, the books they were reading, amusing themselves with stories, while the others quietly ate. When Rosie had cleared the plates, she brought in two apple pies.

Bessie picked up the dessert knife and started to serve everyone a piece. "These apples came from our tree today."

Carley laughing said, "This proves the old adage that the apple does not fall far from the tree. Look at us, we are all here as family and close to the tree that feeds us tonight."

Howard spoke quietly, with his wine glass in hand, "That may be true for tonight, Carley, but I will soon be leaving my apple behind."

Papa, straining to hear, said, "What did you say, son?"

Howard raised his voice, "I said that I will be leaving soon."

Papa leaned forward toward Howard and said, "Did I hear you right? Did you say you are leaving? You just found a job and have settled your family. When are you going to stop this gallivanting life?"

"I don't see it as gallivanting. Mrs. Kidder wrote and said that her foreman has died and she needs me to take over. After all, I am not taking Bea away this time from her family."

George put down his fork and with irritation in his voice said, "I thought you didn't get along with her?"

Bea shifted in her seat uncomfortably and lowered her eyes.

Howard sharply replied, "Whether I get along with her or not is not the question. The answer is that the job will provide well for my family. That is what I am most concerned about. I want to provide a comfortable living for my family."

"You should have thought about that years ago when you first married. What have you been thinking all the years in between? You've been living on the family money ever since. This time it's the money from the other family." George pushed his chair back, threw his napkin on the table and angrily left the room.

Howard picked up his glass and drank the rest of the wine. "It's a great wine Papa. I wish we could have enjoyed it under better circumstances."

Bessie turned to Bea. "Why don't we give Rose a rest and clear the rest of the table. I'm sure Papa can take Carley and Howard into the library while we're busy."

Carley jumped up to help Papa with his chair. "I have to get my earphone. I believe I left it on the sidetable in the parlor. I want to hear more of what Howard plans to do."

"I'll get it," Howard said and left the dining room. He found the earphone, looked out the front doorway and saw there was a full moon as the garden was softly lit. He took a breath of the fresh evening air and returning to the library heard Papa talking to Carley.

"Where do you think George is? I would hope that he would join us."

"I'm sorry Papa," Howard said, "but I don't think he has anything more he wants to say."

"I'm sorry to hear that. I was hoping we could all rationally discuss the situation."

"There really is nothing further to say. We will be leaving as soon as I can make the arrangements."

Carley cleared his throat. He tried desperately to keep a rule not to intrude on family matters. But Howard's turbulent life had kept Bessie awake night after night with worry. Especially now that Howard had children. He knew Bessie carried tremendous guilt specifically her family's financial burden now a valueless mine on the family's hands. His shenanigans were stressing the family's future. Who knew how long Papa and Mumsie would live and possible extra medical costs if severe illness hit. He was willing to assist from his own purse which was not overly bountiful. He had his own children to worry about. He cleared his throat again. "Howard, understand I do not usually interfere but you have brought your decisions to my table and I cannot help but be concerned. It has not been kept from me how much you have weighed in on the family for advances way beyond what you were able to shoulder responsibly. Can you leave Boston with your heavy debt stowed in your luggage?"

"I do resent your reminding me of my debt as if I am ignoring it. There is such a high and mighty attitude that pervades this house as if no one can fail and if they do, God have mercy on their soul while under this roof."

"Son, control yourself. Your disrespect is unwarranted. We have a lot to be thankful for. Carley has always been a gentleman and gracious to all of us especially when hard times have come. I don't know what your mother and I would do without him and our beloved Bessie."

"Right. Bessie can do no wrong. The guardian angel. Always looked upon and talked about with such reverence. When are you going to respect me as a man?"

Papa put down his earphone. "When you become one."

Rage enveloped Howard. Carley putting a book back on the shelf said, "Howard, I think you've said enough. There was no answer to my question. Take your debt with you and say no more. Make no mistake, I care for the safety and security of your family but will not allow disrespect or disruption under my roof."

Bea and Bessie were scraping the dishes in the kitchen and putting them into a sink of hot water. Neither spoke. Bessie picked up a towel to dry the dishes. "Bea are you happy about going back to California?"

"Bessie, this is your city. I can't imagine myself ever getting use to the extremely different life you lead here. I admire you for handling such a large household and still maintaining your interests. I could never do that. My mother spoiled me too much. I really never had to do anything. Actually, until I married, I never even had to do dishes. I've had to learn a lot quickly and I'm afraid that I don't do it very well."

"My dear, you have had to deal with a lot of hardship that would cause any woman to throw up her hands and pray for help. Having those babies in the middle of nowhere is unimaginable. I never heard of Prescott, Arizona until Howard told us. That's the last dish. Let's sit out on the back stoop to get some fresh air. God only knows, we need it."

Bessie flounced out her skirt and settled on the top step while Bea sat on the step below. "Bea, I don't blame you for wanting to go home. My mind ran up and down the stairs when I heard that he was leaving Grass Valley and going to Arizona on this 'get rich quick' scheme of digging in the sand and finding copper. You should have given him a pan and told him to go panning for gold on the weekends and let him get it out of his system."

"He did find a nugget once. Look!" Bea pulled on a gold chain that hung around her neck and pulled out an attached gold nugget that lay hidden in her bosom. "That's as far as it got. It was a little beneath him to crouch down in the water all day, sifting and looking and doing it again and again. Too much for Howard! He had bigger dreams and I couldn't stop him. It was not the life I dreamed of. I didn't know what else to do. I'm so sorry Bessie about the debts he piled up with your family. I don't know what to say to any of you." Tears started streaking down Bea's face.

Bessie slid down a step and put her arms around her. "You don't have to say anything. It was not your fault. None of us have any anger toward you. You have brought us two marvelous gifts."

"What gifts?"

"Betty and little Bea."

Bea leaned over and hugged Bessie. "Those are the kindest words I've heard. I trust you so much with my children."

They were interrupted by some violent noises coming from the garden. Bessie jumped up in alarm and ran around into the side yard. Bea trundled after her wondering what could possibly happen now. She heard what she thought was Howard yelling. Bessie ran toward the men.

Howard's voice erupted through the night with curses. "You s.o.b.! Who do you think you are challenging my life? What the hell about yours? Where is your wife? Off again, traipsing around Europe. At least, mine is here with me."

Bessie stopped in horror seeing George smashing his fist into the side of Howard's head. He staggered backward a few steps and then threw himself upon George.

"Oh, my God!" screamed Bessie.

Carley ran over and reached down to pull them apart but they continued in a fierce struggle. Bessie, putting her hands up against her head saw Papa in the library window watching. Bea was kneeling on the ground sobbing uncontrollably.

Carley kept yelling, "That's enough!" He was able to get them up off the grass but Howard took another swing crushing his fist into George's jaw.

Suddenly Bessie saw Papa walking toward them. He stopped within a short distance. "Carley, get the hose. If they want to act like dogs, then treat them like dogs. Did you hear me boys. Carley, go now!"

Carley backed away and turned toward the garden faucet. George and Howard stood panting, glaring at each other. Then they flew at each other again. Coming back with the garden hose turned to full force, Papa grabbed it and sprayed Howard and George. Fighting off the water, they parted from each other and Howard fell down upon the garden bench. Papa handed the hose back to Carley who stood in amazement at the scene. Papa with great disgust in his voice said, "I never in my life thought I would see my two grown boys behave like silly children in a schoolyard. Both of you have upset the house. Get out of here NOW!"

****

HOWARD

September, 1911
Grass Valley, California

Dearest Mumsie and Papa,

I know it has been a disgraceful long time that I have not written. Sending a telegram about the birth of Thomas Wren Ward 3rd, although a joyous event does not excuse my not putting pen to paper. Many a night my prayers have asked forgiveness for upsetting my beloved family but courage seemed to evade my writing. I never meant to leave under such horrendous circumstances. Your kind guidance toward us during all our growing years would never have given cause for George and my excessively bad behavior. My thoughts have been that life had just strangled us both to unconsciously act out our frustrations. I have not heard from George, but do pray that he has forgiven me also, as I him.

But now we are settled. Mrs. Kidder has given us a beautifully shaded, thick walled, "adobe" house, near her, and just beside the railroad. We have again actively become part of the social life here and everyone adores the children. We have taken up tennis once more and have undertaken some musical shows for charity. I usually have the comic lead and as probably you do, I wonder myself, why? I never thought of myself as a humorous character but obviously it shows through on stage, and I do enjoy it. I expect my enjoyment comes when for a short while I can pretend to be someone else and make a character who I want to portray.

As to my job here as supervising the railroad, it has its difficulties especially dealing with Mrs. Kidder.

The Narrow Gauge was earning dividends regularly and Mrs. Kidder received a nice income from the road, but little is being done towards the future or toward meeting the increasing competition of automobiles. I feel that something should be done toward broad gauging the road, which would greatly increase its value and the chances of getting a buyer for it. I have argued the point with Mrs. K., but she, always suspicious, seems to think somehow I am scheming to get the railroad away from her.

Nevertheless, the happy news is that Bea is expecting again. I know it seems so soon after having Tom, but children so much bring joy into life at times when we feel we need them the most. We are so lucky to have a marvelous nanny to lighten Bea's work. Bea has her reprieves when she goes to San Francisco with her mother on shopping trips. I give my best efforts to make life good to her.
I must close for now.
Your loving son,
Howard

Howard put down his pen and looked out the office window. He watched the workers replacing some of the old trestles under the hot sun. They wore kerchiefs around their necks and some had an extra one sticking out from their pocket. The workers had come mostly from the eastern mountain areas looking for a better life along with a few negroes. At the stroke of noon, the tools were laid down and the mountain men drifted off to their own private tree. The two Chinese workers and the negroes sat beside the rails in two separate groups while the Chinese pulled out their reed baskets and chopsticks and hurriedly started to eat as if the food was going to be snatched from their mouths at any moment.

The negroes watched them with amusement. These men have hard working lives but little is ever said between the groups. Howard leafed through the papers on his desk but his mind wandered to the men outside. The Civil War seemed not to change anything. We are still a divided country. What little pittance these men receive when they line up before me on Saturday to get their pay. But they seem to survive. I wonder what it would be like to step into their pants each morning? Do they get up looking forward to the day? Do they really believe they will have a different future? Are they free? I haven't read anything that makes me believe that those negroes and Chinese can come and go, live and work wherever they please. Even those mountain men are talked about as if they were fools. But who really are the fools? We? The so-called American aristocrats who dialogue continually about the virtues of democracy? Howard leaned back in his chair and smirked. Well, who am I to speak? Born into the tinseled aristocracy from which I have tried a lifetime to brush from my shoulders. It fit my family but not me. He looked out the window again. Could I be one of them? God, I'm restless.

The door swung open with a thud as it hit the wall behind. Howard jerked his head around and saw Bea standing there with an anguished look. "Howard, what have you said to my mother? I can't understand what she is ranting about but it has something to do with you. I couldn't calm her down. Do something!"

"It's okay, Bea. Calm down. You don't need to get yourself so upset especially in the state you're in now."

"What state is that?"

"You're carrying a baby. What else?"

"Of course, I am. I'm aware of it all day long. That's why I want you to stop arguing with my mother. Can't you just do your work and let us live in peace?"

"Peace! You want peace. How can anyone have peace around here with your mother obviously swallowing something that makes her irrational? I've tried to talk some sense into her about a reasonable business plan but she thinks I just want to steal the railroad from her. Listen, Bea. If she doesn't want to expand the gauge and make it competitive with the future, we might as well pack up now and go. The business will collapse without investment and we will just be here to pick up the pieces."

Bea stared at Howard in disgust. "Haven't we already done that? I remember picking up the pieces in Arizona."

Howard kicked the wastebasket and yelled, "Go back and coddle your mother. I can't do anything more."

Bea stepped into her mother's sitting room and found her in the rocking chair with her eyes closed. "Mother!" There was no response. She put her hand on her mother's shoulder and shook it gently. "Mother, Mother, are you okay?" She shook her again causing her mother's head to fall over to the side. Panicked, she ran down the stairs screaming, "Someone call the doctor." No one in the house responded. Grabbing the telephone she dialed the operator. "Operator, I need a doctor immediately!" she shouted. "I'm Bea Kidder and my mother is not waking up. Please, please, hurry!"

She barely heard the operator's response. Running back upstairs she grabbed the water pitcher from the sidetable along with the handtowel. Hastily, she poured water on the towel and washed it over her mother's face. She could not keep her head up so she lifted her forward and pulled her down on the floor. Grabbing a pillow from the chair she placed it under her mother's head, pleading, "Mother, Mother, please wake up." She kissed her on the forehead imploring, "Please, please, Mother, I need you. Don't leave me."

She heard loud talking and footsteps hurrying up the stairs. Looking up she saw Dr. Woods with Howard right behind him. Dr. Woods bent down toward Mrs. Kidder and took her pulse. Taking out his stethoscope he listened for a heartbeat. Glancing up at Howard, he said, "She seems to have a steady heartbeat but I think her pressure is low. Help me get her to the bed." Bea heard the children running up the stairs and not wanting them to see their grandmother, she hurriedly left to take them outside again.

Dr. Woods and Howard managed to settle Mrs. Kidder on her bed. "Start rubbing her arms rapidly." Dr. Woods slapped her cheeks. "We have to get the blood flowing to get her pressure back up." He reached into his bag and pulled out some smelling salts. He placed it under her nose and in a few seconds she started to cough and shake her head. "I think she'll be fine now"

He turned to Bea who had come back into the room and asked her to tell the maid to bring up some hot tea. Dr. Woods pulled a chair up next to the bed and slumped down into it. He took a deep breath then whispered to Howard, "That was a close one. Truly, her heartbeat was barely audible. Have you noticed anything wrong with her lately?"

"Well, she has been acting very erratic. She seems angry all the time and I have difficulty just talking about daily things. She does stay up here in her sitting room most of the day. That's very unlike her. So I don't know."

"I'll sit with her awhile. Maybe she will come around enough for me to talk with her. You might as well go back to work. I'll call you if I need you."

"Thanks for coming so quickly. Your being here

will comfort Bea."

Howard passed Bea coming back upstairs. "Don't worry Bea. Dr. Woods said she will be alright."

Bea ignored Howard's comments and went on up to her mother's room. She picked up a handkerchief that was on the nightstand to put down the tea tray. Putting the handkerchief in her pocket she noticed that it was wet and seemed to have an odd smell. Bringing it up to her nose and whiffing it, she suddenly felt faint. "Oh, my God, I think I know what it is. Could it possibly be?"

"Dr. Woods," she said as she handed him the handkerchief, "Could this be laudanum? It smells the same as when I was given it for the birth of the babies."

"Good God, I think you're right. Why would she be taking this, Bea?"

"I don't know. I really don't know."

"Has she been complaining about any pain?"

"If she has, Mother never tells anyone. You know her. She will never let on that she is sick."

"Has she been drinking?"

"Just her usual sherry in the evening, I think."

"Where does she keep it?"

"Down in the sideboard in the parlor."

"Let's go have a look."

Bea opened the sideboard door where the sherry was kept. Dr. Woods saw a half empty bottle of sherry. He scoured the room thoroughly opening every drawer, searching every nook and cranny and finding nothing he asked, "Is there any other place where she might have kept some liquor?"

"No, not that I know of."

"Let's look around her sitting room."

They went back up to the sitting room where Dr. Woods scanned the room carefully. "I would be willing to give odds that there is another bottle in this room.

He spotted a knitting basket next to the rocking chair. He threw the skeins of wool out of the basket and reached into the bottom. Withdrawing his hand he showed Bea an empty bottle of scotch. Gasping, she turned away in anguish, not wanting Dr. Woods to see her cry.

"Why don't you go out to see if the children are alright? I'll go sit with your mother. We are going to have a serious talk as soon as she is able."

Dr. Woods had begun to nod off when he was awakened by rustling sounds. Mrs. Kidder, while trying to sit up, was mumbling something that Dr. Woods could not understand. "Sarah, you're going to be alright. Here, let me help you sit up. We have some talking to do."

"No, no! Leave me alone. I can do it myself and why, in heaven's name, are you here?"

"That's what we're going to talk about, Sarah. First, let me fix you a cup of tea to help clear your head."

Mrs. Kidder pursed her lips as she watched Dr. Woods pour the tea. He handed it gently to her and sat back in the chair.

"Now it's time Sarah. Tell me why you are taking laudanum and not to put it politely, swigging booze from hidden bottles?"

"What foolishness are you spouting? I do nothing of the sort."

"I'm not sitting here, Sarah, just to make polite conversation. I was summoned to find you passed out and barely breathing. You're lucky that I was able to get here quickly. I don't know how much of that scotch you drank before you inhaled that laudanum but enough of it would have killed you. You keep on and I'll be signing your death certificate."

Sarah rose up from her pillow and hurled her teacup at Dr. Woods. "You get out of here and don't come back! I will do what I want to do and no one is going to tell me different. Did that sneaky son-in-law of mine call you? You know he's trying to get my railroad? I'm fine. I just have to keep my eye on him."

"Sarah, I think we all will have to keep our eye on you. Remember you have a daughter and grandchildren who love you. Would you want Bea to find you dead in your rocking chair next time?"

"Get out!"

Dr. Woods wiped the tea off his vest then closed his satchel. "May God look after you, Sarah."

On his way out the front door he found Bea on the porch. "I'm sorry Bea. I did the best I could. She denies all of it. Unfortunately it is going to be up to you to watch her. But call me if things get out of control again and maybe I can have one of my colleagues help out. This is not a medical condition as much as it is a mental condition. You take care of yourself now."

Bea sat on the porch sadly watching Dr. Woods' car go down the drive. Tears came splashing down her cheeks as she rocked patting her stomach where a new baby was growing. The laughter of the girls sprinkled across the garden and floated on the gentle breeze. Her head lay back and she gazed at the approaching dark clouds and whispered as if someone was listening. "Life is going to change again and I am dragged through the world like a tired rag doll. I can't bear it!"

Suddenly her back stiffened. Her hand reached around to her lower spine when a prolonged sharp pain wrapped around her body. My God, the baby. The baby is coming. She awkwardly pulled herself up out of the chair and called through the foyer, "Someone call Dr. Woods right now."

Several hours passed before she smelled the scent of laudanum softly enter into her body and she thankfully let herself drift. She heard troubled talking. Something about the baby. Not wanting to hold the baby or speak to anyone, she drowned herself in sleep. Upon waking she found herself alone and the house quiet.

****

BESSIE

The doorbell rang insistently. Not expecting anyone, Bessie apprehensively opened the door.

"Telegram, ma'am. Would you sign for it?"

"Certainly." Bessie scribbled her name quickly and murmuring, "Thank you," stepped back into the parlor ripping open the envelope. Her eyes fell on the indelible words: **Moved to San Francisco. Bea, children and I fine. Address. 136 Fillmore Street. Will write soon. Howard**

Bessie felt the scream rising in her throat. Throwing her head back, she silently implored, "Please God, not again! Not again! Tell me it's not happening."

Hearing the front door open, she was surprised to see Carley come into the parlor. "Good grief Bessie, what's the matter with you? You look like you are about to faint. Sit down. I'll get you a glass of water." Carley noticed the telegram in her hand and took it. Fury flashed across his face. He poured her a glass of water from the pitcher on the sideboard. Handing it to her, he said with an unusual forcefulness, "I want you to understand and understand this well. You are not responsible for your brother. This is the life he wants to live and you cannot change that."

Bessie choking up, uttered, "But what about the children?"

"What can you do about the children? They are his, not yours."

"But they must be terribly confused."

"We're all confused. We never know what to expect from him. Bea will have to nurture the children, not you. She is their mother and we have to pray that she can handle the situation. I think we have to support her, not your brother, whatever happens."

"How do I tell my parents? Haven't they had

enough? It's not only Howard but Mumsie is so worried about George. She wants to know why Justine is not with him and I have no way to tell her that their marriage is over."

"Let me talk to your parents. I believe I can discuss this in a calmer, more matter of fact, manner. I'm going to go say hello to the children first. Calm down and remember that you have your own family to take care of. Remember you are carrying another child and it needs you to worry about it and that includes me!"

Bessie sipped the water several times, thinking how adamant and insistent Carley was in his choice of words. "He rarely involves himself in family affairs except the terrible situation the last time Howard was here. And what was that remark about her having to worry about their family which she readily agreed, but worry also about him. Why should I have to worry about him? Is there something happening that I don't know about?"

Sounds of giggling children jolted Bessie awake. Startled that she had nodded off, she sat up and straightened her dress wondering what time is it? I had no idea I was that exhausted to have fallen asleep in a chair. It must be close to dinnertime. Looking into the kitchen she found Rosie bustling about.

Wiping her hands on her apron, looking hassled, she said, "I had dinner almost ready, Bessie, when Carley came in telling me to put it off for half an hour. He said something about talking to your parents."

"Oh, dear! Then don't rush. I'll go up and see. Get off your feet for awhile."

Bessie tapped on her parents' door and carefully opened it not wanting to interrupt. Papa, in a voice filled with strain said, "Carley has told us the news and we have made a decision. Come sit down and I want no opposition to what I have to say. Your mother and I have decided that we must take a strong hand in this unfortunate situation. We are not on our death beds yet and I for one do not expect to be for some time. I am remorseful and I might have retreated into a retired life with my books and left the shenanigans of my children to others. The reality of Howard, and I do not exclude George, in the outcomes of their decisions have jolted my senses to use a stronger patriarchal hand. Bonpapa never let his hand drop but I, unfortunately, did not follow his example."

"But,"......

"I want no 'buts' Bessie. You have done enough. I have an extraordinary deep respect for all you've done but now is the time for me to take back my authority. Mumsie and I will be taking the train to San Francisco as soon as arrangements can be made."

"Mumsie?" Bessie said with surprise. "Mumsie? Papa, that is a long trip."

"Dear, I think I should go with your father. We will have a compartment and I do want to see the West. I have never been but have heard marvelous stories and after talking with Bea, I am sure San Francisco is a civilized city."

Papa laughed. "Yes, I don't expect to be involved in some shootout on the street with some drunken cowboy. I understand that the streets are paved now. The world moves on." He picked up his pipe.

"I guess there is nothing I can say?"

"No, nothing. It's settled."

Mumsie picked up her embroidery. "Now, go get some sleep."

****

GEORGE

George pulled his overcoat tighter across his chest. Snow started to lightly flake across his shoulders. He picked up his pace as he walked down Fifth Avenue toward Delmonico's. He glanced at his watch and realized he was late. His mind flashed across the short note he had found on his desk when he returned from lunch. It had read: *Dear George, I have arrived home to New York from France. I would very much enjoy your company for dinner tonight. I do think we have much to talk about. Would you be so kind to meet me at 6:00 at Delmonico's?*
Justine

He had read it over and over trying to read between the lines. "There are so many questions. Home, for instance. What did she consider home now? What did she really want to talk about? And then she just signed her name, 'Justine'. That was unlike her. No sentiment." He had telephoned the Cutting home and was told that Justine would be in later. He left a message that he would meet her at Delmonico's at six. Now it was six thirty. It was very unlike him to ever be late but his footsteps dragged as his mind raced over what he wanted to say. Reaching the glass front of Delmonico's he glanced through the window. He saw Justine sitting alone, her fingers bending a flower from the vase on the table. Sadness consumed him for a moment as he thought how beautiful she is. I don't think I ever told her how the beauty of her carried me through every day.

He handed his overcoat to the maitre d' and slipped into the chair across from Justine. A wispy smile crossed her face. "George, you look good and it was nice of you to come."

"Why wouldn't I? Am I not still your husband?"

Justine lowered her eyes. "Yes, of course, you are."

George, with a sense of impending sorrow, tried to find words. He leaned across the table and pulled a rose from the vase. Taking Justine's hand, he placed the rose gently in it and closed her fingers over it. "Is my being your husband the reason why we are here?"

She slipped the rose back into the vase. "Why don't you tell me what has been happening with you. I truly would like to know. Then I will tell you what is happening in my life. Can we start there?"

George straightened his shoulders and swept his hand over his hair. He motioned to the waiter to bring some menus. "Why don't we order first?" George opened the menu and pretended intense interest but he could not keep his mind focused.

Justine felt the uneasiness in George's demeanor. "I'll have the filet mignon with the asparagus. I understand it is the best thing on the menu."

"Oh, yes, yes!" He placed their order with the waiter and requested the best bottle of Chateauneuf de Pape.

"Well, now, tell me about your law firm. It is your old firm, isn't it?"

"It's doing fine. Nothing much changed and as is usually the case law can be dull and the cases plod along in their own good time. Nothing exciting." George tasted the wine and nodded to the waiter that it was fine. He filled their glasses and George raising his said, "But I have just been named as the new Commissioner of Parks."

"Really! That is exciting news. Father will be so delighted to hear. He has always been involved in making New York a better cultural and beautiful city."

"I don't expect to be seeing your father. Your parents were never fond of me. I expect they enjoy having you back in their home. Are you going to stay long this time?"

"That is my news. I have been asked to put together my ideas on Gregorian chant and music in general for publication. I cannot help but say I was astonished that someone had taken note of my years of work. As you may have seen it as foolishness, others saw value in it."

"How can you say I saw it as foolishness? I did not! But I am aware, as you certainly are that it did interfere in our marriage. I thought we had a marriage. I played my part but you did not take seriously our vows and made a life outside this sham of a marriage." George took his napkin and ran it roughly over his mouth. He looked around the dining room with slight embarrassment for fear that someone had heard his raised voice.

Getting control of his anger, he said, "Excuse me Justine. My emotions are on edge. I did love you so very much but you have been scraping that love from my heart for a long time. We both had a love of music but you made it your life alone without me. How can you explain that and where and what am I to do now?"

Tears welled in Justine's eyes as she held her head down and dabbed at them with her tiny white handkerchief. She clutched it in her hand and speaking with tinges of sadness. "George, I floated along in a dream with you when we were young and the music lulled us into what was never meant to be. I could never blend my life with yours. Gregorian chants beguiled me into their world, not yours. I'm so sorry. I can't bear to see your anguish. And I am the cause of it." Justine tucked her handkerchief away and slid out of her chair. "George, I will carry you in my heart but I must leave."

Struck as if he could not take another breath, George watched her wend her way through the tables. He emptied his glass of wine and motioned to the waiter for the bill. Out on the sidewalk, the snow was coming down with a heaviness that caused him to lean against the building. He stared upward, not moving, not thinking, as New York passed him by.

****

George walked along the packed red dirt road hearing the distant roar of the ocean. "How good the fresh salt air feels on my face. I could live every day inhaling the scent of the Atlantic mist." He lengthened his stride now anticipating seeing the weathered grey shingled house overlooking the cove. He raced up the steps and banged on the knocker wanting it answered quickly. "C'mon, c'mon, it's cold out here."

Bessie opened the door and witnessed a shivering George standing before her. "George! What are you doing here? Come in before cold death grips you."

"I can always depend upon you to turn a tired phrase. Yes, it does seem to have me in its arms."

"I'll get you some hot coffee." Bessie picked up a decanter and poured some applejack into a snifter. "Here, drink this and go warm yourself by the fire while I brew the coffee."

George stood in front of the fire rubbing his arms and sipping the applejack. The strength of the alcohol made him shudder but he felt warmth travel through his body. He looked out the large bayed window and watched absentmindedly as wave after wave filled the cove. "Ah, water, it seems the perfect cradle to lull you into the grave." He leaned his head against the window and imagined himself sliding over the rocks into the water.

Bessie placed the coffee pot down and settled herself in the overstuffed chair beside the window. George, not speaking, poured himself some and sat down in the other chair and watched again the waves.

"You don't have to say a word, George. I'll wait. It's so unexpected to have you here. It's lonely here in the winter. It's soothing just watching the barrenness of the cove without a soul's footsteps in the sand. It mesmerizes me into such a blissful state. Believe me if you can, I think only of me while I sit here."

"I'm sorry if I've crashed your secluded nest but I didn't know where else to go." Bessie noticed George's hand shaking as he tried to lift his coffee cup. "Where's Woodbury? I expected him to be here. I thought I might pick up some paints and try my hand."

"You must be teasing. I've never seen you pick up a brush. Charles is off in the Caribbean. He has found a new muse to follow there."

Bessie pulled a shawl off the footstool and wrapped it around her shoulders. She noticed George's face gather a wistful look as he watched the cove.

He emptied his snifter, picked up his coffee and said, "I had dinner the other night with Justine."

"I gather it did not go well by the look on your face."

"Of course not! I've suffered so much in my efforts to control my emotions concerning this marriage. I've walked miles on the sidewalks of New York, not wanting to go home. Home! What an empty word. As if I have ever had a home since our wedding. I can't understand why. For years I've felt abandoned moving here and there trying to find a place I could call home but it is always empty. I keep a great distance from friends because the embarrassment is just too much for me trying to make excuses about the whereabouts of Justine. Sometimes I don't even know. I don't know! I came because you are the closest being I have that might have some understanding. I want to go on but my feet are mired in this mud of a marriage. I want to wash away this part of my life. It has drained me physically and emotionally and I will not be alive again until I rid myself of its oppression. You as a woman must have some insight. You married Carley and I think it's a good marriage, or am I wrong?"

Bessie snuggled down in the chair, and bent her head. She contemplated the situation she suddenly, unwantedly, found herself in. How do I answer truthfully?

"I don't know how to tell you, George, but women feel differently about marriage. Not in the beginning though. The life we are born into dictates to us very early on that we are expected to be married, expected to bear children, expected to maintain a home. Expected! Expected! Expected!" Bessie sat up straight in her chair. Her face tightened, in not quite anger, but a sense of wrongness. "And what we live are those expectations but inside, deep inside, some of us resent and many of us rebel against those expectations."

"But you have not rebelled. And I didn't think you bore any resentment about your life."

"And how do you know that?" Bessie got up and poured herself some applejack. She moved toward the window, grabbing her throw from the chair.

"I just thought… " George's words evaporated as he looked disconcertedly at Bessie.

She stood staring out the window pulling the throw tighter over her shoulders. "That's what everyone does, they just think, therefore it must be. Is it shocking that some of us might want it different? Do you know what happens when the kisses are gone; the thoughtful little acknowledgments that we are loved fade? We watch the flowers fade and lose their petals knowing how much like us they are as we fade into age. Bessie sagged down in the chair again. "Have you noticed George that I am pregnant again? Have you? I start all over again, nursing a child, watching over their rearing, their education, praying for their lives to contain a modicum of happiness in this insane world. When is it over for me? And now you are here asking what happened?"

The moments ticked off the grandfather clock that stood near the door. The ticking started to bang in George's head. He held his head and put his hands over his ears. The chimes announcing the hour bounced off the walls. He grabbed his handkerchief and wiped his glasses. Without looking up he wiped the handkerchief across his eyes. He was embarrassed that he could not hold back his emotions. He waited until he could catch his breath again. "Bessie, I never meant to bring you grief. I've always held onto the idea that you, as I have always known you, could keep me close in your thoughts. Have I gone from that? Have I not understood you as I have not understood Justine? I thought you were different than Justine. I believe that Justine never wanted children and I believe now she never wanted a home with me. I thought you could tell me why she married me?" George wiped his eyes again and tucked the handkerchief back in his pocket.

Bessie also became aware of the ticking of the clock. She wondered how much of her life was ticking off. Sometimes it seemed to stop and then pick up the pace faster and faster as if there was little time to live. Maybe it was her heart that was beating faster and she could hear it.

George stepped over to the chess table and noticed an unfinished game. He stood seemingly concentrating on a possible move. Finally, he picked up the queen and studied the board. Suddenly, he slammed it down on the board in front of the king and angrily blurted, "Check and mate! That's what she's done. Game over!"

"A game! You saw your marriage as a game?"

"No, but I believe that Justine was playing a game. Maybe a cat and mouse game."

"If it was a game, then were not you the cat? I seem to recall how persistent you were that she marry you. You said that you both loved music so well that it would be in your life together. She kept it in her life and is pursuing it with an enviable passion. You became a lawyer and left the music behind. Have you forgotten the newspaper engagement announcement, although I shudder knowing that it was written with a soiled hand wanting to titillate the readers. But it did say that you had remarked that if she didn't marry you, she wouldn't see you again. Was that a threat?"

George flinched in anger. Bessie picked up the queen from the board. "Look at her, George. The queen may have all the power but sometimes she succumbs to her own demise in order to protect the male. Maybe Justine does not want to give up her power anymore and I, for one, respect that." Bessie put the queen in George's hand. "Look at it again George and think of the life of a woman."

"I will be working with Justine on her new book on music. I hope to put the music back into my life. I want to hear it again." Bessie picked up her shawl that she had thrown on the chair and said, "You can use the guest room upstairs. I hope we can have a pleasant dinner together."

****

HOWARD

Howard paced up and down the train platform, tugging at his hat and nervously rubbing his hands. The train was supposed to be on time and he had reflected on what he was going to say to his parents, especially his father. We're still living in a rooming house as I have not yet been able to find a house with no money coming in at the moment. Having worked for the railroad I had all kinds of privileges and prerogatives. Free transportation passes over all railroads, free telegrams and free express company "franks"; so I could ship ourselves and our chattels wherever we wished without expense. When I put in an invoice for this move to San Francisco I hadn't told management that I had resigned my position. Crossing my fingers I had hoped that I could get the family to San Francisco before they found out. I knew of no other way of leaving Grass Valley without funds. We are existing on the little monies I have left from my last pay check. Howard placed his hand in his pocket and fingered the few dollars he had left.

His mind wandered to Bea's situation and the bill they now owed the doctor when a train whistle thundered through the air. Howard looked down the track and saw the oncoming train. Flashing through his mind was the realization how easy it would be to stand on the tracks and let what happens, happen. Bringing himself back to reality as the engine pulled past him, he scanned the windows finally seeing his mother's worried face. He moved toward the window then noticed how gray lined her face seemed to be. She was always so beautiful I guess I never saw the years passing, always seeing her as my mother. He saw his own mortality in her face. It must have been an agonizing trip for her. He choked back his emotions as he came face to face with the fact that this might be the last he would spend time with them, especially his mother. Suddenly, she spotted him and started to wave. He waved back and jumped on to the train to help his father with the luggage.

"Howard!" his mother cried. "Oh, Howard, I thought we would never get here. One would never know how big this country really is."

His father shook his hand and asked him to retrieve some of the bags from the overhead. The conductor grabbed two valises and his father had two. Howard picked up two more and was stricken with the idea that with all this luggage they must be expecting to stay for a long time. Oh, God, he thought, I hope not. I have enough family to deal with.

Howard managed to get his parents settled into their hotel. His mother seemed quite pleased with the accommodations and pulled back the curtains to look out upon the city. "My, Howard, it's quite beautiful. I didn't expect the hills and the water wrapping around the city. When do we get to see Bea and the children?"

"Tomorrow afternoon, Mumsie. We are all going out for lunch. Why don't you settle yourself in your room and Papa and I will go down to the lounge. You can have your dinner here in the hotel. I will see you tomorrow." Howard bent down and kissed her on the cheek.

She grabbed his arm and looking up said, "I'm so glad we are here. I just wanted to make sure you were all right after your having left Mrs. Kidder."

"I'm fine, Mumsie. There is nothing to worry about. Papa, would you like a drink?"

"Certainly I could do with something strong at the moment. Let's let your mother rest and we will find the bar. I'd like to see how bars are in the ole' West," Papa said with a wink.

Howard and his father settled themselves into some comfortable chairs in front of the hotel's fireplace and ordered brandies. His father pulled his chair closer so he could be sure to hear Howard. "I'd like to hear your plans, son. We all thought you had finally settled down in Boston when you up and left for a position with Mrs. Kidder again with whom, as I understood from you, that you had problems working with her from the beginning. Was your judgment so clouded that you thought Mrs. Kidder had changed? We older people do not tend to change. Your mother and I are here for one reason and one reason only, and that is to make sure you will present yourself well as a concerned husband, father and especially an adult. And we will be staying until the time we can be assured that you have a permanent situation and your family is safely ensconced in a community that will afford them a proper education and an avenue into polite society."

He had great admiration for his father and a conscious love though he had never found the words to express it. It had lain dormant for all his years. He was now, more than ever, reluctant to tell him how he felt and about the life his father had chosen. He recalled fondly the stories of his days of wandering through the Amazon in search of animal or new plant species. He sat stunned glancing at his father while slumping down in his chair. He felt like the scolded child again who had dared to leave the house during the snow storm. He cleared his throat and gave an effort to speak but nothing intelligible came. He took a large gulp of his brandy and waved to the waiter to bring another.

Papa's eyes fell on the second brandy that the waiter had brought. He waved him off when he asked if he also wanted another. "And why do you need another, Howard? I have a suspicion that you are having difficulty in explaining your plans."

"I've been trying my level best but I've found that I have fallen into the trap of believing in what people tell me. I'm too trusting and they sense that and seize the opportunity to take advantage. I have kept my integrity and they find it easy to blame the business failures on me. Yes, the money is gone but not to my doing. It lies in the pockets of the deceivers and I have no way to retrieve it. Dear God, I would love to pay you back and someday I will." Howard leaned his head back and slid his hand into his pocket. He felt the wrapped object and a feeling of assurance crept over him. With a sense of resolve he said, "Be assured Papa, I will pay you back."

Papa folded his hands on his chest and let his eyes circle the room. He noticed an eclectic group of people, some well dressed and others who seemingly had searched their closets for something presentable. There were strings of pearls dangling across some French laced bosoms and skirts of silk. He was struck by how many of the men were dressed in leather pants, even sporting leather jackets. He wondered how many of them might be sporting a gun tucked inside their jackets. After all, wasn't this the Wild West? But most of all, it appeared that many of them postured the aura of wealth. It was no secret since the gold strikes of 1849 had made many prosperous and some to extremes of wealth. "Why has not my son, a geologist, been able to make even a modest living?" He looked at Howard fiddling with something in his pocket and said, "Son, I am still waiting for an answer. Where do you go from here?"

"Remember my childhood friend, Junius Brown?"

"Yes, I do. Fine young man. You mean to tell me that he is here in California?"

"Junius introduced me to his brother-in-law who has decided to open an agency to sell various products mostly for the home. He invited me to join him in a partnership and I accepted."

"What kind of salary is he offering?"

Howard took another gulp of his brandy. "I'll be working on commission until the company grows a solid financial base." He felt choked to tell him the rest. "And I will have to live with them in Los Angeles until that time when we feel the company is growing enough that I can bring Bea and the children down."

He dropped his head not wanting to see or hear anymore from his father. "I gather what your mother and I are here for is to take care of your family. And that is what we will do, no more, no less can you expect from us. It is up to you to make this new position a success on your own. I will hear no more whining. You take responsibility. No blame!"

Howard glanced at the door to the lobby and pleaded for a moment he could escape but he was left paralyzed in the presence of his father. Papa pulled out a five dollar note and dropped it on the table. "Pay the bill with this. I have to go see if your mother is ready for dinner. We will see you tomorrow and have plans set for us to find a home for your family." Papa rose and pulled at his vest, buttoned his jacket and strode through the bar toward the stairs. Howard watched in utter defeat.

****

The horn of the boat blasted across the pier causing the people waving to suddenly cover their ears. Howard saw Bea and Betty with their hands over their ears but little baby Tom, now nearly two years old, kept waving and waving as if it was the only good thing he could do. Howard surprisingly felt an intense emotion at the spectacle of his beloved children seeing him off for the first time. He had tried to explain to the girls that he would be back soon but they questioned him again and again why he had to go. He watched his parents wave for the last time as the boat pulled away from the dock. His father had shook his hand and wished him well rather curtly. His mother hugged him several times, wiping her eyes often, and telling him over and over to watch his health as if he was going to die in some far off place. Bea just muttered goodbye and brushed her lips quickly across his cheek. His father had leased a large home in Berkeley and hired a nanny for the children. They did not tell him how long they planned to stay but he knew they would not leave unless his little family was safe and well cared for. The boat slid farther out into the bay and Howard waved for the last time. He wandered toward the bow watching the ocean crashing its waves along the shore. As the shoreline disappeared, and the horizon seemed endless, Howard breathed in the salt air, awed at the boundless Pacific. He felt free.

****

BESSIE

Sounds of trills could be heard from the piano as Bessie's fingers flew up and down the keyboard. With a loud chord, she stopped and looked at Justine who was hovering over a paper penning notes. She was so intent on the paper that she had not noticed the music stopping or heard what Bessie deemed was the final chord. "I'm done, Justine. All night I lie awake trying to link art and music together in some common sense, creative manner but it eludes me."

"I've faith in you Bessie. You'll create something in that marvelous mind. I'm depending on this collaboration and we will publish this book. Don't worry because remember I've not been given a due date for its completion. We have time to work and play."

Bessie swirled around on the piano stool and noticed skirts of snow surrounding the evergreens. She lifted the window slightly and reached onto the sill for a handful of snow. She watched it melt and drip through her fingers onto the carpet. "It's strange, Justine, for I know snow is cold but at times it feels warm. My hand is still warm. The snow did not affect it at all. I'm just throwing around senses. Somewhere there is that connection between the canvas and music just like the cold and warmth, my fingers and the keys and the brush and my hand." She stood and watched the snow fall. "They say no two flakes are alike. Let's go out and see if that's the truth. Can you imagine if we find two flakes and could freeze them for a second and be witness to the truth. Are there two alike or not?"

Amused, Justine said, "I'd be willing to see you try."

Bessie pulled on her coat and boots and was out the door before Justine could find hers on the coat rack. "Come on, Justine. The snow is delicious. I want to throw myself on top of it."

"Don't be silly, Bessie."

"Silly! Silly who? Who is going to see us and why should they care? Come on, no one is home so let yourself fall."

Bessie fell backwards on a slope and began moving her outstretched arms up and down. "Who cares, Justine? It's us. I want to be girls again and make angels. There has got to be more angels in the world. No more snowmen!"

Justine impulsively picked up some snow, packed it in her hand and slung it at Bessie. Bessie leaped up, gathering snow, chased Justine around the big oak tree. The snow flew back and forth while the skies grew darker. Gasping for breath, Justine collapsed on the garden bench.

"So you've had enough?" Bessie threw back her head and opening her mouth let the snow fall on her tongue. "Just like I said. Delicious."

Justine opening her mouth too exclaimed, "Oh, the taste is delicious!"

"I know just the place to taste delicious life some more," Bessie said, pulling Justine up from the bench.

"Where?"

"Across the pond."

They plodded through the snow that was pelting them until they came to the road that wound around Jamaica Pond. The pond was just beginning to lace over with icing. Justine felt content soaking in the youth of the moment. She took Bessie's hand as they turned up the stone driveway and through the gate to the porch of Amy's home. Bessie banged the doorknocker insistently.

"I know she's home. Wait until you hear the intriguing tales of her trip to England. Besides we can't go home now. Look how heavy the storm has become. I guess we'll just have to wait it out. Let's savor the day while we can."

The door opened and Bessie was confronted by a surprised Ada.

"Bessie! Come in and who might your friend be?

"Ada, this is Justine. Justine is my sister-in-law. I've told you about her and our collaboration together."

"Yes, certainly. I'm so pleased to finally meet you Justine. Let me call Amy down from her private aerie. You already know, Bessie, her meeting with Mr. Pound did not go well and she is still muttering over it, determined to write something that will outdo his arrogance."

The recognizable boisterous voice of Amy could be heard from the top of the stairs. "Oh, my Lord! You're just the people who can brighten my day. It couldn't get any darker," Amy said descending the stairs and hugging Bessie and Justine. "This old, cold, haunted house. We need a good roaring fire to warm my family's shrouds and these old walls and once they're settled we can talk. Just we girls with that storm roiling outside, a fire and a drink should inspire us. You know, girl talk. Just what I need. Let's have some female energy around here and wake the dead. Look at you Bessie. You look like your bursting. Let's hear it."

"Justine and I came looking for some inspiration and you usually have some tucked away here."

"Don't know if you can find it here but we sure as hell can try."

Amy got the fire stoked and Ada, Bessie and Justine pulled some chairs closer to the hearth. The maid had brought in some hot toddy and Bessie put several spoonfuls of sugar in her cup. "Aha, Bessie! You've stopped worrying about your weight, I see. Are you trying to compete with me again? When it comes to weight, my dear, you can never beat me."

"Today there are no restrictions, taboos or no-no's.

We threw ourselves in the snow, tasted it, fought and danced in it. We have shed the doldrums and now we are here to find inspiration I know you have hidden away in these musty old books.

"Inspiration! Amy tries to find it around here every day. She throws words around like billiard balls banging into each other on a pool table. It's an experience to live in this old house. I never had the pleasure of meeting Amy's entire family but I can hear their voices bouncing off the walls if they were anything like Amy."

Justine cupped her hands around her hot toddy to keep them warm. "Ada, tell me how did you come to meet Amy?"

"Serendipity I guess. I had tired of the London theater and decided to take a ship to Boston. One night I was seated at dinner with a very lovely couple who introduced themselves as Mr. and Mrs. Thomas Ward. Mr. Ward kept my mind off the rolling of the ship and its implications by telling me fascinating stories of his travels and the most interesting of families. At our departure, Mrs. Ward handed me a note writing how much she would be delighted if I called upon her daughter. They, of course, were Bessie's parents. I took advantage of her mother's request and called. She gracefully invited me to a social at her home. Entering the salon, I saw an outlandishly large woman with a boisterous voice enchanting everyone with her stories. So I sneaked into the circle to listen. Bessie handed Amy her new book of poetry and told her to read one. Once she had finished a stunning poem that so moved me about being female in this world, I wanted to sit there forever. And we did. After all the others had left, Amy and I talked for what seemed hours. Bessie had to attend to her family and I'm so grateful she left us alone. Now after all the years of being an actress, married and then widowed, here I am where I was always meant to be."

Ada leaned over and kissed Amy on the cheek and lovingly patted her hand then held it. Justine looked askance over the top of her cup, viewing an odd relationship between the two of them. A sense of an intimate camaraderie filled with their personal electricity. But she felt comfortable in their presence and sat back in her chair, letting herself relax.

"What was it like to be an actress, Ada? I, unfortunately, have not had the pleasure of seeing you on stage. I know you, not well, but enough that I would appreciate your presentation of a character. Especially how you would portray a woman in these times?"

"Well, my Lord, Bessie! I'm suspicious that you have an ulterior motive in asking about a portrayal of women in 'these times'. Is that correct? These times?"

"Yes, there might be. But I wouldn't know unless you answer."

Amy reached over and flipped open the cigar box. Pulling out a panatela, she rolled it in her fingers, adjusted her pince-nez and peered at Ada. "This should be fun. I'm waiting to hear just what it's like to play women of different means. Have you played a woman damned like me?"

"Mercy no! I would never be able to do you justice, Amy. The public would never allow it. The stage would be covered with the red of tomatoes before I opened my mouth."

"Really! And why is that?"

"Justine, imagine yourself seated in the audience and I arrive on stage dressed in a somewhat masculine suit, a pince-nez dangling on my bosom, a cane in one hand and a cigar in the other."

Ada sauntered around the room mimicking Amy's walk and mannerisms. Then she picked up one of

Amy's poetry books, opened it and started to read in a deep, sonorous voice,
*"I am waving a ripe sunflower,
I am scattering sunflower pollen to the four world-quarters.
I am joyful because of my melons,
I am joyful because of my beans,
I am joyful because of my squashes.*

*The sunflower waves.
So did the corn wave
When the wind blew against it,
So did my white corn bend
When the red lightning descended upon it,
It trembled as the sunflower
When the rain beat down its leaves."*

Ada hesitated for a moment with a sardonic grin on her face. "Listen carefully now to the next part."
*"Great is a ripe sunflower,
And great was the sun above my corn-fields.
His fingers lifted up the corn-ears,
His hands fashioned my melons,
And set my beans full in the pods.
Therefore my heart is happy
And I will lay many blue prayer-sticks at the shrine of Ta-wa.
I will give corn to Ta-wa,
Yellow corn, blue corn, black corn.
I wave the sunflower,
The sunflower heavy with pollen.
I wave it, I turn it, I sing,
Because I am happy.*

Ada snapped the book shut. "Now isn't that poem marvelously intertwined with erotic imagery? Beautiful though it be with the rhythm of words, do you think the audience would embrace it? Envision for a moment the looks on those faces. I'm sure the men would be secretly reveling over the words 'his fingers', his hands' and especially 'my white corn bend'. The lascivious smiles would make women squirm in their seats."

"I'm not sure if I understand the eroticism you're talking about. I'm not squirming," Justine said tentatively, not wanting to seem foolish.

"Hell, woman, you have been living a convent life," Amy roared. "We all need a good stiff drink after Ada's prancing performance. I didn't mean to embarrass you Justine."

Amy inhaled heavily on her panatela, blowing smoke into the air. "I have strong convictions Justine that women should do what they most desire to do with their life. You made that decision to lead a life in search of lost music. Unfortunately, you were a little late on the scene and found yourself bound in a marriage. I knew George most of my life and excuse my directness Bessie, since he is your brother, but I could not imagine George allowing a wife to do anything but play the mistress of the home. It took courage to decide your career was not compatible to a marriage and I respect that. How much did it cost George to buy that annulment?"

"Amy, that's enough. Maybe you should have a stronger drink that will numb your wagging tongue." Bessie took some clean glasses from the sidebar. "Besides, what is so wrong with being the mistress of a home, much less a mother? What have you to say to me? Did I succumb?" Bessie poured from a bottle of scotch she had taken from the cabinet. With scotch in hand she said, "Bonpapa always quoted Sir George Lewis, 'Life would be tolerable if it were not for the pleasures.' Aren't we all tolerating the life we have and wrapping ourselves in those elusive pleasures we find?"

Amy lifting her glass replied, "Putting the truth aside for a moment, you two have a great conspiracy. Isolating yourselves where you can listen to the resonant sounds and capture the colors of the day that no one else hears or sees. Unloosening wonderful notes in a music that has been lost in those somber dark apses, naves, and choir lofts of... of." Amy inhaled and let the smoke rise again. Tapping her panatela on the ashtray, her voice slightly tinged with irony continued, "Oh, what do they call that church again? Catholic, I believe. I always thought the word 'catholic' meant universal. That music isn't Catholic. It is universal. It even touches my hardened soul."

She pulled up her pince-nez and glanced at Bessie and Justine with a smidgen of a smile. "I might begin listening to Gregorian chant around here. It would certainly liven up the silence that hangs in this house now. Can't you see us, Ada, flowing around the hallways, the salon, the library, arms widespread, all to the lovely voices of monks? Ahhhh! The sound of male voices is what is missing in our lives. Sweet male voices that is, not the sound of the cantankerous English poets, ranting and raving about the words of women. Assertive, talented, intelligent women I might say. And we all sit here in this room, hopefully in praise of each other!"

Ada had just taken some of her drink when she let out a loud snort, spewing her scotch. "Just like a bunch of Bolsheviks. That's who we are. Plotting against the male world. Let's plot some more and take over the stage. I can say I am really enjoying this conversation." She took another long gulp of her scotch.

Justine feeling a little more courageous just having emptied her glass spoke up a little louder. "Well, I don't know if I agree. Let the men have their silly wars. Let them handle the financial crises. Let them run the markets and have their way. I would just like to be left alone."

"Aha! Easy for you to say. No disrespect but I believe your husband more than likely put some money into the hands of a priest to buy an annulment. It erased your marriage clean as if never existed and he could start clean as could you. If you, a woman, had wanted that annulment, do you think you could have gotten it as easily as George. Remember who runs the churches! Again no disrespect but with your family's wealth, like mine, we can live the life we want. What can the poorer classes of women do? Nothing! Their fate is left in the hands of men. When the poor and the oppressed finally reach their ultimate mental and physical limit, revolution happens and I'm waiting until we women rise like the Bolsheviks."

"Justine, my dear, you're one of my cherished friends, but there is some truth in what Amy said. Your annulment was quiet. Remember what happened to poor Fanny Kemble when she tried to divorce Pierce Butler with good reason? It was a battle royal and the world of aristocrats on both sides of the oceans made it pure gossip fodder. All the parlors in Boston buzzed with glee and rubbed their hands in anticipation of letting their tongues wag. She stood her ground with all the slings and arrows flying in her path. She would not tolerate Pierce's arrogant stand on slavery and his brutalization of his slaves. She, like many of we women, had too compassionate a heart and could not stand to see the violence fall on the heads of those poor innocents. She fought back with a vehemence many of us lack and then we suffer in silence because our tongues are too weak."

Ada swung Amy's cane like a sword. "Do not speak for me, Bessie. My tongue and certainly Amy's has never been quieted by some man who believes he thinks for me. Never, never, never! We must all say 'never again'. Let's drink to that!"

Justine stood up. "I will drink to that. I will say never again." She turned to Bessie stating with a new determination. "Aren't you surprised at me?"

"Actually, I'm extremely happy for you. Yes, let's all drink to 'never again'."

Amy climbed out of her chair and took Ada's arm. All four women stood pronouncing loudly, "Never again!" and drank the rest of their scotch.

The sound of a heavy thud turned everyone's head toward the windows. One lonely thick icicle dangled down from the eave while the broken ones stuck up through the snow like candles on a cake. They all moved closer to the windows and looked with utter amazement at the heavy caked snow laden trees and no sign of a driveway.

"Justine, I think we will need sled dogs to get home. I'll do the mushing."

Amy, putting her arm around Bessie said, "I know a taxi would never make it and I don't know where the nearest dogsled stop is. But never mind, a telephone call home will warn them that we'll be having a slumber party and they will have to fend for themselves. I'm so grateful to the heavens for having silently imprisoned the two of you in my stone castle. I'm sure I can rustle up some prison food." Amy headed off for the kitchen leaving the women to finish their drinks.

****

The moon laid its soft light across the bedroom floor. Justine watched the shadows of the branches gliding back and forth on the walls. Her body relaxed under the warmth of the heavy quilt. Closing her eyes for a moment, she thought how peaceful the room was and how peaceful she felt. Reflections of the evening's conversation strayed across her mind. Her eyes traced again the shadows and she moved her head back and forth on the pillow with the rhythm of the movements as if they were a ballet on a beautiful floor.

"Bessie," she whispered not wanting to wake her if she had fallen asleep.

"Yes, I'm awake."

"I'm sorry but that inner self of mine is just chattering away and arguing with whomever that other stalking woman is. We never seem to resolve our issues. We do battle so intensely that we kill the chance for peaceful sleep. I don't know, Bessie. I try to smother the voices hoping some ethereal music will overcome them and they will dance with each other rather than fight." Justine sat up in bed pulling the quilt under her chin. "Look at the shadows dance. They move like a ballet. See that one branch dance across the wall as if she is the beautiful, forlorn swan? So thin and wistful."

Bessie pulled herself up propping the pillows behind her. "Do you remember when we were young how we would sway across the room believing in that fantasy world. Did we realize it was a fantasy or did we place ourselves into an imaginary life?"

"How would we have known what was real and what was imaginary?"

"There are days I understand what is all too real but want to walk in my imagination. Remember my quoting Bonpapa tonight? 'Life would be tolerable, if it were not for the pleasures.'" Bessie giggled. "The most intriguing thing he said was he had found out why people die; it is to break up their style." Bessie pushed the pillows higher on the headboard. "I think I know exactly what he was talking about. It's so hard to break the path that was made for us, especially at our age. The stones in the path are no longer loose but cemented together so the path is paved. I don't know if I have the strength or the courage to re-walk it."

Justine watched the shadows swaying across the room. "Oh, God, I don't hear the music anymore. I just see the shadows. Dark! Dark has come."

She heard Bessie whisper as she laid back down, "Maybe my path will change."

Sleep finally pulled its curtain on their tormented souls.

****

HOWARD

Howard and the taxi driver struggled to get his steamer trunk out of the taxi's trunk. The driver looked up at the stairs that led to a rather large, magnificent house. He picked up one end of the trunk and said, "Think you will need some muscle to get up those stairs."

"Thanks! I can use some help." Howard did not expect anyone to greet him since he had not told Bea he was coming home. Reaching the top of the stairs he asked the driver how much.

"Just three dollars. Hope you have a good homecoming."

Howard rummaged through his wallet and pulled out three dollars and then handed the driver a dime. "That's for your help."

The driver looked stunned at the dime and sarcastically said, "I think you need all the help you can get if that is all you can scrounge up. Good day!" The driver skipped down the stairs and waved, saying, "Good luck. You need it." Putting the taxi in gear and flooring the accelerator, he muttered, "Cheap bastard."

I think he's right. I need all the luck I can muster. Hesitantly, he rang the bell. He heard footsteps coming down the stairs. As the door opened, he saw Bea with straggling bits of hair down her neck. She had an apron on and looked tired.

"Howard! Why are you here? Has something happened again?"

"Nothing terrible has happened. Are we going to stand here or can I come in?"

Bea backed away from the door to let Howard pull his trunk into the entry. "If you don't mind, I need a stiff drink. It has been a long trip."

"Of course. The whiskey is on the sideboard in the

dining room. I'll get some tea for myself. I need a rest and I'm certainly anxious to hear why you are here. And why you felt it not necessary to write or is the surprise not a surprise?" She threw her apron down on the sofa not knowing what more to say.

She returned shortly finding Howard having already found the whiskey and wandering around the room, looking at old photographs on the wall. "Where did these come from? One of them looks like the old Empire Mine. Is it?"

"Yes, Mother brought them down when she came to visit while your parents were here. She thought they might be interested in them."

"Where are the children?"

"It's their nap time so we have no distractions while you explain yourself. What is it you have to tell me, Howard?"

"You should not be really concerned, Bea. It's just that rascal Reynolds had utopian ideas of business without the funds to create it. I gathered he thought that I would be the money man and I had no intention of trusting another partner with my funds."

Bea straightened up and with controlled anger said, "My funds. You said, 'my funds'. Have you been keeping money from me. Your parents paid six months advance rent for me just in case you did not send any money for our upkeep. They were right. Mother, when she left, put an envelope on my desk with money and I have been using it to put food on the table. Now what are you expecting to do and what are we expected to do?"

"I didn't come home to have your anger thrown at me." Howard took a long gulp of his whiskey. "God, I'm trying to make a life for us but people tend to lie to me and I'm just too trusting a person. I tend to trust people when I shouldn't." He took another drink and stared at the pattern in the rug.

Bea put her teacup down and without commiserating with him, said, "What now?"

"Well, I did hear of a gold strike in Alaska."

"What?" Bea jumped up knocking over the tea tray and without bothering to try to stop the pieces falling to the floor, ran from the room.

Hurried footsteps and the squealing voices of children flew into the room. "Papa!" Little Bea ran toward Howard.

"Careful! Stop where you are. There's glass all over the floor." Howard quickly stood and picked up Bea while Betty, holding Tom's hand stared at their father and the broken tea tray. Bea hugged him tightly. "I'm so happy. I thought I would never see you again."

"Oh, why did you think that? I would never let any of you children go. Come over here and give me a kiss, Betty." Betty obediently kissed her father on the cheek and stepped back. She let go of Tom's hand and Howard reached out to shake it. "My what a little man you've become. One day maybe we can work together when you grow up. Would you like to look for gold?"

Tom shook his head no. "Is it hard? I think I want to stay home."

Howard laughed and hugged him. "That's okay. I understand. Then you will always know you have a bed to sleep in and breakfast on the table. That's smart of you."

Bea came back with a broom and dustpan. Tears were streaming down her cheeks and she swept up the tea pieces. Betty stooped down and put a large piece in the dustpan. "Let me help Mama. Are you crying about your teapot?"

"It's okay, darling. I can manage. You take your sister and brother outside to play. Your father and I would like to talk." She took a handkerchief from her pocket and wiped the tears from her face. Little Bea and Tom hung onto her skirt begging for a kiss. Bea kissed both of them and told them to go out to their swings.

"Tell me now Howard what can I expect?"

Howard picked up his whiskey again and said, "I met a man who referred me to a Mr. Bart Thane who is here in San Francisco. I wrote him a letter with my resume and that I was serious in finding an engineering position that would suit my resume. He responded that they were opening up an immense, low grade, gold ore deposit near Juneau, Alaska, and expected to erect a large converting mill and develop water power. Thane said that there was room for good engineers, and suggested that I accompany him up there. It seemed like a splendid opportunity. I accepted."

Bea's hand flew to her chest.

"You need not cry. Everything will be fine."

Trembling, Bea, in a tearful voice said, "Did you ever once think of me in these fantastic dreams of yours? Why should I be your lamb and follow without question of my own well being or the children's? Remember them? Remember me? What are we to you?"

"You're my little family and I love you. If I don't seem to show it in the way you would want, well that is how I am and you knew it when you married me."

"You never once said to me that I would be dragged wherever you desired to go and, of course, the responsibility of children would be mine. Did you tell me that?"

"How would I know what life would offer me?"

"So far it has offered you nothing. Here I have stupidly been the good little wife, bearing children in godforsaken places and even converting to Catholicism for you. Which of us has given the most to this marriage?"

Howard poured himself another whiskey.

Bea, watching him down another whiskey, said "Howard, have you ever gone to church while you've been away? Have you gone to confession? I sure would like to know what it was you confessed to if you did."

Howard stared intently at the pictures on the wall.

"I've been thinking about a divorce, Howard."

Without turning around Howard said, "You know the Catholic Church does not allow divorce. There has never been a divorce in my family and there never will be."

"There is always a first. My family is not Catholic and I'm sure Mother will support me. According to your church, we will all go to hell. Guess I'd rather be there with my family and especially my father than live this life. He loved me so much." Bea looking at the roses in the garden sadly said, "The roses are so beautiful and yet they fade. I don't want to fade that fast. I'm going to get the children ready for dinner then I am going to bed. Good night!"

Howard stood looking at the photograph of Grandma and Grandpa Kidder with Bea sitting on her mother's lap. He thought how beautiful she looked. She must have been about ten. Yes, I would not like to be on Grandpa Kidder's bad side. I feel that rifle he has would be pointed at me. I wonder if he would understand how difficult it is to make a living in the West. He was damn lucky with his building of the railroads.

The grandfather clock chimed loudly and awakened Howard. The clock was still chiming and suddenly stopped at the stroke of eleven. "My god, I didn't know I was that tired." He climbed to the top of the stairs and saw his trunk in the hall. He turned the knob to the bedroom and found it locked. He sighed and pulled his trunk into the guest bedroom. I wonder how long she will keep this up? He slipped into a nightshirt, pulled down the covers and laid his head on the pillow knowing he was not going to fall asleep again.

****

GEORGE

Mumsie lay asleep on the settee. She had not been well for several weeks and Papa suggested she lie down in the library to be near him. He was enormously concerned this time with her illness because she looked paler than usual and seemed to lack interest in anything. Ever since they had come back from California she had seemed depressed. Howard was her baby and she had asked on the train coming home, "How could he leave his wife and especially those babies? Didn't he seem anxious to go? I just don't understand. I thought we had taught him where his responsibilities lay. Not in another scheme. Oh, Tom, my dear sweet husband. You have had to endure so much from a son you have given so much. I feel heartbroken with his continual escapades." She stared out at the passing scenery for awhile then continued, "It's like Justine. How could she go off and leave George to do what she wanted to do? It was if she never thought of what the responsibility of being a wife was to be. And yet, she and Bessie are such good friends. Why couldn't she have taken the duties of family like Bessie has? We can always depend on Bessie to do what she had committed to do. I wonder if she ever tried to influence Justine to take care of George?" She never said another word the rest of the trip. She was brokenhearted.

Papa reached for the settee throw and laid it gently over Mumsie. He ran his hand down her cheek and thought how very beautiful she still was. He went to the front door to pick up the mail that had been slipped through the slot. Tiptoeing back into the room, he picked up the letter opener. Anxiety struck his chest with pangs seeing it was a letter from George. Any letter now from either one brought anxiety stamped on it. Hesitantly, he opened the folded paper which he noted was written on Union Club stationery.

September 10, 1917
Dear Papa and Mumsie:

I am sitting here in the Union Club in one of the chairs that you or Bonpapa most likely sat in all the years the both of you were members and President. It gives me some comfort knowing your presence is here to contemplate what and where should I devote my life with the knowledge of how full your lives had and have been. I have been in a state of paralysis these last years and have found practicing the law has been a mistaken path and truly not my forte. One wakes up every day facing an adversarial situation. When I sit down before a judge I sometimes wonder if by the look of his face the scales of justice will tip the wrong way only because of latent prejudices which raise their ugly faces depending on the defendant and there are times that prejudice can be heard loftily from the voice in the witness chair.

The distressing world situation with the Germans marching into Belgium has caused us all consternation. I have always had a militaristic bent and have come to the conclusion that I could and should be of service to my country. Therefore, I have applied for a position with Military Intelligence and with hopes you will not be angered, I used the influence of our family name in Washington.

And lastly, before I close, my love for Justine has never diminished and my fears for her since she is in France studying the music of the monks of Solemne, I want to make sure she is out of harm's way. She hears the eternal notes of heavenly music but I fear she is deaf to the thunderous notes of The Ride of the Valkyries as they march through Europe.

> *Do give my love to all and I assure you I will keep myself safe.*
> *Your loving son,*
> *George*

Papa folded the letter and put it back into its envelope. He slid it among the pages of the book he was reading. While stoking his pipe he thought he would not tell Mumsie until he knew exactly where and when George would be assigned. He knew this unsettling information would cause her more anxiety and suffering. Her overwhelming motherly instincts when stressed never allow her a peaceful day. Turning his head toward the door having heard a noise, he saw Bessie beckoning to him to come. Fearing to wake Mumsie, he went into the hall and closed the door behind him.

"What is it, Bess? You look distraught. Please tell me it's not another disastrous situation. We have had to deal with so much. Too much!"

"What do you mean, 'another', Papa? Let's go out on the front porch. Hopefully we can find some fresh air before we both tell our tales we don't want to hear."

They settled down on the porch swing. "Okay, I want your news first," Papa said.

"I had a letter yesterday from Bea and have no idea how to break the news to Mumsie. I know you'll take it in stride."

"Go on!"

"I didn't tell you Bea wrote that Howard came back from Los Angeles with the old tired story how the business did not work out nor did the office in San Francisco so as his custom, he found another outlandish situation in Alaska. Of course, going for gold."

"Alaska! Good Lord! He's always running after

that golden calf. What was he thinking?"

"More what he was not thinking. He took Bea and the children to Seward, then left for the Yukon. I couldn't imagine what life would be in Seward with three children. As it turns out, Bea could not manage it and is sending the two girls to us to care for until Howard comes back." Bessie sat back in the swing completely defeated.

Papa ran his hand down her long tresses. My sweet Bessie, I wish to all the heavens I had a well from which I could draw clean, fresh pure water and sprinkle it on your golden hair and we could start life again without travails and sorrows. I have no well from which to draw the earth's water. Forgive me, forgive us."

Bessie bit her lip trying to hold back her bursting emotions from exploding upon Papa's chest. She pushed the swing back and forth, breathing in and out with its motion. "Papa! Papa! You don't need forgiveness. I understand. I understand!" Wiping her eyes, she asked, "What was your news? Don't tell me if it's unbearable too. Please don't."

"No, I wouldn't call it unbearable. George wrote he has applied for a position with Military Intelligence because he feels strongly that he must make a change and find what suits him best and that is a military career."

"I'm not surprised. He loved his military outfits and always carried himself as if he was an officer and in command. Even as a boy. Maybe this will break his obsession with Justine."

"Justine would be so relieved if that happens. She tells me George's anger still consumes her at times when she desperately needs to work. I would love for both of them to find some serenity at least." Bessie's feet pushed the swing as they both watched the autumn leaves float effortlessly to the ground in silence.

****

BESSIE

Bessie paced up and down the railroad platform constantly looking at her watch in anxious anticipation of the coming train. She wondered how two young girls survived the trip across the country knowing every passing scene was taking them further and further away from their mother. A train whistle pierced the air and people began picking up their luggage while others excitedly peered down the track. "Yea!" one little boy yelled, "Daddy's coming, Mama. Hurry, I want to see him first." Bessie wished she could be that excited.

As the train moved slowly past her before it came to a full stop, suddenly Bessie spotted little Bea waving frantically at her from the window. She smiled and waved back. Finally, a woman stepped off onto the platform, then reached for Bea. Bea ran toward Bessie and wrapped her arms around her waist saying, "I'm so glad to see you Aunt Bessie. I want to hurry home and see my cousins. Are they anxious to see us?"

"Certainly, my sweetheart. They had school this morning but they will be there when we arrive home."

The woman approached Bessie holding Betty's hand. Betty gave Bessie what she thought a somewhat reluctant smile. She leaned down and gave her a kiss, then took her hand. "It will be all right, Betty. Remember you have a home here."

Betty murmured, "I know."

The woman extended her hand to Bessie and said, "I am Mae. I trust that Howard told you that I would be accompanying the children. It has been an awfully long trip but these girls are delightful, as you know. I've heard all about you and your love for them. Please forgive my intrusion in your home. I'll be returning home in three days if that is acceptable for you."

Bessie, not knowing exactly who this woman was shook her hand. "Thank you. Thank you so very much. You have no idea how anxious I was about the girls' journey but they were obviously in good care. You are most welcome. Now we all have to get home quickly to run some warm soapy baths. We've got to scour off all the dust you picked up on that long train ride. I guess Mae will look forward to a bath and clean clothes too."

"You bet I am!"

Bessie climbed into the driver's seat and Mae surrounded herself with the children. Just as Bessie said, the children came running down the front stairs to greet them. After many hugs, Frances took the persona of being the man of the house and told them to follow him into the children's parlor for tea. Anna with a happy look took Bea's hand while little Mary giggled over and over in happiness.

Later that night Bessie came to help Rose put the children to bed. She had decided to put another bed in Anna's room and let the girls be together. As she was helping Betty pull her nightgown over her head she saw a gold nugget on a chain dangling from her neck.

"Betty, what a beautiful necklace. Who gave it to you?"

"Daddy did. He told me never to take it off so I would always remember him."

"Oh, Mary Mother of God, Howard." Not letting the girls hear her. "How could you leave these little ones who have become lost in your wayward life?" She pulled the quilt over the girls, kissing them goodnight. Closing the door she felt the despair for such innocent ones tremble through her.

****

Bessie trundled all the children into the car and waved to Carley standing on the front doorstep. She grasped the wheel tightly in anticipation of the long drive to Ogunquit. The children amused themselves by counting the cows or other animals along the way and cried with glee when they spotted a fox scurrying across a field. Relief overcame her as she turned down the road and saw the ocean and the house ready for some rustling signs of life. Before she had stopped the car, the children were out and running down to the beach and splashing each other with yelps and screams as the cold water hit their faces. At least the children are happy, Bessie thought, as she turned the key in the lock. Pushing open the door, the musty sea smells of the rooms washed across her senses and she dropped down in the chair to watch the children.

Her eyelids closed, her hands caressed her shoulders swaying them back and forth. She felt compelled to open her eyes to see a figure out the window in the distance. She watched it come closer and wondered. "Is it? No! No!" She slipped back into reverie, her mind wandering through images she conjured of memories coloring themselves. The dusky siennas of the cobbled streets and walls of Italy. The tall, slim, grayish green of firs that drew their lines across the hills of Tuscany. The lightness of life that slept through the afternoons, then the cooling taste of a white wine while the colors dusted the skies of evening.

A light tapping on the door, then silent footsteps fell on the carpet. She felt the warmth of lips kissing her lightly on the cheek as if to say, "What colors do you see behind those closed eyes? The blue of the sea, the green of the undercurrent, the gray rocks, the white crests or are they the colors of deep emotions? Did you paint that for me?"

"No, I painted the colors of my life gone by. The

colors of the sea are always with me, days and days, and splashing of waves always roaring in my head. The sound so intimate it holds the tides of my life."

Without a movement of time, she could feel the sand sift through her fingers. Her head nestled in the curve of his arm. She felt whole and loved and her body pressed into the sand as she slowly moved it into his. She could hear the sound of someone calling, "Bessie! Bessie!" drifting in with the wind. "They're not calling me. That is not me! My name is Elizabeth. My name is Elizabeth." She pressed her head deeper into the softness. A low voice touched her ear. "It's okay, Elizabeth. You were born Elizabeth. Without you we would have suffered greatly alone. I am still with you. Take my hand. Take it Elizabeth, do you hear me?"

"Yes. Please stay with me. Love me! Please let me love."

The door banged open and Francis yelled, "Guess who's here, Mama? Guess?"

Bessie opened her eyes and in shock, said, "Oh, my God. Charles! I thought that we..."

"You thought we what? You look pale. Are you ill?"

"No. No," Bessie said, standing up and brushing the sand off her dress. "I thought I had seen you walking down the beach."

Woodbury, with a sly smile, hugged Bessie and whispered, "Yes, it was me."

****

HOWARD

Howard crept into the library hoping not to disturb anyone and made himself a whiskey sour. He had become used to sours in Alaska to warm himself besides cranking up courage. He opened the back kitchen door and wound his way through the garden to find the comfortable bench in the middle of the roses. Sitting on the bench, he found the moonlight throwing its glow upon the roses creating the marvelous shimmers which spellbind one for hours. "How many times had he been here in this house, Bessie's house, not mine, with Mumsie and Papa, Mumsie waiting for death to cover her and let her sleep undisturbed forever? Her lifelong melancholy seeps into you after awhile. You always hear the sighing and its sound will walk the hallways long after she is gone.

He reached over and plucked one of the pink roses that was dipping its head to the ground. He propped it up with his thumb and forefinger and turned it over and over, inhaling its sweet smell. Pink! Pink is the color of girls. My girls. He recalled them that morning running down the steps to jump into his arms, smothering him with wet kisses. They hugged their mother and grabbed their brother Tom's hand to take him into the house to their rooms to show him all the things they had done and made over the past year. They had grown so much and came to the dinner table with the graces of young ladies. Betty proudly wore her gold nugget necklace. When Bea noticed it she threw an angry glance across the table at him. She had been looking in all the nooks and crannies in the house in Seward and was rather frantic that she could not find it. He never told her that he had given it to Betty when they were sent East. He didn't care. He just showered in the loving eyes of Betty when he put it around her neck just before the train left.

He drank the rest of his drink, smelled the roses one last time and started back toward the house. He would be telling Betty and Bea tomorrow they would be moving again. The door to the library was open and the last log was slowly spitting out its glowing ashes as they slipped through the grate. He stepped in and put out a live ash that had fallen on the carpet. His eyes fell upon the chess set and his hand reached out to pick up the queen. It was a model Bessie had a local potter make that appeared to be the missing queen. Howard's hand fell to his jacket pocket and he patted it softly. He tiptoed up the stairs, slipped under the covers and let his eyelids fall. He longed to reach over and feel the soft skin and the smell of a woman close under the quilt with him. But those times had long passed with Bea as she wrapped herself tightly in the sheets avoiding any possible contact with him. There had never been an intense love between them but their intimate nights had given him three children which he would never allow to be taken from him. He fell asleep with the images of them floating in his dream.

****

Morning sun had now replaced the light of the moon and it streamed into the dining room which had been set for breakfast. Howard, having awakened rather late to find Bea already gone, and hearing the noise of the children decided to dress slowly hoping that everyone would be well into their breakfast by the time he came down the stairs. He greeted everyone with a "Good morning" and "I hope we all can enjoy this day together."

The children were anxious to go outside and giggled as if they had an unspoken agreement between them.

Howard poured himself a cup of coffee from the sideboard and sat down across from Bea who kept fiddling with her eggs. Mumsie was having her breakfast in her room as usual. Papa was buttering his toast. "It warms my heart to have my family, especially my mischievous grandchildren at our breakfast table. I wish it would happen more often."

Bessie pouring her coffee said, "Now that you are here in Boston, where will you be settling? Close by again, I hope, so that Bea and I can pick up our friendship from where we left off."

Ignoring Bessie's question, Howard trying to distract his father said, "We have not talked about George. What is he up to?"

"In a minute. I want to hear your answer to Bessie."

Little Betty, who had been on her way out of the dining room with the other children, stopped in the doorway. She looked at her mother who was staring down at her plate and wiping her mouth with her napkin. Seeing the nervousness of her father, she said rather matter-of-factly, "Papa, where are we going to live?" She walked over to his chair. "Where, Papa?"

Howard put his arm around her waist and kissed her. "Don't worry, dear. You'll love New York."

Bessie slapped her napkin on the table. Pushing back her chair, she stood up glaring at Howard. "Don't even tell me what wild scheme you've got up your sleeve again. I don't want to hear it, don't want to know about it, and least of all, I don't want to know what your plans are for the children. God only knows they have been through enough!" She slammed the kitchen door behind her.

The morning light slowly edged its path across the white linen tablecloth.

****

GEORGE

Holding on to the doorknob, George scanned the room which had been his office as Park Commissioner for several years. It had been a comfortable position and felt he had given the city his greatest accomplishment by preventing any invasion of the parks by commercial enterprises hoping to advertise their firm by what he thought were offensive signs. Business does not have to implant their ugly footsteps on property that was ordained for the people's enjoyment. Now was the time to move on. He closed the door, walking out onto the city streets pondering the new life he was about to embrace.

Germany had marched into Belgium bellowing its caustic voice demanding its unfounded sovereign right against what they claimed was aggressive tyranny. What tyranny? What real threat? In God's name why would the western European countries impel their young men into war? Why not let the Rhine forever run between them but still the black boots come?

He had written to Bessie and his parents that the opportunity had presented itself to join a commission and he was commissioned as a major in the Officers Reserve Corps and assigned to the aviation branch. He was to be attached to the General Staff in France and would be doing liaison work with the British and French high commands in Paris. He felt the sense of Paris in his steps as he gazed up at the windows of the edifices of New York. As he walked north on Park Avenue noticing the brownstones, the mothers and prams on the sidewalks, he understood the fascination of New York with its diversity of peoples and places, but it had not the romance of Paris. There was no Seine where one could linger on one of its many bridges with lights and slow moving waters below and watch the boats move in rhythm to the song of the city. No, this was not Paris. He quickened his steps anxious to pack. He thought better of not stopping on 84th Street where Howard had ensconced his family while he had already taken off for Paris. Should I meet up with him in Paris? I don't have to make that decision now. I know that time will come.

****

HOWARD & GEORGE

, *June 1917*

St. George Hotel
Paris
Dear Papa and Mumsie,

Forgive me for not writing earlier but I have been inundated with business deals which have required my complete attention.

The National City Bank had a small company known as the Allied Machinery Company of America that exported machine tools - lathes, grinders, shapers, presses and such machines. With the war had come a sudden demand for this class of machine, and the little company had become swamped with orders and disorganized by too much business. The management of this company was handed over from the bank to the new American International Corporation. One fine day, an expert accountant, Hartley, and myself, were asked to spend a few days investigating the company and to make a report on its condition and suggest how it could be best reorganized so that it might function better. We made our reports, and two days later I was told that I was appointed as its temporary manager, and to go ahead and take charge. Besides the main New York office, we had branches in Brussels, now held by the Germans, St. Petersburg, Paris and Turin. I had much to learn, and was tremendously busy evolving new forms and methods and changing and enlarging the personnel of the company.

I was promised a vacation of a fortnight, but recalled a week later. When I entered the President's office, he calmly welcomed me with "Hello, Ward! Can you sail for France next week?" I sailed five days later, after a hasty farewell to the family, hurried purchases and packing, dashes here and there for passport and visas on La Touraine of the French Line. I was off to reorganize our foreign offices. The trip was uneventful, but exciting because of boat drills, target practice with the soixante gauge and the dangerous possibility of our being torpedoed by German subs. Our office was near the Gare du Nord, and after a week or two I discovered that I was powerless to do anything because the local manager, who was a vice-president of the company, thought that he was running the whole show. So I took the next boat back to New York to explain the situation, after which I too was made a vice-president, and after a few days in the States I made my third crossing within a month.

I did not see my "little family" since they were vacationing with you at St. Kittery. A month later the other officer was called home and I was left free to carry out the reorganization without his interference. I got a little room with "pension" near the Etoile and am very comfortable. Each day after work, I usually walk home down the boulevards and parks. Paris during wartime is interesting but not amusing. Disabled and convalescing soldiers are everywhere, but there were no able-bodied men except foreigners. All possible work is being done by girls and women. All work stops from noon till two o'clock for lunch. The cafes are open, though sugar, white flour and other supplies are short, and some of the theaters are open to give some variation to the inhabitants and amusement to soldiers on leave. At night only a few street lights are lit, and these are instantly extinguished if notice is received of an expected air attack. We have had three, but no damage was done, and the display was interesting - searchlights, anti-aircraft guns popping, and an occasional boom of a bomb in the distance. France itself is more interesting, even in peaceful areas. German prisoners are used on construction and road work. The women and old men are working in the fields whenever there is enough daylight. Military motors and camions are hurrying everywhere. Where the Germans are not occupying the country, it is beautiful, with tilled fields, tree lined roads, occasional woods, and little cuddling towns - but elsewhere it is another story.

Two other colleagues and myself with the assistance of the French government were assigned to examine as many destroyed factories as we could reach; some of them just behind the front. We were given a big military car and captain to escort us, and as we whirled over the roads in a cloud of dust, everyone stepped aside and tipped their hats as if we were generals.

Our route lay along behind the lines to the northeast of Paris. We saw miles of once fine roads that had been torn up and the bordering rows of beautiful old trees cut down, torn fields with their little sticks erected supporting a bit of cloth to mark unexploded shells. Small and large cemeteries with simple wooden crosses to mark French soldiers graves, but only stones over German graves - old gun emplacements, acres of tangled barbed wire, now being cleaned up - little villages with houses and church wrecked by bomb or shell fire - immense factories a mere mass of fallen brick or rock and a mass of twisted machinery. Behind the active front were troops without end, camions everywhere, and occasional aeroplanes overhead. Once a bomb was dropped just where we had been standing five minutes before. Desultory firing could be heard, but no attack was in progress. We visited aviation fields, artillery emplacements, signaling points, hospitals, and everything else that we could reach that seemed of interest without losing too much time. We returned to Paris in the evening through heavy thunderstorms, and that night my intestines began a distressing upheaval.

Do have to close sending my love and hopes that all are safe and sound at home. I do not know when I will have the chance to write again. Expect to see George soon. He must certainly like his position in intelligence. If anyone ever wanted to be a military officer, it is George.
    Your loving son,
    Howard

George pulled his coat collar up as a bracing wind blew down the Seine bending the trees on the Ile St. Louis. He had agreed to dine with Howard feeling obligated to maintain a relationship with him although not feeling brotherly in the least. He passed in front of Notre Dame making the sign of the cross quickly hoping it would help him control his temper which might burst if conversation of family spread across the dining table. He found the small inviting brasserie tucked in a narrow street. Stepping inside he found it filled with patrons chatting with great enthusiasm. He gave his name to the maitre d' who seated him at a table near the window. He ordered a cognac and waited for Howard. He glanced around the room when a conversation caught his ear. Four men, obviously by their uniforms, members of the French army were raising their glasses and toasting the United States. Strange. I didn't feel we were all that welcome. We've been remaining neutral to the distaste of many Europeans. We're neither fish nor fowl, although the Allies have accepted us as a sort of necessary evil. Neutrality has made many of us in the offices feel craven and debased. It's such an uncomfortable situation hanging like an albatross from my neck. Can't you kill the damn bird Wilson!

Howard burst in the door, shivering as the maitre d' helped him with his coat. He shook his shoulders shaking off the cold and then spotted George at the table. With a big grin he sidled past the tables and all too loudly for George's senses said, "Brother! Brother! How great to see you looking so fine as one of our proud American officers." The four men at the other table instantly turned toward them. One of them announced, "A toast to the Americans, our allies and friends to the end." They all stood up and in unison cried, "Vive l'Amerique! Vive la France! Hooray!"

George looked at Howard and then the men in utter disbelief. Howard with a sly smirk said, "By the look on your face, George, I believe you don't know the news. You've been hunkered down in that dark office of yours all day obviously pouring over God knows what kind of so-called secret papers."

"Obviously! What? Okay, sit down and tell me why they keep grinning at us as if we are heroes of some kind and take that smirk off your face."

"So I have the upper hand for once. Waiter, bring us a bottle of your best champagne, s'il vous plait. For once, I'm going to enjoy telling the great news." Grinning, Howard held up his glass. "President Wilson declared war on Germany today." Then he gulped down the champagne. "If only you could see the look on your face. I wish I had a mirror but you are the one who always has one in his pocket."

George took umbrage at the cutting remark but took his goblet and drank. "I'm shocked that headquarters would neglect to inform us. After all, we are the American Intelligence group. Someone slipped up badly. At least I feel I can finally wear this uniform with some pride." He straightened up, pulled his shoulders back and lifted his glass to the French soldiers. "Vive la France! Marchons!"

Howard leaning over the table, winked and whispered. "Wait until they see Pershing arrive! Can't wait to see the look on these frogs faces then."

George pulled back disdaining the pejorative remark. Disdain was acceptable but pejorative language was used only by lower classes who usually have no sense of propriety. "So when is the great General suppose to arrive?"

"Some time before the Fourth of July. My company has asked me to represent them and meet him at the boat. I've a great deal of information for him concerning the destroyed factories and those that are still in operation. I'll have the opportunity to accompany one of our great heroes. Imagine! I'm sure he will be interested to hear what I have to say. He'll be impressed." Howard poured himself more champagne and offered some to George.

"No, I'm fine for the moment." Howard nodded with a smile to the Frenchmen again. The waiter pushed his cart over to their table and poured cognac over two breasts of duck and lit it with a swoosh. Ladling the fiery duck onto their plates, he said, "That's what we fellow comrades will do to the Germans. Light them on fire and strew their remains as fertilizer across our fields. Maybe they'll make good potatoes. Bon appétit!"

George picked up his knife proceeding to cut the duck and vegetables on his plate into small bite size pieces. Howard looked on in amusement cutting a slice of duck and popping it into his mouth. George, still cutting his dinner and without looking up said, "I interviewed Nellie Bly the other day."

"You interviewed Nellie Bly? Is she a spy or not?

We're all talking about her."

"Shush! Can't you ever keep your voice down?" Looking over at the other tables to see if anyone had heard, he whispered, "It's Military Intelligence after all. I thought I would mention it because I, for one, was also surprised to be involved and she is a curiosity and certainly the talk of New York and Paris."

"Talk! Remember Papa always talking about her and her writings in the New York World. He seemed to be enamored of her. I suppose anyone would. Aren't you?"

"I can say she is interesting and strong willed."

"You seem to be intimidated by her."

"Certainly not!" George stabbed his fork into a piece of duck and chewed vigorously.

"Okay! So you were not." Howard, in the lowest tone he could muster asked. "Is she a spy?"

"That's up to Intelligence. I submitted my report to them. She wants to meet with President Wilson because she believes she can help him better understand the culture of the Germans."

"Really! So she thinks that she is the authority on German culture? Interesting what silly notions come into a woman's head."

George tried to compose himself before responding. "Dear little brother! I thought that after all these years you would have learned something about the contributions of women in our world. Especially with the relationships that Bonpapa had with some brilliant women who could outmatch us any time."

"Huh! Like whom?"

"Margaret Fuller. And after meeting Miss Bly, I do think she would have your head in a contest of ideas, world, cultural or whatever." George lay down his fork and summoned the waiter. "May we have two coffees please?"

They drank their coffee in silence. Howard turning his head every once in awhile to see if any people were trying to catch their attention. George pulled out his wallet and glanced at the bill the waiter had put down on a tray. Paying the bill, he said, "I apologize for having to cut our time short but I do have another appointment this evening and I don't want to be late."

"Really! And you saw no need to tell me?"

"Yes, I saw no need. If you see the family before I do send them my best wishes and sentiments."

The maitre d' helped them on with their coats and they stepped out into the brisk evening. Howard shaking George's hand couldn't help but ask. "And who is this person that has caught your attention so much that you couldn't wait to leave? After all, we see so little of each other."

"Not to offend you but I have met one of those intelligent women who does not have silly notions. I don't want to miss the opportunity of enjoying an evening of enlightenment with her."

"Do you mind telling me her name?"

George pulled up the collar of his coat and turned away toward the Pont Neuf bridge. Howard barely heard him say, "Edith."

****

HOWARD

Howard carefully placed the picture of himself standing behind General Pershing as they disembarked from the ship in Calais under several of his ironed shirts making sure it would not be damaged. He took one last glimpse of the photo and glanced at himself in the mirror admiringly as he slammed down the top of the trunk. He sat down at his desk, flipping his pen into the inkwell, he penned his last letter from Paris.

August 1918
Paris

Dear Papa, Mumsie, Bessie, and Carley,
When I arrived here the U.S. and President Wilson had been neutral in the war, and we who were abroad hated our status. As George told me at dinner, we were neither fish nor fowl, and though the Allies accepted us as a sort of necessary evil, we felt thoroughly craven and debased. But the day after we declared war every employee embraced me and greeted me as a friend and ally. We had at last found our honor again. And then Pershing arrived with his emblematic handful of men, and paraded on July 4th before the enthusiastic French. That night I went to the Opera Comique and at the end of the First Act, General Pershing and his staff entered the middle boxes of the balcony which were draped with American flags. A tremendous ovation greeted him, and Madame Cheval enfolded in a French flag, sang the Marseillaise with magnificent spirit, kneeling on the stage with her hands outstretched to him. Little chills of emotion ran up and down my spine. General Pershing was tall, straight as an arrow, well set-up, strong featured, the best looking army officer I have ever seen.

On the 14th of July the Allies paraded - a small group from each contingent at the front, carrying their battle flags. It was impressive. During the war, only military masses were celebrated in the churches, and at the Elevation, instead of a tinkling bell, there blazoned forth overhead the thrilling notes of a bugle. I visited several times the marvelous U.S. military hospital at Neuilly, and every day found myself wishing that I was in active service, and doing my part more valiantly than by helping to supply the Allies with more shell-making machinery.

I do have a surprise photograph tucked in my luggage which I am sure will impress you. I did have dinner with George but unfortunately that was our only time together. I wonder if and when or where we might meet again.

I am boarding the ship tomorrow morning and anxious to see my little family in New York.

Your loving son and brother,
Howard

Howard leaned over the bow of the French liner, Espagne, and watched the longshoremen loading cargo and luggage. A sense of loss and remembrance swept through him as he saw the ropes unleashed from the dock and felt the movement of the deck as the liner began its voyage across the Atlantic and he again wondered what lay ahead.

Days had flown by when he heard the smack of the bow as it hit the wharf in New York. Trudging down the pier pulling his trunk along the walk he hailed a taxi. Giving the driver the address, he sat back and contemplated his reunion with his family. He was anxious to see the children but concerned with how Bea might greet him. "Joy or anger?" As the driver was putting his trunk on the staircase platform, Howard rang the bell. After having no response to his ring, he rang the super's bell. A haggard older man opened the door appearing very aggravated about being disturbed.

Annoyed, Howard asked, "Mr. Wells, my family does not seem to respond to the bell. Have they gone out?"

"Out? Yes, they went out several months ago. Didn't you know they moved?"

"Apparently, not! Do you know where they went?"

"Yes, yes. Come in for a minute and I will try to find the forwarding address your ole' lady gave me."

Howard's ire rose at hearing his wife called an ole' lady as he motioned to the taxi driver to wait and stepped inside. Angrily he sat back in the taxi, as he watched the scenery go by on his way to Nutley, New Jersey. As the taxi pulled up to the curb he could hear the squeal of young children. He opened the gate while bushes could be heard swishing from around the corner of the house. A young Bea came running with Tom following her and throwing himself forward, touching Bea yelling, "Tag! You're it!" Suddenly their eyes fell on Howard. Bea, startled for a moment, rushed forward and jumped into his arms, crying, "Papa! Papa!" Then she began to sob. "I thought you were gone forever."

"Oh, never, never child," Howard said, hugging her tightly.

Then he saw Betty standing there with a grim look on her face, not moving. "Then why did you not come back when Mommy was so sick? We needed you."

Howard put Bea down gently saying, "I'm sorry, I did not know Mommy was sick."

"I guess you were too busy for us."

Then the sound of the screen door opened and Bea leaning on a cane, stepped onto the porch. "Are you home now? Or are you going to keep your trunk packed ready to go again?"

"Now don't be harsh with me. Remember there is a war going on and letters move slowly."

"Oh, did you write?"

Howard ignored the sarcasm and turning toward the children said, "Okay kids, show me the house. It looks big. Is it haunted?"

Young Tom giggling said, "I hear awful noises at night but Mummy just tells me to go to sleep, it is just the trees. I don't think so."

"Well, let me go throw those goblins out." With that they all ran into the house with Howard in tow.

****

GEORGE

The butler carefully handed George a glass after being seated in Mrs. Wharton's home. "Merci," George eyeing the light green drink suspiciously asked, "What kind of concoction is this?"

"Absinthe sir. Don't you have it in America?"

"If we do, it hasn't been served in my home. Please go on and serve the others." He had never tasted absinthe but knew the stories of addiction and the Degas painting of the woman seated with a glass in front of her with the heavy sadness of where life had dragged her. Observing the painting, convinced him that drinking absinthe led to lingering addiction. "What the hell! Might as well see what all the fuss is about." He took a sip and winced.

Edith Wharton extending her hand to George said, "I'm so pleased to have you here and the ear of your good friend and colleague over at Military Intelligence, Ronald Simmons. We will have a tryst later tonight so I can push, pull and probably torture the both of you into spilling your secrets."

George shifted uncomfortably in his chair. "What kind of secrets do you think we have Mrs. Wharton?"

"Oh, please call me Edith. This is not New York or Boston. It's Paris and Paris has changed because of this ugly war. We can drop all the stringent military protocol for a night. We are all familiar with each other here, George. Now I certainly want to know all about that infamous woman Nellie Bly."

"Ahem! And how would you know that I know something about Nellie Bly?"

"George, there are no secrets in Paris. Haven't you learned that yet?"

He took a taste of absinthe, winced and took another sip trying to understand its fame. Edith, who had taken a seat next to him, covered her mouth with her gloved hand trying desperately not to laugh. "Ah, so this might be your first taste of absinthe, my dear?"

Embarrassed, George said, "I guess it's obvious. Why would someone become addicted to this? It has quite a bitter taste and bite.

"Beware 'la fee verte'. She is twinkling her toes on the rim of your glass. She is beckoning you to dive in." Edith pulled off her elbow length gloves and laid them on the sidetable.

"La fee verte! Isn't that 'green fairy'? Why in God's name would they call this a green fairy?"

"Now watch that George. Addiction comes all too fast. One never knows what one might desire later after the bite is gone. But don't you worry. I'll be here for you and take the glass." Then she took the glass from his hand and took a sip without a wince. "See, one does get use to it."

"I thought it had been banned. For God's sake why would any country ban something that tastes like licorice that has been soaked in iodine?"

Edith laughed heartily surprising those around who were chatting. "Please go on with your conversations." Continuing, she said, "They say it's addictive, George but I can tell by the look on your face, you won't succumb. Don't think the ban will last too much longer. People are getting their senses back after the horror of this silly war." Edith motioned Ronald to sit down next to her on the settee. "We all need to be addicted again to great wines, elegant food, and the coterie of ingenious writers and artists, like Ronald here. Aren't you anxious to get back to that blank canvas and swirl your imagination across it?"

"Thankfully, Ronald is using that imagination to help us create a truly operative Military Intelligence. If that is possible with the mangled disorganization that is going on." Displaying his hands upward, George in aggravation said, "It is the saying that the right hand does not know what the left hand is doing. Utmost frustrating to all of us."

The night wore on with intense conversation about the horrors of the war. Edith was now working with the refugees and orphans trying desperately to find help for them and build schools. People stopped drinking when speaking about who they had lost. The laughter had stopped and sorrow seeped through the walls. Guests started to leave. Gaiety had been all too brief.

Edith pulled her gloves back on.

****

November 12, 1918
Paris

Dear Bessie, Papa & Mumsie,

I hope this finds Mumsie well. And the rest of you joyous over the Armistice which was finally signed yesterday. I believe I can tell you now since the sworn secrecy should be no more. I became involved in an incredulous situation with Major Churchill. On November 7th, we received a report that an Armistice had been signed. The news was sent to us and they insisted that it was correct. I was convinced that it was physically impossible for the signing to have happened so soon. I contacted General Pershing's headquarters that we had received a notice from the French Ministry of War that the Germans had signed that morning. Unfortunately, the false news got to the people and celebrations began all over and I understand in the U.S. also. I have no realistic idea why the Major and those involved would state that an armistice had been signed. I believe it was a terrible gossip grapevine event that escalated once they became aware that the Germans were being defeated along the lines of war. They will have to live with the damage to their careers the rest of their lives.

Forgive me for not writing as often as I should have. My life here has been one of an incredible opportunity to be involved with the effort to create a viable permanent Military Intelligence Service for the U.S. It had been a herculean struggle with Major General Hugh Scott but with the perseverance of Major Van Deman he finally managed to have us sent here to Paris.

Luckily for me, I believe my fluency in French and working knowledge of German allowed me the privilege of being an intricate member of the Service here and being involved with "counterespionage", something new in our previous intelligence gathering. Now I think I have found my place for a life career which allows me not only to be involved in the development process of a strong Service but with the blessing of living a French lifestyle with all its intellectual curiosities. I have enjoyed my compatriots immensely but the death of my good friend Ronald Simmons has lessened the joy. He had been an aspiring American artist here when the war broke out and Van Deman recruited him to work for us. His effectiveness in organizing a viable American system of intelligence in just six months left us all in awe. It was a pleasure to match wits with him. Then last February he was assigned to set up a section of the Military Service in the south of France with its headquarters in Bordeaux. After a very short time there he became ill with double pneumonia and died within three days. It could be said that war took him all too young. I miss him to this day. Do not want to end on a sad note but war has left its mark of grief on my heart.

My promise is to write again soon. I am anxious to know myself where life will send me next but I am determined to stay in France.
Lovingly,
George

****

HOWARD

He pushed the library door open slightly and saw Bessie and Woodbury on their knees placing canvases along the library shelves. No one had answered the door so he had come in hoping to surprise them. He kept quiet interested in watching the scene evolving. Bessie kept picking up canvases, gazing for a minute and then putting them down.

"I don't know Charles. It's so important to choose canvases which are so compelling that people cannot turn away. Funny that I should think that everyone shares my emotions when I look at your canvases."

Woodbury threw his arm around Bessie. "I've always trusted your emotions. You hide them so often but when you finally unleash them, the good ones caress me. I'll trust your eye and emotion." Giving her a kiss on her neck, they heard the squeak of the door as Howard pushed it open. Bessie scrambled up quickly when she saw Howard. Embarrassed, her face reddened. "Howard, I didn't expect to see you here."

"Obviously not!"

"We were just trying to select the best of Charles' paintings for a gallery opening."

"It looked like a little more than that."

"Howard", Charles said, "Give your sister a little more respect than crudeness. Come in, sit down and I'll go get some tea."

Howard settled himself in the library desk chair and swiveled around to confront Bessie. "So what is this with you and Woodbury?"

"What is what?"

"It appeared to be a little close."

"You're so tiresome. I didn't expect you but now that you are here, I can imagine it's another crisis." Bessie collapsed into a chair, her hand picking up a rosary that had been left on the tea table. She started fingering the beads.

"No need to say a rosary for me. Although I do feel like Job the way life has been treating me. God or some creator seems to continually enjoy putting stumbling blocks in my path. All I want is some success, for once. But again it's another turn in the road for me."

"Certainly it has had a lot of hairpin turns. Your driving has been bad! Okay! So what is it?" she asked dropping the beads back onto the table. "First of all tell me about the children."

"They're fine and quite happy, thank you. The girls are going to the School of Sacre Coeur on 81st Street and Tom is in elementary school in Nutley. Bea appears to be over her medical problems and is out and about. I tend to believe that her mother is sending her money and Bea is hiding it from me."

"Well, it's nice that she has pocket money. After all, you seem to be gone all the time. Surely it gives her peace of mind that she can rely on her mother."

"There must be a well of money. You know Mrs. Kidder sold her shares in the railroad and moved to quite a nice mansion in San Francisco."

"Good for her. She deserves it. Remember Howard that is not your money."

Howard bristled. He opened his silver cigarette case and withdrew a cigarette. Turning his head away from Bessie he lit it, then inhaled deeply. The library door was pushed open and Woodbury held it with his foot while trying to maneuver the tray.

"Here, let me help you with that, Charles. It's kind of you to think of me with hot tea. I can use it especially after that long train ride and I wouldn't mind a shot of whiskey with it if you don't mind, Bessie?"

"I think we can manage a little whiskey, can't we

Bessie?"

Bessie said nothing. Woodbury poured Howard a shot and after handing it to him picked up one of his ocean paintings. "You always have an opinion Howard so what do you think of this for the show?"

Howard took the painting and scanned it. "As always Charles, you have an intimacy with the ocean that I don't share. It looks extraordinarily beautiful on canvas but crossing it is always a harrowing experience. I'm still shaking from my last trip and the experience still tears at my nerves."

Woodbury took the painting from Howard and placed it back against the bookshelf. "Ah! The immensity of the ocean with its vibrant greens and blues, crashing waves assaults my senses. I can't help but love it. Okay, so you have no love of it but why were you so shaken?"

"Yeah, my nerves are fine now." Howard took a draw from his cigarette and forcefully blew the smoke toward the ceiling. "The story is that we had some stormy weather, and I had just tucked myself in when I heard the whistle sound and saw a white flash accompanied by a tremendous crash. I was sure we had been torpedoed. When I got on deck I found that a freighter had rammed us a glancing blow on our port side. I ran below again and put on some more clothes, and stuffed my pockets full of what I least wanted to lose. It was a cloudy night, not much wind, but the seas were still heavy. We all had on our life preservers and stood beside our lifeboats, ready to embark if necessary. All that raced through my mind was 'Titanic! Titanic! Who could forget that horror? Anyway, sorry but I couldn't bear to have that night staring at me from one of your ocean paintings on my wall."

"That's too bad. I was just about ready to give this one to you."

Bessie with a slight smirk, laughed. "You deserved that, Howard. What have you missed? Oh, heavens grace, you still don't know what is of value in life."

Howard took a swig of his whiskey then picked up his tea cup. "Hopefully that's not true. All I'm asking is a little bit of help. I don't want to burden Papa. I find myself at wits end again through no fault of my own. Money just seemed to fall into everybody else's hands but mine. I think I deserve more. I have fought but there are people out there who only had their best monetary interest on their minds. They have no conscience!"

"There is never a situation that is your fault. How many times have I heard that story?"

Howard stood up and grabbed his hat. "Maybe I should go? I thought we were family."

"Sit down, Howard. I went too far but my tongue can't always be held in check when exasperation becomes my shadow. You've handed me so many responsibilities and pressures in the last few years. Bea and those poor children have had to cope hopelessly on their own. Finally I have had a brief time to enjoy something I want to do. Just me! And I have a conscience."

Woodbury had taken the tray back out to the kitchen when Howard asked. "Is that conscience involving Woodbury?"

"Yes, if you really want to know. He's not only been my mentor, but a friend, my loving friend for years. Though all his efforts have failed in making me a credible painter, but at least I have the joy of knowing him. Yes, I dare to make room for him in my life. Enough said about it! I'll make some phone calls for you." The sound of the door slamming brought

Bessie's head down, her hands covering her ears. "I don't want to hear anymore! Please! Please! Please! No more."

****

Carley tapped lightly on Bessie's bedroom door. Hearing her weeping, he opened the door and saw her lying face down on the bed. He bent over and kissed her hair, then stroked it for a moment. Sitting on Bessie's favorite soft cushioned paisley chair he hated and reached over and took her hand. His thumb brushed across her fingers and he felt the gold wedding band that had been on her hand for so many years now. How remarkably beautiful as she ascended the staircase in wedding gown and crossed the room, all the time smiling at me. If I could only relive that moment and recapture the life that I had planned for us. We walked over the threshold of Nutwood, this home where I had grown up with all my hopes and dreams of a quiet life; Bessie with children and me with my drawings of buildings and homes I hoped would beautify the landscape of Boston. But it didn't happen.

Bessie turned her head toward the wall and did not acknowledge his presence. Carley realizing she wanted no part of his comforting, fell back into his state of apathy waiting to hear the hearse come up the drive. It was no surprise that Mumsie died quietly in her sleep. He had rarely known her to be an active woman but always the albatross around Bessie's neck. I wonder if she is weeping from sadness or relief?

In his mind he heard the laughter of children, the stairs creaking, doors banging, seeing cars come up the driveway. I always seemed to be a passive observer. So much energy, so much activity overwhelmed me and I, unfortunately, receded into my sanctuary... my office with my drawings.... calm, serene, surrounded by my walls. I was born when society took for granted that it was a man's world. Carley picked up a photograph of the children from the dresser. He turned it over reading their names on the back and their ages at the time. They are all grown now and I never really thought of them as moving on into such a different world. Bessie was frustrated all her life wanting avenues opened to her that were closed. I knew that, but women had their place, right or wrong. Who am I to say? I've been aware of the subtle indoctrination of our daughters creating what Bessie hoped would assist them in the making of a life they choose and not chosen for them. They didn't have to follow in her footsteps. She did not want that for them but she let them choose. At least Nancy seems to have gotten her message. My surprise was so evident when she told me that she wanted to be a doctor. I could not wrap my mind around such a crazy idea. It took me awhile to close my gaping mouth. Bonpapa pulled some strings and off she went to Columbia Medical School and with her attitude I'm sure the young men students were in awe. Looking at the photo of Nancy he had an image of her bossing them around with her rather staunch demeanor.

Carley tiptoed out of the room, leaving Bessie to grieve.

****

With Mumsie's death and many of the children off to college, Bessie and Carley decided to move the family into Oakwood, a much smaller home that Carley had built on the property. Having income from renting Nutwood, helped Carley deal with the always cumbersome finances. Papa, realizing the move had been done because of financial pressures thought about his conversation with a mine promoter. This man had told him that he had obtained the other half of the bankrupt Mt. Tritle operation and had offered him a reinvestment if Papa was willing to put up a portion of the money. He was considering it. After all, he could do no worse than Howard. Maybe this man knew what he was doing and then he could help with the family finances. They owed so much to Carley for his generosity over the years taking care of all of us. No one should be asked to do so much.

The sound of mail dropping through the door slit shook Papa out of his reverie. "Pray thee God that it's a letter with good news." Glancing at the writing his hopes were dashed wishing it could have been a friend as he laid it on his lap. He rang the bell for Rose and told her to please call Bessie down.

Alarmed seeing Papa's state of dejection, Bessie said, "Papa, is something wrong?"

"I don't know, dear. I hope not." Picking up the letter, he handed it to Bessie. "I know by the writing who this is and I just couldn't open it for fear....."

"For fear of what, Papa?"

Shaking his head and in a voice with a slight tremor, he said, "Whenever a letter arrives from Howard I can't remember a time when it was good news. Always trouble. Please, you read it and let me know if I should know."

Bessie ripped open the letter and sat down in the window chair. After reading it she wondered, "How do I phrase this. If anyone can bring sadness, sorrow or trouble into this house it's Howard. I think I sang too many mad insane songs to him."

"This letter is mailed from New York and all this time we thought he was in Denver. It seems he did quite well there and was offered to come to New York and straighten out their district office. Unbeknownst to us, he is sharing an apartment with Francis and Nancy. This will be news to Carley and certainly we knew nothing of it. I guess they thought they would save some college expenses by sharing but didn't tell us knowing we might object. Surely they would be right. He writes that Tom is now at Carlton Academy in Summit and he is very happy to be near Betty and little Bea at the convent."

Bessie, putting the letter down scanned the books on the shelves not knowing how to explain the rest of the letter.

"Why is Tom in Summit? I thought he was with his mother. She didn't go with Howard to Denver, did she?"

"I don't know Papa. She stopped writing and didn't answer my letters. I became so weary of their marriage but knowing at least the girls were safe in the convent, I didn't pursue the matter."

"There is something more in the letter that you're not telling me."

"Bea asked for a divorce and he agreed on one condition. He gets the children. It appears that he did not think Bea was serious in her conversion to Catholicism and he wants the children to be raised Catholic. She has remarried a cousin from the Clark family. I think I can understand. She wanted to be back in the bosom of her real family. Maybe she can find happiness and security there. I do hope so. She certainly did not find it in this family.

"Bessie, sweetheart, you tried so hard. I'm sorry. I'm so sorry. Oh, my sweet Bessie." Papa took his handkerchief from his pocket, taking off his glasses, he wiped his eyes. An untouched tear lightly fell on his cheek.

Bessie tore the letter in two. Getting up she dropped

it in the wastebasket. She wrapped her arms around her father, kissing him on his forehead, pleading, "Papa, forgive yourself. You and Bonpapa have been angels in our lives but one child did not hear you. He deafened to your wisdom, but I have not and I have loved you both."

"Oh, dear God, why does life make one's heart feel such pain. One day I'll close my eyes forever. At that moment, oh, at that moment..." Papa's head bowed.

****

HOWARD

He opened the closet and sighed, looking over his clothes thinking, "Should I take a trunk or just two valises. How much clothes am I going to need in New Caledonia? Well, it's a French society so I expect I should take at least one set of formal wear." After piling the clothes on the bed, he decided to take the trunk. Finally placing his shaving gear on the top, he picked up a packet of ribbon tied letters. He opened the top one and began to read, *My dearest Howard.* He smiled remembering when he first met Mae Boyle out West. They had been introduced by one of his mining buddies and he was instantly charmed by her open smile and friendliness. She was a frontier woman proven by her forthrightness and knowledge of the industry unlike most of the women he knew. She resembled Mrs. Kidder but without the personal baggage.

As he read on, she reminisced about their last time together talking about the hopeless prospect of the Bully Hill mine which Papa had invested and lost his money. I had told her that I had no idea this man had visited and convinced Papa to invest. "Another charlatan! I would have known better." Then she wrote how she had joined Howard heading south with a mining geologist.

Sitting down in his big leather chair, he remembered at San Diego they had taken two automobiles, one of which Mae nicknamed "The Desert Queen". It was old and dilapidated, but it certainly could run. We carried spare tires and many extra cans of gasoline tied to the running boards, as we were going far, in a barren, dry country. My god was it hot as we headed east for some sixty miles, then turned south across the border into the land of tequila and mescal, that hot, fiery drink, but the mescal was milder and more palatable. All day we followed that pretense of a road, over shoulders of mountains, across valleys with dry washes and creeks. It was such a vast, semi-barren mountain country with lots of cacti and occasional thin forest of trees. I remember arriving at the Venezia mine about midnight. Funny, how on the way, one of our cars ran out of water, ran hot, and we had to stop to cool off. Our "Desert Queen" continued to the next creek, filled some cans with water and started back to give aid to the other car. In the meantime the other car cooled off, and they thought they would move ahead a bit. We met at a sharp turn, and missed a head-on smash by inches. Curious, that the only two cars within a hundred miles should almost wreck each other. Life has its narrow escapes. I hope I can escape the next one.

With a wry grin he placed the letters on the top of his clothes. Scratching his head for a moment, he wondered how close a relationship he might have with Mae. He had to write her that he had tried vigorously to float her International Minerals Syndicate to handle her Mexican and other properties but to no avail. Mae had some Idaho-Maryland stock in California which had great possibilities of producing gold. We shall see. I sure would like to hold a gold nugget in my hand again. Well, it's not California here I come. New Caledonia here I come!

****

1929

Darkening clouds gathered heavily over Copley Square as the hearse slowly moved toward the open doors of Trinity Church. The pallbearers took their places beside the casket and began the procession into the church. Bessie, taking her father's arm, walked slowly down the aisle, glancing up at times at the congregation. Suits and dresses of black augured the somberness of death. She settled herself in the first pew and acknowledged her children, including Howard's, Betty, Bea and Tom sitting behind her. Bessie lifted her black veil as her eyes took in the richly carved wood of Trinity Church. She lowered her head as her eyes fell on the casket. Bessie bit her lip, closed her eyes. Her chest tightened. It had not been the life that she expected but there was no bitterness from all the years she had spent with him. Twenty-five years difference in age in the beginning did not seem to matter. Then the years flew by. Age seemed to grasp Carley and he retreated from the vigorous, boisterous family and a seemingly diaphanous curtain fell between them and life drifted on.

Wiping a tear away she heard the soothing sounds of her favorite composer, Sibelius drift down from the apse as the organ began the service. The music lifted the darkness of sorrow and she let herself drift into the other world she had so covertly inhabited beneath her life of husband, children and all the family who attached themselves to her, needing the safety, security and especially the warmth of her arms.

I don't want to turn my head and look. I have to believe he's here. Papa has said nothing to me. He always noticed me changing into excited expectation whenever the doorbell rang and Charles stood there. We then talked hours into the day to dusk about Charles' new obsession with the Caribbean. Papa smiles after Charles' departure and usually asks, "And how was your discussion today?" knowing all too well that I can't keep my secret from him. In his world, he hears me well and speaks no word that would cause me pain. Even here as I look around, some would deem me 'playing with damnation'. In this church of worship, tongues wag and not always in prayer.

Bessie squeezed her father's arm and let her head rest on his shoulder. She felt the pressure of his hand enclosing hers and she saw him give her a wink. "He, my silent ally, knows all too well my emotions live on in a man who paints life. Vibrant life!"

Woodbury surreptitiously had come down the side aisle and slipped into the end of a back pew. His eyes swept over the mourners and noticed Bessie with her head on her father's shoulder. He felt apprehensive and helpless but did not want to intrude.

The priest stood up and intoned the words of the mass. As the last Latin word was spoken, he praised Carley as a staunch Christian man who fathered his children well and cherished his wife. He went on to speak about Carley's life and contributions to the people of Boston. Bessie stared at the priest as his words pushed on. "How little one knows about his reality, his disappointments, his struggles. And his final loss, losing his leg and the frustration with a wooden leg which beleaguered him every day. Age harshly broke his spirit."

A streak of sunlight glinted on the gold plaque on the casket brightening the lettering... Charles Bruen Perkins. Bessie grimaced, realizing how many men named Charles had become part of her life. Not only Carley but Howard had actually been named Charles Howard Ridgely Ward and finally Charles Woodbury, the Charles who late in her life embossed the name on her heart.

Looking at the plaque she thought, the one Charles that affected Carley's life the most was Charles Callahan Perkins, his father. It is as if his father had given Carley his name never knowing the burden it would become on his son's life. The prominence and acclaim of his father were so attached to Carley's mental core his entire life. Every morning he put on his father's name and carried it with him in his own attempts at success which did not come with the glory of his father's career. Carley had to wear his father's cloak. That cloak etched away his pride years ago and left us, just the two of us together, husband and wife and nothing much else. I hope death opens another door for him and youth comes back.

The priest blessed the coffin and the congregation and the mass was over. Bessie stepped upon the landing and knelt, lifting her veil she kissed the coffin. Running her hand back and forth across Carley's nameplate, she whispered, "I did and still love you, my very dearest Carley." Leaning her forehead against the wooden casket, kissing it lightly, "I hope you will let me go as I have you." She stood up and motioned to the children to come forward. Saying their goodbyes, Nancy, holding her mother's hand, led her down the aisle and into the sunset hues casting its soft light on the hearse as Carley's body was laid in the back. The waiting cars pulled forward and Bessie, taking her father's arm again stepped forward as an arm passed across her and opened the car door. Bessie, without looking, said, "Thank you." and heard the response, "You're most welcome." Startled she looked up and saw those intense blue eyes of Woodbury. Her hand flew to her chest when Woodbury carefully whispered, "Someday you will see the blue of the Caribbean. I promise you a new life." Bessie felt rattled and glanced at her father who showed no apparent surprise.

"Sir, allow me to help you into the car."

"That would be most kind of you. Years do take their toll on this old body."

Once Papa was settled in the car, he turned to Woodbury standing by the open door. "I would be very honored if you would accompany us to the cemetery. You may brighten our day."

Woodbury without hesitating took his seat beside Bessie. The cortege moved on.

****

BESSIE

1928

She pushed the gate of the iron fencing that surrounded the Lowell family plot. Nothing pretentious about this gravesite. All plain and simple just like the family wanted. Finding Amy's small headstone, she fixed the red bow wrapped around a small green potted plant. She fingered the tendrils so they would cross the ground of Amy's grave. Laying a small blanket in front of the tombstone, she set herself down. "Amy I brought you a plant. A lovely leafy brilliant green plant. Just my small gift to our friendship. Our loving friendship although I can't think of you as dead. I think of you as just taking off in that old car of yours heading north and I'm just missing you being here. Do you hear me?" Bessie ran her fingers over Amy's chiseled name. "I need you to answer, you stubborn woman. My house is so quiet now with all the children gone. Imagine Nancy finished med school and is now on her way to a little town, Waterloo, in New York to be their town doctor. She was so headstrong and had a will that no one was going to fence her in with houses and children. I'm so proud of her. Those townspeople have no idea who will be doctoring them. And of course Francis is in New York as a film critic for the Herald Tribune. Everyone seems to be treading their own path. I envy them."

Bessie twisted herself to lean her back on the stone and let her gaze fall on the names that clustered around Amy's tomb. "You certainly are surrounded by this family of Lowells."

"You'll never know how all of you intimidated me with your deference. I would lie awake at night before

I came to visit hoping some incredible muse would come to me and fill me with some unique observation but if she did, it never passed my lips. Here you are Amy and they're not so intimidating now."

She reached into her bag and pulled out a book, flipping quickly through the pages. "Amy, tongues have been wagging and you would shake with that raucous laugh of yours, if you are not now already doing so. You would be proud of me. Maybe that frisky spirit of yours fused with mine because I no longer care. This time in my life, I am here sitting above your blessed ground, and taking on this judgmental world, or our little minded society, and dancing your pattern.

"Woodbury was so generous to put my name on this book with his as if I really had something to do with his theory. He's always talking about seeing as if people are all blind. Maybe they are!" Bessie sat for a moment turning the pages slowly. "I guess we are all blind when it comes to relationships. When we were young, remember that time we thought and talked so many days and nights about whom we knew and who they loved and we romanticized so often when we were so unaware of the tenuous undercurrent of those relationships. I saw nothing but deep affection and love Bonpapa had for Bonnemaman and I know to this day it was real. I mistakenly thought we could find the same loving bond."

Bessie choked back a small sob. "I miss them and you so much that the pain stuns me and that pain, that deep pain like daggers in my chest. It takes me time to breathe again. Time to move my mind into a quiet place. It is times like these I wish it were all a dream. Wake up! Please wake up."

She opened the book again and leafed through it finally stopping at a sketch of a man and woman dancing. She ran her finger over the sketch. "Didn't we Amy? Didn't we think we could find that romantic love? Silly girls we were. A romantic love like your beloved Keats? Hmmmm! You found Ada but you had so little time together. George deceived himself believing that he had found an eternal love. He lost it but he still embraces himself in a memory of a love that never was. I hope he's found a sanctuary in Nice. Suzanne Carrolton, remember her family in Baltimore? She lives nearby and I expect keeps him company. The French have decorated him with every medal imaginable which we all are proud but I envision him still walking the streets with the desire that Justine will come back. Sadly he will never leave France in search of that elusive love."

Bessie picked a blade of grass, twirling it in her fingers. "Justine and I have a great friendship but why she married my brother is something we don't talk about. I wonder if Papa thought he had found his great love. He still lives in that often silent world of his but he's found strength in a world where he's content. Even before Mumsie died I realized that I was the link in their marriage always bowing and running to Mumsie's needs and not my own. Papa was there but then again he was not. Hmmmm!"

An elderly couple, arm in arm, stopped for several minutes across the path, bowed their heads in front of a grave and laid a white rose in front of the stone. Dabbing her eyes with a lacy handkerchief, the woman took her husband's arm again, leaned over and kissed him on the cheek. Turning they noticed Bessie, nodded and smiled then slowly moved down the path. Bessie, out of curiosity, picked herself up and walked across the path. Seeing the name on the stone, she drew in a sharp breath. Bessie dropped to her knees on Amy's grave. "Amy, her name is Elizabeth and she was born on the same day and year as me. She was a baby when she died. I lived and she died. It says 'Never will you be forgotten'. Amy, she has that sacred love that dwells in that small casket with her."

A nearly indecipherable whisper fell from Bessie's lips, "Charles, you're my sacred love, secret in my heart."

****

August 1935

Dusk had fallen and the intense light from the lighthouse slithered back and forth across the
dark, nearly black waters of the Bay of Fundy. Bessie fascinated by the light wondered how the whaling ships captains' hearts must have jumped when the light appeared across the top of the water and they knew they were on their way safely home again to Grand Manan. Woodbury was painting in his studio indulging in effort to mix Caribbean colors onto his palette. She wrapped her knitted shawl tightly around her shoulders, shivered a little, then reached into her bag and found the letter her niece, Bea had written. Seated on a garden bench outside the cottage, she opened it.

The envelope had a return address of Auburn, California. Bessie recalled Bea marrying Donald French Bennett several years ago. His family had lived in Dorchester when Bea met him at a party at Dartmouth. He had been a fun loving, party going, young man and Bea insisted on marrying him although he was out of their social class. Shortly after the wedding, Donald sadly was diagnosed with tuberculosis and had spent the last several years at Estes Park, Colorado, hoping for a cure. It has seemed a futile effort. She had heard that Bea when the baby was due planned to go to Auburn where her father now had an assay office. Poor Bea! Of Howard's children, Bea had been the curious one, mischievous at times but so needy. She didn't so much miss her mother as her father. She made a fantasy of Howard... her knight in shining armor who would ride into town with wild stories to shower her with, plighting love for his little family and then off he would go again. She never seemed to blame him. Bea loved Manhattanville College in New York and to my amusement, always playing the sophisticate. But why shouldn't she? Betty was the responsible little mother wanting not to be seen too much and I think haunted by the past. She just wanted life to be simple. And Tom, well Tom was and still seems to be the baby, squired away to all those boarding schools. I don't know what he thinks of his father. He never says much.

She finally began to read.

March 20th,

Dearest Aunt Bessie,
I trust you received our birth announcement. Don and I are so blessed to tell you about the birth of our son, Donald Ward Bennett, on March 16th. He appeared into the world with that look of, "Where am I and who are you?" I know we will be answering questions of "Why? Why? Why? for years to come.
Unfortunately, Don is not recovered enough from our stay at Estes Park to be near the baby. The doctor and his wife have taken him to their home until we can find a good nurse to travel with us on the train back home. Don's mother, Lydia, who has the energy of a new puppy, came out to help. She is certainly feisty and I could not keep up with her. I am sure the baby will inherit some of that feistiness. Lydia, in her matter of

fact way, there is no argument with her, said that Don will stay with them in his old room and she will nurse him until his health comes back. Truly, deep in my heart I don't know how he will survive this tuberculosis.

I trust I can ask of your love to allow the baby and me to stay at Oakwood just until I can find a place of my own. Of course I am going to have to find work and I do not believe my degree in French is going to be of much help. We will have to stay in Boston so Don can see the baby once in awhile and the Bennett family surely must see him.

With my fondest love to return home to Boston. The West, though beautiful, lacks soul.

Your loving niece,
Beatrice

Oh, it would have been such an easier life for Bea if she had accepted Mrs. Kennedy's offer to be her personal secretary. She spoke to Rose on the phone and politely declined. She was so in love with Don, nothing would have changed her mind. How can I deny her love for him when I struggle with my choices in life. Lord, keep me from being a hypocrite. I cried so often in my pillow. Here I sit loving another man and kept it secret for years. I did love Carley for his quiet fortitude through all our years, withstanding all the problems of my family but he is gone now and I feel his spirit went with him.

As the wind blew up and started to whirl the leaves around her, Bessie spoke into the wind. "I did love you Carley. I pray your spirit has found loving arms. Mine still long to be around you. No matter I am with another!"

"Have I caught you shouting to the wind? Has it answered you?" Woodbury sat down on the bench. "Never mind, shout what you will."

****

JUSTINE

May 1936

    She settled herself down on the low wall in the cloisters of the Monastery of Solesmes. She bent her head as she heard the sounds of Gregorian chant enwrap the cloisters. As the deep male tones of the monks singing those long, long notes she thankfully thought, "They do stop the chattering and painful thoughts of my mind. How calming the sound. What peace it brings for the moment. I know since I was young that it was this sound I was meant to find.
    Justine opened her chant book and picked up the unopened letter she had gotten from the Post on her way. She had seen the return address and was pleased it was from Bessie. She had missed her so much since moving from her home in Ardsley and anticipated hearing Bessie's news, hoping Bessie had written about her accomplishments and work with Charles. Bessie was not a person to take living alone easily without male companionship even though her father still lived in her home with his beloved books.
    Opening the letter, two other pieces of paper dropped on her lap. Startled, she unfolded the letter and saw the words, 'son's death'. She felt faint and her heart started racing. She opened Bessie's letter.

June 1st
Oakwood
Jamaica Plain

My dearest Justine,
    Yes, I have a broken heart and these words are difficult for me to write, knowing that you always kept a place in your heart for George. We, since being

childhood friends, know your love of music and later your determination to make Gregorian chant your life's work. I understood why your marriage was not to be and I never wanted to cause you any grief. But I cannot keep the grief of George's death from you.

Papa and I had no knowledge that George was suffering from pneumonia. He, of course, thought it was of no consequence to tell us. So we were so saddened to receive the enclosed letter. I knew that you did not have a telephone, so I wanted you to have the letter with the details of George's death. Of course, we replied to Suzanne that we kindly accepted her favor of having George buried in Menton. Suzanne also enclosed a poem written by Bonpapa which she found on George's nightstand. These were probably the last words he read and I believe he carried them with him into his death.

I know he would want to be buried in his beloved France. America never really seemed to be home for George. Maybe that is still the bond between you and George. You love France as much as he did. You were kindred spirits.

And I do miss you.
Lovingly,
Bessie

Tears fell gently on her cheeks as she quietly sang with the monks, 'kyrie eleison'. Holding on to the last notes she let them tremble down to the deepest part of her. She wrapped her arms around herself as the tears continued to fall. As difficult as it was, she began to read.

Sunday, May 17, 1936

Villa Himalaya
Boulevard de Garodan
Menton A.M. France

My dear Mr. Ward:

Here are some details of your dear son's death. I heard he was ill, so I went to his office. Mr. Dube, his partner, told me that he had double pneumonia but that he was not in danger. However, his secretary, who was in the office, said "Mrs. Carroll, you had better go to see him."

Knowing from a previous talk I had had with him about death, I thought it best to go and see him and propose to him the help of our Catholic religion. After waiting a long time in the hall, I insisted on going to his room accompanied by the bell boy. I reached his room, but did not go in, in case he did not wish to see me. The boy said I was waiting. The door of his room was opened, and I heard him say, "Pray thank Mrs. Carroll for her kindness." So the nurse came out in the hall. I asked if he was in danger. She said, "No, but he has double pneumonia and is seriously ill." I said "Tell Col. Ward to get well as soon as he can and come to Menton to stay with me."

I gave my telephone number, but little did I think that the next morning at eight o'clock I would receive a phone message that he had departed this world.

On receiving the message, I at once went to Nice and decided about the ceremony and offered to have him rest for always in the mausoleum I built for my dear husband. You cabled that you were satisfied, and I represented the family at his funeral and accompanied him to the Menton Cemetery, where we, Mr. Dube and myself, laid him at rest.

He was ill less than a week, and he little suffered. All his friends came to the Mass and expressed to me their deep regrets.

If you decide to let him rest with my poor husband, Charles Carroll of Carrollton, in this beautiful cemetery at Menton, I would advise that I should put a tablet mentioning his presence, relating some of the great services he rendered to the Nation. I shall myself be buried there, and the thought that we shall be all united is a consolation.

Pray let me know what else I can do for you. The mausoleum stands in the Cemetiere du Chateau, Grave No. 5, at Menton, Alpes Maritimes.

Yours sincerely,
Suzanne Carroll of Carrollton
Nee Suzanne Bancroft

Justine sitting against the cloister column, glanced up at the dawning morning light. She opened the other letter with a stifled sound of anguish when she saw a faded rose fall to the ground. Instinctively she knew it was the rose she left at the restaurant the last time she had seen George. Whimpering, she held it against her chest. Trying her best to regain some composure she began to read the poem written by what appeared to be Bonpapa's hand.

The Shield

The old man said, "Take thou this shield, my son,
Long tried in battle, and long tried by age,
Guarded by this, the fathers did engage,
Trusting to this, the victory they have won."

Forth from the tower Hope and Desire had built,
In youth's bright morn I gazed upon the plain,
There struggled countless hosts, while many a stain
Marked where the blood of brave men had been spilt.

With spirit strong I buckled to the fight,
What sudden chill rushes through every vein?
Those fatal arms oppress me – all in vain
My fainting limbs see their accustomed might.
Forged were those arms for men of other mould;
Our hands they fetter, cramp our spirits free;
I throw them on the ground, and suddenly
Comes back my strength, returns my spirit bold.

I stand alone, unarmed, yet not alone;
Who heeds no law but what within he finds;
Trusts his own vision, not to other minds;
He fights with thee. Father, aid thou thy son.

    Laying down the poem, Justine cried, "I did love you George. But I could not love you enough. Please, please forgive me."

****

BESSIE

1939

"BLUE, Blue, blue, blue, blue! Wrapping around me. Drowning in it. Take me with you, flowing in and out. Water, so intensely blue." Bessie put her brush in the blue paint crushed on her palette and moved it around and around. Frustration and usually not prone to cursing, she said, "Damn it! How can I capture the power of this water? I'm so damn inadequate! Inadequate! Where in my selfish mind did I have the notion I was capable of capturing what I see. I see it. Fool I am, I can't do it!"

Feeling a light kiss on the top of her head, Bessie looked up and saw Woodbury dressed in white pants and white loose shirt. "I can see you have taken on the Caribbean way of life. Funny how dressed in white your body could lose itself in the shores' white sands with only your blue eyes glistening in the light."

"Well, it's warmer than the white snows of New England wrapped in heavy coats. You should see my swimming trunks."

"Are they the color of the water?"

Woodbury put his arm around her and kissed her cheek. She quickly raised her hand to her cheek. "Charles, what if someone saw us?"

"You must be joking. Who would see us here on St. Lucia, my little island and who the hell would care? If someone did see us, what would they see but two grey haired people enjoying each other in this paradise. Isn't it about time we love each other?"

Bessie laughed. "Yes, everybody is gone except dear Papa. Remarkable, his life, his patience and his wanting me to be happy. Never, never a disparaging word from his mouth to me. I truly am his little girl, though look at me now. I can't even braid my hair. I would think he would want us to enjoy our time together, however little it might be."

"Yes. Yes. How little time. Let it not slip. Let's paint the daunting taste of ourselves." Charles yelled at the sea, "Hold back that time, damn it."

Watching the waves slide on to the shore, gracefully ebbing back and forth Bessie hesitantly asked, "Charles, do you still miss Marcia?"

Woodbury waiting for a moment, said, "Always! Why would I not? Even after nearly fifty years, I see her, hear her, smell the essence of her in those clothes she left behind. She went too soon and I couldn't save her. But here you came into my life and now with your beautiful silver hair streaming down on your shoulders and me, with my greying hair, why can't we love? Living does not stop nor does it erase the memories but lets us feel our aliveness. Without that, how could I paint?"

Woodbury turned Bessie's face toward him and kissed her. Her heart was racing. After many years she felt the blood of sexual feelings course through her body. Pleasure overcame her and she lay back on the sand. Woodbury lying beside her softly kissed her neck and his lips moved over her body as Bessie's arms enwrapped his. As rapture embraced them, they drifted off while the sun began its descent.

****

1940 April

Walking through the halls, the rooms, and the library of Oakwood, no voices of children, mothers, fathers, or intimate loved ones could be heard. In the room where Charles had died, Bessie envisioned his face again and again as he lay in death. Sadness burdened her as she thought how Papa had died so shortly before in his room. Death had stalked her home dragging its memories of those who had passed on. Her body still felt the warmth of Charles' love. His hand caressing her face. "Release has to come! 1 have to let go. Let go!" Inspiration waking her reverie, she pulled the valise from her bedroom closet, threw some clothes into it and snapped it shut. Locking the front door, she hurried to the car. Hours flew by before she pulled into Perkins Cove. She took the small package sitting on the seat and walked slowly to the edge of the cliff. She opened the package and pulled out the chess queen, turning it over and over in her hand. Why had Howard taken it from Bonpapa's set? Bonpapa had put the game away in a cupboard where it sat for years waiting, hoping the queen would appear again someday. I couldn't bear to part with it when Bonpapa died. I never understood why the missing queen meant so much to me. Howard kept it so carefully wrapped in a soft cloth obviously not to scratch or mark it. How perfect she remained. There she was when I was going through his trunk of possessions Mae had sent thinking that I would want them. Did Mae know about this? Strangely it was tied to all the letters I had written him. Just mine. The other letters were tied and kept in a separate box.

The wind started to pick up and waves were mounting as they crashed against the cliff. I'm here. Alone! Now, in this moment, alone. Have I always been alone? Carley, you married me and we were blessed but so many times I was alone even with you lying next to me. And my heart, Charles. I gave you my heart. But your constant travels to your beloved Caribbean so often left me alone with the coldness of New England.

Bessie moaned softly. "Hear me, Bonpapa! Oh, your sacred chess queen is still within me. She has all the power and moves any way she desires. Except those damn dancing knights. They dance swathed in their masculinity. Two steps forward, one step side. Or one step forward and two steps aside. They dance to their own rhythm. Can I, like the queen really choose to dance to her own rhythm? Who were my knights? Charles? Bonpapa? Who were other knights? George? Howard? They all had their own steps. Mine, allowed only to stand in front and protect all, like the chess queen. All these years I've been moving through the mist of their lives finding no anchor of my own. Only fighting to save my knights. The king! I don't know who that is or was! Whoever he is, he just watched me struggle. No more sits a king by my side.

Bessie shuddered. She looked at the queen in anger as an emotional sea rose in her. Standing up, as the waves crashing fiercely against the rocks, an unknown strength overtook her. With a scream she threw it as far as she could into the sea. It split in two on the rocks below. A white crested wave crashing in swept the queen out to sea.

Shouting into the wind, "No more am I the chess queen. No more! It lies on the ocean floor. I've swept my life away. No more! No more!"

****

Picture Gallery

**George Cabot Ward
later Lt. Colonel Cabot Ward**

Oakwood home-Lenox, Mass. 1884

**Top boy on banister-George Cabot Ward
Girl on top of umbrella-Elizabeth Ward Perkins
Girl on stairs-Louise Thoron Endicott (cousin)
Older boy-Ward Thoron (cousin)
Young boy-Howard Ridgely Ward
Man-Samuel Gray Ward (Bonpapa)**

**Bonnemaman, Anna Hazard Barker
Ward, wife of Samuel Gray Ward**

Mumsie, Sophia Howard Ward, wife of Thomas Wren Ward 1911

Papa, Thomas Wren Ward

**Father and Mother Kidder
with adopted daughter, Beatrice Clark Kidder**

General Pershing arriving in France June 13, 1917 with Howard Ward in background in formal black dress and bowler hat

Picture signed by Auguste Rodin given to Mrs. Charles Bruen Perkins by Anna Seaton Schmidt-student of Rodin and friend of artist, Elizabeth Nourse

Family of Beatrice Kidder Ward with children, Elizabeth Perkins Ward, Thomas Ward, and Beatrice Howard Ward

**Elizabeth Ward Bruen Perkins
1952 (Bessie)**

Bessie with Anna, Elinor and Francis

**Sitting-
George Cabot Ward, and brother
Howard Ridgely Ward**

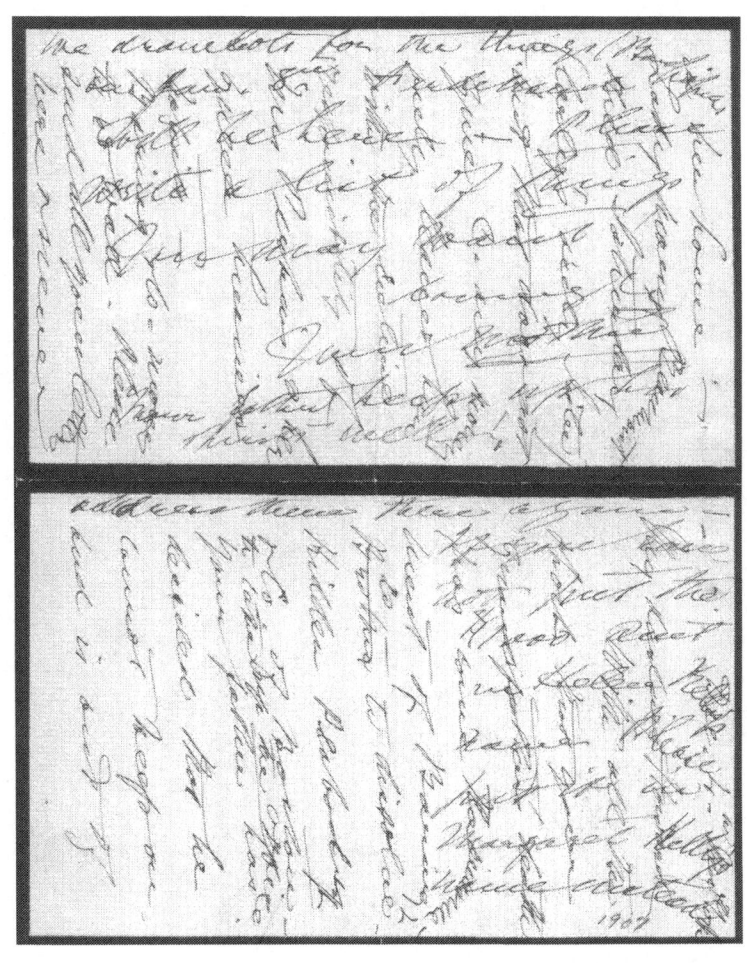

A letter written by Mumsie to Howard
(Many letters written at the time were written with crossing over lines…saved paper.)

WORKS CITED

Allen, Gay Wilson. *Waldo Emerson: A Biography*. New York: Viking, 1981. Print.

Allen, Gay Wilson. *William James: A Biography*. New York: Viking, 1967. Print.

Baldwin, David. *Puritan Aristocrat in the Age of Emerson: A Study of Samuel Gray Ward*. N.p.: n.p., 1961. Print.

Capper, Charles. *Margaret Fuller: An American Romantic Life*. New York: Oxford UP, 1992. Print.

Combe, Pierre. *Justine Ward and Solesmes*. Washington, D.C.: Catholic U of America, 1987. Print.

Deiss, Joseph Jay. *The Roman Years of Margaret Fuller; a Biography*. New York: Crowell, 1969. Print.

Emerson, Ralph Waldo, and Charles Eliot Norton. *Letters from Ralph Waldo Emerson to a Friend, 1838-1853*. Port Washington, NY: Kennikat, 1971. Print.

Emerson, Ralph Waldo, Bliss Perry, and Bruce Rogers. *The Heart of Emerson's Journals*. Boston: Houghton Mifflin, 1926. Print.

Fuller, Margaret. *Woman in the Nineteenth Century*. New York: Norton, 1971. Print.

Greenslet, Ferris. *The Lowells and Their Seven Worlds: Occasionem Cognosce with Illustrations*. Boston: Houghton Mifflin, 1946. Print.

James, William, and Elizabeth Hardwick. *The Selected Letters of William James*. Boston: D.R. Godine, 1980. Print.

Lewis, R. W. B. *The Jameses: A Family Narrative*. New York: Farrar, Straus, and Giroux, 1991. Print.

Lowell, Amy. *Men, Women and Ghosts*. New York: Macmillan,

1916. Print.

Lowell, James Russell, and Charles Eliot Norton. *Letters of James Russell Lowell*. Vol. 1. New York: Harper & Brothers, 1894. Print.

McAleer, John J. *Ralph Waldo Emerson: Days of Encounter*. Boston: Little, Brown, 1984. Print.

Novick, Sheldon M. *Henry James: The Young Master*. New York: Random House, 1996. Print.

Perkins, Elizabeth Ward. *Mrs. Gardner and Her Masterpiece*. New York: Scribner's Magazine, 1925. Print.

Porte, Joel, and Saundra Morris. *The Cambridge Companion to Ralph Waldo Emerson*. Cambridge: Cambridge UP, 1999. Print.

Richardson, Robert D. *Emerson: The Mind on Fire*. Berkeley: U of California, 1995. Print.

Woodbury, Charles H., and Elizebeth Ward Perkins. *The Art of Seeing; Mental Training through Drawing*. New York: C. Scribner's Sons, 1925. Print.

Woodbury, Charles H., Joan Loria, and Warren A. Seamans. *Earth, Sea and Sky: Charles H. Woodbury, Artist and Teacher, 1864-1940*. Cambridge, MA: MIT Museum, 1988. Print.

Woodbury, Charles H. *Painting and the Personal Equation*. Boston: Houghton Mifflin, 1919. Print.

Made in the USA
Lexington, KY
10 January 2016